THE WALK
INTO MORNING

THE WALK
INTO MORNING

Mildred Barger Herschler

TOR®

A Tom Doherty Associates Book
New York

The lines of "Walkers with the Dawn" by Langston Hughes are from DON'T YOU TURN BACK by Langston Hughes. Copyright © 1969 by Langston Hughes. Reprinted by permission of Alfred A. Knopf, Inc.

All other lines by Langston Hughes are from SELECTED POEMS OF LANGSTON HUGHES by Langston Hughes. Copyright © 1959 by Langston Hughes. Reprinted by permission of Alfred A. Knopf, Inc.

THE WALK INTO MORNING

Copyright © 1993 by Mildred Barger Herschler

This book is printed on acid-free paper.

A Tor Book
Published by Tom Doherty Associates, Inc.
175 Fifth Avenue
New York, NY 10010

Map by Ellisa Mitchell.

Tor® is a registered trademark of Tom Doherty Associates, Inc.

Library of Congress Cataloging-in-Publication Data

Hershler, Mildred Barger.
    The walk into morning / Mildred Barger Herschler.
        p.   cm.
    ISBN 0-312-85425-0
        1. United States—History—Civil War, 1861-1865—Fiction.
    2. Slavery—United States—Fiction. I. Title.
    PS3558.E776W3   1993
    813'.54—dc20   92-42577
                                                 CIP

Printed in the United States of America

0 9 8 7 6 5 4 3 2

To my brother Bob Barger
my fiercest critic and my guiding light,
and to my daughters and my son:
Michal Mays, Janeen McCloud,
and Brian Herschler,
from whom I've learned so much.

ACKNOWLEDGMENTS

I want to thank my editor extraordinaire, Harriet P. McDougal, for her enthusiasm, direction and stimulation; the staffs of many public libraries, especially the Louisiana Division of the New Orleans Public Library, the Schomburg Center for Research in Black Culture, Harlem, and the Huntington Public Library, Long Island, New York; William F. Messner, historian, for his definitive work I've quoted herein; Mike Meier of the National Archives, Military Reference Branch, Washington, D.C., for his help; the late Langston Hughes for his life and work; and my loved ones—Betty Barger, for her constant encouragement, support, and prodding, Donald Kepler for his methodical help with research and his mapping of our lives, and all my family—Ellen and Charley and Bob, their children and mine, who keep the faith.

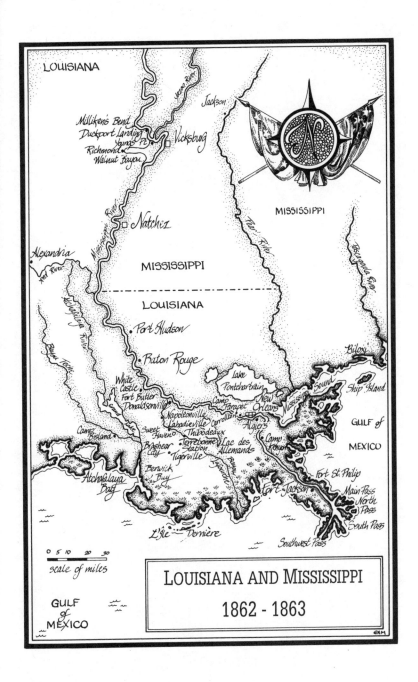

LOUISIANA

Yazoo River

Jackson

Milliken's Bend
Duckport Landing
Young's Pt.   Vicksburg
Richmond
Walnut Bayou

MISSISSIPPI

Tallahatchie River

Big Black River

Natchez

Pearl River

Alexandria
Red River

MISSISSIPPI
- - - - - - - - - - - -
LOUISIANA

Port Hudson

Baton Rouge

Atchafalaya River

Bayou Teche

White
Castle
Fort Butler
Donaldsonville

Camp
Parapet
Napoleonville
Labadieville   Camp
Sweet   Carrollton
Haven   Thibodeaux
Brashear   Terrebonne
City   Station
Tigerville

Lake
Pontchartrain

New
Orleans

Algiers

Lac des
Allemands

Camp
Kenner

Berwick
Bay

Atchafalaya
Bay

Bayou Lafourche

Bayou Grand Caillou

Fort St. Philip

Fort Jackson

Pascagoula River

Biloxi

Mississippi Sound

Ship Island

GULF of

MEXICO

Main Pass
North
Pass

South Pass

L'Île Dernière

Southwest Pass

0 5 10   20   30
scale of miles

GULF
of
MEXICO

LOUISIANA AND MISSISSIPPI
1862 - 1863

Being walkers with the dawn and morning,
Walkers with the sun and morning,
We are not afraid of night,
Nor days of gloom,
Nor darkness—
Being walkers with the sun and morning.

—LANGSTON HUGHES

PROLOGUE

I am in hope of capturing a contraband.
I shall not then miss my horse as much . . .

—A WISCONSIN COLONEL, BEFORE THE
ATTACK ON NEW ORLEANS, MARCH 1862

When the bullet hit, he rolled over and over, over and over
down the levee.

A corporal ripped his trousers off, put a hot wet rag against
him. The surgeon, a brawny old blacksmith from Connecticut, cried, "Give this here nigger soldier a dose so I can cut
that iron ball out."

So it was that far up the river at Milliken's Bend, Chad
began to float above the big live oak on Sweet Haven's lane
over two hundred miles south, as Laurel plunged the knife
into his hip . . .

Climbing to the top of the live oak, he can see the whole
world. At daybreak, as the slaves wind over the path past the
cottonwood tree, past the elms and sugarberry and clumps of
pine to the fields, he can see the mist, thick and grey blue,
rising after a night on the bayou behind him and the fields far

ahead. He can see ratooning sugar sprouts painted bright green by the first arm of the sun, the sugarhouse with its tall smokestacks waiting for the grinding and boiling of harvest, and rows of long, low slave quarters huddled like great slugs in the mud. He can see the shacks of the house servants tucked by the jutting kitchen, and burly mules pulling carts carrying pails of hominy and molasses to the fields. He can see the fine carriage house, the barn and stables past the near mansion that's white against the fog, the orange trees and date palms circling the gardens, and behind him, the willows that rim the yard on the old dirt road that follows Bayou Lafourche. Over the fields he can see the woods, so deep the trees look like one tree, and if he looks hard with his sharp eyes, he can see beyond to the swamp, the haven and hell of runaways.

Give the *peent* of the nighthawk.

That's Uncle Blake's voice talking to a tight circle of men the night Chad, under ten, stumbles onto a big escape. He's half-awake in the corner of the longhouse when he hears the quiet movement, the footfalls so light only an ear close to the ground can catch the sound. He gets up slowly, scarcely breathing, stepping over and around warm bodies sprawled on mats of Spanish moss, slips out of the quarters almost into Uncle Blake. Three men are suddenly beside Uncle Blake, four pairs of eyes turn toward Chad: Stay and watch, boy. He knows what that means and he knows that runaway slaves seldom look to the faraway North but set out for the wild, dense islands of the swamp, and then follow the Gulf shore through Texas into Mexico. Now the three go, moving swift and low, clothed by the dark of the moon. In the distance he hears a hound yelp a sleepy complaint, and a chill runs through him. *Are you going, Uncle Blake?* What'd I say, Chad— not without you.

The swamp's attraction deep in his mind, he's a smaller boy, cross-legged, all ears: *Tell me.*

Outside the longhouse under the moon, a heavy delta wind bringing good salt air, Uncle Blake settles back against the rough wood, sighs away the long day in the fields, says, The swamp's a trap without an Indian to guide you.

Tell about us. He gives Blake the biscuits Laurel sneaked him, lies, *I'm full up to here. Now tell me.*

Well, we'll get us a Chitimacha, knows his way, we'll follow him through that trackless swamp, then we'll stick to the shore through Texas, go into Mexico till we reach free territory. Then maybe find us an old Conestoga wagon and go clear to San Francisco. (Chad sees the very name bring Blake's breath faster, for Blake's papa was a sailor full of San Francisco tales.) He looks hard at Chad. You heard it all before—an edge on his voice—and maybe it does you no favor, for a free man can be sold on the block, and runaways get hunted and torn by dogs. He sits up straight, takes hold. That's enough of dreams, he says, and Chad gets that choke-tight throat: *Say it ain't a dream . . .* oh, lordy, say.

The small boy's curious. Yes, says Uncle Blake, black families are fixed and kept by the slaves, only the masters divide them. Chad goes to Uncle Noah.

You know your mama die in the birthing, the old man says.

Did Papa die, too?

Lean as a walking stick, gaunt eyes in sun-wrinkled face, Uncle Noah stares at the floor, shakes his head like it needs screwed on: Maybe Granny Martha say sometime.

Chad's great-grandmamma, the oldest slave, sits mute in her chair, her dull eyes staring. Was a time Granny Martha took care of Chad, of all the children whose folks were in the fields. Now she sits and stares.

Uh-huh, says Uncle Noah, she sure enough shoot the overseer come in her bed one night, they never did find the gun, no sir. His eyes fill up as his voice goes on: After your great-grandpapa die, I guess I be her best friend. Wasn't only time drove her to that corner. When a person live so long and hard, she got a right to her quiet and a right to be heard if she break it.

Still, misty night, she rises from her bed, stands tall and frail and mighty in the center of the longhouse, slaves gathering around. One tallow candle lights her thin, wrinkled face, where Chad's gaze is fixed. A hush over the shadows, the veil of age yanked off: Grandchild Belle birthed a son, golden dawn ten season back, writ on my mind, she says, Belle hold her son and name him Chad, writ on my mind, she says.

He sees that face, that old chin lift, her heart swim in her eyes as she reads him the record of his springtime birth, gives him the gift of his age. The shadow of her bony fingers is a question mark on the wall.

Chad asks, *My mama's mama sold away?*

Beyond the carried word, she says.

Moans, then silence fills the room. Now his untold papa crowds his head, is coming out his mouth—but Granny Martha clasps her hands, nods at him and at the candle, and he blows it out and holds his tongue.

Meet you at the tree, says Clay.

I have to learn my lessons, Clay, I can't play now, Chad's child-voice says.

Clay's mad, his white face is red, he buzzes around: You can do that any day.

Sunday's the only day Uncle Blake's not in the fields.

You like him better than me, your blood brother?

No, Clay, course not, but I'm learning how to read and write.

I can just see Papa if I'd tell him Blake can read and he taught you!

Hush up, here come Logan.

What's the trouble, Master Clay, the overseer asks, boy give you sauce?

No, sir, says Clay, no, sir.

Well, let me know if he do. Walks off, that Logan, looks over his shoulder, his eyes cruel and aimed at Chad.

He'd sure fix Blake, whispers Clay, wouldn't he?

* * *

Laurel paddles the pirogue Chad and Clay hollow out of a log from a fallen cypress. She leaves her dress on a stump, hurries it on when old Mammy calls, hides up in the live oak on the end of the lane to the house, while Clay swears he hasn't seen his sister all the livelong day. The thin, sharp-eyed house servant never looks up. Clay hears his tutor's carriage lumber down the road and makes it into the tree, gets out of his French and his arithmetic, too, while Mammy looks everywhere but up.

Sitting atop the live oak is akin to freedom, the hope that's sown like the seeds of Indian corn into each day. First time Laurel climbs that tree, her blond hair catching the sun like a goldfinch on the wing, she says she'll never be able to think of pieces of Sweet Haven again. Everything at once changes things, she says, lets you see how God must feel, looking down. Chad doubts if God can see as far as he can, or as much.

Two small boys lie lengthwise on thick branches. Clay gasps, Look, Chad, look at that. A shallow-draught boat moves like a phantom up the bayou. People are crowded on, shackled back-to-back, feet in manacles. Their staring eyes, their faces, solemn and still, speak sorrow so deep, so personal, Chad looks away. The swamp cypress, wading knee-deep, reaches pale arms toward them.

Uncle Blake says, The Lafourche ain't sluggish like some of the bayous, it ain't covered with lilies or that green satin scum. It's a good road for smuggling brand-new slaves up from the Gulf.

Stir it around, says Uncle Blake, weigh and sift, don't take my notion as truth. He leads Chad away from the world of the great live oak to the wide, open road of the mind. He smuggles in newspapers to teach Chad to read, maps to show where he is, fetches paper scraps and pencils so the boy can write big, bold letters, thoughts of his own. Says he never saw such impudence in a child, wanting all that learning.

Riding to Labadieville, riding in the wagon that rolls up the road to get flour and salt for the master's table, fuel for the master's lamps, Chad and Clay loll with the empty barrels, spot canecutters and snakes along the way, keep score. *That ain't no swamp rabbit, it's a clump of brush, Clay.* How you see a cottonmouth in that curly branch, Chad? Laugh, laughing, rolling on their bellies. Stop the ruckus back there!

Clay goes to the great house for his meal. Chad smells the supper cooking in the great kitchen as he passes on the rim of the gardens. He stops at the door where the corn is boiled to get his bit of hominy and molasses, then goes back to his chores in the stables and the carriage house and the black-smith shop where the iron is forged. Tools and horseshoes in his hands, scarce little in his belly.

On his mat in the corner of the longhouse, he sets his mind to thinking. It conjures away his hunger, is private, his stock-ade. Yet it, too, craves to be fed—by the flowers, the birdsong, the shades of green, weeping, yawning, crawling green, by words to read and words to write from his secret, captured thoughts. But the thought that feeds it most is freedom.

Empty stomach stilled by sleep, he dreams nagging snatches that begin in a nightmare of sopping underbrush and end on a road along the wide river he's never seen. The Mississippi swells and sighs, calls to the wind, the wind calls to him.

The whip cracks in the stables. Chad sees the old stable hand lashed, can't contain his anger: it rises in a slow bubble from the white-hot pool below, and when Clay comes down all ready for fun, he calls him Master Clay. Clay goes straight up.

Chad says, *Well, it's proper.*

Propper-cropper! Who's been talking to you? Sweet little Cecily? Clay's sweet face, worried, makes the bubble settle, the whirling world be still.

Cecily, a blur in his mind, a persistent voice, pesters her sister by the bayou, rubs mud off her shoes with spit, looks at Chad the way she looks at bugs. She begs Laurel to come home and play, whines at Clay for playing with Chad. I ought to tell Papa to sell him, she says, and Clay's face wrinkles like a prune, mass of red wrinkles with blazing eyes, tight fists offering to hit her. Don't mind little Cecily, he says, she's just talking . . . talking . . . talking.

Clay's the mimic, waltzes around back of the longhouse: Come here, Master Clay, poor Miss Cecily want you this minute! Clay-ton! . . . You must learn how to waltz, Clay-ton, you going on four-teen! Older by half a year, Chad laughs till his belly aches. Then comes Uncle Blake, face twisted with pain, whip marks black and dripping red, the picture wavers, hangs over the world. Logan's bad, all right, says Clay, his oval eyes open wide. Logan only holds the whip, Blake says . . . Thunder rumbles but it's too far off to tell if it will shape into a storm.

Abraham Lincoln president, South Carolina on its own, racing through his head. Clay prances like a proud wood duck, says Fort Jackson here he comes. Uncle Blake talks New Orleans, where ships ride above the streets with the North's spring thaw, like whooping cranes line the docks. *Will we go there together?* the older Chad is asking. Sure enough, we're partners, ain't we?

The U.S. flag comes whoosh down the pole, Master Wycliffe's heel twists it in the ground: Everybody gather round for the raising of the flag of the Independent State of Louisiana, the pelican flag, the sovereign state.

War comes on the wings of spring, and Uncle Noah, his brow agleam with sweat, doesn't say a word. But someone lit a lantern in a room behind his eyes.

Logan stands big and tall, his voice sharp as the knife: Don't y'all fret, you be protect from the demon Yankees till all's back to normal. Old weasel's pale gaze rests on Blake and then on Chad, eyes glint like polished iron.

He hates seeing you with Master Clay, says Uncle Blake.

You do, too, Chad's voice wails.

Blake just smiles his easy smile: The way things be, you only ask for trouble.

Papa's in a snit, says Laurel, long yellow hair damp around her neck, I declare I miss you, Chad. He's sixteen now, looks down on her. She puts biscuits in his hands and lays her hands there, too. Her new slave girl has her eyes on him—Anna's gaze stings him like a slap—and he draws his hands away. Laurel steps close, leans, brings her lips to his, his heart starts thumping as if it wanted out. His voice comes up from a hard climb and it doesn't sound like his: *It ain't safe here no more, things change fast sometimes.* Slowly, she says, they change slowly, you just don't notice till it's time. His neck is burning, his pants are tight, he walks her to the path and then he takes off, running, to the bayou.

A year later and Captain Farragut's fleet is at the foot of New Orleans. Clay comes, his arms swing loose, flies hang their buzzing on the heavy air. The closer he comes, the farther away he is, stands tight-mouthed. They pick words like half-ripe berries. Then Clay says, Laurel ain't supposed to come here anymore, it ain't fitting.

She's my friend, same as you.

She's not a little girl anymore, you ought to know that, what's wrong with you, anyhow?

Chad's shoulders arch and the blades meet.

Clay looks at the dirt and sighs. When his air's all out, he's limp and sorry: I'm in a bad mood and taking it out on you. The manager's leaving and Logan wants the job and I bet he can't even add. I asked Papa to fire that Logan and all I got was a lecture on Laurel. Papa swears she's got no convention in her.

Chad rubs his tongue across the back of his teeth, thinks how smooth they are. He finds a small stone and throws it in the bayou, tries to salvage him and Clay: *See how the pebble skips across the water? It don't hit the rough spots, where it might sink.*

Clay smiles, shakes his head: Same old Chad, talking in riddles.

Uncle Blake says, When I was new here, you was just a mite and sticky as a june bug, I couldn't shoo you off. I swear you're made of printer's ink, the way you read and write now. Look what I brought. In Chad's hands he puts a copybook full of lined pages, fine blank pages looking to be filled. And something else, he says. I went by the rubbish pile and I said that's what he needs, that book the poet wrote, goes like this: "But our poor slave in vain / Turns to the Christian shrine his aching eyes." A Yankee must've left it, now it's yours.

Poet Whittier's *Voices of Freedom* is in his hands, in his cache beneath the longhouse floor, in his bandanna bundle, in his carpetbag, in his Union army knapsack, long after Blake is gone . . .

Two dates and an orange Laurel sneaked him wait for Uncle Blake. Uncle Noah puts a hand on his arm: I have a message.

Uncle Blake?

He went, says Noah.

But we're going together, him and me.

Noah says, Time was short.

Angry buzzing in his head closes down his ears while the old man mumbles.

A commotion outside, two white men in the longhouse: Where is Blake? Master Logan's short neck sinks like a setting hen's into his round shoulders, his eyes dart into corners. Master Wycliffe's nose is long in the light of the lantern he carries, his oval eyes settle on Chad's face: Where is he, Chad? *I don't know.*

Logan raises his whip, the master stays his hand, yells, Better tell me, Chad! Blake's new master's waiting in my parlor, and a pretty penny he paid for him. I know all about the two of you, reading and writing and plotting against the hand that feeds you. Where's he hiding? *I don't know, I don't know . . .*

Through his pain he hears Noah say, You ready for the message? Blake say it ain't a dream. Meet him here when the South's cut in two.

The dream goes wild: Blake like a giant, carrying an axe, cutting, slicing, chopping the South—big map of the South, big blocks of green cane and white cotton—set it over there, this chunk. Then Blake becomes Logan, the axe a whip, red-rimmed eyes gleam, the whip cracks . . . the hip throbs.

Gone the pirogue, its rope untied and gone with it, and the old grey cypress leans over the empty mooring. *He took it,* he wails, *took it and went without me.* He can see Blake paddling, paddling through the wilds, maybe to the city that coming from Blake sounds like a cluster of stars.

Will we go there together? Sure enough, we're partners, ain't we?

I can just see Papa if I'd tell him Blake can read and he taught you, Clay's voice whines.

Down Clay comes, won't meet Chad's eyes. Stands first on one foot, then on the other: I'm sorry about Blake. Clay has that red-wrinkled baby face, looks about to cry. An eagle circles overhead.

It's hard to speak with fury in his throat, a wedge driven fast between them. His voice comes hoarse and prickly as a hedge-hog: *I'm glad he's gone.*

Clay sighs, nods, puts out his hand, but Chad's gaze is fixed on the eagle, the circling, soaring eagle.

Evening and the field hands scarce, Colonel Wycliffe gazes at Chad's long arms, long legs, shakes his head and paces, mutters about changes clean overdue, walks and gestures, makes no sense. Too long, he says, gone too far. Small white man carries power like armor, his presence looms like Logan's whip. Chad stands still, a proper slave, his eyes and ears wide open. Before the master stalks away, he shrinks Chad's world, down, down till it's only a space a yard long in the close, hot arms of the cane . . .

. . . hot cane to hot iron, hot iron from hot cane, how it all began.

ONE

At certain seasons, so sturdy, so thick, tangled and towering seemed the stalks, that one could hardly refrain from pitying the poor blacks who had to cut them down. And yet this task was to them a labor of love, and they appeared to enjoy the fun. Although the necessities of the crop demanded almost incessant exertion, and allowed no time for rest or recreation, the slaves preferred it to any other employment, and always looked forward to the grinding season . . .

—HENRY C. CASTELLANOS, *NEW ORLEANS AS IT WAS,* 1895

September 1862

Taller than a man, the cane formed archways from its furrows, framing row upon row of hot alleys that wouldn't cool down until the stalks were cut. Dark clouds rimmed the horizon. Almost every day around noon the skies let loose a hard, drenching rain that stopped work until the sun reached down to lift the pooling water through the air.

Chad scanned the brush along the wagon road, then walked to the cart that held the water cask. A parched silence hung on the air. No rustle of leaves, no birdcall broke the torrid hush. Only the thuds survived the heat, hoe thuds on the heavy clods of earth, a sound he knew he would hear forever, if only in his sleep.

The silence of the slaves was brittle. Unlike the deep quiet that lay on the fields before Captain Farragut's victory brought General Butler into New Orleans that spring, this silence cracked with every rumor, every hope of the war's moving closer. But the overseer's whip was a constant threat, and from the back of his pony he was quick to catch a whisper.

The cask was still throwing its shadow on the hot boards of the cart as Chad poured water into the common tin cup. He drank, swung around, then poured another cupful. Logan's beady eyes weren't on him. The old weasel was making the rounds of the plantation running a good mile and a half back to the forest that stretched into the swamp. He had left Master Dolan in charge. Dolan paid more mind to his jug than to the field hands, didn't see much through the whiskey's glow, although his very daze was a trigger and he'd lash out with the whip to show he hadn't missed a thing. Now he sprawled out under a tree on the rim of the field and drank deeply from the sweat-coated jug.

Soon the cane would be heavy with juice. Before it flowered, they'd begin cutting the thick stalks near the surface of the ground, stripping the leaves with their knife hooks and trimming them at the top near the last joint. Then they'd pile them in windrows to cart to the sweltering sugarhouse each day of the endless days of grinding and boiling and pouring the molten mass in the crystallizing sheds. Across the plantation they worked night and day from mid-October into January, without a Sunday off until the job was done. He knew how it had been for Uncle Blake, how deadly it could be if the overseer saw fit, and old Uncle Noah repeatedly warned, "Come harvest, you best be gone."

Uncle Blake, gone with April, had taught him how to use his mind, but the fields had shown how strong he was, how his muscles worked together to protect each one, how they answered his need even when his energy ran out. His body could

endure and renew itself, but could he take relentless whippings?

Yesterday the lash curled around his ankles at the water
cask as Logan stood snarling behind him. "You take your
good old time and want more," yelled the overseer. "I'll give
you more!"

He's only my driver, not my doom, Chad had written in his
copybook, and he repeated it silently. The cowhide whip
cracked against his back. Blood surfaced and oozed as he took
the blows with pursed lips, counting them. When it was over
he staggered back to his row where Uncle Noah was out of
breath from matching the whiplashes with angry clouts at the
base of the cane.

After dark, Uncle Noah paid him a visit. "That man Logan,
call hisself massa,"—the old man's words caught halfway and
came out in sudden rushes—"he won't let up till he see you
dead. What you gon do?"

"Nothing."

"You don't moan and cry. He don't like that."

"Too bad."

"I know, I know. But you special, done come late to the
fields, playmate of Massa Clay—uh, uh, uh!"

They drag the pirogue they made up the bank, turn it upside down:
Voilà, *an altar! Pushing a long, thin vine through a needle's eye,
looks right smart, his Clay, in the careful morning light. "When
two Chitimachas mix their blood, they're loyal all their lives," Clay
says. He holds the green-tailed needle, pricks his finger, a red
bandanna around his head, two red blotches on his white
cheeks—"I, Clayton Wycliffe, promise to henceforward..."—kissing the needle, passing it to Chad—"I, Chad Creel... and never
to forsake...*

... forevermore..."

Uncle Noah put a hand on his arm, getting his attention:
"Mark my words, son. Come harvest—"

* * *

Gone, Chad thought now, wiping the sweat off his face as he scanned the wagon road and drank his fill of water, gone to fight for freedom.

The heavens opened and the rain filled the ditches, ran through the alleys, soaked him to the skin.

Two

Thousands of hogsheads of sugar at the value of at least a million dollars ought to pass into the hands of the United States together with much other property.

—MAJOR GENERAL BENJAMIN F. BUTLER TO EDWIN M. STANTON, SECRETARY OF WAR, REGARDING THE LAFOURCHE DISTRICT, NOVEMBER 14, 1862

October 27, 1862

He lifted the rough floor board in the semidarkness of the slave quarters and reached into the space above the damp earth. His arm slid easily through the narrow opening, his elbow plugging the hole at each thrust. As he retrieved his possessions one by one, he glanced around the inside of the longhouse, barren except for a few chairs drawn around a slatted table and a long line of worn mats loosely stuffed with Spanish moss. At the far end, the open door let in the tired, filtered light of the delta's short dusk. No one was there but Granny Martha, sitting by the entrance, stiff and still. His smile drew no hint of recognition, no turn of the lines around her mouth.

He stuffed his newspapers, pencils, map of Louisiana, his copybook and dog-eared volume of poems into the old red bandanna, tied its four corners, and stopping only to kiss the top of her head, walked past the old woman into the evening.

The world had waxed into a somber show of light and sound after the greycoats fanned the dust of the road up the bayou in the night, circling the house, spilling over the grounds. The sound of footfalls, horses' hooves, wagon wheels made Chad's heart race. They'd passed by morning, but the distant grey smoke and gun-thunder kept the fields untended, and if anyone moved about the master's house, he'd noticed no curtain pulled aside to show it.

He knew it was coming, the battle of this October day: word was the Union was brewing a caldron to pour down the bayou. Then yesterday morning Yankee General Godfrey Weitzel steamed up the river with transports protected by gunboats to Miner's Point near Donaldsonville, marched into town as big as you please, and began his advance down Bayou Lafourche. Last night he bivouacked near Napoleonville while his pickets skirmished and blacks from the countryside cut roads up the steep bank of the bayou. They worked through the night making a pontoon bridge out of shallow-draught flatboats, and it was towed down the stream for the passage of troops from one bank to the other, as scouts reported the greycoats were encamped on both sides. This Chad heard from the active grapevine, the eyes and ears of the plantations, eyes that watched Rebel General Alfred Mouton come to call on the planters, ears that heard messages from the Union lines. News about troop movements passed like lightning from plantation to plantation as the war moved in.

All morning Chad sat in solitude against the longhouse as Rebels fought the Yankee regiments just above Labadieville. Most of the slaves stayed inside, speaking low as the battle raged. When at noon the big guns quieted, the stillness sat like a vulture until the word was passed: the victory belonged to the Yankees. The spent Rebels commenced their march down the road. Now as the sky darkened, only a few hollow-eyed stragglers trudged by, and Sweet Haven's doors were closed against them.

The air was close and soft. Uncle Noah napped under the

sugarberry tree next to the pair of tall cedars. Chad knelt before the spare form and the old man opened his eyes. "You going now, Chad?"

"How did you know?"

"I feel it in my bones." He stretched. "Besides, the Yankee general done fight his battle, just like they say he would."

"Say Mouton's clear down at Terrebonne Station, burning all he can on his way back to Berwick Bay. We sure done see the last of him."

"Um-hum." Noah frowned. Chad remembered the September day the news came that President Lincoln had issued a paper saying he would free the slaves come January. It set off a night of talk, songs, and prayers, but Uncle Noah went to bed early. Now Noah said, "It ain't over yet."

"No, but we're winning." He put a hand on the old man's arm. "I'll be back to get you and Granny Martha and go out West, California maybe. We'll have us a cart and a horse or two, and you can ride up front or take a snooze in the wagon."

"Bless your heart, Chad. I'm mighty glad to see you go. I don't want you hurt."

"We're free, Uncle Noah, no one can hurt us now."

The old man put a hand on Chad's knee and looked from side to side before he spoke: "Mind Logan, boy. He can taste your blood."

Noah's thin face was so full of concern, Chad put out a hand and touched it.

He's already late as Laurel stops him on the path at daybreak. He takes time to gobble up the good ripe fruit she's brought. Then he runs like the dickens, crouches behind the bushes rimming the near field to see if he's been missed, whistles a birdcall and catches Uncle Noah's eye. The old man looks toward Logan, who's dismounting, and passes the word to the others in his row, who are doing Chad's work and their own. When Noah nods, he comes running, and he takes over his share of the work before Logan scans the field. He can feel the vein of relief run from one field hand to the other, and Uncle

Noah gives a loud sigh that brings Logan to attention, angered and confused. A baby cries from the shade of a bush and its nursing mother hurries to it with the old weasel shouting from his red face, "Damn you, sucker, mind your pickaninny!"

Uncle Noah got to his feet. "I want to give you something." He went into the longhouse and when he came out he put a stone onto Chad's palm, mumbling something under his breath. He smiled and you could almost see the years fall off his face. "That stone come over the water. I bring it tween my toes."

It was deep red, small like the pebbles of the delta, and smooth from years of rubbing. Chad hugged the old man, hard enough to hear him gasp, then went to the tree to add it to his bundle. When he turned to wave goodbye, Uncle Noah was gone.

He headed for the mansion. Through the window of the kitchen out back he saw the cook talking to a helper. If he asked Aunt Cora to give Laurel a message, like as not he'd be sent packing. Anna walked into the room then, and stood on the hearth against the mantel, her chin out, her lips holding a pout.

She's tall and skinny, wiry and proper, up against a tree. Her mouth's a mere slit, her hair's plaited close or in a tight bun. She could be an old field woman, stony-faced and patient, but she's young, no older than the mistress she's awaiting. She pesters Laurel, "Didn't you hear Miss Cecily call?" He tries to pretend she's not there, so he won't meet her eyes. Laurel keeps on talking to him, she doesn't care. "My shadow is watching, Chad," she says, laughing that ripple that grows and fades then grows again.

With constant staring he caught Anna's eye: she might not help, but she wouldn't tell on him. She looked startled but said nothing as she walked coolly toward the door.

"Don't go wandering, girl," called the cook. "Can't tell what's out there now."

"Don't you fret," she said, her voice strained and stiff. "I have nowheres to go." When the door slammed behind her, she turned to Chad. "Well, the big man finally turns up! Where you been all this time, boy? Don't you know your honey's bawling her eyes out for you?"

She looked like an owl, speaking the crisp, hard words and glaring at him. "What you looking at?"

"Nothing. I was thinking about Laurel."

"*Miss* Laurel, honey, Mis-tress Laurel."

He talked into those awesome eyes: "I need a favor. I'm leaving tonight."

"Is that right?" Her voice softened. "Where you headed?"

"New Orleans."

"Sounds like you won't be back here nohow."

"Will you go tell Miss Laurel to meet me out here behind that magnolia tree?"

"I allow so, if you do something for me."

"What?"

"Take me with you."

"You're crazy as a loon."

"Crazy as you."

"In the fields they say no house servant want to be free." Her dark eyes flashed. "They lie."

"Well, you can do what you want, but you ain't going nowhere with me."

Her chin went up and she rubbed the palms of her hands together. He wondered if she'd hit him but she said, "I'll get her," and swept into the kitchen. Chad saw the cook shake her head toward her and say something low to the woman peeling potatoes.

Laurel was dressed in dark blue and she moved in the shadows, but her smile was bright until she saw his bundle. "I was afraid of that, so I brought a chicken, a whole one. You can tuck it in your kerchief." She glanced at the house. "Clay saw me coming downstairs and he wanted to know where I was hurrying to. I don't know if he was satisfied with my answer. Is there somewhere we can go?"

There was somewhere and he led her there, straining his eyes into the darkness of the forest.

"Promise not to tell anyone, not even Uncle Blake," says Clay as they build the fort in the woods. "Can you get more nails and boards?" Chad nods, he has chores in the blacksmith shop, in the shed, the stables, all over the world. "I won't tell Laurel and Cecily," he says, "but why not Uncle Blake?" Clay stops hammering. "You best stay away from that old fox," he says.

She made little surprised sounds around the fort, then slipped inside. "What a playhouse it would have made if I'd known what you were up to."

"It used to be bigger."

Laurel's laugh turned into a sigh. "Oh, Chad, what will become of us?" She put her hand on his cheek, then sat down and rested her head on her knee where the uneven roof let in a moonbeam. "You can't imagine all the awful things happening. I can't stand to think about it. Why, when the Yankees get ahold of our slavefolk, they harness them to carts like oxen! I declare, they're devils."

"Some folks say they's angels."

"Don't tease, Chad-wick." Her voice got low and damp. "You're all I have, you know. Mama's not herself so I can't talk to her, and when Papa is himself I sure can't talk to him. He's got to be right, won't lend an ear to Mama's ideas, let alone mine. He pats my hand, just pats me away." She shrugged. "Then there's Cecily, too busy putting on airs and pinching her cheeks to be much company. All the uniforms have her in a tizzy. And Chad," she whispered, "I have the oddest feeling when I confide in Anna. Why, I treat her like a sister, but she's downright sullen."

"You have Clay." It was true, she had him even if he'd lost

him. A wave of sadness washed over him as Laurel's voice pushed through: ". . . Grinding should've begun two weeks ago, but Papa was pacing the floor, wondering what to do about the war. He refused to go to Texas like some, and now he says he'll get the crop out even if he has to sell it to the Yankees. It makes no sense to me at all!"

She gave a sob that stepped up high, then slid down. "I feel so alone."

"Clay's still here."

"Not for long, I fear. Papa and Mama pull him this way and that, and he tries his best to please. After the manager left last spring, Papa would have put Mr. Logan in charge of the books if Clay hadn't said no sir, he'd do them, and it's such a dreadful job, no wonder he wants to go to war!" Suddenly she was laughing. Funny, how that laugh affected him, maybe it had a life of its own, he didn't know, but he felt good when he heard it. "I used to hear music from the house and part of it was that laugh of yours," he said.

"Oh, those parties! They make me ache inside. Promise me we'll never have a party"—she leaned her head on his chest—"when you come back . . ."

She was so close he couldn't think, couldn't think of thinking, and he didn't know what his hands might've done if a sound hadn't come from outside the fort. It was a crackle, a discord, and he sat upright, his muscles tight. Laurel grabbed his hand and didn't move for the long moment before the old door creaked and Clay stood before them, stock-still.

Chad stood up. "You go along, Laurel. Clay and me, we have some business."

"You two!" she cried. "I'm not leaving till *you* do—you and your old fort!"

"Master Clay and I have business."

"*Master* Clay? What's got into you? Have you lost your senses? Clay, tell him. Tell him nothing's changed."

Clay turned his gaze on her face and shook his head. His hand went through his hair and he opened his mouth and closed it again.

"I'll be going now," Chad said softly. He tucked his bundle under his arm. Tears streamed down Laurel's face. At the narrow opening Clay stepped aside, gesturing awkwardly. "Goodbye, Chad. I'm sorry it had to turn out this way. It isn't that you're not my blood brother. I figured it all out. It's just that the times ain't favoring us anymore. That's all it is. We're all controlled by the times."

"That's one way of thinking, Clay." *You wouldn't have guessed, the way they talked, wouldn't have ever guessed they were slave and master . . . some even said they looked alike . . .*

Clay put a hand on Chad's shoulder, and he stiffened against it. "I was hard on you about Laurel, wasn't I? But here she is, just the way she always was. You been downright tolerant of her and I oughta thank you."

"I'm the one brought her here," he said.

Clay would not be roused. "The times don't favor us, that's all it is." He held out his hand and Chad saw it shake. "Blood brothers?"

His hand wouldn't go to Clay's, his arm stayed stiff by his side, but his voice came up strong around the anger, through the grief, echoing a past that was black and white and false and gone: "Forevermore," he said.

A whiff of burning wood from a nearby plantation's sugarhouse made him think of the hundreds of trees hewed down by Irish workers contracted to Master Wycliffe every fall. Full of wood chopped and stacked, full of countless cypress stumps, autumn was as final as dying. He remembered Logan's face after the battle, as he ordered him to be at the sugarhouse at midnight to build the fire that would not go out until the end of harvest. "No one's free 'less I say so," he'd said, as though he'd read Chad's mind. The old weasel's eyes were red as the sunset's flame, seemed to say *I've got you now.* Uncle Noah was right about it: Logan hated Chad for his friendship with Clay, maybe even thought Chad was behind Clay's pestering to fire him. Through the incessant labor of

the grinding season, the slavedriver could have wrung re-
venge, but the joke was on Logan, for Chad was on his way.
He ran from the fort and the forest, over the fields toward the
longhouses, putting the past far behind him before he slowed
to a walk.

The night was dark—no moon, no stars—and a sharp chill
came with a sudden breeze. Up ahead was his row of longhouses along the path leading to the lane that passed the
house and went out to the bayou road. As he neared the row,
his footsteps broke a strange, abrupt hush, like a slice of
silence before him. It's in my head, he said, the night bugs are
rubbing their wings and humming, everything sounds just
right. Then the chill pushed in, firm as the body of a snake,
and the night sounds stopped. The leaves on the trees seemed
to bunch together, creating deep pockets of utter cold. He
slid his bundle under his shirt, looked over his shoulder and
around about. A candle from an open door in the row of
doors cast a wavering half-light on the path. The hairs on the
back of his neck crawled and his breath came short. Then he
saw Granny Martha, sitting in the chair outside his longhouse,
her arms half covered by a shawl across her lap, her wide eyes
staring toward him, her body still and stiff as a corpse.

He nodded ahead to the woman in the chair, hoping for a
sway or a wave of the hand, something to soften the thud of
his footsteps, his harsh, short breath, something to weaken his
rising fear lying now with the creature in the chair. If he could
get past, past that chair, he would break into a run. Drawn as
a moth to a burning pyre he kept on walking, looking straight
ahead. Her eyes were like a bird of prey, trained on the path
he walked. He looked beyond into the dark, but sweat beaded
his brow as he neared the chair. Then suddenly she rose, rose
slowly and turned toward him. From the corner of his eye as
he passed her, he saw her scarf slip to the ground: what was
it she held with both her hands?

A shot rang out, one loud report and a sickening thud.
Granny! He swung around. Sprawled on the ground by the
dark space between the longhouses, his white face caught

grinning, was Master Logan, a crimson hole where his heart should be. Near him lay his cold, cocked rifle. Still as a marsh quail stood Granny Martha, a smoking revolver limp in her hands.

Oh, my Granny, oh, my God.

A little smile crossed her face, her eyes were bright and full of tears. The old revolver dropped to the ground, atop the shawl that had covered it.

Chad folded her in his arms, held her thin frame gently, kissed her quilted face, her eyes, her ears.

The field hands were gathering, nodding him on, waving him away.

"Say I did it," he called over his shoulder, and one of them said, "No need."

THREE

To fling my arms wide
In some place of the sun,
To whirl and to dance
Till the white day is done.

—LANGSTON HUGHES

October 28, 1862

Anna shifted in her sleep, digging deeper into the pine nee-
dles and threading vines of the forest. The small palmetto tree
at her feet rested its leaves on the still, warm mist of early
morning. She ran a hand over her braids, loosening, undoing.
Opening her eyes, she half expected the red polka-dot curtains, and seeing instead the slim trunk of a nearby pine,
rolled over on her back and saw the sky.

Lazy morning sounds let her yawn, stretch, reach an arm
toward that moss hanging down. No clanging of pots, hurried
footsteps, shouts—no Cora in the kitchen outside the room
where Miss Laurel hung those curtains that caught the day's
first light: stark white in the pale room, red polka dots that
sent a rush of terror through her.

Today was different, unshaped, unboxed, a day so light it

might fly away if she didn't make a form, mold edges, put a lid on. No lid! That was it: she'd just let it be and see what it became all by itself, just wander through it on tiptoe, singing—for she was free!

She loved to sing but Aunt Cora wouldn't let her—*Girl, you sound like a cat on the prowl!*—and she lost her song in Miss Laurel's presence: *Put the tray on the balcony this morning and lay out my pink and white dress. Papa'll never guess where I'm going if I look all ruffly the way he likes, Anna, don't you think?* Think she did, but she said, Yes, Miss Laurel, No, Miss Laurel, I'm coming, I'm coming.

She was Laurel's birthday gift when Laurel turned sixteen. She was sixteen, too, and for the next year she stood in the boudoir with its dusting-powder smells, combing that long flimsy hair, following her mistress through the daylight hours until she dropped into bed at night—doing this, doing that, taking it all in and letting precious little out. *Never let them know what's in your head,* said her mama back in Mississippi, and she'd nodded slyly, thinking, I keep a lot from you, too, Mama, right behind my face. She'd learned the difference. Small peeves she'd kept from Mama, why-did-you's and you-are-so's, little, personal things. Her temper had flared against her own (one to reckon with, her mama said) but when Miss Laurel cooed, *Don't worry, Anna, Papa says we won't let the Yankees hurt you,* she felt no need to show her scorn: *Let them have their say and never let them know.*

One thing tore at her, and even now she groaned, thinking of the way the yellow-haired girl swiped food from the kitchen and went loping to the boy who was sent late to the fields, just last spring, he was so favored. At the thought of his name, her jaw set and her stomach tightened like a trap, confining her disgust at how he looked at Laurel and the way they laughed together. Laurel kept telling her all they said, not noticing how Anna couldn't smile, how she had to push her words out through the cracks: *Miss Laurel, Mammy's calling.*

Chad was his name, the boy who was a man, who looked at her from the corner of his big, oval eyes as if he thought she'd bite. Now she could see to laugh, but then her eyes were tightened on the girl who was a woman, the one who owned her like the dolls in the cabinet, like the clothes in the press, the stack of books, the one who gave her a ribbon or a bow and let her see through a white girl's eyes, live a life not hers. Miss Laurel seemed to feel so generous, giving her a room with a window, a window to the light, and putting up those curtains.

There be two good memories for every bad one if you look, her mama said, and after she was put on that boat rocking in the deep mist, with strangers down in the hold where she slept, slept away the trip to the town where Master Wycliffe's houseboy waited with the cart, she lay many a night in that dank little bedroom *looking.* The memory of her older sister brought great warmth, a graceful image of arms and hands, mostly, for she was very young when Alila would take her to the bayou and soap her body with those slick, warm hands and the cool suds bubbled as the warm hands caressed—then stark white cloth, red polka dots—no! She'd end up holding back a scream, cold sweat running between her breasts as the first light splashed the curtains. Something gone it was, forgotten, yet it blocked her way. It got so hard to find good memories, such a risk, that she had to give up looking.

She got up from her pine-needle bed and, yawning, stretched toward the sky. To breathe the fresh, free air! To see the new sun fleck the leaves, to hear fresh morning sounds! The contrast of things past and present amazed her: *This gloom makes me sick, Anna,* she could hear her mistress say, *Papa's in a dark mood since New Orleans fell, curses this one and that one, never any peace, not much laughter, either.* Laurel's pale face was more washed out than usual, and she laughed a nervous squeak. *Papa goes on so I don't know what to think. Now he's saying, by God, he'll stay at Sweet Haven come Abraham Lincoln himself.* Anna had solemnly shaken her head and— laughed! Yes, a laugh so still you'd never guess bubbled up her throat: picture Master Lincoln ambling through the door with a big grin on his face, *Hallo!*

Though the climate of fear grew strong, she herself was not scared of the Yankees (last thing her mama said was to pay no heed to white folks' loose talk). Still, she didn't want to be there when the Yankee general came marching down the bayou. And the general was on his way, Chad said when he came two nights ago, beckoning to her from the kitchen window, asking her to get Laurel. He'd stood there kind of leaning, as though he'd fall if she didn't help him out, but his eyes stayed right on hers and she had to admit they were calm and clear . . . clear as the night of a killing frost.

He was running away and she should've known he wouldn't take her with him. She deserved what she got, asking. But it was time for her to go and so she went, didn't plan a minute, just set her hands to doing: got a big sack from the kitchen, put a few things in it, jar of water from the Wycliffe cistern, hard old biscuits when Cora wasn't looking. Then she left before Laurel got back that night. On her way through the gardens she stripped a kumquat tree, sour as the day is long. The fruit was the end of her bitter memories, fitting to take along, and all she wanted of Sweet Haven.

Four

You can form no idea of the vicinity of my camp, nor can you form an idea of the appearance of my brigade as it marched down the bayou.

—BRIGADIER GENERAL GODFREY WEITZEL,
UNION ARMY, OCTOBER, 1862

Late October 1862

He wakened to a pair of eyes staring into his. "You in trouble?" asked a white boy standing over him. To the side an older boy eyed him sharply as the younger spoke again: "What you doing here?"

"Sleeping."

Slaves escaping to the Union lines were camped along his way that night: men, women, and wide-eyed children, some with plantation carts and mules, most with nothing but the rags on their backs. Chad had asked, How you feel? not camping with them, just passing through. Across the bayou and beyond wide fields of cane, he'd found a sheltered spot in foliage near the swamp that lay between him and the river plantations to the east. Here he'd slept.

"What you got in that bundle?" asked the older boy.

Their tattered clothing, bare feet, sunken cheeks meant poor white trash, a name Uncle Blake said brought them close to slavery.

"A chicken," he said. "You're welcome to it."

The younger one plunged forward but the older stopped him. "If'n he's telling the truth," he said, "Ma needs it more'n we do."

"Is your mama sick?" he asked, giving the chicken to the older boy.

"She ain't sick and she ain't well. What can we give you for this?"

"A drink of water."

They led him to a shack where the underbrush widened to a swampy field. As they neared, a woman opened the door and leaned on it. She was thin and ghastly pale, her hair straight and sparse, but her smile when she saw them put life into her face. "Come on in," she said. "You running away?"

Chad nodded.

"When my man was on his deathbed, it was the slaves hereabouts that helped me nurse him. One woman name of Ella got whipped bringing us food and medicine. I hide ever escaping Nigra I can, since then."

"I don't have to hide, ma'am. The Yankees are marching down the bayou, chasing the Rebels out."

"Is that right?" She coughed into her hands. "Cross your heart?"

"Yes, ma'am."

"Praise the Lord!" she said, her eyes rolling upward.

Their home put Chad in mind of house-servant shacks where ashcakes baked on the hearths. His gaze went to the pot steaming over the fire.

"You welcome to my gombo," said the woman. "Don't have nothing in it but okra, but you welcome to it. What's that you got there, Elmer?"

"A chicken, Ma, see?" He unrolled its cheesecloth covering. "He gave it to us."

"You sure bout that? Did you give it to Elmer, boy?"

"My name's Chad, ma'am. Yes, I gave it to him."

"Well, I declare, thank you then. Been a while since we tasted fowl. Had a coop of chickens, but couldn't keep them in food when the corn was gone. I said, lawsy, this land's too wet to farm. My, what a treat it'll be."

The little fellow's eyes were on the roasted bird and Chad wished he'd brought two. The woman dropped it in the soup. "There," she said, "that'll make the most of it. Soon's it's brothed a little, we'll have a company meal." She fidgeted with her apron. "Where you headed? Oh, this here's Elmer and the little one's Todd. My name's Missus Andrews. Shake hands with Chad, boys, and say you're pleased to make his acquaintance."

The boys solemnly obeyed.

"He's thirsty, Ma," said Todd, his big eyes showing sympathy. "He want a glass of water."

"You don't say 'he' when the boy's right here," snapped Mrs. Andrews. "You call him Chad, what his name is, or you talk to his face." She gestured with her head and Elmer took a pail outside. "Folks get sick from bayou water, I say. We ain't got the rich folks' cistern, but that there rain barrel been in the family three generations, and no one's died of bad water yet." She stirred the soup. "Where you say you headed?"

"New Orleans."

"Clear down there? That's one place I never been. My mama and papa was, though. Papa was a shrimper fore he lost his boat, yes he was, and Mama had big plans, but you know how it is, bad season, get in debt, and it's all gone. I was just a tyke when we come up here, try to farm the land, lucky to stay alive with nothing but work. This land ain't fit for farming, and I guess that's how we got it. Wore my folks out, it did. I swan, what you going to do in New Orleans?"

"Join the army."

Her mouth dropped open. "You don't say!"

"The Union army," he said.

"The Union army. I declare, that's mighty fine. I know some has sons in the army, fighting for the South. I said why, what they ever do for you, but you know how it is, they hope their sons break away once they in the army, maybe have a chanct, leastways a full belly." She began to cough and it shook her so she had to sit down. Todd ran to get an old shawl off a nail on the wall and put it on her back. Elmer brought her a cup of water. "Pshaw," she said, clearing her throat, "anyone coughs now and then. You boys tend to your company and stop fussing over me."

She got up, pulling the shawl around her, and stirred the soup. "Make yourself at home, sit right down at the table. Won't be long now."

Chad asked about the swamp between them and the river and the woman shook her head, said a man could lose himself in that morass. If he stayed in sight of Bayou Lafourche until it wound to the river, his trip would be longer but his way sure and his step dry. The boys looked on as Chad laid out his map of Louisiana and read some of its landmarks aloud. "I'll be going north to go southeast," he said, his chuckle lost on Elmer and Todd, who stared at him soberly. Mrs. Andrews sighed. "Seems like I been doing that all my livelong days, but I never get around to getting nowhere. Look at my young sprouts—no schooling or chanct to get it. Where you learn to read?"

"A friend taught me. He taught me to write and figure, too."

"Hear that, Elmer? Ain't that mighty fine," she said. "Not many Nigras know all that, and that's a fact." She scanned the map for a while, moving her lips as if she were reading it, then declared how fine it was laid out and how true to the country, like the ones her pa used in the old days. She avoided his eyes and Chad looked at the map until it was time to eat.

They sat around the table. The woman gave a blessing first, thanking her God for Chad and his chicken and Elmer and Todd at the table. She talked while Todd gobbled, staring at Chad, and Elmer stared into his soup. Finally she said, "Elmer, tell him how well you know this country."

He raised his head. "I know it," he said.

Another spell of coughing overtook her and she turned from the table as it tore at her, motioning the boys to stay seated, as riled as she was wrung. Finally she turned back to the table, her shawl to her mouth, her face the color of the ashes on the hearth. In a little while she said, "Once we had one of them itinerant teachers come by and he couldn't get over how much Elmer knows and how quick he is to learn, could he, Elmer?"

"Don't make no nevermind, Ma," said Elmer, finishing his soup and staring into the bowl.

"Sure it do. Why, they say that fellow Lincoln start out just like you."

Color spread over Elmer's face but he said nothing.

"I swan, all you need is—" She held back a cough.

"Please, Ma," said Elmer, his eyes still down, "he don't want to hear."

"Sure he does, don't you, Chad, sure you do."

Todd laughed. "He sure don't have a say in it the way you are, Ma. I say he's a real nice man, though. I like him."

Elmer nudged him, and Mrs. Andrews put up her hands. "What did I say about talking to his face?"

After the meal, Chad filled a small jug with water from their prized rain barrel.

"You welcome to stay on for a while," Mrs. Andrews said. "We ain't had a man around here since my poor husband passed away, God rest his soul, and an educated man like you be good for the boys. I don't have time for learning them, myself. But I do make them mind their manners, don't I, boys?"

"Yes'm," said Todd, and Elmer looked at the floor. "Let him go, Mama," he said.

"Thank you kindly, ma'am," said Chad, "but I have to be on my way."

"Well now, of course you do." She was leaning on the doorjamb but now she straightened and there was a mix of pleading and sorrow in her eyes as she turned to him. "Mebbe though, you could use some company along the way, someone good at tracking game, good worker, good thinker, too—like Elmer."

Chad was stunned. Elmer spoke up: "No, Ma. I won't leave you and Todd."

"Listen to me, Elmer—"

"No." He walked off.

"When Elmer gets like that, there ain't no moving him, just like his pa," she mumbled, then her voice got shrill: "Come back here, boy, and mind your manners, I'm still your ma!" She put her hands on Todd's shoulders and smiled a shadowy smile that spoke beyond her words: "We got company to say goodbye to."

It seemed as though the country had stopped spinning its daily webs of work and sun and pain. He passed through Indian corn and cane fields waiting for the knife, and wooded land lively with the abrupt song of the golden-winged swamp warbler, the drawn-out notes of the lark, and the loud medley of a mockingbird, putting on a show. He took a long, slow breath. The camellia trees were laden with new blossoms, just as they were at the advent of spring. When last he saw their lush display, he was turning seventeen, Uncle Blake escaped, and he was sent off to the fields. He looked up at the blue sky and whooped: no other spring would be like last spring, and no other fall like this one.

From a distance came a growing rumble like thunder in the ground, and he climbed a tall cottonwood to get a view. Up the road dust was rising from more commotion than he guessed the little town of Labadieville had ever seen.

Down the bayou on both sides came the Union brigade: cavalry, infantry, field artillery, every soldier with a black man to carry his supplies. Along came the freed, the men and women and carts of children, walking, running, limping with the army down Bayou Lafourche. It was such a sight, a driving, frolicking, crazy sight. He ran, zigzagging at the throng's edges, veering to the swamp in his impulse to get away, panting with a certain frenzy, glad he was going in the opposite direction.

He climbed a live oak and peered into the distant east, hoping to see the river, but the morning sun's rays fooled him: a hundred rivers shimmered through vine and field. He ate the sweet fruit of the alligator juniper and the coco plum and followed the bayou toward Donaldsonville. Before darkness closed in, as the bullfrogs sang their lives away and mosquitoes hummed, he wrote down the day.

Two nights and another day's beginning, and he was running toward the rising sun, crossing the fields near Donaldsonville, into the wetland, going east toward the Mississippi. The glazed surface of a swamp pool took him by surprise, and he found himself in water deep enough to swim the few long strokes to its edge. He shook himself, glad he'd thrown his bundle as he took the dip, sparing his belongings. The swamp might be full of tricks but it was narrow here, and he came out to a cornfield and a longleaf pine forest beyond.

The forest was thick with undergrowth, but he forged through to the other side and stopped, breathless. There, only a few yards away, was a great green mound, stretching like a serpent to his right and to his left as far as he could see. He climbed the levee to stand tall above the mighty river.

"I made it," he called. "Y'hear? I made it!"

He thought he heard his name on the wind and turned as the voice came again: "Chad?"

Anna! Her swept-clean face, upward turn of the jaw, shoulders ready to shrug: "Is that you, Anna?"

"Seems so," she said, out of the forest now, at the foot of the levee. "I swear, I thought I'd never lay eyes on you again."

He ran down the slope, happy to see her in spite of himself. "How did you get here?"

"I been on the road since I gave Miss Laurel your message. Couldn't stay there, a-sittin' and a-waitin' for the Yankees."

"Didn't you see them on the way?"

"Passed right by their camp. They didn't mind. Some folks said I should stay with them, but not me."

"Me, neither."

She looks different out in the open, he thought, and he asked, "You hungry?"

"No, I brought lots of kumquats, almost cleaned out a tree, and I picked a mess of fat pork on the way. The sack's right there, help yourself."

As his mouth puckered with the sour kumquat and recovered with the sweet, wild figs, her face opened up and shined on him. "Get on, now. Maybe I'll see you in New Orleans," she said, waving. She walked over the levee to the water's edge, took off her blouse, splashed her face and arms. He watched her, knowing he wasn't going without her, now that she'd come this far.

FIVE

Tell me, O dream of utter aliveness—
Knowing so well the wind and the sun—
　　Where is this light
　　Your eyes see forever?
　　And what is this wind
　　You touch when you run?

　　　　　　　　　　—LANGSTON HUGHES

November 1–6, 1862

He liked the way she ate. She made a business of it, enjoying it so much he had to laugh. This made her toss her head and glare at him. He turned to the fruit in his lap, grateful it was there, and then she giggled. "You look so funny when you think you done wrong."

"What did I do wrong?"

"Make fun of me."

"No, Anna, I wasn't, honest. I like watching you is what I was laughing for."

She cocked her head. "Say that again. Bet you can't."

"Could if I wanted to, but I don't."

"I'm glad." She looked serious for a moment, then giggled again. "I mean I'm glad of what you were laughing for."

"So am I."

She leaned on an elbow, looking happy, looking pretty. "How far do we have to go, Chad?"

"Far as we want to," he said, feeling pretty good himself.

She kind of pulled herself in. "I mean, how far is New Orleans, Mister Chad?"

He cleared his throat. "Not many days ahead. I think we're close enough to let down a little—far as the danger goes."

She looked at him with that turn of the jaw, so he showed her the map, pointed out where he thought they were. "New Orleans is right down here, across the river."

Their road was the winding Mississippi, where the Union flag flew above warships. When the guns were aimed closely at the land, they knew it was Rebel-held and kept close to the earth, skirting the jetties, and at night they slept in heavy foliage. Near Lac des Allemands, where the Louisiana state militia, guerrillas, and civilian patrols spilled out from the lake to the river, they traveled at night near the rim of the swamp, lest they be seen and captured. In the first morning light, they often stopped to pick nuts and berries, and her smile was so bright he thought he needed blinders.

Now, gazing at their likely position on the map, "Suits me fine," she said airily, as though she would change it if she could. Then her eyes were suddenly deep. "What you gonna do first off?"

"Sit on the dock and eat shrimp and watch the boats come in and load up."

"Miss Laurel, she says—" She sniffed and looked away from him, a funny twist around her mouth. "Well, I know better than to take it serious, but she says Beast Butler is a bad man, as soon shoot a Nigra as look at him."

"She's talking through her papa's mouth. It ain't so. We'll be just fine in New Orleans, free as anybody. Why, Old Cock-eye Butler's raising a black brigade, and I'm going to join it."

"Join the army? What for?"

"To fight for our freedom."

Her face looked full of questions but she just said, "Oh."

She fingered a surface tree root and seemed so far away that he touched her hand. There was something he suddenly wanted her to know: "When the South's cut in two, I'm going to meet Uncle Blake back at Sweet Haven."

"Cut in two, huh? Why back there?" She pulled her hand away and made a face.

"It's where we started. It's where Uncle Noah and Granny Martha wait for us, a place we know how to get to. We'll have a horse and a mule and a covered wagon with a floor curling up on the ends and cooking pans hanging on hooks." He looked up where the treetops were trying to reach the sky. "Even if he don't get a chance to meet me, I'll have a wagon like that for the old folks."

"You dream, you do."

"It ain't a dream!"

She faced him quickly. "Oh? Says who?"

"Uncle Blake."

"What else he say?"

Her tone had changed, had that brittle lilt, but he went on anyway. It made him feel good to talk about Blake. After all, it wasn't his fault he had to leave so fast, was it? Uncle Noah just happened to be there, maybe even told Blake he'd better take the pirogue, knowing Chad wouldn't mind. Things would be different now if Clay hadn't betrayed them, telling on Uncle Blake and him—but different isn't always better. He took a big breath. "Well, he say we'll go to California, maybe San Francisco, where a black man name of Philip Bell has a newspaper called the *Pacific Appeal.*"

"How you know that?"

"I read the newspaper, that's how. Blake's papa was a sailor and he gave it to him. Blake got a newspaper from New Orleans, too. He knows I like to read."

"Sounds like your Uncle Blake knows a lot for a field hand."

"Sure he does, and he tells it all to me."

"What would he tell me?"

"He don't even know you."

She tossed her head. "I don't care to know him! I don't need his advice, or anyone's not ever. I can sure enough make my own way."

Her arms were crossed, her mouth a slit the way it was before he knew her. He guessed she wanted to be with him in New Orleans on that dock eating shrimp. He cleared his throat. "Once we get inside the city, Anna, we'll find a place for you right off. It's best we go our own ways then."

He'd meant it kindly, but she stiffened like a canecutter whose time has come. "Who you think you are, anyway? You think I want to follow you, do you, and fall all over you like your ladylove, huh? Well, you—are—wrong!" She spit out the words with fire, jabbing him in the belly as she spoke. "Just cause you got that white ass so nice and easy don't mean you have the least bit of charm for me!"

The top of his head suddenly pulsed with rage. "Don't you dare—" he cried, grabbing her arm. "That ain't true and it ain't fit talk."

"What you know about fit talk, nigger?" She moaned as he gripped her arm. "I can say what I want to and you can't stop me, what you think you are, my master? Why, you're the same as the whoring white man—and you know it!"

He raised his arm in fury and it hung in midair.

"Go ahead, hit me," she yelled. "I wouldn't be surprised a bit. You learned a lot from your little white whore. I was sure enough wrong to tag along with the mistress's boy!"

He was on her then with all the passion he'd harnessed with Laurel, all the anger, all the hurt and love gone wild. He heard her dress rip as he pulled it up and the ripping sickened him but he didn't stop, maybe couldn't, sure enough didn't want to.

He shut his mind and held her hands though she'd gone limp and there was no need. Then he found the place and it was done, and for a moment he lay still, feeling her heart race beneath him, feeling the warmth, the tight enclosure. Slowly, slowly, he began to move and she moved with him. It was as if her body were a mold of his, yet in contradiction, and for the first time in his life he was not himself alone.

When it was over he turned onto his side, his back to her, and wept.

SIX

I wish I had wings to
Fly like the eagle flies.

—LANGSTON HUGHES

November 6–12, 1862

She watched him silently, feeling she might fly apart, split into a thousand miserable bits, for he had cried when she felt like singing. She wanted to sink into the ground right on the spot, just be sucked in without moving: moving might rustle the air and the air might rustle him, bringing his eyes to hers. She thought about it, planned it out, and ever so carefully, one motion at a time, edged away and made ready for sleep.

They traveled on the fringe of dense swampy forests, one and another headed by a sea of stumps. She wondered where the trees had gone and as he told her, he looked down or past her. She watched his every gesture as he built their small fires, climbed trees, scanned the map, lay in sleep. A few short days ago she could have touched his hand, before she let pure fancy rule and in her fit set Laurel smack between them. Oh, Anna, she said to herself, how could you?

* * *

"Ain't you hungry, Anna?" he asked. He'd skinned a bull-frog's legs and roasted them brown and tender. He was telling her what he expected they see when they reached the city in the arm of the river. It was more talking than he'd done in a while and a light was in his eyes.

She was so enthralled his question made her jump, and she began to eat. "This sure is good, real good." She licked her fingers and saw him smile. "Go on, tell me," she said.

Now he smiled broadly. "I'll bet there's something around that bend up ahead."

He was right: a small jetty of framed woodwork stretched from the levee out toward the larger wharf across the river, where an old, empty barge and a small fishing vessel were moored beside a gunboat. A large river steamer inched toward the dock. Anna stared across at the small buildings standing on piles over the water, and a cluster of white houses with large galleries, small gardens, and chicken coops. Some had a cow or a goat tied to a tree.

"Where are we?" she asked.

"There's not enough there for it to be New Orleans, but Uncle Blake told me you work down to it. There's homes on the skirts, he say, and lots of woods. But if we keep to the river and keep walking, we can't miss it."

"What are those buildings out over the water?"

"That first one has a sign—say 'Bath House'—and another one say 'Billy-ard Rooms' and I can't see the first word on the other one, but the next word is 'alley.' "

Then Chad took her hand, rubbing her fingers as he held it, and she thought she'd break when his eyes met hers. "I'm dreadful sorry, Anna," he said.

"No time for that," she cried, pulling away her hand, mustering all the merriment she could. "You go your way and I'll go mine, and I'll see you sometime maybe." She ran her hand over her hair: she'd let it out, river-washed and full, with hardly a thought to how it must look, and her clothing was frowsy, her shoes apart at the seams—what a sight she must be! "I can hardly wait to walk into that town in the arm of the river," she said, wiping her eyes, "just walk in and find me a—a bath and stay in it for hours, like a lady!"

He looked her over, smiling that smile of his. "You are a lady, Anna," he said.

SEVEN

I've known rivers:
Ancient, dusky rivers.

My soul has grown deep like the rivers.

—LANGSTON HUGHES

November 12, 1862

Bone-weary, Jerry Labarre rested a dark arm on an oar, the Mississippi and his rowboat behind him. He searched the faces of the young man and woman as they approached, thinking here they come, stars in their eyes, heading for New Orleans and a peck of trouble. "Take you for a picayune," he said.

The young man shook his head before he spoke, scanned the riverfront, didn't look directly at him: force of habit, he supposed, the mark of a slave. "We have no money. I could make a raft, maybe."

"You'd never get across her," he said, nodding toward the wide river. "There's a tricky one, calm on the surface, cranky underneath. Takes a while to learn her."

"I could owe you then."

"*Oui,* you could."

The tall young man, all muscles and bones, plucked from the fields like a ratooning sprout, had earnest oval eyes, a high forehead, and the whisper of a smile on his long, thin face. The woman's pretty face was full of sass and verve, her jaw set, and she stared back at him. She put him in mind of Suzanne, the way she was when he met her, the way she stayed until the day she died. It shook him a little, but he tried not to show it, tried hard not to gawk at the young woman. "Where are you headed?" he asked, as if he didn't know, as if so many others hadn't passed by that way.

"New Orleans," said the young woman. "I'll pay you back soon's I get work."

Jerry thought of the crowded contraband camps growing in the woods near the city and shook his head. "We'll call it even, if you row us over."

"We don't want no favors," said the youth, shifting from one foot to the other.

"Fiddlesticks. I live over there, and I'm all fagged out. You'll be doing me a favor." He reached out his hand. "I'm Jerry Labarre."

"I'm Chad Creel. And this is Anna."

He shook her hand. "You are a lucky man, Chad. The fever took my wife in '53. The world is not the same without her." The world isn't the same, anyway, he thought, and sometimes he was glad his wife missed the worst of it. He couldn't imagine Suzanne living in the cabin he built after he had to sell their house. But more than that, she would've bristled when law after law was passed against the black Creoles during the years leading to the war. *What do they mean, prohibiting manumission?* he could imagine her saying, her chin stuck out in defiance. They'd never had the pleasure of children, and Suzanne had been known to buy a young girl on the block, keep her as a servant while tutoring her for several years and perhaps sending her to finishing school, then emancipating her to live her life as she chose. This law alone would have caused his wife grief. He'd wondered many a time if they would have emigrated to France or the Caribbean Islands, as had a number of their friends. No, he thought now, she'd have wanted to stay and fight. Anna's eyes showed that kind of spirit, too. He couldn't help smiling, and he knew his smile looked out of place, coupled with a lament for his wife.

Anna sat stiffly in the boat while Chad took the oars. Jerry directed them across the wide river in a diagonal path that gave in to the current enough to hold it in check. "Over there," he said, pointing to a spot alongside a moored river steamer, "ease in there." He stood up. "*Bon!* Another yard and I'll tie her up."

It was easy to see Chad couldn't keep his eyes off the steamboat with its big paddlewheel, the fabled riverboat of the racing days. A nearby gunboat seemed to be a lesser curiosity: he'd seen the likes of it before.

Then they said goodbye to Jerry, getting ready to walk into New Orleans as though they were anybody. He had the urge to hold them back, to put them somewhere and tell them something, Lord knows what. "What do you think you'll do?" he asked, knowing it probably wouldn't matter: how could it matter what they wanted to do? They'd be swallowed by a crowded contraband camp *tout de suite*—no papers, no friends—and that was the least of the evils.

"I aim to join the army," said Chad.

"Oh? But it's suppertime," he said. "I wish you would come with me for a bite to eat. I've been saving a large *estomac mulâtre* and now I know why."

"What's that?" asked Anna.

"Ginger cake, *chérie.* I make it from an old recipe my wife got from friends who own a plantation up the river."

Chad shot him an inquiring glance, but he didn't go on. The *gens de couleur* walked in many directions. It would take too long to explain. "I have bottles of *bière douce,* a ginger beer. And there's wine. But beef is like gold now—and who wants to eat gold?" He laughed. "Will you be my guests?"

They turned to each other, and Anna giggled. It was as though his Suzanne had risen from the grave.

Chad explained with a sheepish grin: "First time we ever been called guests."

"It's time you were, then. Come, it's not good to stand, much better to be walking."

They followed the road by the levee, passing through a small crowd of steamboat passengers, mostly army officers and their ladies, making their way to the railroad stop ahead. Chad slowed down, his eyes fixed on the interlocked cars and locomotive.

"Where are they going?" asked Anna.

"They're probably on their way to the St. Charles hotel, headquarters of the Union army. The train will take them as far as the New Orleans terminal, and *fiacres* will carry them the rest of the way. This is the Carrollton station. It's a faubourg of New Orleans."

"I didn't see any Nigra soldiers," said Chad.

"Not likely to, here," said Jerry, walking faster. "See the sign over there? It says 'No loitering.' "

"I can read," said Chad, "and write, too."

"Good," he said, hurrying them into the wooded stretch to his rough cabin. Only his closest friends weren't surprised when he opened the door to his furnishings: a good French chair and pair of loveseats, pretty lamps, two small tables, a cherry *secrétaire* with its glassed-in bookshelves, and three fine prints on the wall. His cot was in the corner not far from his kitchen, and the massive Spanish table he'd managed to build the cabin around stood boldly in the middle of the floor.

Anna was staring at the small, high windows where he'd placed pots of *matas de romero*, the plants his wife had told him brought good luck. When he questioned that, Suzanne had assured him that if he wished to know which families were happiest, all he had to do was find the houses with the greatest number of rosemary plants on their sills. The pots were in his windows in memory of Suzanne, and now as Anna stared at them, he found himself wondering if they might not have brought him a bit of luck, after all. *She could have been our daughter,* he thought, then realized Anna had said something.

Her gaze had shifted to the photograph near the lamp on the table. "It is a daguerreotype of my wife, Suzanne, my *petit chou*," he said, and realized the emotion in his voice was a symptom of age. He hated to see teary-eyed old men walking with heads down, and always pulled back his shoulders and blinked back his tears when they threatened.

But Anna was smiling at him and Chad put a hand on his shoulder. "You have a nice house," he said. "Did you build it yourself?"

"Yes, mostly. When the war took my business I had to sell my house in the *carré de la ville*. Sit anywhere you like."

"What was your business?" Anna asked.

"I was a lithographer and engraver. I had trade in three languages. I might show you some of my work after supper." He got out the bottle of Médoc he had laid to rest under the floorboards, and placed china bowls on the table. The jambalaya he'd begun that morning was ready, except for heating the rice and herbs and adding the oysters he'd bought at the oysterman's hut before his last trip across the river. He was sorry he had no pork to add, but there was his gombo filé, vegetables he'd boiled in a stock of young sassafras leaves pounded to a powder. He didn't mind cooking, but it was no joy when he dined alone. Both the children were watching him, such expectation on their faces he felt a pang of pity: when he and Suzanne were at the threshold, they'd stepped into a friendly world.

"Can I help?" asked Anna.

"I forgot to slice the tomato into the jambalaya," he said. "You can do that. It won't be long cooking, and then we'll sit down together at the table."

"It sure is a big table," said Chad. "Did you make it?"

"Oh no. It's—just an old table we used to like." He found silverware and linen napkins laid away in his chest, and feeling very merry, dipped into the gombo and held the spoon to Anna's lips.

"Um-um!" she cried, her eyes sparkling. "That's good!"

Even her voice was Suzanne's! He poured ginger beer for

his company and a glass of Médoc for himself. Such a long time since he'd tasted wine.

Chad had taken a *Picayune* from one of the small tables. It was a rag full of slanted articles and editorial tommyrot; nothing like *L'Union,* the newspaper owned by Jerry's friend Trevigne. Suddenly Jerry remembered what Chad had told him. "I'm glad you can read, *mon fils,*" he said, lighting his lamps, one by one.

"What's this about the Nigra regiments—the Native Guard?" asked Chad. "It says the soldiers feed and shelter runaways. It says the soldiers keep the police out of their barracks by force."

"Yes, I've heard that."

"What do the police want with runaways? They ain't fugitives anymore."

"We know that," said Jerry, "but the city *gendarmes* don't."

Chad shook his head, whispering an oath. "Then what happens—" he looked at Anna, and they both turned to Jerry—"to freed slaves?"

He faced them squarely. "Some work for soldiers, some become soldiers—and then there are the contraband camps." He took a big swallow of his wine. "Please, eat the hot gombo while I serve the jambalaya."

"What's a contraband?" asked Anna.

"Property won by the victors. Even—people." He was surprised at the depth of his sigh, and quickly smiled. "Please, sit down. After supper we'll talk about it." He didn't know what he would say. How could he tell them that walking through town in their tattered clothing they would certainly be arrested by the *gendarmes,* hustled to a camp by a soldier, or even taken by a fugitive hunter? He wanted them to relax a little, eat their fill, and perhaps stay the night and another day or so. What was their hurry? Perhaps the prospect of joining the army, judging from the response the recruiters received from free and freedmen. When General Butler was goaded into putting his recruitment notice in *L'Union* early in August, over eighteen hundred men enlisted and were drilling within two weeks. The First Native Guard was mustered into the army late in September, the Second in October, and now, with recruits still coming, a Third was forming. But even if Chad made it to the Touro Almshouse, their temporary barracks, it would be no life for Anna, following the army or waiting somewhere behind. From what he'd heard, the Union's promise to supply families with rations was often broken, and women and children were suffering.

"This sure is good, Mr. Labarre," said Chad.

"Please call me Jerry, both you and your missus."

Anna blushed and her chin went up. "I'm not his missus. I'm Anna Mead."

"What a pretty name!" he said, glad to see his mind was still agile. "I hope you're enjoying the meal, too, Anna Mead."

"Oh, yes," she said, biting her lip. Then she turned a sympathetic frown on him. "How did the war take your business?"

Ah, he thought, she was listening, just as Suzanne always listened, even when her attention seemed to be elsewhere. "Shortages, *chérie.* No paper, no ink, sky-high prices. I was foolish; I held on too long. When I paid my debts, I had little left, not even a house." He forced a smile, and turned to the impersonal: "You see, most of the city's provisions are imported, and the Union blockade paralyzed the port. Fifteen thousand bales of cotton were burned on the levee just before the occupation."

"They're good at burning things, the greycoats are," said Chad.

Jerry sliced the Creole ginger cake he unwrapped from its layers of cheesecloth and burlap, and served it with fragrant, steaming coffee. He could tell that Anna had been a house servant: she tried to eat slowly, but he had to smile when she opened her mouth wide for a last enormous bite, and showed her pleasure with a "Mmm." Suzanne had had her moments, too, although she was educated at a fine school in Paris. She was the daughter of a French planter who manumitted her mother and her when she was born, and they'd moved to a comfortable apartment in New Orleans. She'd had no interest in becoming the *placée* of a white man: her independence meant too much to her. She was unspoiled, and able to enjoy herself, sometimes hiding her delight behind her tortoiseshell fan—the one he kept in his chest to fan his memories.

"We ought to go soon," Chad said. "It's getting dark out."

"It's not wise to be out at night. Stay with me and go in the morning. Anna is welcome to my cot, and we can 'bivouac' on the floor." He looked from one to the other as they nodded consent.

"I'll clean up," said Anna, and Chad stood as though awaiting direction until Jerry introduced his table full of books, papers, and periodicals near the *secrétaire*. "Why don't you read a while, *mon fils*? Did I hear you say you can write?"

Chad nodded.

"Do you ever get a chance to practice?"

"My friend gave me a copybook to write in, and I have it almost filled."

"Really! What do you write?"

"Things I think. Goings-on." He smiled. "How it is, the most."

"That's very good, Chad. It makes me think of Paul Trevigne. He publishes a newspaper he calls *L'Union.*"

"I know that one, sir. Uncle Blake let me read it."

"Paul's a good friend. You could learn a useful trade from him."

"Trade? Onliest time I traded something, I got an apple for a snakeskin."

"No, no—it means a way to make a living." He'd forgotten how untutored a man could be. He'd had a formal education by the time he was grown, and had taken his place as a respected artisan. His father was a full-blooded African, his mother of mixed ancestry from Haiti, both manumitted slaves who settled in New Orleans. They were part of the *ancien population* who built the city. His heart went out to Chad, who had learned so much under conditions that might have conquered his own ambitions. Here was the fabric of a fine man. "Chad," he said, "you must never stop learning."

The youth had a question on his face, but Jerry turned to Anna, who was asking where the napkins went. "We didn't soil them," she said. "They sure too pretty to use."

"You like pretty things," he said, more to himself than to her, and he saw her look at her torn dress and purse her lips. "Of course you do," he added, thinking he might have sounded surprised, "and someday you will have all the pretty things you may want." His heart swelled as he looked at her, and he wished he were in fact her father.

Chad held up a newspaper: "*La Misachibee*. That's a funny name," he said.

"It's the Indian name for the river, but it's a far cry from an Indian newspaper. Isn't it a beautiful word?"

"I like the real name better. Sometimes I say it over and over, just to hear it."

"I like it, too," said Anna. "It sounds like a song."

Jerry thought of the slaves who used to sing and dance in Congo Square, *"Dansé Calinda, bou doum, bou doum,"* to the rhythm of the tam-tam and jawbones. A crowd would gather to watch and listen, and in the evening, as the gentlemen with their gold-headed walking sticks and the ladies with their parasols strolled away, the slaves would sing a goodbye to their dance: *"Bonsoir danse, soleil couché."* He wondered if there were such dancing and singing on the plantation. "Did you ever dance the bamboula?" he asked.

Both heads shook *no*, both pairs of eyes widened with wonder.

"Peu importe," he said. "It's an old dance, not important."

"I want you to see something," said Chad, taking from his pack *Voices of Freedom* and passing it to Jerry. "This is a book full of songs," he said.

Jerry drew in his breath: Whittier, the slave's poet, a book hard come by in the South, one he'd bought on a trip to the North, and treasured. "Let me see," he said, " 'Hoarse, horrible, and strong / Rises to Heaven that agonizing cry / . . . da-da, da-da, da . . .' "

" 'Filling the arches of the hollow sky,' " Chad read, and with him Jerry cried, " 'How long, O God, how long?' "

Their burst of laughter filled the little cabin as Anna clapped her hands and danced about, making the floorboards squeak. Jerry collapsed, laughing, to a chair, tears rolling down his cheeks. "Sit down, children," he said at last. "It is the shank of the evening, and suddenly I am not tired at all."

"But you must be," Anna said.

"Give an old man time to enjoy you," he said, getting up. "You haven't tasted my brew yet—they call it *la bière du pays*, as it's made of the common apple, pine, and ginger root. It has a little kick, so be careful."

As they sipped the beer of the peasant, Jerry's mind began to wander over streets of the past. He told them about the old days in New Orleans, the lively dock, the brass bands playing "Hail Columbia" as the steamboat races to St. Louis began.

"I heard about the riverboats," said Chad, "and the ships from England and France and China—"

"*Oui.* It was a sight you cannot see now. And the *Place d'Armes*—now you see soldiers there, and a few solemn beggars, people hurrying to the market, not stopping to chatter. The square used to be alive with the ice-cream vendor in tasseled fez, Indians selling sassafras roots and blowguns—and there were booths with tropical fruit and roasted peanuts and pastry—*bière douce* cooling in tubs." He sighed. "I used to drink *chocolat* and play dominoes at the old Café del Aguila—and the opera, *mon Dieu,* how Suzanne loved it! We didn't live lavishly, but we had a garden as lush as any in the *carré de la ville*—jasmine and roses, pomegranate trees. Sometimes we went to the Gulf for the 'dog days' to escape the heat and the fever. If only we had gone in '53 . . ." He closed his eyes and rested the back of his head on the high-backed chair, thinking of Suzanne, of their trip to L'Île Dernière on the lower delta, the island resort that was destroyed by a hurricane in—was it '56? "The white sands are dazzling, dazzling . . . and the sunsets! We took our blanket out at night, my wife and I . . ." He opened his eyes, embarrassed. Chad's gaze was riveted on him, but Anna stared at Chad, her inscrutable face undone by her telltale eyes. It was the way Suzanne had looked at him. "Do you know," he said, changing his tone, "you are about to enter one of the first American cities to have gaslighted streets?"

"No," said Chad.

"I swan!" said Anna.

Jerry laughed. Such an attentive audience! But there was a dress to mend and plans to be made. He gave Anna a needle and thread. "I know a place where you can stay. My friend Henriette Delille runs the Convent of the Sisters of the Holy Family on Rue Orleans between Royal and Bourbon, where the ballroom used to be. It must be twenty years old by now. The sisters—all women of color—take care of the sick and poor, and they house orphans. I think they have a school, too. Can you read, Anna?"

She tossed her head. "Never wanted to."

Jerry patted her hand. "No matter. You'll make a good nurse, I'm sure. I hear Henriette is ailing, but any of the nuns will be glad to receive you."

"I—I'll go there, I guess," she said, snipping a thread between her teeth. With her dress on, she couldn't sew it well, but he thought a clumsy mend would be better than a rip. "Thank you," she said, glancing at Chad. "I will go there."

"And you, Chad, I think you should go to the office of *L'Union* and ask for my friend—I'll write down his name. Tell him I sent you. I think you should stay with him as long as he'll have you."

Chad frowned. "I want to join the army."

"I know, and so you will. But the things you'll learn there won't feed you when the war is over. Besides, you'd make a capital newspaperman!"

"I'll pay your friend a visit," Chad said slowly, and Anna added, "It's nice of you to want us safe. Thank you."

"Thank you, *ma petite,* for listening to me and my memories. I try not to dwell on them. I can't afford to think too much."

Anna shrugged. "Thinking ain't good nohow."

"It's what they couldn't take away," said Chad, and Jerry

Labarre nodded. "Sometimes," he said, "it seems they can take everything else."

Jerry woke with the dawn. It was foraging time. By eight he would be ferrying customers across the river. He had ordered his life: a time for this, a time for that, leaving very little room for the past. But last night he'd been flooded with memories, sitting in the company of Chad, with his wide-open mind, and Anna, a replica of Suzanne, her mindfulness, her quick grasp. The road ahead of them lay full of chance, full of trials he could only imagine, given the wobbly shape of the world and all he knew of power. When he passed his cot where Anna lay, he thought how like a child she looked, her face ajar with sleep. Suzanne would have loved her, taught her, given her a good life! Last night in his dreams his wife was with the three of them, giggling behind her fan.

The coffee was brewing when Chad appeared in the kitchen. With a shy smile he told Jerry he had seen the day-light and wondered why the bell hadn't called him to the fields. Then Anna was up and they had bowls of blackberries and sagamité with their coffee. Anna called the hulled and boiled corn porridge, and ate it like a lady.

Now he pulled his chest from beneath his cot and drew out the beautiful tortoiseshell fan. He gave it to Anna and she took it, holding it gingerly, closing and opening it, her eyes wide and wonderful.

"I have some walking shoes that were also Suzanne's," he said. "If they fit, I wish you would wear them. They don't fit me."

She slipped her feet into the brown leather shoes and smiled.

"Ah! *Cendrillon* has found her *pantoufle!* Let's hope you may find your Prince Charming, if indeed you haven't already."

The color rose in Anna's cheeks and her gaze never left her shoes. Chad was smiling.

Jerry then put slips of small-change paper money in their

hands, telling them the "shinplasters" had been issued by local merchants before the occupation, but could still be used to buy small items. He gave them streetcar tickets, also a medium of exchange, and warned them not to board any but the "star cars" designated for blacks. "Now that the bluecoats have come, you'd best have a few coins as well." He dug into his chest.

Chad looked flabbergasted and shook his head wildly. "We won't take money from you!"

"Fiddlesticks. Having money in your pocket could keep you from being arrested or picked up by fugitive hunters, and I won't let you go without it." He gave them directions, first to the convent, then to *L'Union,* and they listened, Chad, excitement written on his face, Anna with her curtain drawn, except for her anxious eyes.

"Remember I am here, if you need me." He gave them each a swift embrace. *"B'jour,"* he said.

When they'd gone, he was only a weary old man, leaning on an oar.

EIGHT

[The blacks] manifest the greatest anxiety to educate their children, and they thoroughly appreciate the benefits of education. I have known a family to go with two meals a day, in order to save fifty cents a week to pay an indifferent teacher for their children.

—GEORGE HANKS, SUPERINTENDENT OF NEGRO
LABOR, DEPARTMENT OF THE GULF, 1864

Mid-to-late November 1862

Anna said goodbye to Chad outside the convent. He offered to see her in but she wouldn't have it: she allowed she didn't need help from anybody. But the look of him, striding away with that stride he had, glancing back to smile that smile, was enough to hollow her stomach. Watching him go in the sunshine, she felt a rush of panic so strong she almost ran after him: *Oh, God, what if I never see him again? What if . . .*

She couldn't go through the big double doors while her nose was stuffed with tears and her eyes rimmed in red. She ran across a street and through an alley into a wide open space edged by solemn buildings. Hedges and flowers ran wild in the center, orange and lemon trees and climbing vines spilled over the walls, everything was tall and beautiful. A few women hurried by with black servants talking French. Soldiers walked in pairs, and outside the buildings guards stood ready with guns. There were no vendors of ice cream, no ginger beer cooling in great tubs, no peanut stands or laughing people. Uneasy, she retraced her steps and stopped before a large spired building, right out of Laurel's picture books. A black coachman rested atop a carriage near the entrance, where a lame white child with a tin cup stood. Music, low and stern, came through the great open doors. She stared into the dusky light until the coachman called to her: "That's St. Louis Cathedral, missy. A church. There's no service now—go on in. Anyone can."

She'd gone to church with her mistress at Sweet Haven only when Laurel coaxed her papa into it, and she'd sat in a back pew with other house servants during the Sunday morning service. She'd come from a cotton plantation in Mississippi where preachers gave sermons in the ginhouse, but Master Wycliffe, along with his neighbors, felt that religion might "lead slaves astray." Still, its practice wasn't punishable the way reading was, so Anna had seen the inside of a church. Not like this one. Its carvings and painted windows and high ceilings bore no likeness to the plain walls and windows of the white frame building in the country.

She walked down the center aisle in the dim light, looking straight ahead, and when she reached the end, knelt on the bare floor as others were doing. All her kneeling had been at white folks' feet, she was thinking, and they'd sold her away from her family when she was on the brink of womanhood, sold her into silence. She raised her head to the altar and her eyes fixed on a statue of a calm-looking woman. Was she sold into silence, too? The floor was hard but she lingered in the curious place until the low, insistent music reached into her, smoothing out, filling in. After a while she roused herself to leave.

* * *

The convent was larger than it looked from the outside, rooms tucked here and there off a central parlor where the wide stairs spiraled upward. The black nuns were crammed into stiff white gowns and their heads were covered with starched white cloth that held their faces fast. They were friendly except for one, who kept looking at Anna as though she had stripped her kumquat tree. Finally, standing among the others, that one spoke: "I am Sister Clarice, in charge of the school. Will you be wanting to learn to read?"

"Yes, ma'am. But I want to nurse the sick even more."

Sister Clarice frowned. "Classes are conducted around their needs." She turned and left.

Mother Superior smiled. "We're all happy to see an able-bodied woman like you, Anna. I declare, most of the women who come from the plantations are half-starved and worn out. We are full past capacity with orphans and the ailing, and if you couldn't help, it would be hard to fit you in."

Another of the women, introducing herself as Sister Denise, took Anna by the hand and led her away, talking as they went. She had a nice smile above a double chin, and she stepped lightly, her plump hand warm around Anna's.

The first hospital ward was a surprise: thin aisles separated lines of pure white cots, and the moans and heavy breathing of the very ill mingled with laughs and conversation. The sun made paths through the windows that bordered the court-yard, where a few people sat and children played. The sisters moved in and out of the aisles lined by children's cots, where often lay a child on each end. A listless, propped-up little girl was fed small spoonfuls of soup, her eyes on the climb of the spoon from bowl to lip. Across the room a nun held the hand of a gasping man. A woman on a nurse's arm crumpled into bed with a great sigh.

"You'll be scrubbing floors and doing errands today," Sister Denise was saying in her spirited, breezy way, "and tomorrow, I allow it'll be all that and more, as you see what's needed. Do you think you're up to it, being with such illness?"

"Oh." Anna shook herself. "I was just thinking how—cheerful it is."

"Bless your heart," said Sister Denise. "I'm glad you see it."

Anna began school in a sun-drenched room. Sister Clarice could have been a china doll at the head of the class, except she moved around, and spoke from that placid face. She paid little notice to Anna after her greeting, and Anna counted it a blessing.

Whole families were in school together. Grandparents sat with open books by little ones who sometimes poked fun at each other and giggled into their hands. One fat, sickly woman let out a whoop when she read a new word right, and when Anna gave an answering whoop, Sister Clarice said with a stern mouth, "Anna, this is a classroom, not a circus."

Most of the time everyone was still and polite, except for Sammy. He was only five or six but his very presence was disturbing. He was smaller than the children she reckoned were his age, but he seemed larger. His eyes stood out in his slender face and his jaw was clenched. He was downright mean: pinched the children who sat by him, edged over to stick his slate pencil in the ones who didn't. Sister Clarice said nothing and looked at him with nothing in her eyes.

Sammy's eyes never met Anna's, so she couldn't tell what was in them. She only knew the boy liked to make other kiddies squeal, and when their mothers hissed at him, he seemed to shrink to half his size. She moved to a desk right by him and when she saw him make a move toward a child nearby, whispered, "Look out what you doing, boy." He turned a confused face to her and jabbed his pencil in her hip. It was such a shock she cried out loud, and Sister Clarice glared at her. "If I have to remind you one more time that this is a classroom, not a circus, Anna, you'll be expelled. Now move back to your desk."

She looked back expecting to see Sammy laugh, but he was sitting stiffly, his jaw clamped shut.

Now he was everywhere, moving like a lizard, his eyes on her when she turned her back. She'd turn fast but he'd dart away, leaving her with a knot in her stomach. If she looked for him, he wasn't there, but she knew he was somewhere behind her, staring. The children ran from him, so he sat alone.

"Oh, he's a pitiful one," said Sister Denise. "Our kindly treatment lets loose his anger, but punishment just won't do. He had a brutal master, saw too much, his mama said, and he himself was lashed."

"What for?"

"His mama said he was full of wonder, wanted to explore the world, but the master tarred the fence around the fruit trees, and every time Sammy got tar on his clothing he was whipped for stealing fruit." The sister sighed and ran her fingers over her brow. "He clung to his mother like a young wolf spider until she died six months ago. And now he seems—so lost."

Anna remembered feeling lost: it was attached to sorrow, and she felt it first as a small child when her sister Alila was gone. A shiver ran through her and the nun put a hand on her shoulder. "There, there, Anna. Kiddies abide. He'll be all right."

Tending the kiddies was Anna's favorite task. Their arms around her neck felt wonderful. The sisters taught them manners but not timidity: most of them looked you in the eye and spoke their minds. She found the ones who had seen too much of slavery were the hardest to love, often sunken into themselves and shifty-eyed, mindful only of survival as they saw it. But no other child was like Sammy. She wished she could forget him as the busy nuns seemed able to do, wished she could center on the ones who gave her love right back, but she was drawn to Sammy.

She watched him from the corner of her eye as his gaze followed her. Once she turned to face him as he stood in the background, taking him by such surprise she caught him looking wistful. Twice she took an orange from the kitchen bowl and, passing him, put it in his lap. He threw the first across the room, fear and confusion on his face, the next he snatched, and running, sank his teeth into the rind like a starving animal. Sometimes he sat in the corner, so far away she wondered where. But she knew the power of her concern, for his eyes were always on her.

She was learning to read and write. She took her schoolbooks to bed with her each night, studying whenever she found a shaft of moonlight or the pale glow of the outside lantern. Sometimes when the nuns who shared her room were on their knees in prayer, she would kneel by her cot to write in her copybook or work on her reader, the Bible. There was a time when she was not interested in learning, when Laurel's books held little fascination, when in fact, they represented all she despised. But now she felt her mind stretch with a skill she craved: imagine reading and writing a letter—to Chad! Her fifth day there, an old man showed her a letter from his daughter on a plantation near Mobile, and his eyes failed him, he said, could Anna read it aloud? She was right in the middle of mopping, she said, and called one of the sisters to read the letter.

Turning now with her mop, she saw Sammy staring in the window from the courtyard. How beautiful he looked! She longed to hear him laugh, or even cry. All she'd ever heard him say was *No!* and that was not enough. He did not disrupt the class lately, but he wasn't learning, for when his turn came to read there was only silence before he was skipped.

Then one day stolid Sister Clarice lost her composure in class. She stopped in the middle of a lesson, sat smack down at her desk, head in hands, and bawled. Everyone stared open-mouthed. The sickly woman began to cry. Anna slipped over to Sister Clarice. "It's Mademoiselle Delille," murmured the nun. "She's sure enough going to die."

Anna went with the teacher to the room where Henriette Delille, the founder of the convent, lay ill. Sammy was behind them and he stood against the wall in the hall as they entered.

In her haste she paid him no mind, although she noticed the fright on his face.

The room was plain, adorned only with tokens of the faith. Miss Delille lay still, her breathing loud and harsh as if she were running up a steep bank. *When she gets to the top,* thought Anna, *she'll stop breathing.* She looked parched on her pillow, and her skin seemed stretched across her cheekbones, but she didn't look old, not at all.

The nuns were gathered about her bed, waiting. A priest murmured something into his beard, fingered something in his hands, gestured over her at intervals. *They're waiting for her to climb that bank,* Anna thought, *and I'm not a part of it, I don't even know her.* She turned to go. As she opened the door, Mother Superior put a hand on her arm and said, "Mademoiselle Delille wanted to know all about you. She would have asked to hear you read if she hadn't worsened."

Sammy wasn't in the hall. She went to the hospital ward and filled all the bedside cups with fresh, cool water, then sat down in the kitchen. After a time, Sister Denise came in and announced, *"Elle est morte."*

"You mean she's dead?"

A sorrowful wail came from under the kitchen table. She stopped and Sammy came out, running. She caught him but he broke away, kicking, screaming, biting her hand. She watched him flee down the hall to the parlor and up the staircase toward the orphans' room.

Lying awake in the dead of night, she wished Sammy was where she could reach him. She got out of bed and crept into the hall, a candle lighting her way to the orphans' bedroom. She passed down the line of cots until she saw him, curled on his side, his face loose and calm. She touched his cool forehead, his neck damp with good, deep sleep. He stretched, turned over, and his sweet child's face, streaked with tears, glowed in the candlelight. She kissed his hair and tiptoed away.

*　*　*

Death is room temperature. She was expected to kiss the forehead of Henriette Delille, and that's how she found out. Many of the town fathers came to the funeral—a big important doing with music from a marching band—and she was glad she was one of those who stayed behind to mind the convent.

Once a week she took groups of orphans for an outing in the square, the wide-open space she'd found that first day. She watched while they romped, and made up games to draw them all in. At these times she would glance about her, out toward the levee and back toward Royal Street. Surely the town was small enough that she might see someone she knew, she thought. It was not uncommon to see people hug upon meeting, as though they hadn't been together for a spell. Still, she would not think of wandering about with such a scheme, and was content to take her air in the courtyard except for her weekly stroll with the children.

Today for the first time she brought Sammy along. No, he came. No one ever brought Sammy. Still, it was at the insistence of Sister Denise, who, because Anna asked her to, fairly pushed him out the door. He scowled and hung back until they got to the square, and then suddenly he was gone.

She drew in her breath, calmly scanned the area, then fanned the children out to look for him, this way, that way, meet back here. She ran to the levee, calling, searching.

The children in groups of two and three returned looking scared. "Nowhere," said a boy who never could stand Sammy, "he ain't turned up nowhere, Miss Anna. He's vamoosed."

"Maybe somebody shot him," said a little girl gravely.

"We're late getting back," said Anna, her voice hoarse. "We have to go."

"We can't go without him!" said the same boy, and the others echoed, "No, we can't!"

"Don't fret," Anna told them, "we'll look along the way, and I'll come back again when y'all are safely in."

They gathered in lines and walked soberly through the alley. Her legs were weak and a cold sweat washed over her as they reached Royal Street. When they were crossing the street to the convent's corner, she heard a sharp call—"Anna!"— and Sammy raced from far down the road into her arms.

Falling to her knees, she grabbed his head and kissed his cheeks and his nose, hugged him and stood him out to look at him. "Are you all right?"

His gaze was fixed on her face and suddenly Sammy was crying. She took him in her lap and held him, gently rocking, weeping with him. The children ran circles around them, laughing, shouting, "Sammy's back!"

"Did someone steal you, Sammy?" asked the grave little girl.

"I got lost," he said, "and I couldn't get back, no matter where I went."

"We fretted, didn't we, Miss Anna?" She reached out to touch him and he flinched, rolled out of Anna's arms, curled into himself as though he thought the little girl would hit him.

Anna grabbed his hand and got up. "Time to go home," she called, and the children began to walk in pairs. She kept Sammy's hand, holding him close to her skirts all the way. He cut loose when they walked through the convent door, but she smiled to herself, for she knew he wasn't going far.

NINE

Consider this case: General Bragg is at liberty to ravage the homes of our brethren of Kentucky because the Union army of Louisiana is protecting his wife and his home against his negroes . . . these colored regiments of freemen, raised by the authority of the President, and approved by him as the Commander-in-Chief of the Army, must be commanded by the officers of the Army of the United States like any other regiments.

—MAJOR GENERAL BENJAMIN F. BUTLER, COMMANDING,
HDQ. DEPT. OF THE GULF, TO BRIGADIER GENERAL
G. WEITZEL, NOVEMBER 6, 1862.

Mid-November 1862

It was the right thing to do, but it didn't feel right, leaving her. The convent was a good place, Jerry Labarre had said, and Chad couldn't have a woman with him where he was going, even someone as plucky as she. But despite his urge to get on with it, to explore the dock, to visit the *L'Union* editor, to join the army, walking away from Anna was the hardest thing he'd ever done. He walked fast and didn't look back. But as he neared the great New Orleans waterfront, he wished he'd told her to stay at the convent until he came for her. Then he reckoned what a folly that would be, how she'd utter a cutting laugh and give him for to know who was in charge of her!

A crowd was gathering up ahead, and he quickened his pace until he stood with the throng on the Front Street levee, where he could see passengers stare down from the bow of a docking ship. One of the white fellows standing by him said it was the *Marion*, a mail steamer that took regular trips from New York, making it in eleven days nonstop. Pushing through with his aide, a tight-lipped, smooth-faced army officer went on board before the gangplank was secure, and the fellow—he was MacElroy—whispered, "That's Beast Butler. His missus must've come back this trip."

The passengers spread onto the wharf and Chad heard a man grumble that the cheery, bustling port had changed: not a barrel of molasses or a cotton bale along the nine-mile stretch of levee.

MacElroy said a crew member told him there hadn't been cause to use the six light pieces aboard the ship. "The *Marion* ain't never met a gunboat, and lucky, too," he said. "It'd be easy prey for a real warship like the *Alabama.*" He'd heard the ship was so overcrowded they had to build berths in the luggage room. He stared at Chad. "Two or three steamers a week come down from New York, but that's about all the excitement we can offer a newcomer, anymore."

It seemed to Chad a big lineup of ships: a half-dozen gunboats (the man said they were passenger steamers with added guns and ironplating), the *Essex*, called a steam-ram, and several coasters that used to carry freight.

"Any work on the docks?" Chad asked.

"Hear that, MacElroy?" another man at Chad's elbow chuckled.

MacElroy's thick eyebrows raised and seemed to bristle. "If there was, there sure wouldn't be room for a stranger."

Chad backed off as the crowd thinned, and there before his eyes was Jerry Labarre's town: stores mostly empty, merchants talking in doorways, white soldiers everywhere. But no one was questioning the *Marion's* passengers making their way into town, and no one stopped him. A couple of men called to him, hey boy, where's a hotel, but a black newsboy on the corner pointed the way.

He was taking in the sights, the narrow streets, the carved iron-work gates and railings, when the newsboy came over and said, "Sure 'nuff better keep moving."

He asked how to get to the office of *L'Union.* The newsboy was from the *True Delta,* but he gave Chad directions and even wished him luck.

A plump, sallow-skinned woman told Chad Mr. Trevigne was busy in the back, but if he would wait, she would try to pry him loose. She glared at his ragged clothes, then went behind the curtain covering the doorway and held a loud conversation in French. Then *"Entrez,"* she said, parting the curtain and letting it fall between them as Chad crossed into the large, high-ceilinged room: a newspaper office! It was like his first trip to Labadieville, so much to see and learn.

Paul Trevigne was a slight, brown man with a little mustache and spectacles halfway down his wide nose. He wore a headband with a beak, and wide bands on his arms kept his shirtsleeves up. His vest was unbuttoned, and high suspenders pulled his trousers above his waist. A shaded gaslight hung by a chain over the table where he worked, and when it swayed, shafts of light fell here and there. He was lining up little pieces of metal into a frame, and when he'd finished a narrow alley of them, he looked at Chad over the rim of his glasses. "Madame Trevigne tells me Mr. Labarre sent you," he said. "That right?"

Chad nodded.

"How well do you know him?"

"Met him on my way down here."

"You just off the plantation?"

"Yes, sir."

"Can you read?"

"Yes, sir."

"Know French?"

"No."

"Want a job?"

The words stunned him, took his breath clean away.

"Well?"

"Yes, sure I do."

Paul Trevigne looked down at his work. "I can't hire any-one. But if you need a place to lodge, you can sleep and board here. Mr. Labarre's a fine man and if he sees you the way he must, it's good enough for me."

"I learned to read off your newspaper."

"That a fact." He didn't look up.

"I'll work my way."

"Hand me one of those trays over there."

They were as heavy as the iron slabs in the blacksmith shop back at Sweet Haven. With the metal frames of newspaper pages, the trays filled two long tables.

"Look here," said the man. "I'm making words—setting type. See?"

"They—they're backwards."

"Right." He stopped to show Chad the printing press, a huge machine that took up almost half the room, and how the words met the page. Then he went back to work.

Hands in his pockets, Chad watched the skilled hands slip type into place. Finally, the editor said, "Pull that stool up for me and get one for yourself. My feet are tired."

Chad obeyed, setting his stool where he could see what was going on beneath the light. Now and then Mr. Trevigne shot him a sharp glance that he answered with a smile.

A page was finished and the editor was halfway through another before he said, "I can use an extra hand for errands and delivery, but as I say, I can't pay you. Takes all I have to keep going. So if something comes along—" He studied Chad above the rim of his glasses. "Nothing's apt to." He sniffed. "There's a lot to learn here, if you like words."

"I do," he said. "I write them."

"That so?"

"When I set words down, I can look at them and tell if I have things right." He shook his head. "I mean—"

"I know what you mean. It helps to clear your mind." He looked up and his eyes were piercing. "Why did you come to New Orleans?"

"I want to join the army."

"You do. Well, you could." He fastened his eyes on his work, never moved an eyelash except to blink. "Might be worse things than that. Can't say as I can think of them, though."

"How's that?"

"To begin with, black soldiers *don't get nothin' from nobody.* Their uniforms are hand-me-downs, their knapsacks don't have straps, most of them don't have haversacks, and their rifles are antique. There are plenty of supplies, but the quartermaster ignores their requisitions for arms and mules and what-have-you. To top it off, they haven't been paid. My young friend André Cailloux is a captain—it's a name you should remember if you enlist: Captain Cailloux—so you see, I've got it all from the horse's mouth."

"Golly. Where are they fighting?"

"They're not." He pointed to another tray of type and Chad got it for him. "They're digging ditches."

Chad thought of Uncle Blake with a shovel in his hand. "I know a man joined the army, I bet."

"Um-hum."

"He escaped back in April, long before the general marched down the bayou."

"That a fact."

"Yes, sir."

Mr. Trevigne looked up. "The bayou—you mean Bayou Lafourche? General Weitzel?"

"That's where I come from."

"The First was sent there after the victory. Weitzel said he didn't want them, for they frightened the planters. I got ahold of Butler's answer to Weitzel, and I was gratified to see he read his general a proper lecture, putting him to shame. Went to the edge of asking which side Weitzel was on. Let him know in no uncertain terms he has to command the First Native Guard."

"The First sounds like there's room for more."

Mr. Trevigne looked at him. "The army's the only thing I know of, has no limits. The Second's almost ready to leave, and the Third's about to drill at the Touro Almshouse."

"Touro Almshouse?"

"It's the old house built for the poor by the philanthropist Judah Touro, a Jewish friend of my father's." He wiped his hands on a greasy rag.

"The Third!" said Chad.

"Yep. *Mon Dieu*, they were raised fast! Butler's notices in my paper in August started a stampede, beginning with freemen from New Orleans. General Butler still says it's all free or freedmen. Hogwash! But he wants to head off objections to enlisting slaves."

"Who wouldn't like that?"

"It would be easier to say who would." He cleared his throat. "You don't want to know about politics, do you?"

"Sure enough, I do."

Mr. Trevigne started on another frame. Chad waited until the backward words separated by slugs were all set for a headline, then asked, "What about politics?"

The editor grunted. "Well, the U.S. government wants to make loyal citizens out of the planters, so it likes to please them, but it wants slaves in the army by hook or by crook. The planters don't want their slaves joining the army, no sir. And General Butler has to please the U.S. government."

"Gee rod!"

"So General Butler figured out how to say the men he was enlisting were not slaves by government definition. To recruit from some of the plantations, he used English and French laws forbidding their subjects to hold slaves in foreign countries. The French consul hated that"—he chuckled—"and he used the Second Confiscation Act to recruit others."

"What's that?"

Mr. Trevigne was setting another headline. He asked, "What's what?"

"The Second Conversation Act."

"Confiscation. It's a law that says slaves owned by Rebels where the Union's in control are free, but it's never been enforced. Doesn't matter. Any able-bodied man who applies gets in, long as he swears he's free."

"I guess I can swear that."

Mr. Trevigne didn't say a thing, just kept working.

From the corner of the room came a clicking sound. Mr. Trevigne hurried over to take a telegraph message, then turned to Chad. "A few newspaper offices have their machines in the front. People stand around all day waiting to hear the South's won the war." He went back to work for a short time, then slipped off his stool. "I'm finished here. Let's go upstairs and see what Madame Trevigne has prepared for dinner."

The stairs, hidden behind a door at the back of the room, led to a parlor, where pots of mint and rosemary lined the windowsills.

Without a word, Madame Trevigne brought the meal to the table near the balcony doorway. The editor filled the plates with fried crawfish and sweet potatoes, passed around the best bread Chad had ever tasted, then seemed to slip into his thoughts, eating slowly, sipping a glass of wine. His wife ate with gusto, and then sat, hands folded on her lap.

Chad gulped his portion, trying to sit small and unseen, swallowing hard trying not to. Finally the mister touched his napkin to his lips and smiled across the table at his wife. "Thank you for a good noonday meal, Madame."

Chad opened his mouth to thank her, but his tongue froze before her icy stare. She began to clear the table, wagging her head toward him, speaking to her husband in French.

"He'll sleep downstairs if it is all right with you, Madame. Perhaps the cot—"

Shrugging, throwing up her hands, she disappeared into the kitchen.

"I don't have to stay here, Mr. Trevigne," Chad said. "I just stopped by."

"You'll find the cot comfortable, and you'll be here to alert me when messages come in."

A sound from below shook the floor.

"It's the old press starting up. Clangs around like a street-car. Would you like to help deliver the paper?"

One man was, in the editor's words, feeding and pampering the machine. The short, fat man stared at him, but Chad couldn't take his eyes off the press. Steam-power driven, a revolving cylinder pressed each sheet of paper against metal plates of type. "It does eleven hundred sheets an hour when it's in good repair and has a fast feeder," said the mister, "but it's as old and cantankerous as I am."

Another man pulled a mold off a framed page on the table, poured a hot liquid over the mold and placed the instantly hardened plate on the press. "Nelson's stereotyping, makes a mat or mold of plaster of Paris from the page, and pours melted lead over the mat to make the boilerplate he's inking. Over there feeding sheets is Tom. They're reporters till it comes time to get out the paper every week. Then we all pitch in. You can help me fold."

Nelson walked over. He stood tall and thin, about Chad's eye level. He looked like a sapling that needed props. "Where's he from?" he asked.

"He's new in town," said Paul Trevigne.

"He doesn't have the carriage of a slave."

"You sure are good at stereotyping, Nelson."

They ain't, Chad thought, *talking to my face.*

Nelson laughed in short, breathy spurts like a panting hound. Then he turned to Chad with a smile that let him know he was welcome.

When the afternoon's work was over, the newspapers lay in stacks by the door. As Chad carried the last out to the cart where Nelson waited, the editor gave him a small square of heavy paper. "Your press card," he said.

*   *   *

He got up from his cot across from the printing press and made his way in the dark beyond the curtain to the shop front, to the pale moonlight coming through the windowpane. *The big storefront window plays tricks,* he wrote in his copybook. *The light comes in strained, could set my mind awhirl and cut me off.* It was another world—apart from anything he'd ever known. Even Uncle Blake had never seen the inside of a newspaper office! He wished he could talk to Anna. He'd tell her how this place made him feel like a fresh sponge, and then he'd watch the way her eyes looked, her chin moved, the way she smiled, or didn't. He could tell how she felt without her saying a word. He had watched her out of the corner of his eyes all the way down the river, and he'd wanted to say, Come on, Anna, let's talk about it, but he couldn't. He remembered the day one of Colonel Wycliffe's visitors rode into the field, whistled shrilly with two fingers in his mouth, pointed out Maria, dismounted and waited in the brush while Logan fetched the young slave. It was the first time he'd seen this, and his skin had crawled with disgust. That memory was roused as he lay in the brush with Anna, that and others like it, and ashamed, he'd shed bitter tears. It was god-awful, the way it came over him. He couldn't change the fact that the anger, the ornery cussedness that brought it about was akin to the white man's whoring ways. But not all of it: making love to Anna was untouched by ugliness, the loving itself, pure and right. He went back to his cot wishing he'd been able to tell her that, instead of saying he was sorry.

TEN

Them cool green leaves
Is waitin' to shelter me.

O, little tree!

—LANGSTON HUGHES

Mid-to late-November 1862

Mr. Trevigne brought down a table and lamp for Chad to
read by. Then he said, why disturb you when you might be
reading, come mealtime you might as well take a plateful and
have your fare right here. Chad agreed. Madame Trevigne
put him in mind of the master's wife. When Mrs. Wycliffe
came to the stables, she would stare through, above, and
around but never at him. He always kept his face stiff but not
lowered, because he wanted to look at the pretty mother of his
friends. She'd greet the coachman, even praise the stable
hands, all except Chad. But Madame Trevigne's scorn was the
busy kind. She had the voice of Laurel's mammy, sharp and
scolding, carrying down the stairs like the winds of a storm.
French à la cyclone he called it, to make Mars laugh.

He'd been there three days, soaking up his surroundings,

learning things he planned to use someday. A trade, Jerry had
called it, but he called it fun, cramming a lot into his head
fast. He was reading a book about the kinds of type and
minding the front office when he first met Mars. This forlorn,
ragged black man kept standing outside looking in. His eyes
had a hungry stare. Finally Chad couldn't stand it any longer
and he waved him in, sat him down, and gave him the sandwich he'd brought down for supper. The man was ghastly
thin, his cheeks hollow and pockmarked, and when he
opened his mouth, words came out in halves at best. He
smiled when Chad made Mars out of the sounds he gave for
his name, and so he was Mars. The worst of it was how
ashamed he looked when he tried to speak, beads of sweat
coming out on his forehead, a flush on his peaked face. Chad
came right to the point: "What happened to your tongue?
Sounds like you got it caught in something."

Mars looked at the floor and Chad saw a tear roll down one
cheek.

"Lordy," he said, kneeling. "I sure didn't mean no disre-
spect."

Mars had stopped chewing on the sandwich and from the
looks of him, he might be going to be sick. Chad led him to
the cot in the back room, laid him down, covered him with the
light blanket.

When Madame Trevigne came home, Chad grabbed her
sacks of groceries and hurried her up the stairs so she
wouldn't notice the form on the cot. But when the mister
came down to set a galley, he saw first thing. "Who—is—
that?" he asked, slow and spaced, like a too-short headline.

"That's Mars. He was outside and I got him in."

"What for?"

"He's pretty sick."

Paul Trevigne glared at Chad and went immediately to the
cot. "It isn't fever season, thank God." He looked Mars over,
sat him up, stared in his mouth, and put him down. Mars's
face had the look of doom. "Ah—goo," he said, trying to get
off the cot.

"I think he means he'll go," said Chad. "He can't talk right. He almost threw up my sandwich."

The mister shook his head. "Wonder it didn't kill him. I'll get some broth from my wife. It'll be a few days before he's ready for solid food."

Chad could hear Madame Trevigne's French through the stairway door. Her cutting tone was unhappy about the soup, about Mars, about Chad. But the most her anger could do was send him away. It couldn't cut part of his tongue out, which is what they saw had been done to Mars.

The editor fed Mars his first bowl of broth. Then it was Chad's job to wash him. The next day Mars was able to do those things himself, but it would be a while before he could think right. Malnutrition starves the brain, the editor said, and you could see the poor soul had been a castaway. Chad didn't like *poor soul:* Mars could smile from the inside out, could stand up straight and keep his eyes off the floor. But he wouldn't sleep on Chad's cot. He curled up at the foot of it like a lanky hound, making a fluttery sound in his sleep.

Chad could see Mars had a keen eye on the world and the mister must have seen it, too, for after a few days he decided the bright-eyed man he called Maurice didn't have to leave. "Maurice," he said, putting it a different way, "we'd appreciate it if you'd stay a little while and lend us a hand."

"He'd be obliged," Chad said, butting in before he could stop himself. Mars smiled.

Chad wondered if the shop men would take to the newcomer, and wasn't surprised when Nelson, always talkative, spoke easily to Mars. But Tom didn't even try. Chad could swear if Mars had been gasping on the floor, Tom would have stepped over him. *Tom isn't a bad man*, he thought, *just used to his own window and afraid to see too far out.* Neither of them had much to say about the newspaper: Mr. Trevigne was boss.

"Wha' dow?" asked Mars when he saw Chad reading by the gas lamp.

"I'm reading the newspapers."

Mars grinned. "Ow louw!"

Chad read from the *Picayune*'s editorial complaining about the "impudent airs which the spoiled negroes are beginning to put on." He laughed at that, and Mars slapped his leg and howled. "Mo?"

The papers were full of accounts of work slowdowns and walkoffs as ex-slaves demanded wages and better hours, even calling for Christmas off. Some planters said their workers were in a "state of mutiny." Others said their hands had stampeded into Union lines or joined the army.

Mars's eyes were bright. He'd been sitting on the floor and now he stood up and pulled a trigger of air. "I wa ah-m-ee— ba-m, ba-m."

"You can't join the army, Mars. They'd say you ain't fit."

Mars acted out how fit he was, complete with marching and shouldering arms, and soon had Chad laughing out loud. He was like Clay that way, athirst for Chad's laughter and a good mimic. The longer he knew Mars, the more he put him in mind of Clay, not only in action, but the kind of man he was: gentle, and able to skim over the facts, making everything seem to come out all right.

One day after Chad finished cleaning and straightening up the tables and Mars swept the floor, they went out for a walk. The streets were crowded and they kept to the curb. Three black soldiers were walking down the middle of the sidewalk, and Chad was about to stop and talk to them when a gang of white men came along and pushed the soldiers into the gutter. "Look at the niggers, all dressed up," yelled one man and another cried, "Goddamn mokes!" But the soldiers weren't taking it and fists were flying. Chad and Mars stood next to the building by an alley as the city police moved in with clubs and hauled away the soldiers.

One of the policemen came over and asked Chad for his pass. The officer took a look at his press card, and then directed his attention at Mars: "Let's see your pass there, varmit."

Mars showed his card and the policeman shook his head. "What you do at the Nigra newspaper?"

Mars was on the spot. Chad saw that doomsday look on his face and said, "He does errands and cleans up."

"What's the matter, cat got his tongue?" said the officer. "Let him say what he does."

Mars opened his mouth to say God-knows-what when Chad began to stare across the street. The officer turned to look and they made for the alley. They heard him yell, heard his foot-falls behind them, but they hid in a doorway and their pur-suer lost heart for the chase. Mars thought the whole thing was a lark, laughed so hard he peed his pants. Chad got a little sore at him and they cut their walk short.

He couldn't stay mad at Mars, not because he felt sorry for him, but because he liked him too much. He had the kind of innocence Clay had, and his acceptance of his lot in life, his absence of anger, was what Granny Martha would call brave. She'd say it was right for Chad to look after him, for you had to speak for the weaker ones.

That night, as he listened to Mars flutter in his sleep, he knew she was right.

Mr. Trevigne put Mars to work feeding the press the next day. "You are a fast folder, Maurice, and I know you can do it." Mars beamed. He was getting along fine when a sheet got caught and bollixed up the whole press. Tom glared at him, but the editor said sheets got stuck a lot when the press was new to the feeder. After that Mars did so well the mister shook his hand.

That night, after they'd delivered the papers and cleaned the shop, Mars sat on the floor looking out the big window. Chad came from his cot to ask what was wrong, and he said nothing was.

"Are you sure nothing's wrong?"

Mars got up and did a pantomine, twirling and twirling on his toes, pulling his smile all over his face, turning it into a show of glee. Chad felt a little foolish and went to bed.

The next afternoon Mr. Trevigne told Chad that he could see Maurice someday freeing Tom from his job on the press. Then he looked at Chad with a certain gleam, something you didn't often see in the editor, and said, "You show a different kind of promise. We'll talk about you tomorrow."

Chad was excited at first, then sad. Mr. Trevigne had plans for him, and any other time it would work out fine, for he liked the editor, liked all the learning, liked newspaper life. But he had to take his chances with the Native Guard, *had to,* and his copybook words agreed: *It's time.* He'd say goodbye in the morning.

Then a funny thing happened: Mars up and left, just like that, that night.

There was silence in the darkness when Chad woke up and turned over. The second time he woke, he missed the fluttery breathing at the foot of his cot, and looked for Mars. Sitting up, he saw the blank floor in the first faint light.

He left a note for the mister: "Mars is gone and I have to find him. I hope he will come back and be your pressman, but I have to join the army. Thank you for all you did for me and tell the Madame *merci beaucoup.*"

He went out into the quiet of the grey dawn.

ELEVEN

Reach up your hand, dark boy, and take a star.
Out of the little breath of oblivion
That is night,
Take just
One star.

—LANGSTON HUGHES

Late November 1862

The drains along the sidewalk stank, and a cat arched its back
as Chad passed by. Dogs foraging for food stayed away from
the alley cats: maybe they wanted the ditches rid of those
long-tailed vermin wallowing in the garbage. It was worse in
the summertime, Nelson had told him, and just before the
occupation, the city let it pile up till it drove more people out
of town than the Yankees. One thing Butler did right off was
clean the canals, flush the drains, and send men armed with
brushes and brooms to scour the French Market, where the
fever started. His zeal was purely personal: he'd gone out in
his *calèche* to inspect the canals and when he saw how they
were plugged up with dead cats and horses, he came back
ready to puke. He was smart, waited for a norther to blow

water out of Lake Ponchartrain, the draft it created pushing water from the basin through the canal, as the workers used hoes, rakes, and shovels to clear out the filth. Any good strong norther would lower the lake a good two and a half feet, Nelson said, and a south wind would bring water back into the lake from the Gulf.

Closer to the dock, the cleaning crews were already at work, and Chad figured by the time the ladies with their parasols were out for a stroll, the air would be clear.

He walked down the narrow streets and then to the wider avenues following the river to the west, looking for Mars. Delivering newspapers had given him a knowledge of the city, and he planned to cover as much of it as he could. He went out past the St. Charles Hotel, the Union headquarters, standing elegantly next to a truck farm. Soldiers guarding it gave him no more than a passing glance. On the town's outskirts he doubled back at the Café du Faubourg, and came to the railroad station. Half-asleep horses were hitched to the fine carriages Jerry had called *fiacres,* a new name among the many he'd learned in the stables and carriage house of the Wycliffe plantation. He sat down by a spittoon to think, but was told to "git" by a policeman who gave him a swat on the butt, making him jump like a fool. That cleared his head. He would be more wary now.

The day was waning as he came to the reedy, trackless swamp they called *la cyprière,* lying north to the lake. It was dismal in the quick twilight, but he was tired and stopped to rest. Did something move where the bushes and trees were thick at the swamp's edge? He thought it was a shadow cast by the changing sunset, but when he saw it again, he stared into the thicket, never intending to go in. But here came Mars with his big strides, waving his arms. "Wha oo, Aad?"

"What do you mean, what am I doing here? How about you? Why did you go like that, sneak out in the night that way? Why, I'm heading for the Touro Almshouse to join the army, but I wouldn't have gone without saying goodbye to you!" He pressed forward, getting things said: "Do you know what Mr.

Trevigne told me? He wants to make you the main pressman. That's what he said, and he don't loose talk, no, sir. You got to go back, Mars, got to!"

Mars gave a faint smile, but his attention was elsewhere. They were quiet then, and as the night took hold they lay down in the grass. Stretching his long arms in a wide arc, Mars drew a star above his head, and pointing to the heavens, mapped out great pictures in the sky.

Chad lay thinking how he'd laid things out as though Mars had no sense. He'd ask some questions, find out some things, in the morning.

The first thing Chad heard at daybreak was a mockingbird singing its life out in the cool dawn. He listened with his eyes closed, waiting for his friend to blow an answering call through his teeth—an incredible sound Mars had worked hard to produce. When there was no movement near him, he opened his eyes and saw that Mars was gone.

He moved toward *la cyprière,* then stopped in his tracks and slapped his thigh. "I should've known what he was up to! And I even told him where the barracks is!"

Outside a confectionery he caught a star car to the Touro Almshouse.

"Nope, I ain't seen him," said the sentry, "but we just changed guard. Go on in. You might find somebody who did."

The hall inside was big and high-ceilinged. Chad stood in its center until a passing soldier asked, "What you doing here? You in trouble?"

"I'm looking for somebody, a friend of mine, can't talk right. You seen him?"

"What makes you think he's here?"

"He was aiming to join the army. I told him he couldn't, but he didn't listen." He stopped, realizing the soldier was looking at him funny.

"Where you from?"

"Up the river and down a piece."

"You have a place to stay?"

"I'm going to join the army, but not until I find Mars. I have to find him, that's what I have to do. He ain't fit to be running around alone."

"Come and have a bite with me. I'll ask some men for you and we'll see."

The soldier brought his ration to share. Then he went to talk to a line officer standing at the door, and he pointed and glanced back. The officer came over and sat down. "I'm Corporal Jeffries. Private Collins there, he say you looking for someone name of Mars, can't talk right. That so?"

"Yes, sir."

The soldiers in the crowded hall came and went.

"He your brother?"

"No, my friend. Is he here?"

"Don't think so. You can stay here if you need a place to sleep."

"I can't do anything till I find Mars. I want to talk to all the soldiers who guarded the door since last night."

"Can't see that you can."

"Why not?"

"They's on duty somewheres else."

"Ain't there a list of duties?"

"Naw, I don't see how you can ask for that."

"I want to see Captain Cailloux."

Jeffries raised his eyebrows but his voice stayed soft. "You pulling rank and you ain't even in the army. Besides, that cap'n done left with the First. What you say that fella was to you?"

"My friend. He's a cripple, kind of. Had his tongue cut out on the plantation. He's smart but he can't talk. I gotta look after him, speak for him."

"Speak for him, huh?" The corporal looked at the floor. "What you do if you see he ain't here?"

"Keep on looking."

"What if—he's dead?"

Chad jumped. "I—I guess I'd want to know."

"Wait here a minute."

Jeffries came back with the private and they both sat down. "It ain't an easy thing to explain," the private said, "but sometimes if you been picked on all your life, you get mad, and when someone come along you can pick on, you do. Maybe you don't think about it, you just do it. Seems like you was out of your head."

"You hurt Mars?" he whispered.

"We didn't," the private said, "we ran to break it up. That big sergeant over there saw it first. Sergeant Blair, he is."

They caught the soldier's eye and he came over. "You talking about what happened this morning right after roll call," he said, "damnedest unholy thing. Them two privates picking on that poor soul, jabbing him and laughing and tripping him up. I went to pull them off and the poor thing ran babbling down the street fast as he could go, and then—mercy—them two didn't mean for nothing like that to happen, their faces turned so white they could've passed." He shook his head. Then he said in his slow, pebbly voice, "This policeman, he yell stop, stop or I'll shoot, and the poor nigger didn't stop and the man took his revolver and shot him up. There had to be more holes in him than I swear I ever—"

Chad was shaking and the sergeant saw it, whistled through his teeth: Jesus. I guess I said too much. He patted Chad's arm and walked away.

He slept almost two days and when he got up he walked smack into a wall. He couldn't cry, he couldn't eat, couldn't seem to see. All he saw was Mars full of holes. All he could do was wait until Mars moved over and he could see beyond.

The men in the barracks just brought him water and most of the time let him alone. When a few days passed and he could tell where he was going, he helped in the kitchen like a wooden toy.

After a while, he could feel the soft wind, taste berries, hear thoughts. Mars sat down in a quiet corner.

When he joined the Second Regiment of the Louisiana

Native Guard, they didn't ask his age or if he'd been a slave, and they could see he was fit to be a soldier. Taking the oath of allegiance to the Union army, he thought of Anna, of how it would be to fold her in his arms, and at last he could say yes, that's me.

TWELVE

[But] the blacks, by militantly asserting what they considered
to be their rights as members of the federal military, had es-
tablished a precedent, one which would be acted upon countless times throughout the war by other black men who viewed
the army not as a means of black control, but rather as an in-
strument of black emancipation.

—WILLIAM F. MESSNER, HISTORIAN, *FREEDMEN AND THE
IDEOLOGY OF FREE LABOR, LOUISIANA 1862–65*, 1978

Early December 1862

Reveille was at sunrise. The men turned out under arms, the
first sergeant called the roll, the rifles were stacked and the
men broke ranks. Chad hurried to write in his copybook
before breakfast. Later in the day he would wash and pack his
knapsack with his poetry book, newspapers, map, pencils, his
printer's manual and composition book, and his smooth African stone. Then he'd scrub his canteen and brush out the old
haversack someone had found for him. There his rations and
cartridge box would go when the regiment moved out in two
days.

A week ago in Congo Square, Chad began company drill:

"Ten-shun! Shoulder arms! Right—shoulder—shift arms! Countermarch by file right and file left! Quick ma-arch!" He found himself with his gun on the wrong shoulder, marching the wrong way. The drill sergeant cursed. Later, Sergeant Moore, the man with the gravelly voice, detailed Corporal Jefferies to drill him during off hours. "They's gon put you in the Third Regiment that's just commenced drilling if we don't get you shaped up," confided Jeffries, a tall, handsome man with a short beard and a big smile. He had been around when Chad was in bad shape. He was that hulk by the bed, shaking and rousing and prodding with that soft voice, *drink this*.

"I don't want to be left behind when y'all fall out," Chad said.

"*Move* out," Jeffries corrected. "It wouldn't make no never-mind if Sergeant Funk wasn't such a doggone stickler for drill. You'd sure enough learn by yourself in a few days, but he ain't a-gonna wait. You make one more mess of his column and we all be sorry."

He didn't. Corporal Jeffries was a good teacher and Chad got the routines down pat. The next day he showed so much improvement the sergeant blinked, but kept on cursing until the drill went smooth as a lady's silk glove.

Then their orders came. Anna was the only one he wanted to see before his regiment moved out, and he was excited as he approached the convent. Still, outside he hesitated, almost afraid.

She had just left for a stroll with a group of kiddies in her charge, a nun told him. "I'm Sister Denise. Would you care to wait?"

"No, ma'am. Just tell her Chad was here, Private Chad Creel."

"I'll tell her, Private Creel." The sister's smile was as bright as a candle's flame. "I'm sure she'll be very sor-ry she missed you."

He backed through the huge wooden doors that closed heavily, protectively. It was all he wanted to know, wasn't it: Anna was safe and sound.

* * *

She must have looked disappointed when Sister Denise told her of Chad's visit, because the nun added, "I'm sure he'll be back."

"No he won't," she said, tossing her head, "but I don't care."

"Isn't he a friend?"

"I didn't know him at all back where I come from. Didn't like what I saw of him."

"But why did he visit? He must like you."

Anna couldn't help blushing and couldn't stand herself for it. She snapped "You like to conjure something up?" and stamped out of the room, ashamed that she'd said it but unable to turn back, needing to make it even worse as she went: "Go to blazes!"

She couldn't tell what came over her lately: why did she feel so mean, always ready to snap when someone was only being decent? She burst into tears on her bed and didn't want to stop crying. That made her angry. She pounded her pillow with swift, hard blows.

"Anna," came a voice from the doorway of the room she shared with three nuns. It was open just a crack, but she could see Sammy's slight figure leaning on the doorjamb. She splashed her streaked face with water from her washbowl as he pushed open the door. "What you doing, Anna?"

"None of your business, child. You want me to ask you that every time you breathe?"

"No, ma'am." He looked so solemn, kind of perched in midair.

"Come here, lover," she said, and wrapped him in her arms. "What would you like to do tomorrow?"

"Can we go for a walk, just us?" They were fast friends, but he was still a little shy with the other children.

"Well, I don't know why not. It ain't our day to take the whole gang. Might do us good, the two of us."

"Will you read to me?"

"I told you, just as soon's I know how well enough, I'll read to you. But you have to learn, too, so's you can read right back to me."

Sammy laughed. "I will. I like reading. I can write my name: S-A-M-M-Y N-O-R-T-O-N. Did you know that?"

"No! You can? Why, child, I'm proud! I say I—am—proud! You bring me your name tomorrow, all printed fine, and around noon we sure enough will take a ride on the street-car."

Sammy drew in his breath, gave her a swift hug, and ran from the room.

She was reading when the nuns came in to bed. "Good night, Anna," they said hoarsely. She said good night but didn't look up. She didn't need their friendship, never asked for it. She undressed quietly and went to bed.

The next morning she ate breakfast with her three room-mates, the same, she thought, as eating alone: they talked among themselves in their subdued voices and she kept her eyes on her plate. She was bathing patients and changing beds when Sister Denise came by and asked, "Are you still mad at me, Anna?"

She looked at the nun's sweet face and into her eyes, free of anything but inquiry. "I'm so bad," she whispered, "I'm just so bad I don't see how you stand me."

Sister Denise took both her hands and squeezed them. "No, you're not bad, you just act mean sometimes, same as anybody."

"I can't help it."

"Maybe not. When you can, you will." Anna watched the sister's smile spread across her face. "Sammy says you're going to take a ride on the streetcar."

"I promised. I have some tickets."

"Well, why don't you go early? I think they drill at Congo Square around nine-thirty."

Anna couldn't help laughing. It was such a silly thing for the nun to say, so silly. Yet she'd been wondering all night if they would see anything important when they took that ride up to Basin Street. She sought out Sammy, exclaimed over his name written in bold letters and tucked the paper far into her blouse.

"When we going?" he asked, and she said, "Why, now."

When Sammy asked why they had to ride on the car with a star on it, she said, "It's prettier, boy," and he giggled. Nothing could daunt them today, she thought, not even the devil himself.

Congo Square was full of black soldiers, lining up, marching around, showing off. Sammy's eyes got big at the sight. "Can we watch?" He ran ahead.

They found a bench they could stand on and see clear over the heads of the soldiers, right into the eyes of some. Anna searched as the lines came and went and finally she saw him: "There he is!" she cried.

"Who?"

"Your Uncle Chad," she said, holding Sammy up and pointing. "Right there he is, on the end of that line back there!"

"Why don't he wave?"

"He can't, silly, he's got to swing that gun around, and— look at his bayonet!"

"I see it! I see it!"

Finally the sergeant yelled, "Present arms! Shoulder arms! Order arms! R-ight face! Break ranks, march!"

Chad marched right over to them. "Hello, Anna." She thought he'd ask right off who Sammy was, but he kept his eyes on her. "You look pretty, Anna."

"You do, too," she said, staring back, and suddenly he kissed her, just up and kissed her, hugging her to him like she belonged there. She kissed him back, not caring that a crowd of people was in the square, not even caring that Sammy was there.

It was a while before they looked at the boy, either one of them. He was standing with big eyes and a funny smile, and Anna grabbed him up and pushed him at Chad. "This is Sammy, my sweetheart," she said.

Chad raised him high and put him on his shoulders, not

saying anything, just looking as happy as Anna ever saw him. "We're moving out, Anna," he said, "tomorrow."

She felt as though he'd hit her and she stood there wishing she could fade away without blinking an eye. "Fine," she said. "Ain't that fine, Sammy?"

She reached for the boy and he came to her smiling so wide and open she thought he'd melt in the sunshine.

"What you say, Sammy?" asked Chad.

"You my Uncle Chad?"

Chad looked at Anna and she thought she'd melt, too, just be a puddle right there in the square. "Sure I am," he said, "and I'll always be your Uncle Chad. Don't you ever worry bout that."

"I can write my name!" Sammy reached into Anna's dress so fast she couldn't stop him, and pulled out the paper. "Look-a-here!"

Chad looked as though he'd burst before he'd laugh. "Ain't that something!" he cried. "Mighty fine writing! Got anything else hidden away?"

Anna was blushing but she didn't mind. She just stood there like a fool, blushing.

Chad put out a hand and touched her warm cheek. "I gotta go, Anna."

She bit her lip.

"Smile, Knucklehead?" His eyes pleaded and looked so suddenly old. He gave the absurd name a soft, sweet meaning and she felt so warm, so close to him. But there was no time now, and when there was, it was all they admitted to having. What fools they were, playing parts they didn't feel, too choked to speak their minds. She laughed and tears rolled down her cheeks.

Chad folded her into his arms. "Anna, oh Anna, I'll be back for you," he said, "I promise."

Over his shoulder she said "I'll wait," and "Goodbye, Chad," looking at the trees blowing in the wind.

He knelt to hug Sammy, not even knowing who Sammy was—just like him, wasn't it—and left.

They looked after him and Sammy said, "We gonna miss him, ain't we?"

She looked down at Sammy, the small boy standing at her side like a new shoot in the sun, and she knew: whatever lay ahead, whoever came and whoever went away, marching, marching, they'd be together, she and Sammy, watching it all.

THIRTEEN

They [the free blacks of New Orleans] are intelligent, energetic and industrious, as is evident from the fact that they own one seventh of the real estate in this city.

—GEORGE DENISON, CUSTOMS COLLECTOR FOR
THE TREASURY DEPARTMENT, TO SECRETARY
OF THE TREASURY CHASE, AUGUST 26, 1862

April–May 1862

From the time Blake was taken from his mama in Kentucky and sold to the Wycliffes in Louisiana, he'd kept apart, afraid to form ties that could be broken by the wave of a slave-holder's hand. He might have gone mad at Sweet Haven if it weren't for the boy who kept at him, never letting him slip into himself, where there was only loss. Chad was like a candle flame that brightens when you blow on it, like a lightning bug that glows in the warmth of your hand. Gradually, Blake began to spin his dreams for the boy, the dreams his mother had spun for him, and his father had tried to live.

Blake's mama doted on him, her only child, taught him to read and write and figure, and to dream. His papa, a sailor in the U.S. Navy, was kidnapped in Memphis, sold on the block to the Kentucky cotton planter, never settled down to cotton

picking. He'd managed to hide away a treasure of souve-
nirs—a bit of bamboo from the Orient, a string of beads from
the South Seas. The place he'd loved was San Francisco, and
he'd given Blake a copy of a newspaper run by blacks in that
improbable town. Blake loved his papa when he spoke of his
travels. Then his eyes sparkled, his voice rang. Much of the
time he was silent and far removed, or as thorny as an Osage
orange hedge. After he'd gone, Blake and his mama lived
with the dream of his coming back, as he'd said he'd buy their
freedom when he got back to the ships. Now Blake thought
if they'd been able to say he'd be gone forever, his mama's
grief might have eased. But they'd kept the dream alive. And
his mama kept the man alive, talking of his daring ways.
"Freedom can't be sold, it's in the soul," she said.

Blake had passed the dream to Chad, the dream of freedom, the tales of travel. And always in the background was his
mother: though the door had been shut between them a long
time ago, in his heart he'd expected to open it, to find her
there. Then, over ten years ago, news came of his mama's
death. He told no one, not even Chad. He would have written
his mama if his master had permitted, and run by night to see
her if the distance had allowed. But his plans like hers were
only dreams, and what is the use of dreaming?

He'd stopped in the middle of Chad's prodding, *Tell me,
Tell about us,* stopped when he came to the San Francisco
part: it sounded like his papa, who never made it to the ships,
sounded like his mama, who never let him go . . . That's
enough of dreams, he'd said, and Chad's face wrinkled like a
prune: *Say it ain't a dream,* he'd said.

Reading and writing took the time he had to spare, learning and teaching Chad, and helping slaves escape. No more
tales of travel, no more loose talk, horseshit, dreams.

When the war brought New Orleans into view, *Will we go
there together?* Chad had asked, his face taut, his eyes aflame.
We're partners, ain't we? Yes. They were partners, friends and
family. He'd never go anywhere without the boy—until the
day he had to.

Now, after paddling down the bayou into the waterways of

the lower delta, he fished for dinner and immediate plans, watching the skies of war. He was free, and freedom had come from the most unlikely source: the master's son.

He was grateful for the pirogue he'd maneuvered down the bayou, down through the wild, bright country, past dense forests, to the shore, moving slowly east through a great bay dotted with islands, pushing on toward the river's mouth. The pirogue was weathered and strong, hulled out of a cypress trunk by Chad and Clay Wycliffe. Clay was near Chad's age and Blake had balked at their friendship, warning that it was asking for trouble as sure as sunrise. But Chad wouldn't listen, had stuck with Clay—saw something in him Blake couldn't see until the night he left.

"Come with me," Clay said, standing at the edge of the field in the pale of sundown, his eyes pleading. "You can't go back to the quarters, Blake, or they'll take you. He's come— the man who's bought you!"

They cut through the brush to the bayou, Uncle Noah puffing behind them, Clay talking fast: "My sister told Papa how Chad could read and figure, thinking he could help me with the books now that the manager's gone to Texas. She thought she'd do us a favor, me and Chad." He panted through the words, but kept on talking. "Papa asked where Chad got all that learning and Laurel told him 'Blake.' He got hopping mad. I tried my best to stop him and I thought awhile I had, but I should've known he wouldn't listen, what with Logan adding to his fire!"

They reached the bayou, and Clay stood there looking as bad as Blake ever saw a white man look, and sorrier. "I can't say my sister cares a whit about you—any more than I do— but it sure was not her plan to get you sold. Take the pirogue, Blake, and go."

"Why?" Blake had to ask. "Why you doing this for me?"

Clay smiled. "I'm doing it for Chad," he said.

"When you tell him how you helped me—"

He shook his head, looked sheepish. "I can't tell him. He'd be mad as a hornet he wasn't here." Defending, commanding, his voice rose then: "There wasn't time! Now go!"

Blake went, but not before he left the message, turning to old Noah: "Tell Chad it ain't a dream," he said.

The bombardment of Forts Jackson and St. Philip was at its height when he got there. On the sandbar of the Southwest Pass, he watched the awesome spectacle, bombs bursting above the leafage that lined the river beyond the pass. During the long nights, Rebel fire-ships sent to collide with the attacking fleet came blazing down the current, precious near the army transports anchored at the river's mouth. Smoke blotted the sun by day, the sky flashed, and Blake was in a twilight world. Then, on April 24 (he'd taken care to mark the days) the shelling stopped: the fort had surrendered. Ship by ship would soon begin its voyage up the river, past the warships, past the mortars up in front, up to the Crescent City.

He paddled for all he was worth to a nearby troop transport full of white faces. He was taken aboard the *F. W. Farley,* and sent—skat!—down to steerage. He learned that a general called Old Cockeye had with him on these ships eighteen thousand soldiers to march into New Orleans. Eighteen thousand whites and me, he chuckled to himself. A few black sailors aboard made him think of his father, made him resolute: he'd fight for the freedom his father had lost. But the thought of killing chilled him, and when he heard talk of Union spies waiting in New Orleans—the number grew bigger every time he heard it—he knew that was for him. How to find the one to work for was another thing: what officer would want a black man telling him what was what?

Dragged behind a tugboat, picking its way through cluttered waters, the *Farley* reached the levee at New Orleans. Old Cockeye Butler's steamboat, the *Mississippi,* was docked by its side. Its deck high above the wharf, the transport finally lowered its long slippery ladder in the evening of May 1. Blake was the only black man to climb down.

The crowd met the troops with angry hoots and jeers, with a few smiles of welcome and salutes. One old Irishman whirled his shillelagh around his neck, giving the Union flag a bow. Tattered whites begged among the crowd. Marching to the tune of "Yankee Doodle," Blake and the Union army entered the Crescent City.

On a deserted street, he fell behind to stare into a book-store window. An *a-hem* made him slowly turn, coming face-to-face with a young black man dressed in gentleman's clothing, carrying a cane and smiling. "I see you can read," he said.

Blake looked the fellow in the eye. "Yes, I can. Can you?"

The man gave a nod and extended his hand. "I am André Cailloux."

"I'm Blake Durand," he said, shaking the hand, uncallused but firm.

Soon Blake was sitting in the Café des Réfugiés, before him something called *le petit Gouave,* a drink Cailloux said had originated there. Blake thought it could stay there for all he cared, though it had a way of lifting spirits. The patrons were all shades of yellow and brown, and at tables and the bar, they discussed the occupation. One man kept straightening his tie and repeating, "We might even see business pick up." Another vowed it would be a long time before commerce was back to normal even if the Yankees poured in supplies and traded with the Europeans. Then a sallow-skinned man, brimming with spirits, slapped André on the back, calling him "my man." Gesturing toward Blake, he asked André why he had taken up with a ragged black.

Cailloux stood up. His hand went to his side as if feeling for a sword, the blood vessels bulged in his neck, his jaw tightened. "I demand an immediate apology to my friend, monsieur, and to me," he cried, "for I am the blackest man in America!"

The whole place stared at Cailloux and the sallow man, whose mouth was ajar. "Why," he said, "I do declare, no offense meant to you, my man, or—or to your friend. I shall be on my way." He put on his hat and sped to the door, bumping into chairs along the way, mumbling apologies to the chairs.

The café resounded with laughter and the bartender said

the drinks were on the house. Blake, feeling out of place, kept drinking what was set before him. One nearby man grumbled about the caste system, saying he hoped it would crumble under the yoke of the North, and Blake coughed until the bartender brought him water. He couldn't tell how long it was until his new friend turned to him with the news that it was time to leave. "I should have warned you. When the spirits start flowing in these places, generosity becomes a trap." He looked at Blake and smiled. "I see I'm too late."

Blake knew what his friend meant when he got off the stool. All he remembered about the walk to Cailloux's home was a big fat rat running across his feet into the smelly ditch along the curb.

He woke up under a white ceiling in a bedroom where flowers bloomed in great pots and a breeze came from a small balcony. His heavy head rested on a pillow, and the odor of strong coffee made his stomach swim. He feebly readied himself and climbed down a winding staircase outside the bedroom. Through open glass doors to a sunny courtyard, André smiled at him. "Mother and I are waiting breakfast," he said. "I was about to come and see if you survived."

Madame Cailloux was a stately woman, like Grandmama Martha if you added elegant clothing. She sat in a wrought-iron chair at a small table, a pretty fan on a jeweled chain in her hand. She smiled the way he remembered Mrs. Wycliffe smiling, kind of looking through him, until he sat down across from her and her eyes probed into his. "My son tells me you are from a plantation on Bayou Lafourche," she said. She poured him coffee, complaining that it was a dollar and a quarter a pound. "I daresay you have no preference—cream and sugar, I mean. I'd advise a little cream, no sugar, perhaps a drop of liqueur from the looks of you."

"Have a ginger cake," André said. "It will ease your stomach."

Blake took a bite and chewed slowly.

"I've heard of great suffering at the hands of planters in your area," said Madame Cailloux. "Is it so?"

He nodded, put up his hand to catch his head and saw André smile.

"The whip is barbaric. Have you—" She stopped, staring at him.

Would his head at last topple off? He tried to hold it level and look sensible. André seemed to be enjoying it all, but when Blake's eyes met his he said, "I'm afraid, Mama, we had a rather late night, and perhaps our friend—"

"Of course." She got up. "I shall leave you to your miseries." She hesitated at the doorway. "It is best to practice moderation in all things."

When she was gone, André said, "Mama is sometimes overbearing, but she has a warm heart."

Sunshine splashed through the flowering trees and Blake shook himself. "I have to go."

"No, please. You are a guest in my city, and I've led you astray. It was not intentional." His eyes were now as earnest as the turn of his mouth. "Have you been here before?"

"No."

"New Orleans has always been full of paradox. Black businessmen have prospered, sitting on the edge of slavery."

André's gaze was unnerving, and Blake didn't know what to say. Then André sighed, and his mouth twisted. "Many of us seem to have lost sight of our origin and show no responsibility to our brothers. I'm sure you saw that last night."

"Last night is dim in my mind. If I'd been with a man showed no responsibility, I might've woke up dead."

André laughed and it was such a good sound, Blake joined in. Sobering, his friend's face settled into the sad earnestness that seemed to be his nature. "Do you like to read?"

"Yes."

"Come see our library."

The walls of the large room were lined with books. It was like walking into a world of words. "Thank you," Blake murmured. "I don't reckon I could ever learn what's in all these books."

André pulled out a volume and leafed through it. "I'll

never know what you know, Blake. Your knowledge is far greater than mine."

The streets weren't deserted when they went out that afternoon. Women with parasols strolled, soldiers strode, streetcars lumbered by, and everywhere ragged people begged. As they walked along Decatur Street two grim-looking, well-dressed white women came up behind them. He and André stepped aside to let the ladies pass, and as a Union officer ahead of them did the same, one of the women stepped up and spit in his face. The lieutenant looked stunned. André hurried to offer him his handkerchief. "Drat it," said the officer, flushing, "I thought the morning reports of this sort of thing were exaggerated."

"One can hardly exaggerate such an insult," said André. "Let me apologize for the behavior of my countrymen."

"Oh, the men are all right, it's the women, ladies they call themselves. Why, when Flag Officer Farragut came ashore to have breakfast with another officer, a woman threw a bucket of dishwater from a balcony onto their heads." He burst out laughing, said, "Excuse me," and flushed again. "The—ah—reports of such displays of contempt have been coming in all morning."

"What are you going to do?" asked André, shaking his head.

"What can you do to a she-Rebel?" The lieutenant cleared his throat. "Thank you, thank you very much," he said, and sped off.

It was dinnertime when they returned to André's home, and Madame Cailloux had set three places at the table. The conversation was lively as they told her about their day.

Then André said, "I want to fight. It's the only way I can reconcile my complicity with the slave system."

"What do you mean?" asked Blake. "You don't own slaves."

"No," said André, "but I've come to believe that the responsibility for the existence of the slave system rests with the people who don't like it but turn their heads. Even buy its products."

"It's hard for me to see through your eyes," Blake said, "but don't—don't keep the past ahead of you."

André smiled. "But I have to make it as right as I can. I aim to prove what I said last night. Maybe my skin doesn't show it, but I'm the blackest man—"

"And the most foolish," said Madame Cailloux. "Let them fight their wars without you." As she served *café brûlôt,* she turned her eyes on Blake. "You're welcome to stay another night."

"Merci," said Blake. "I'll leave in the morning, then."

"Farragut welcomes black sailors," said André, with a smile.

"The Navy's not for me," Blake said. "I promised to be somewhere when the river's free."

"So what will you do?"

"Maybe go to General Butler, see if he needs a spy."

Cailloux shook his head. "Too soon for him to know much."

"Then I'll have a look around till I find someone who does."

Before he went to bed, Blake turned to the books in the library, reading late by a gas lamp. At midnight, the *grande dame* appeared with a glass of warm milk and a pat on the hand. "Good luck, *mon cher,"* she said. "Do not get hurt in this damn war." She sighed. "No one can say a war belongs to him, unless he would, with Satan, own hell."

FOURTEEN

Despite Butler's hesitancy to arm the black population, throughout the summer of 1862 various Union commanders in the Gulf Department enlisted the military support of fugitive slaves. Leading the way was General Phelps, the balky brigadier, who never ceased drilling his black regiment at Camp Parapet.

—WILLIAM F. MESSNER, HISTORIAN, *FREEDMEN AND THE IDEOLOGY OF FREE LABOR, LOUISIANA 1862–65*, 1978

May—September 1862

General Butler's answer to "she-Rebels" came on May 15 with his Woman Order, stating that any woman who displayed contempt against his men was liable to be treated as "a woman of the town plying her avocation." Despite widespread uproar against the general, the women were cowed, though Blake had to say they could still bring more of a chill to the streets than a soldier could. Then Mumford, one of the white fellows who pulled down the Stars and Stripes Captain Farragut had raised over the Mint, made the mistake of wearing a piece of the flag in his buttonhole, parading it with a mob outside Butler's headquarters. Now he was in jail. Everyone was talking about Mumford and some placed bets on whether he'd be hanged. One old black man, standing on the street under a balcony with Blake, confided that no one seemed to notice how clean the streets and gutters were since Butler put the unemployed to work on them, or that the starving would've surely died if the general hadn't passed out food.

Blake had spent a week visiting the crowded contraband camp south of New Orleans, and another on city streets. He'd walked and talked and listened, staying in the shadows of the groaning town, when he heard of General John Phelps. The name was praised in *L'Union,* taken to task in the *True Delta.* Stationed at Camp Parapet near Carrollton, Phelps was striving to put freed people to work, trying to give them decent shelter. One article said he'd brought in teachers.

That was enough for Blake. Wearing the clothing André Cailloux had insisted he take, the suit he allowed had kept him out of jail, he headed up to Camp Parapet.

The approach was alive with zealous spring insects—small millers and soft, green-winged bugs that got in his eyes and stuck to his sweaty face. Mosquitoes hummed and bit. He attracted attention, though his suit was wrinkled and damp. Refugees, squatting in crude leaky shelters of cane or rails in front of the rampart, called to him, asking permission to stay. Most of them were in rags and barefoot. Children ran about over soggy ground, their clothing sticking to them if they had any on. Some of the people smiled at Blake, walking like a white man, and others scowled. All of them stared.

A sentry looked him over and let him by. He stopped a white soldier to ask directions to the general's headquarters, and the fellow grumbled, "I'll show you." The soldier glanced from side to side with distaste as they walked by the refugees.

The grizzled general was standing at one end of his small cabin, looking at a hanging map. He stood well over six feet, and his limbs were long and loose. "How is it you got yourself through the guards and announced to me with nothing but your name, Mr. Durand?" drawled Phelps, turning toward him. Deep-set eyes in a long swarthy face looked down into Blake's.

"You are the only one can make me a scout and a spy, sir," he said. "I had to."

"I see." The general scratched his chin. "You say you want to be a scout and a spy, too? Then tell me the news."

Blake recounted newspaper reports and all he'd heard in the camp and in the city.

The general nodded. "In my opinion New Orleans ought to be brought to the hammer. Will you have a spot of whiskey?"

"No, sir, thank you."

Phelps poured into a tin cup and took a swallow. "Truly one fifth of my troops are drunk for days after payday. I abhor overindulgence, but I know if the men don't have whiskey, they'll die of country fever; quinine alone won't prevent it. We're beginning to lose some already. I fear we may be halved by fall." He looked into his cup. "Exercise and perspiration. They need those, too. It heartens me to see my brigade drill: my men are good. Of course I am also blessed with a number of greenhorn regiments from Maine, New Hampshire, and Connecticut. They are ignorant of etiquette, dress sloppily, don't salute an officer." He eyed Blake. "Let us get down to business. I'm a Vermonter. Where do you hail from?"

Phelps's gaze was piercing. Blake was able to keep his eyes level as they talked, although it was the first time he had met those of an older white man on purpose.

Phelps slid into the chair behind his narrow, makeshift desk, and motioned Blake to take one near him. "I think you'll be pleased to know I am commencing to recruit freedmen." He leaned forward and put a hand on Blake's arm. "By July I expect to have a tidy regiment of ex-slaves and a healthy number of men sent downriver to General Dow to train as artillerists. He told me he's sure they'll make very respectable gunners, and I agree." His eyes twinkled. "Don't you?"

"I do, sir," said Blake, and before he could stop himself he asked, "What about Butler?"

"*General* Butler?"

"Yes, sir."

"I suppose General Butler will object."

A private stuck his head in the doorway of the cabin.

"Come in, Private, come in and tell me what you want."

The stocky white soldier inched in, hat in hand, and the general's face reddened. "Put on your hat, salute me, and state your purpose!"

"I—sir—just want some requisition slips for the captain to fill out—sir."

Phelps took several papers from a stack on his desk, and handing them to the soldier, gave him a curt salute. The soldier pulled back his shoulders, and left saluting.

Blake tried not to smile, and Phelps threw up his arms. "That is a mere sample of the problem. The other day I fell afoul of a gawky lieutenant with a red shirt and bare feet, sitting on the head of a barrel, eating an apple and gossiping with a sentry," he said. "His conduct and his appearance were unbecoming a private, let alone the rank conferred upon him. I halted my stroll and glared at him. He did not rise, but he did salute. I read him a lecture and sent him on his way." Phelps shook his head in grave despair. "I wouldn't have been so angry with the fool lieutenant," he drawled, "if he hadn't saluted me with his apple core." He let out a slow and convulsive burst of laughter, in a falsetto that seemed to shake him apart. "You see, Durand, I am an officer of the regular army, not one of those ninety-day volunteers. I try to make them mind their manners."

"Yes, sir," said Blake, smiling.

"Enough of this," the general said. "Tell me about yourself. Everything."

Blake picked his words awkwardly, trying to pull out pieces of his life that would meet the general's aim: how hard he worked, how he had sense, and learning, and knew the ways of men. He thought he'd failed, but the general clasped his hands before him and nodded his head. "I see, yes, I see. And you've no wife and children?"

"No, sir."

"Well, let me see. Your first assignment will not be critical, but there's nothing of that nature that I need, and you need practice. I'd like a survey of the people in the camps and on plantations. Ask them what they want—land, money, education—now and after the war, how we can compensate them and get them on their way to independence, how best they think their needs may be met—and their dreams fulfilled." He sighed, and Blake felt a kinship he had no yardstick for; he'd never felt close to a white man. "Go as far as you can up the river—stay below Port Hudson—and as far down the river as you see fit. Take all the time you need, and tread softly where the Rebels hold the land. Be dumb, if you must, and wary." He tapped the desk with a pencil. "Anything you may learn of military value, report to me at once. Now, you'll need rations and an advance in pay—and clothing. Shoes." He wrote an order for the quartermaster and a Letter of Protection in his long, sweeping handwriting. He told Blake where to get his pay, and then bade him goodbye, pumping his hand. "I pray the nefarious slave system will be brought to an end and the slaveholders suffer their just punishments," he said. "We owe it to justice and humanity to proclaim the immediate abolition of slavery throughout the South." He smiled and his voice softened. "Good luck, Durand."

Blake gave a proper salute, even clicked his heels, but in the doorway he turned to wave goodbye.

General Butler was muttering over the London *Times* when Blake was ushered into his office at the St. Charles Hotel. The room was elegant. The man behind the massive desk had a smooth, fair complexion with a slight flush, sparse grey hair combed back behind his ears, thin lips and clear eyes, one slightly out of line. He squinted at Blake, and waving him to a chair, continued grumbling about his critics, how reaction to his Woman Order and Mumford's execution had been slow to die. "I am as careful to assess what I see as you, a scout, must be. But I must also pay attention to the climate of the country, indeed the world"—his smile was charming—"for its judgment can end a man's personal advance."

It was September. In July Secretary of the Treasury Chase had urged Butler to enlist blacks, and now the First Regiment of the Louisiana Native Guard was ready to be mustered in and the Second was beginning to drill. Old Cockeye never did anything halfway: he commissioned black officers, mostly lieutenants, a few captains, and one major, a surprise action that Blake felt would never be repeated, given the climate of the Gulf Department.

Butler smiled that charming smile, showing his white, even teeth. "I want to welcome you to my command, Durand. I've heard all good things about you. Are they so?"

"Yes, sir."

"Good. I like that. You are without the constraints of modesty and can therefore be trusted. Do you know how few I can trust in this lonely post? Yet I can ride the streets between Chalmette and Carrollton without incident from the Rebel citizens. I said I would make this a Union city or a home of the alligator!" Squinting his eyes, he went on to decry the insubordinations of his officers and the disadvantages of his office, how he must play to one politician or another, and his smile flashed as though on a string he pulled. "The Northern attitude is pessimistic," he said, tapping his desk, "and no wonder, the way McClellan and Pope let them down. Incompetence. In the Gulf Department, we are doing well despite the recent retreat from Baton Rouge and the antics of General Taylor and his merry band of men. Our problems are small but frustrating. I am plagued by requests from my officers for leaves of absence, such bad examples have they become."

Blake settled into his chair. He had grown used to being a listener for lesser officers. Often they mused about this and that, almost as though his presence inspired them. He was a black man in their midst, yet they spoke of "the niggers" and the nuisance they were, of the trials of the military handling "the savage hordes." Could they not see him? Sometimes he wondered if he were a shadow, or a man without a voice of his own. Only when he'd reported directly to Phelps had he felt he was part of a cause.

Now Butler was talking as though to himself, but this was a commander whose approval could make or break a man, and Blake's new immediate superior.

Suddenly the general took a paper from his desk and, squinting at Blake, said, "Listen to this statement from one of my prized generals, if you will: 'While I am willing to prepare African regiments for the defense of the government against its assailants, I am not willing to become the mere slavedriver which you propose, having no qualifications in that way.' " He tapped his desk. "That is Brigadier General Phelps's reason for resigning. What do you think of it?"

Blake was struck dumb. Phelps had told him of his transfer without a word of his own plans to resign. He'd thanked the general heartily, had taken the transfer as a sign of his good work, as an earned promotion. Promotion? To what? And why had it seemed so grand?

"He complains he has not trained his troops for the purpose of hard labor in the swamps, that they fall prey to disease and exhaustion. Are they not used to it? I asked. But some men are stubborn!" His eyes narrowed. "Well, Durand, you worked under him, and so you should know him. Is he worth fighting for? What should I do?" Butler's gaze fastened on Blake's face, and Butler's cold eyes spoke.

Blake bit his tongue and his skin crawled. "Let him go, sir," he said.

"Good boy. We shall surely be better off without the likes of him." The general flashed his smile. "You have good sense."

For one breathless moment, Blake opened his mouth to speak his mind, to say what was in his heart, but the general was around the bend: "I am toying with the idea of offering President Lincoln asylum in our fair city, along with the archives and treasures. How does that strike you?"

Blake's palms were cold and wet. "Fine, sir," he heard his voice say, like an echo against the walls.

"I like you, Durand. Now, tell me, what is our friend Mouton up to?"

Blake was in the open at last. He described the Confederate general's position, the size and nature of his force, and added that General Taylor, in command of the District of Western Louisiana, might later send Mouton up Bayou Lafourche to establish a fort at Donaldsonville.

"Ah-ha! Excellent, excellent. General Weitzel and I have our eyes on Donaldsonville as well. Keep close watch on those wily sons-of-guns, Durand, and let me know their positions and their plans." His white teeth gleamed. "You are talented, my boy, and blessed with good judgment as well. Seldom have I witnessed such precise detail and sound preparation of a report. You will be my trusted spy from now on."

Blake rose and saluted. He had won the general's approval and his own discontent.

Fifteen

One of my men has been detailed as guard over two large
plantations, his duty being to drive off plunderers and to make
the Negroes get in the sugar crop. The owners are humbly
thankful for his protection; they have given him a pony, a
hogshead of sugar and a barrel of syrup; and they allow him
to bring me poultry at fair prices and vegetables for nothing.

—CAPTAIN JOHN W. DE FOREST, U.S. ARMY, NEAR THIBODEAUX,
DECEMBER 7, 1862, *A VOLUNTEER'S ADVENTURES*, 1946

December 1862–January 1863

Noah watched as the soldier put his rifle between his legs,
took a pouch from his pocket and pulled out a chew of
tobacco, looking off into the distance, paying no mind to the
two men standing at his side. The man in the wide-brimmed
hat was talking, and Colonel Wycliffe was all ears.

Noah sat outside the bare longhouse as he had since the
occupation began, when the field hands left in a body with
only the clothes on their backs, the married ones piling their
children and whatever was in their shacks onto plantation
carts. All of them said they were going to the blessed Yankees,
the Deliverers.

"Why don't you come along?" his old friend Virgil asked. "No use you setting here."

"Setting is what I want to do," he told Virgil. "I ain't had time to set and listen to the world since I was taken."

"Then I say God be setting with you."

The only ones with Noah today were the yawning soldier and the man talking to Colonel Wycliffe over there. It seemed that the plantations hereabouts were now in the hands of a three-man commission set up by General Butler, and the man was saying he, as a member, would supply workers to Sweet Haven. All the colonel had to do was swear allegiance to the Union and honor the wage contract. How many hogsheads of sugar were waiting out there to be harvested?

Colonel Wycliffe said some of it was cut, lying in windrows. Some bloodthirsty slave shot his overseer the night of the battle, he said, and when the army marched in the next day, his field hands up and ran after it. He'd always vowed he wouldn't budge, and now he was glad of it, and mighty obliged to General Weitzel for the guard that kept out the pillagers. He knew planters who ran, and their mansions were now in shambles. Others housed lavish-living Union officers who didn't mind drinking the wine cellars dry and sending off silver to their wives.

Ah, said the commissioner, the ravages of war, a pity, a pity.

The colonel asked what was going to happen to all that cane on abandoned plantations, and the commissioner said there were plenty of blacks in the contraband camps and at the army posts, plenty to go around. The colonel muttered that he supposed the profits would go to the Union. The man with the soldier chewing his cud didn't say a word.

They walked around a while, peeking in the quarters and saying next to nothing, and then Colonel Wycliffe pointed to Noah as a *loyal Nigra*. Noah's stomach turned loops and he wanted to speak up, say he wasn't loyal, just old, but they turned away before he could do more than stare.

Well, the colonel said, the present company doesn't seem the sort to take advantage, we'll ride out to the fields now and then you'll stay to dinner.

Noah shook his head: plenty of blacks to go around! Chad might be back sooner than he planned. Lawdy, he whispered, I hope not.

They arrived in droves, most of them new to Sweet Haven. They stood in family circles, looking for shacks, settling for longhouses when the shacks were full. They were barefoot and tattered but had a spring in their steps and a glint in their eyes. They told Noah they didn't want to work the fields unless the land was their own, but ex-slaves on abandoned plantations labored for the Union for nothing, and they'd have none of that. Here they'd get ten dollars a month, and when the crop was harvested they'd be free to leave and find other work. Noah went with them to sign up at the barn. When Chad came for him and Martha he'd have some money to help out.

He told Martha what he was going to do. She cocked her head and her eyes looked in on herself, her lips moving. He thought he heard her say something to Chad. "It's me, Martha," he said, taking her shoulders and looking into her face. "Noah."

What a smile he got! It was enough to send him off light-hearted, reeling to the fields with a song he'd thought was long since stilled.

He'd watched Martha from his very first harvest, how she moved, how nothing seemed to bother her. He was deeply troubled, yearning for home, uninterested in becoming what he was forced to be, on the way to that space in himself that would close like a man-eating plant.

She must have known, for she took his hand and taught him words he had to know and ways he must remember. Roan, her husband, sat in the background, a silent, stalwart man, and Noah saw the two of them as the single framed picture on their wall: hearts joined by an arrow. It kept him to one side but it did not keep him out. He glowed in their warmth, and every time she smiled at him he felt rewarded.

He never married or kept company, for no one was like Martha. She could come out of the fields looking fresh, her sweat just sparkling on her face. She could be caring all night for a sick child and push up the sunrise with a stretch and a yawn. She could tell a tale as a great unfolded secret and weave her words into a net that caught and dragged you in. "Noah," she'd yell, "come sit with us," and then she'd tell stories he'd heard back home and new ones as time went by.

But that wasn't all of Martha. She was the recordkeeper, the one who knew the times of birth and death, the year Cora came from Georgia and Fred left for Alabama. Her head was so full and her heart so ready, he wondered at her. And at night as he lay on his mat in the longhouse he wondered what she would feel like in his arms. It would be too much, he said to himself, like the sun setting in my lap, like a star in my fist: I'd burn and freeze and lose my sense, I'd never know another day.

The night Roan died some ten years ago, a calm settled round about her. One day he found her holding the picture from the wall. "I see the mistress throw a bundle in the trash pile and something big and red is there," she said. "I tell Roan and we go fishing. He laugh at it, say Ouch, hearts shouldn't be join by pain. I say what else? And then he—" She drew in. "That was one year after the day we marry, and today is that day, many year after."

"You amaze," said Noah. "How you know that?"

"Writ on my mind," she said. Then she smiled at him and the whole world lit up, just as it did today. There couldn't have been a finer send-off for a man going out to earn a wage.

The smell of burning wood mixed with a hint of boiled cane, barely a smell but a feel in the air, a knowing, a tinge of brown sweetness sent up taut and scant from a thousand juicy stalks ground and bubbling in the fire: harvest was underway. From the time Noah first got his bearings at Sweet Haven he could tell how far into the season they were by how the air felt. When his eyes burned in the fields and he could breathe his breakfast, harvest was almost over.

Virgil, heavy and short of breath, reached out his hand in greeting. "I couldn't get work, and you can't eat stars and stripes even if they stands for liberty. I said I'd sooner work here with you than go off to another farm, so"—he shrugged and his bones creaked—"here I is." He stood big as life beneath the trees along the path to the fields so you had to believe him, here he was, and you didn't know whether to laugh or cry.

The overseer and the soldier stood on the rim of the fields and the soldier spoke: "By order of General Butler, Commander of the Gulf Department, the wage agreement will not affect the rights of either master or slave. It is not concerned with emancipation. But the contract must be honored by worker and planter alike. Refusal to work will be punished by imprisonment in darkness on bread and water." He looked over the crowd standing motionless and then went on: "Guards have been stationed on all plantations to see that there is no cruel or corporal punishment, and to enforce other provisions of the contract."

They had been waiting for that part—no whippings—and now they looked at each other and smiled. Noah winked at Virgil, who looked tired before the work began, gobbled his ration of hominy and molasses so fast Noah gave him some of his.

There were problems: they often worked longer than the contract said they had to, and they didn't get paid the ten dollars a month they were due. The grapevine said it wasn't much better up or down the bayou. He heard of farms where they got their pay, but on most it was work and wait, and no wonder, when you saw how thick the Union guards were with the planters. He and Virgil talked about quitting, but they kept on working.

Toward the end of harvest, Noah couldn't keep up. He

asked if he could work half days, but the soldier said the master told him there would be no special cases, you either work full time or you don't get paid. He hadn't seen any money, anyway, so Noah quit.

He spent his days sitting in an old chair across from Martha. He would have talked to her, but he hadn't anything to say she'd want to hear, so he let her be.

Virgil came by almost every evening and sat a while. Some flesh had fallen off him and he looked right peaked. "Come January," he said one day, "old Lincoln will set us free. He won't go back on his word, too, will he?"

Noah frowned. He told Virgil he hadn't seen any slaves in a long time, no sir. The hands were a different lot now. No one said they were free, that's the truth, but they weren't slaves. Why, they could hardly wait till the end of harvest so they could collect their pay and leave this place.

"Whoa!" said Virgil. "I didn't mean to get you going. I say, we ain't slaves but we ain't free neither."

When the crop was harvested and sent to market, Noah went up with the hands to get his money. Colonel Wycliffe said they were free to go but he had nothing for them. The work shoes were worth three dollars and the rest of their money had gone for food.

Virgil's smile was a little forced when he said goodbye, and he was a little cow-eyed, too. "You gon be all right, Noah?"

The question was plumb silly coming from a man who looked as old and tired as his friend did. "Dandy. You know me," he said, feeling sorry for Virgil, not for himself. All he had to do was sit and wait.

Sixteen

There are patrols all over the city and every preparation has
been made to meet the insurrectionists . . . General Banks is
not like Butler, he will protect us.

—NEW ORLEANS CITIZEN, *JOURNAL OF JULIA LEGRAND,* 1862

December 1862

The sky was all scummed over the day the Second Regiment
crossed the river to Algiers, boarded the railroad, and went
about twenty miles over the tracks where it made camp. It was
one of those sticky days when he wished it would clear up or
rain but it sat on the fence and dozed: nothing he could do
about it.

Chad was glad to leave New Orleans, a city het up over its
new commander, General Banks, who right off issued a litany
of "public safety" orders that put a stop to the planned celebration of the Emancipation Proclamation, little more than a
week away. He let Jonas French, the provost marshal of the
parish and police chief of New Orleans run amuck, and he
sent so many patrols over the delta no freed or free black was
safe on a country road. He came right out and said the
Preliminary Proclamation had no force and if the final state-

ment came the first of January, President Lincoln would surely spare the Gulf Department. The whites, of course, were glad to hear that, even gladder to get rid of General Butler, and they heaped praise on Banks for—what had the man in the tavern said last night?

Chad had gone to the Pig and Whistle with Jeffries and Collins to celebrate before battle, something soldiers had to do. The streets were crazy with whites who hurled more cock-eyed words at them than he'd heard in the fields, but the tavern was full of blacks. Seemed it might be the final congregation of more than three (final, according to another order) and they were going to make it last.

The man sitting by Chad at the bar was a clockmaker, and he bought the whole gang drinks and did a lot of talking. Chad listened and laughed: wasn't General Banks a frightened man?

"You bet your boots he is," the clockmaker said. "The planters tell him there will be an insurrection come January one, and he swallows it, hook, line, and sinker. He's forcing some back to the plantation—illegally—and locking up as many as he can, saving the poor slaveholders from us savages."

Jeffries and Collins made fun out of that. Then the man said, "I want you soldiers to know I stand behind you," and Collins crooned, "I'd just as leave you'd stand in front of us when the battle begins."

They didn't know then that they would be guarding the New Orleans and Opelousas Railroad somewhere between the river and Bayou Lafouche. But here they were, out in the middle of nowhere looking after a cold steel track.

The jeers flung by white soldiers on the trains passing through added to their gloom. It was getting harder and harder to shrug off the Union soldier. Chad's friends met the bullying in different ways: Jeffries, veteran of the cane fields and somewhat older, took it in stride most of the time, but Collins, who had been a New Orleans slave hired out to the docks where he was allowed to keep a small fraction of his earnings, could not abide it. He'd pace at the campfire at night, swearing softly. But Chad had never been one to look at the bottom of the bayou when something might be floating on top: he told himself that after the black brigade fought one telling battle, the Yankees would come around. Calling off his feelings was another thing. He remembered Granny Martha telling him that anger could eat him alive if he let it fester. "Learn to pity when you can't see sense," she said. "It won't make right from wrong, but it make *you* right, and who you gon live with, anyhow?"

He turned over on his blanket in the dark and let out a sigh that made Jeffries take notice. "I know," the corporal whispered from his bed, "we all want a chance to fight."

The country lay flat and untrimmed except for the cornfield that ran almost into the railroad tracks. It was a damp night, the mist so thick you could lose your hand on the end of your arm. Chad's lantern looked like a big lightning bug as he headed out for guard duty.

The sentry was getting off his belly. When he saw Chad he yelled, "Throw your lantern!" A shot rang out and Chad dived, his lantern landing six feet beyond him, still blazing.

"Put out the lantern," said the guard, "and keep moving. Someone's shooting from the cornfield. It ain't pickets, it's too fretful, but they ain't fooling neither."

"No way to fight a battle," said Chad.

"Listen, you fight any way you can," said the guard, moving away. "I'm gon get some men to cover you in case they comes closer."

Chad peered across the railroad into the fog, kicked the tracks to see they were there. Now and then somebody's rifle sent a shell through the thick air and he returned the shot, moving swiftly so he wouldn't be a target. Then four men arrived carrying no lanterns, and every time the snipers sent bullets flying, they sent a volley back.

Sometime after midnight the shooting stopped. The next

morning, Jeffries said the Rebels weren't within miles of the line. A contingent searched the cornfield and found only the space cleared for a bivouac by a company of the Eighth Vermont Regiment that was camping below them until it moved out during the night. Chad felt his throat tighten.

"Who the hell they think they are?" cried Collins.

Sergeant Blair said simply, "Don't fuss. When we shows them we can fight, they gonna show us some respect: mark my words."

All they had to do was find the war.

SEVENTEEN

. . . a general roundup of all blacks on city streets ensued . . .
A visitor to the city jail found fifty black women packed into a
cell . . .

—WILLIAM F. MESSNER, HISTORIAN, *FREEDMEN AND THE
IDEOLOGY OF FREE LABOR, LOUISIANA 1862-65*, 1978

December 1862–January 1863

"Where we going, Anna?" asked Sammy in the crowded
wagon. At first she didn't answer, just stared ahead at the two
soldiers who sat behind the horses. But when he nudged her
gently and asked, "Are we going to see Uncle Chad, Anna?"
she shook her head. "No, Sammy."
  "Why?"
  "He's fighting the war, honey."
  "There's soldiers driving the wagon. See them?"
  "I see them."
  He leaned forward and looked them over. "Are they Uncle
Chad's friends?"
  "No, they don't even know him."
  "Where they taking us, Anna?"
  "To a plantation where I used to live," she said. "Chad used
to live there, too."

"But he said he'd come for us back in New Orleans, Anna. Why we leaving?"

"Hush, child," she said, "hush, now."

"Why?"

"He'll find us, honey. Try to sleep. It's a long ride." She put her arms around him, felt him relax against her, and closed her eyes. It had been a long day, a long two days, a long, long month . . .

The pale light spread through her bedroom at the convent the morning she fainted. Everything looked blue grey, even the brown washstand and the white bowl, until the dark folded in from the edges and her light went out. On the floor, coming to, she could see three forms bent over her, three faces full of concern. "You've been going too hard lately, Anna dear," said Sister Mary. "Yes, dear," said Sister Adelaide, "stay in bed this morning and we shall bring you breakfast." Said Sister Marie, "Yes, dear, do." It was the most her roommates had ever said to her.

The thought of breakfast made her deathly ill. She threw up in her washbowl and climbed into bed. The nuns were solicitous. Sister Denise put a cool hand on her brow. "You don't feel feverish," she said. "Thank goodness. It must be exhaustion." Mother Superior peeked in with a cheery "Good morning, Anna," and a serious "I'm sorry you aren't feeling well."

By evening she felt hungry. She dressed and went to the dining hall for dinner. Everyone was glad to see her but they wondered at her foolishness, getting up so soon and eating a regular meal. The next morning when she was sick again, they said see, you should have stayed in bed. That night, ravenously hungry, she waited until all but the night nurses were sleeping, then crept into the kitchen. Sitting there eating a large slice of bread, she began to wonder. No, she said, it can't be, can it?

The next morning when she felt she was going to be sick,

she didn't let on. When she vomited, she hid the evidence until she could dispose of it herself, and went about her chores as though she were recovered. After all, she said to herself, this malady is likely to last nine months—and no one, no one must know.

It was a fretful several weeks, her sickness rising and falling, so bad sometimes she had trouble hiding it. Sister Denise looked hard at her and even Sister Clarice, the stolid teacher, asked how she felt. At night she lay wondering what to do, where to go. Even if the nuns found it in their hearts to be good to her, their disgust would show: she could feel their eyes on her now. Even if she explained that she and Chad were going to be married, or lied and said they were, she could hear their whispers. She was so miserable she wanted to cry, and so excited, so happy, she couldn't.

She did not know, when she went out that chilly January night to walk and talk with herself, that her answer would be found in jail.

The two militiamen grabbed her on Royal Street and thrust her into a wagon where she huddled with the others at the feet of the armed guard.

"You can't—" she said, knowing they could. She cried "Let me go! That hurts!" as though there were someone to hear.

They pushed her into a space so crowded she had no room to move, could scarcely see the other women or know them as anything but bodies. The cell door closed.

The breathing of those pressed against her seemed to be her own. There were whimpers: no movement. It was too close, too hot, too important to stay still. They stood like statues, each a part of the whole, staying intact. No one gave instructions, but she knew the unspoken fear: should one woman try to stretch an arm or move a leg, the ripple would widen and clash against the others and smash against the walls until all would be lost. As a carnivorous fish may feed on its young, the large body would crush the small, helpless creatures within. Breathing was quiet except for moans and shudders that rocked the body with fear and were followed by harsh silences. Sweat rolled off one and onto another and gathered in the puddles of pee on the floor.

She could not think of it for fear of fainting, of causing the ripple that would become the quake. She could not dwell on where she was, or surely her chest would stop drawing in the heated air. Instead she thought: Chad, oh Chad, where are you? From her head to her numbing toes she called him and cussed him and held him fast. He was her focus, her only sane thought, and she clawed at him without letup, kept him at her center, hugged him to her breast, grasped him all night long.

When the night was through and dawn spread in from the high barred window, the stillness was so deafening she wondered if the women were dead. Then one by one they were taken away. When there was room to faint, she fainted, and was laid on a cot and given water.

There were questions and she answered them all: her name, her former master's name, the name of his plantation and its location. No one cooperated more, some much less, a few were so stubborn they were thrown back in jail. Not Anna: she knew what she was doing.

"Anna?"

"Yes, Sammy."

"We gonna be together, ain't we?"

"Yes."

"We'll miss Uncle Chad, won't we?"

She looked at the small face, the eyes that fear was touching again, the nose crimped against her arm. "We'll miss him," she said, "but we got each other, and you have to promise you'll take care of me, same's I take care of you."

"Yes'm." He closed his eyes and soon his weight against her knew no boundaries as he slept.

EIGHTEEN

The principle is not that a human being cannot justly own another, but that he cannot own him unless he is loyal to the United States.

—*LONDON SPECTATOR*, COMMENTING ON THE
EMANCIPATION PROCLAMATION, JANUARY 1863

January 1863

Chad didn't hear the news until the morning of January 1: the Emancipation Proclamation came with the new year, right on time. He had always imagined cheering, singing, celebrating the way the Northern abolitionists were going to do, but the telegraph at his outpost was not manned at night and no one was sure there would be a message, anyhow. In his copybook he wrote: The great Proclamation fell with a thud on the cold iron tracks.

On January 20, a chill was in the air and he couldn't sleep. He couldn't get warm and he couldn't keep his mind from clicking like the telegraph, so he wrote in his copybook all about Anna. He thought he'd start with Laurel and his feelings for her, but he couldn't see her face, couldn't see a picture of her that wasn't blurred, couldn't hear her voice. All there was was Anna, and her presence was so strong it scared him: Anna, leaning against a tree, petulant and still, waiting for Laurel and making him squirm; Anna, switching from scorn to interest outside the master's kitchen; Anna, calling his name below the levee, her smile as wide and gusty as the wind. He thought of her eyes, always telling him something different from her words, the way her fury changed to fire the day he lost control—how they met in the square, their eyes, their thoughts, their hearts. Standing in the square in the sunlight, he'd known he loved her, had loved her for a long, long time. Somehow it made it easier to leave her, not harder, but now he had a feeling he shouldn't have gone.

The feeling persisted. He got up and walked along the tracks, watched the iron rails catch shafts of moonlight. He thought of his regrets, how the window he was behind kept him from seeing into hers, kept him all wrapped up in his own plans, not even trying to see what hers were or fit their plans together. Now her presence was overwhelming. She seemed to push against him and he could hear her call. He looked over his shoulder, all around. Oh, Anna, he said, I never should've left you.

"Halt! Who goes there?" The sentry shook his head when he saw Chad. "What you doing out here this time of night? I could've shot you."

The next day the telegraph clicked with news: there had been a general roundup in New Orleans.

"What does that mean?" he asked Jeffries.

"Five or six hundred got arrested last night. Seems the old police chief said all blacks on the streets without a pass after eight-thirty would be jailed, but he didn't post the order."

"Sounds like something Jonas French'd cook up," said Sergeant Blair. "Um-um-um."

"How did it ever get on the wire?" Collins wanted to know.

"Me and this operator got a grapevine of our own," said Jeffries. "He say free people had to pay a dollar and a half this morning to get out of jail, and the freed slaves will be carried back to their old owners, if they can find out who they are. I'll bet they'll play hell doing that. They plans to sell the freed people back for one dollar and twenty-five cents."

"We is depreciated!" Sergeant Blair howled. "Four, five months ago I was worth one thousand five hundred dollars—in gold!" He warmed his hands at the campfire, chuckling. "When I was a house servant, the bookkeeper used to get me to add columns for him. I didn't know what I was adding till one day I looked and saw it was money coming in, all this money, lots and lots of money. When he saw I knew what I was doing, he didn't ask me to do it no more, and before long the master had to get a new bookkeeper." He laughed hard then. "He couldn't tell on me, couldn't say the houseboy knew how to figure or he'd lose his job—and he done lost it, anyhow."

Chad faced Jeffries. "Anything else? He say anything else?"

"He say fifty women was packed into one little cell. That's about all he say."

Chad caught his breath: Anna!

When everyone was sleeping but the sentries, he scribbled a note to his friends and changed to the old clothes he kept in his knapsack. He left his haversack for Collins—who'd probably been the one to give it to him in the first place, back at the barracks. If he could only make it to New Orleans before they found out where Anna came from, he could save her from going back to Sweet Haven. And then he'd be on his way. He didn't know how far he'd have to go, but he'd find an army outfit that was getting something done. And he'd help do it.

NINETEEN

Better a thousand times that New Orleans should be today in the hands of an open rebel than of this man [General Banks], who makes our war a crime and shame before the world.

—*BOSTON COMMONWEALTH*, FEBRUARY 14, 1863

January 1863

Jerry Labarre opened the door a slit, then flung it wide. "Chad!" he cried. "Come in! *Mon Dieu*, you're a sight. Come and get out of those wet clothes before you catch your death."

"I buried my knapsack on the other side of the river."

Mr. Labarre was running around like a mother hen, laying out his bathrobe and slippers, fanning the flames of the stove to heat water and something in a pot. Chad could tell he hadn't been up long: his age lay on him like a wrinkled blanket. "I overslept today," he said, "or I would've been there to row you over."

"It's good to see you, Mr. Labarre."

The old man shot a glance at him. "Should I call you Mr. Creel?"

Chad thought of Mr. Trevigne, how he'd even forgotten the editor's first name. He didn't care what he called a man, as long as it wasn't *master*. He smiled. "Jerry," he said, "Jerry."

Then they were eating sagamité and drinking coffee so thick Chad thought he'd choke.

"Do you want some water in that?" asked Jerry. "It's a little worse for the wear." He was looking at Chad with more than that question in his eyes.

Chad got some water and began to talk, telling about Mr. Trevigne, the army, and then that sleepless night: the eerie pull to Anna, the weight he'd felt. "It was like Anna was sitting on my chest." His voice got louder: "I have to find out if she's all right. And if she's there, in jail, I have to keep her from getting carried back to Sweet Haven."

"And you left the army for this?"

"I left a string of railroad tracks, that's all I left."

Jerry looked into his bowl. "I wouldn't want you going to the jail. Things are worse than ever."

"Then I'll go to the convent—they'll know."

"If they knew, they'd protect her, Chad. I don't see—"

"I have to know," said Chad, slowly, wearily. "Some people can do two things at once, maybe, but I'm not like that. I can't fight a war and worry about Anna."

Jerry gave a sigh that ended in a smile. "I'm glad of it," he said, "and Anna will be, too. Did you see her before you left New Orleans?"

"I saw her." He squirmed a little, couldn't help it, and it brought another smile from Jerry. "Well," said the old man, clearing his throat, "there's not much time. You can't go into town. Your press card won't do now. Everything's awry. I must be careful myself, not to be carried off somewhere as if I were a Rebel. But I do have a pass and I can go to the convent."

"There's a boy, too, from the convent, I think. He's part of Anna now: a nice little boy named Sammy."

Jerry looked closely at Chad's face. "Two nights and a day without rest can leave you prey to illness, *mon fils*. You must sleep while I'm gone."

Chad shook his head. "I think I'm too tired to sleep."

Jerry dressed in an old black suit and plain blue tie. He

stood before his gilt-edged mirror and tipped his hat. "These used to be my work clothes," he said. "It's like old times."

In New Orleans smiling whites congregated on street corners, talking about the way the chief of police had rid the streets of the "spoiled Nigras." He hurried past them to the convent, stopping only to buy a newspaper on the way. A plump, cheery nun greeted him and bade him wait for the Mother Superior. He had memories of the sunny room: here Henriette Delille had poured him tea.

The Mother Superior greeted him warmly. "What can I do for you, Monsieur Labarre?"

"I came to inquire about Anna Mead. I believe she is here with you?"

"She was. I regret to say she is no longer. She was carried back to the plantation."

"No! Then Chad was right."

"We were sorry to lose her. She was bright and very helpful. It was unfortunate, but her choice."

"What do you mean?"

"Perhaps I should call Sister Denise to tell you about it. She was the closest to Anna."

After the nun arrived, the Mother Superior excused herself, leaving the two sitting on stiff wooden chairs facing each other. Sister Denise, who had answered the door, no longer looked cheery. She fingered a handkerchief on her lap, her face a mask. "What is your interest in Anna?" she asked.

"Oh, I'm sorry I didn't explain. That was indelicate of me. Anna has a dear friend named Chad Creel, who is worried about her. I came in his place to find her. They are both friends of mine, fine young people."

As he spoke, the sister's face relaxed and her eyes lit up. "Yes, I met the young man, and I think I know—well, what happened is very strange, nevertheless."

"Tell me, *s'il vous plaît.*"

"It was a warm night and Anna asked permission to go for a walk alone. When we heard what was happening—the arrests—I went to search for her but it was too late. I couldn't find out if they had taken her. There was such a crowd, so much confusion, so many being loaded onto wagons, everyone alarmed and the police very hostile—well, I came back here." The sister looked down. "The next day, early, she came back, telling us they were waiting outside to take her back to the plantation and begging to take Sammy with her."

"Couldn't you have gained her release?"

"Mother Superior was willing to try. I believe, even though they were waiting for her, our influence would have been felt. It is hard for me to imagine a government that wouldn't recognize us."

"So?"

"Anna would have none of it. She said, rather flatly, that it was time she left here, anyway." Sister Denise's sad eyes met his. "Ordinarily, we would not let a child go with a *single* woman who was going back into *slavery*—" She gave a helpless giggle at the absurdity, and wiped her eyes. "But we did, we did because Sammy would have been lost without her, and she so wanted him."

The silence that fell between them was not uncomfortable. Finally, Jerry said, "I believe she will make a fine mother."

"Yes. But I declare, we'll miss her." She smiled. "There is one bit of good news. I hear General Banks is laying out plans for the plantations similar to General Butler's. Former slaves will sign all-year-around contracts, they say, with wages, hours, and conditions. So Anna's return to slavery will be short-lived."

Now Jerry rose. "Sister Denise, I am your servant. I'm sure Anna profited by her stay here."

The nun lifted her chin and her eyebrows at the same time. "Yes," she said, "she did indeed."

"Why?" asked Chad. "Why did she do a fool thing like that?"

"I don't know," said Jerry, "but I suspect, for whatever reason, she was right."

"How can right and wrong enter in? It don't make sense."

"I trust her judgment, Chad, and I think you should, too. I hear she'll soon be working for wages."

"But I said I'd be back here for her."

"You didn't say when. You were going off to war. Think about it."

He was so tired it was hard to think about anything but how he'd felt her near on the night of the roundup. "She was in that crowded pen, I know she was. She needed me real bad."

"What will you do now?"

"Sleep."

"You know," said the old man, "I think there's hope for you."

Chad woke in the middle of the night and didn't know where he was. He sat up, looking around, until the windows became windows and the walls walls and the floor where he slept became Jerry Labarre's floor. Then he settled down on the blankets again and closed his eyes. Of course, he thought, he should have known: he told Anna he was going to meet Uncle Blake at Sweet Haven after Vicksburg fell. She remembered that, she must have, and she knew he would come. He could see her now at the plantation, all fired up and asking for a wage.

At breakfast, Jerry scanned the newspaper he'd bought in town. "The *Picayune* says the roundup is looked on 'with favor by a grateful community.' Listen to this: 'Colonel French, our indefatigable Chief of Police, is beginning to take the contraband bull by the horns, with a view of teaching him a salutary lesson.' " He sighed. "Well, *L'Union* quoted the Boston *Commonwealth* last week. It called Banks a 'turveydrop.' It speaks for the good senator from Massachusetts Charles Sumner, I hear." He chuckled, then frowned. "White soldiers attacking black soldiers in the streets! That kind of thing is handed down from the top, Chad, not by orders but by attitude, mind you, attitude. People can tell when it's all right to express their mean streaks and they just let loose. These are ugly times, Chad, ugly times."

"I know." He was feeling better about Anna, but at odds with himself. Here he was, away from the army and his friends, back where he started. He waited until his friend put aside the *Picayune,* then, "What now?" he asked.

Jerry didn't crack a smile. "Are you sure you want to fight this war?" He poured coffee into Chad's cup.

"Want? I allow I *have* to fight if I can find somewhere they'll let me."

"Well, Jim Lane's First Kansas Colored Volunteers are sure enough fighting, and blacks and whites fight side by side in the army of the Frontier. I'd say to go to Camp Parapet about four miles from here, but General Phelps has been replaced by a man not half his size. You'd be felling cypress in the swamps and catching smallpox. It's a sorry song, there." He brightened. "Do you know where that friend of yours is, the one who tutored you?"

"When he ran away he left a message, said to meet him at Sweet Haven after the South is cut in two, and I'll be there, by golly, even if he ain't." *We're partners, ain't we, Blake says, smiling.*

The silence grew before Jerry said, "Ah, well, Chad, how can one predict? If he's not there, you must trust there's good reason."

"Sometimes folks don't stand up under strain," Chad said and he heard his own voice harden. "They look after only one man when there's trouble. Even if you've mixed blood with them, seems like they shy away with a snap of a finger or a change in the wind." He sighed, and Jerry's questioning face spurred him on: "Not even just shy away, no, that's the least. Your blood brother can turn on you behind your back and sell your best friend away."

"Chad—"

He was suddenly ashamed. "It's all right. I oughtn't to have said all that, but now I have, and it's said."

"If I can help—"

"I can never pay you back for all you've done already."

The old man's face was pure concern. Chad wanted to wipe it clean, to make it spark the way that face was meant to. Jerry shook his head. *"Mon fils,* you remind me of my youth. I want the best for you and Anna. That's all."

Chad took the rowboat and dug up his belongings while Jerry went to get passage on a Mississippi steamboat up to Baton Rouge, the port the Union took back from the Rebels in December. It was just below Rebel-held Port Hudson, and as far as the steamer went. He brought the ticket, a surprise for Chad. "This will start you on your way to Vicksburg, Mississippi, the Rebel stronghold the Union has its eye on. Last year Farragut tried to take it by water, and Grant and Sherman tried by land. They failed. If it's taken, Chad, the whole river will fall to the North, and the South will be—indeed—sliced in half. Something big is brewing there now. If you can't find a battle up there by the time you get there, a lot will be wrong and it won't be me." He motioned Chad to the table. "I'll draw you a map."

"I have one, Jerry, right here. I think it goes up a ways."

"Fine. Spread it out. Now let's see. From Baton Rouge you'll be traveling on foot upriver. Given the rough land and the way the river curls up like a snake—see?—it may take months, Chad. You'll have the Confederate army to skirt, and the Union army to watch for signs of colored troops. But always follow the river. It's a hard road, but the only one."

"The only one?"

"Out of here. To Vicksburg." He pointed to a little dot on the map, and saw the youth frown. "Mark my words, Chad, it's important."

He pulled out his sturdy carpetbag and traded it for Chad's knapsack. While Chad packed the bag, Jerry wrapped food: ginger cake and corn pone and salt pork he'd saved. "There are *gendarmes* patrolling close by today," he said.

"How do you know?"

"I can tell. The sounds are different, the wildlife full of rumor. Be shy. Stay at the edge of the woods on the way to the boat." At the last minute, he took the chamois-wrapped snuffbox from his old trunk.

Chad raised his voice: "I can't take that! It must be worth—"

"Yes, and I have no use for it. It's as pure as gold can be, and it will keep. That's why I'm giving it to you. For here-after-this." He stuffed it into the carpetbag and whispered, "Go!"

Chad grabbed him, fiercely hugged him, cried, *"Au revoir!"* He stepped lightly into the dawning and like a deer sped away.

Jerry hurried after him, not to be seen but to see. As the big steamer pulled away from the shore at last, Jerry untied his boat and rowed to the other side of the river.

TWENTY

Better than nobody
In this lonely
Land.

—LANGSTON HUGHES

Late January 1863

They stood in the yard by the kitchen, Sammy holding onto her skirt. Before long Laurel came rushing out, her hair gleaming yellow in the sunlight, and she grabbed Anna and kissed her. "Isn't it nice to be home! I declare, I've missed you and worried about you. When Papa said you were back, I was just overjoyed." She looked down at Sammy. "And who is this, Anna?"

"Sammy. He's mine."

"Yours?"

"The nuns at the convent let me have him."

"Oh, I see." She looked into his face. "Well, we'll be good friends, won't we? I'm sure we can find chores for a fine boy like you. Your new mama is going to have her own room off the kitchen where only our best folk stay, and we'll put up a bed for you right there. Would you like that, Sammy?"

Holding fast to Anna's skirt, he took a step backward and looked up at Laurel.

"He don't take to white folks much, Miss Laurel. I'm just here to ask what the contract say about pay and hours."

"The contract?" Laurel cocked her head. "Oh, yes, the contract. Why, I overheard Papa say this morning he's forced by that new general to pay three dollars a month to mechanics, two dollars to first-class hands, and one to other hands and house servants."

"Gawd," breathed Anna.

Laurel nodded. "Isn't it a crying shame?"

She felt her face tighten. Laurel went hurriedly on: "Of course you'll get your dollar. Right on time, too, along with the others still at the house—Mammy and Cora and old Horace and Chorly."

"I ain't your maid no more," she said. "I'm working in the fields."

Laurel stared. "Don't be a goose! You can't mean that!" She crossed her arms and began to sputter. "I don't see—I can't imagine—I don't *think* you have that choice." Her voice was loud but uncertain.

"Don't bother your head, Miss Laurel." She turned on her heels. "I know what choice I have, and I choose field work."

Sammy strode beside her, looking back at Laurel with a big grin.

Noah, standing nearby, saw Miss Laurel stamp her foot just as Cecily appeared from around the house and asked her sister what the matter was.

"Anna's going to work in the fields," she said. "She flaunted off so sassy I could spit!"

"I'll get her," said Cecily, starting to run. "She can't get away with that!"

"Stop, Cecily!" Laurel grabbed her sister's arm and held her. "I don't care. She's changed so, I don't want her anymore, anyhow."

Noah had to chuckle: he'd never met Anna, but he reckoned he would. He watched Cecily smooth her skirts. "Well, she shouldn't be allowed to put on airs," she said. "If Clay were here, I'll wager he wouldn't allow it."

"I don't know if he would. But he's not here and Chad's gone, too."

Cecily regarded her sister with disgust. "How can you talk about them in the same breath, Laurel? Why, Chad's just a no-good Nigra and you know it!"

Laurel's face reddened as she stood staring after Anna and the boy Sammy, skipping at her side.

The first time Anna saw Uncle Noah to know who he was, he was sitting in the corner of one of the longhouses where the single field hands were putting up. They were having a meeting about wages, and the big woman standing in the corner of the room was talking about the contract. "We got to complain to the provost marshal," she said. "He's a federal official, sposed to look after our rights." And then one of the men grunted, "He told me if I don't sign the contract, I has to work for the army on the levees or a government plantation for nothing."

Uncle Noah stroked his white beard and said, "Sorrowful."

Anna made sure who he was before she went over and sat cross-legged on the floor by his chair. "I'm Anna Mead," she said and he smiled as if he'd known it all along.

"Look over here at Noah," the woman said then, turning her heavy frame toward them, "worked hard so many year, now that he's worn out they pays him no respect, won't let him work part time."

"That's so," he said, smiling at Anna, his eyes bright and sharp with life.

"It's all right," she said softly. "I mean, you don't have to work. You're going out west with Chad."

"How you know that, child?"

"I—we talked, Chad and me. In New Orleans."

"I swan," said Uncle Noah. "How's he feel?"

"Fine, I allow. He's gone somewheres to fight. But he'll be here after us all as soon as the river's taken, you'll see."

"Never had a doubt."

Sammy came running and plopped himself onto Anna's lap. "This is Sammy," she said, giving him a hug. "Say hello to Uncle Noah, honey."

Sammy's smile spread over his face. Noah took his hand and shook it like a pump. "Well, now. What a fine boy you is!"

"We're going to be a family," she said. "Sammy belongs to us, don't you, Sammy?"

"Sure do," he said, and trotted off.

"He's exploring," said Anna, "but he won't go far from me. He used to get whipped for getting tar on him."

"Uh-uh-uh," said Noah. "I hear you was a house servant, Anna."

"I was Miss Laurel's birthday present." She spit out the words like bullets, but Uncle Noah's calming eyes were on her and she smiled. "May I come and sit with you a while this evening, Uncle Noah?"

"Sure enough," he said. "I'd be happy to have company. Old Virgil ain't come back and lawdy, I been lonesome. Hardly nobody to talk to, except for Granny Martha."

"I saw her outside," said Anna. "Her eyes look almost dead."

"Dead? Naw. She still in there, just farther down, that's all. I spect she hear it all—just don't want nothing to do with the world no more. Huh-uh, had nough."

"I want to tell you a secret," she said, sitting at his feet again that evening.

Noah looked into her eyes, put out a hand and touched her hair. "What is it, child?"

"Chad's going to be a papa." She spoke slowly, softly, the way he guessed she felt about it.

He sat a moment, then said, "That kind of secret has a way of getting out. You happy, Anna?"

She smiled, and he could swear the sun came out. "Yes, I guess I am."

"Then I am, too. How bout Chad?"

"He don't know. I didn't know it when I saw him last."

Uh-oh, he thought. "He know where you is?"

"He don't have to. He'll be here after you and Granny Martha and the one he calls Uncle Blake. You know him?"

"Chad was like his own. Them two was close as peas in a pod till Blake run away. Don't know as Chad ever forgive him for not taking him along."

"Things die hard in Chad," she said, "and they grow slow."

"Maybe the way it should be, leastways the growing." He looked at her and frowned. "No childing woman ought to be out in the field. I never did like it—that sun got no mercy."

"I'll be fine, Uncle Noah."

"You never did no field work, Anna. Why don't you want to work at the house?"

"No!" She said it with such force he jumped. "House work keeps you right under their thumb. I had enough of that!"

"Don't upset yourself. I allow you know what to do if you don't feel good in the fields. Where you staying?"

"Longhouse next door. Sammy and me have a corner in the back."

Now he scowled. "No. We find you a shack. When the time come for birthing, you gon have a place."

There were unoccupied shacks now, families having left after harvest to find work elsewhere, and Noah found the best one he could. He carried the mattress from the longhouse and Anna carried Sammy, half-asleep and clinging, down the path. Two windowless rooms lay beyond the doorstep. One room had a fireplace, and Noah cleaned it out. A few tin pots lay in the ashes and he got some leaves tangled with Spanish moss and cleaned them, too, while Anna swept the floor with the broom she found behind the door. Noah told her he would make a table and chairs, just go into the forest and chop some good pine and get to work the next day. "I has my knife," he told her, "and I can borrow an axe from the shed. I'll build a chicken coop out back, too. You got to eat plenty, not just what they puts out. I know where I can get a good laying hen and maybe a few chicks."

Anna took a deep breath, seemed a little taken aback. *Thank you* came out fine, but he could hear a strain in her voice.

"Better get to bed now," he said at last. "Lord knows how long your day will stretch now that planting's begun, maybe past dark if the moon's bright."

"That's too many hours, Uncle Noah. We ain't putting up with that no more. The contract says ten and if they force more on us, we'll walk off."

"Watch yourself now. You looks a little peaked."

She patted his arm. "I feel fine."

Lying beside Sammy, she looked at the days ahead. Uncle Noah might be pushing to help faster than she could receive it, but he was Chad's chosen kin, and so he was hers. Besides, she could imagine what this godforsaken place would be without him.

Sleep settled over her calmly, but her dreams were full of uncertainty, and the fear that began on the bayou with her sister long ago was in them. She woke in the night with stiff limbs, her heart beating wildly, her throat closed against a scream.

TWENTY-ONE

The planters and overseers do not sufficiently appreciate, or regard, the change that has taken place, especially in respect to this institution of slavery. The negroes come back on to the plantation, with altogether different feelings from those of former times. They have obtained in the camps, and wherever they have been, and they exhibit, a spirit of independence; a feeling, that they are no longer slaves, but hired laborers; and demand to be treated as such . . . This feeling is, in many cases, either entirely ignored, or not sufficiently respected . . . and the consequences [sic] is trouble.

—J. ELA, A LOUISIANA PARISH PROVOST MARSHAL,
TO PROVOST MARSHAL GENERAL J. BOWEN, 1863

February 1863

Sunday's dawn was slow to come, a thunderstorm blackening the sky and sending wind so strong the wallboards creaked and strained against it. Her muscles knotting as she stretched, Anna lay in bed until the rain that gathered in puddles here and there on the floor subsided and a cold wind pressed through the cracks in the wall. She got up stiffly and built a fire, watching the smoke curl up the small chimney at the back of the shack. She had nothing to heat but herself, and she longed for a cup of sassafras tea. Then Sammy stirred and she sent him out to fetch their rations of hominy and molasses, remembering the kind of breakfast she had eaten in the kitchen of the master's house—biscuits and gravy, often ham and eggs, always plenty of butter. But here was little Sammy, back already, gobbling his hominy as if it were buckwheat cakes good and sour from days in the crock. She patted his knee. "I don't have to work today. It's Sunday, lamb. Would you like to study your lessons with me?"

"We don't have books or paper or pencils."

"That's the truth, we don't," she said, "but I'll see if I can get some from the cook. I used to know her."

Uncle Noah peeked his head in the door. "Sammy, let's us make that coop today, so a hen I know'll have a nice place to roost."

Sammy was already on his feet, a smile spreading from ear to ear, looking at Anna for her consent, and she said yes, thinking she might tumble back into bed. But Uncle Noah had to remind her of the meeting. She sighed and felt her hair: she'd plait it, she thought, tie it at the ends with the bits of ribbon she'd had ever since she was Laurel's maid.

Everyone knew there were black soldiers in the area. Some companies worked in abandoned fields, others were building bridges and roads for the army, and a lot of them were in camp awaiting orders and foraging for the Yankee officers. So you never could tell who might be out there, who you might meet purely by chance, could you, she thought. She'd get out those ribbons.

There were meetings all over the plantation. Anna chose the one in the longhouse up the path where Uncle Noah lived. The woman Hilda would be there, and her friend Alcibiade, the two Anna liked the most. Hilda was big and busty and had room for everyone. She worked beside Anna in the fields and kept a wily eye on the short, stocky overseer. He was a Southerner named Kane, approved for the task by Corporal Allen, who was assigned to guard the plantation, and he kept a horsewhip in the cart beside the cask of water.

Last week, as the evening stretched its shadow long and thin and it was time to unhitch the plow and put down the hoe, Kane came out with the news that they had to work until dark. Hilda and Alcibiade were the first to throw down their hoes, then everyone did together as if it were planned, but Kane held his ground. "I'll have to report y'all," he said, his face as cold as it was white. Alcibiade—long and lanky and likable (he was from an abandoned plantation on the river, and Colonel Wycliffe classified him first-class hand)—told the rest they'd best stay now and consider what to do later. Hilda picked up her hoe and said, "We meet Sunday morning."

As Anna went back to work that day, the setting sun was a red orb and the brown earth stretched and quivered before her eyes. She mopped her brow with her sleeve, feeling half-sick. Hilda saw her sway and took her arm. "You need time out and water, honey," she said, leading her to the cask.

"Get back to your rows," yelled Kane, "or Corporal Allen will be *in*formed."

"Go ahead and tell him a woman had a mug of water!" retorted Hilda, and Kane bristled, shouted, "Y'all has to be taught the good habit of industry and respectful deportment like the good general say." He cracked his whip at Hilda's feet and the workers in the field stood still, some bent over, holding their hoes in midair, all eyes on him.

"Let me catch you lazing again, and you'll get it!" he shouted, turning tail.

Hilda shook her head. "He's itching to use that whip. Just can't stand the notion we ain't slaves no more."

"Don't see how being slaves is much worse," Anna said.

"Just wait till our meeting, honey."

Now it was almost time for the meeting and Anna braided her hair. She was glad Sammy was with Uncle Noah today. Last night he'd come running to meet her with a wave and a shout: "I got a friend!"

She'd put her arm around his shoulders. "See? I knew you would. Didn't I say so?"

"He's a-sittin' by our house a-waitin' for us."

Sure enough, he was. Anna looked at the dark man, his knees raised to his chin, leaning against the shack like a fallen tree, his eyes downcast, his large hands folded around his knees. Sammy ran ahead. "Say hello to Anna, Pompée, come on."

The man raised his head and said "Hello" but his eyes darted past her.

"Hello, Pompée," she said evenly. "You and Sammy made friends, I guess. Ain't you working?"

"He ain't a field hand," whispered Sammy.

She breathed that in, looking hard at the strange man and then at Sammy's expectant face. "Well, come on in. I'm worn out."

"I helped Uncle Noah all morning, Anna, and so did Pompée. We helped chop wood and tomorrow we'll help build the chairs."

"That's nice." She eased herself down into a corner and closed her eyes. "What else you been up to?"

"Pompée and me explored the whole place."

"He from around abouts?"

"No, he's new here like us, ain't you, Pompée?"

Sammy's friend spoke so softly Anna could hardly hear: "They're chasing me."

She opened her eyes. "Chasing you? What for?"

"When the leaves turn over on the trees, it's a sign."

Anna's mouth dropped open. "What do you mean, the leaves turning over is a sign?"

Sammy said, "It's all right, Pompée."

She felt the edge in her voice: "That sounds crazy to me, unless you mean it's gon rain."

Pompée's eyes were bright with fear. "You one of them?"

"No, she ain't!" said Sammy. "Come on, Anna. Ain't it time to go get our supper?"

"We're getting fed only two times a day, honey."

She grabbed his hand and brought him down on her lap. "There won't be hominy tonight, but just wait till Uncle Noah gets that chicken coop all done. We'll have eggs, and we-will-have-ourselves a chicken dinner to celebrate!"

"Hear that, Pompée? Shucks, all we got to do is help Uncle Noah."

"If they see the chicken coop, they'll know I'm here."

"No, they won't, Pompée. We'll whitewash it!"

"Oh."

"Sammy, you cut that out!" shouted Anna. "It's bedtime, Pompée, you better go."

He stood up tall as a weathered elm, slender as a twig, and strode away as Sammy called, "Remember, we gotta help Uncle Noah in the morning."

She tucked Sammy in and lay down beside him. "I don't think you ought to play with Pompée, honey."

"Why?"

"He's a man, too old for you to play with."

"Naw, we have fun, Anna, sure enough."

"Just you watch yourself."

She'd been too tired to pursue it. Now, braiding her hair, she only hoped that Sammy's new friend had vanished in the night.

There was one more thing bothering her: when Hilda found out she could write, she'd said, "Well, honey, that's real good. You can keep our records." What if she couldn't spell all the words? Mercy: it was time to go to the meeting.

"Captain Foster's building a jail," said Hilda, standing behind the table. "Some folks is saying it's for workers who give planters trouble, like asking for fair hours, and I say they're right."

Anna looked around the room and saw uncertain faces. Most freed people tended to give the Yankees the benefit of the doubt until a rumor against them was proved, for many such rumors came from the master. Still, Captain Foster, the provost marshal of the Lafourche District and thereby the local representative of the U.S. army, had made it clear he didn't want complaints from the laborers, and Anna agreed with Hilda.

Alcibiade called out, "That jail sure ain't for alligators," and the whole place shook with stamping feet and laughter.

A strange man got up to talk. "I'm from Tigerville and I had to sneak away to come. We got trouble. The soldiers the army has guarding the farms steal whatever we got—chickens and hogs, why, we can't keep a thing. We don't know what to do."

"Have you told the provost marshal?" asked Alcibiade.

"Yessah. He say he don't believe us and look the other way."

Anna said to the man beside her, a very thin man with large muscles and big hands, "Ain't there something better to do than get kicked around this way?"

He smiled a gaunt imitation of a smile. "Well, if you can make enough to buy land."

"I hear an overseer in Ascension Parish gives money to the guard so he can do whatever he want," said Hilda. "Anyone know about that?"

"How about the guard living right here up at the big house—what's his name, Corporal Allen?" said one woman. "Real fancy living for a soldier, I say."

"We's trying to find out how general the trouble is, that's all," said Hilda. "We can be more force if we bands together."

At that, everyone started talking and Hilda pounded the table. It wasn't much of a table and Anna had to laugh when it wobbled. She sat and giggled until the man beside her asked, "How you feel?"

After a while Hilda had them standing one by one to tell what they knew, and she asked Anna to write it all down on paper scraps from the house. They seemed to talk so fast it was impossible to get it all, so Anna wrote bits and pieces.

"In my parish, Captain Darling won't let us have Sunday meeting, can't even hold prayer meeting, never mind preaching and Bible reading."

"Up in Assumption Parish, Provost Wiggins is separating

workers from their families and he won't hear no complaint. He told us we had to sign the contract or he would come and make us."

"We all afraid of Captain Lee. He come around with his rifle on his shoulder and his sabre at his side and make threats and say he won't tolerate no complaint. He send word to the planters to be sure and tell him when the hands is insolent."

"Insolence and indolence," said Alcibiade, "big twin words. The Yankees sure caught the old masters' talk."

The thin man by Anna stood up. "We is not getting enough to eat, and the overseer, he whip us. Some people run away."

"I got a laugh for y'all," said a young woman in the far corner. "A planter down in Raceland up and accused Provost Silbey of binding workers by the hands and hanging them on hooks for any little thing. They say that Yankee provost ain't got long in the parish!"

"Ain't that a turnaround, though." Hilda's breasts bobbed with her chuckle. It was hot and stuffy in the long, narrow quarters, and Anna had to leave. She nodded to Hilda and the very thin man and ran home and threw up. In the small room the moss-filled mattress waited and she dropped down heavily and slept.

As the day waned, she heard comings and goings and pounding out back, but she didn't open her eyes until she smelled salt pork. She thought it was a dream, but Uncle Noah was at the fireplace, frying an egg in the grease.

"Just in time," he announced. "Look what old Hanna lay for you!"

There was just one egg and she wanted to give it to Sammy, but the boy shook his head. "Let the baby have it," he said, looking wise.

"Well, well," she said, "I guess I don't have news to tell you, do I?"

That man Pompée was sitting in the corner looking wildly toward the door, and Uncle Noah sat on the step, smiling back at her like someone who's done something fine.

TWENTY-TWO

[I will not suffer your] self-respect or manliness to be lowered by contact with an inferior race.

—A NEW YORK COLONEL TO HIS MEN AT BATON ROUGE, *NEW YORK TRIBUNE*, FEBRUARY 21, 1863

Late January—February 1863

Chad sat on the deck, looking up at the moon, listening to the water churn through the big wheel near him. Now and then the wind brought a spray from the river, and more than once he sprang to his feet to look down at the black water. He had always been intrigued by the Mississippi, always planned to do more than cross it, maybe explore it down to the Gulf. Now he was going against its current, and it was fighting. The boat creaked and quivered as though it would split apart. Its chimney spouted lively sparks onto the deck and the dark river, like fireflies dying. But the North Star stood in the blinking sky, sending its flame that meant freedom. What would he find traveling northward? He could not count on anything: too much was awry. Looking down at the water, the deep, black water that he could see ahead and behind, but not straight down where he heard it parting for the boat's passage, he wondered if he and Blake would ever meet at the plantation. He saw Blake paddling down the bayou in Chad's pirogue without him, without a hint of going, breaking all his promises. He shook himself. Wait, he said, you ready for the message? Will you ever be ready for the message Blake sent: *It ain't a dream!*

"Get back down to steerage," came a gruff voice as one of the crew passed by. "Skedaddle!"

He grabbed the carpetbag that never left his side and took a last glimpse of the yellow moon.

His pallet was the only one occupied: the other passengers slept in the cabin above, their rooms private and he supposed luxurious. There were a number of Union officers on the boat, several businessmen who spoke like Northerners, and a group of Southern gentlemen. He'd had no trouble keeping out of their way, no need of the coffee and cakes they sold above. Jerry Labarre had seen to that with his packages of food. It would be grand to have Jerry with him here, now, so grand to travel with his friend; to hear his notions and his doctrine of the Mississippi night.

The hilly town of Baton Rouge was swarming with black refugees from the countryside plantations, all looking for work. At the top of a bluff that led down to the water, he caught up with a weary-looking black soldier. "Can I ask you something?"

The soldier slowed his pace but didn't stop. "What you want to know?"

"If I joined up—I mean, have you fought in a battle?"

The soldier took his arm and led him down the steep hill to the river, looking round about them. He said his regiment was sent to reinforce the army after the Yankees moved into Baton Rouge again. But General Grover, newly in charge, would not even recognize the Third Native Guard. They were low on supplies, couldn't seem to get the quartermaster to give them what they requisitioned, and they hadn't been paid.

"This whole town's nasty—downright nasty. Now let me ask you a question: why you so aglutton for a battle? You want to get killed?"

Chad threw a stick into the water. The soldier's gaze made him uneasy. "I just want to fight so I can walk away a free man."

"My advice is walk away now. Double-quick."

"I can't."

"That a fact." The soldier scratched his chin. "How's that?"

"Don't know."

"Looking at you, it's curiosity, I say. You just got to butt in, now that you so free and easy. Why, you can do what you want to now, right?"

"Naw," said Chad. The soldier's eyes held a certain envy. "It ain't so."

"You got a woman?"

"Yeah."

"Got little ones?"

"No."

"I got both. I joined up thinking I could fight the war and get the family took care of, like they promise. Now my wife and kids is in one of them stinking camps and she's working anywhere she get a chance and they's sick and starving anyway."

Chad got up. "Well, I'm heading up North. To Vicksburg."

The soldier stood up, his sad pants baggy. "Don't know that place, but good luck. You're on your own, fella."

Chad slept on the wharf among bales of cotton and barrels of sugar next to crates of army supplies. It rained and he crawled into an empty crate, shivering and cussing softly. Smoke from burning rosin and pitch pine filled the dawning, but no repaired boats needed hands to load them. He tried every day for almost two rainy weeks, went onto every steamboat, saying he'd work for passage upriver, for he'd seen supply ships headed that way. Finally, when he'd decided to leave this sopping port, just walk on, the way he should've done the minute he arrived, a captain whose cargo was food and ammunition said he could use another hand. Chad carried barrels and crates on board.

They hadn't traveled a half day when they pulled over to a small jetty on the left bank and dropped anchor.

As they unloaded, the captain and several of his men peered up the water and scanned the riverfront. Chad asked a black sailor how long they would stay at the jetty before moving up the river, and the man laughed. "This's as far as we go, sure nough. We ain't no gunboat, don't even have one piece aboard."

Union soldiers on shore were loading the crates in carts and taking off as fast as they were loaded.

"Where are we?" he asked.

"Up yonder across the river is Port Hudson. We's lucky we ain't been shot at yet. Come on, now, time to get aboard and get the hell out of here."

"Back to Baton Rouge? No, I'm staying here."

The sailor's face turned blank. "What for?"

"I guess I aim to get North somehow."

"Here on up, the place is swarming with Rebs," the sailor yelled. "You'd be crazy to stay here. Why, the Yankees that took our cargo ain't hung around, sure nough."

"I have to stay," he called, running down the levee into the thicket beyond. The boat's crew stared after him.

TWENTY-THREE

I never knew one of them to steal anything from a Union officer or soldier. They say that they used to feel free to rob their old masters, but it would be wrong to rob a man who hires them and pays them wages.

—CAPTAIN JOHN W. DE FOREST, U.S. ARMY, LAFOURCHE DISTRICT, 1863, *A VOLUNTEER'S ADVENTURES*, 1946

February 1863

The mosquitoes used to come through the gratings in the slave quarters. Nothing Chad could do would keep them out. He often wished they had windows to close, but you couldn't close a grating: cold air in wintry spells, flies and mosquitoes, gnats and millers and big ants with their sting, and sometimes a couple of those big, black bugs that don't bite, just mope around if there's no feed to pounce on. He often wakened in the thick of night with a humming in his ear, and in summer's heat when it poured one minute and not the next, he was always scratching. Still, it was nothing like this. These mosquitoes were bent on war, came in brigades, whined as they attacked.

It was a campfire that sent him into the swamp. He reck-

oned a fire meant Rebels and he skirted it, finding it multiply
and become a legion of campfires. He ran until tangled vines
wove a wet maze through the trees, then he picked his way
around thickets cut through with sluggish streams. The water
underfoot grew deep, and tall grasses and reeds took the
place of crawling foliage. He waded up to his waist, but seeing
no end to it, cut back to a solid footing. The swamp was alive:
alligators slid for cover, bullfrogs bellowed, snakes swam or
coiled on branches, waiting. Shrubs and briers caught at his
ankles. He kept moving in the direction he chanced to
choose, and entered at last a cushioned forest of pine. Here
he rested his feet and slapped at his assailants while a bright
green lizard captured a feast with its whipping tongue.

It was dark when he cautiously approached a deep stand of
magnificent trees. All was quiet, even the air was still and
close. He caught his breath: thousands of tiny, shining eyes
danced through the night, danced wide and deep as far as he
could see—fireflies, fireflies, fireflies! He wished he could
write music.

In the morning he came to a clear, wide stream and con-
sulted his map: the Red River? The nose of a vessel came into
view and he climbed a tree fast. It was a Confederate gunboat,
its crew scanning the bank for any movement, its guns trained
and manned. When it was gone, he climbed down, gathered
wood and vines, and got to work.

He made a raft for his bag and swam it across to a silent,
disheveled plantation, gardens untended and lawns untrimmed. There was not much left to forage, coops and pens
were empty, early vegetables picked. He found a sweet potato
bin and a few ears of corn and went on through such ominous
quiet he kept looking over his shoulder.

Now signs spoke of marching regiments: trampled underbrush and flattened fences, roads widened by hundreds of
footprints in the dusty ground. The merciless cane field was
askew, its thick green stalks at first pushed flat, then as the
field wore on and the marchers tired, the stalks were bent and
leaned in useless, tangled skeins: the cane had met its match
and so had the armies.

He sat on a fallen log and took out the map, wondering if he'd made a mistake. Had he crossed the Atchafalaya River that flows south out of the Red? If if wasn't the Red River he'd crossed, the one that flows east into the Mississippi, chances were he was going in the wrong direction.

"What you doing here, brother?" came a voice behind him, and he turned to see a large, grand-looking black man dragging a mule laden with bundles and a bulging knapsack. He carried three chickens and a hatchet. Chad got up slowly.

"I say, what you doing?"

"Nothing."

"Where you come from?"

"Downriver."

The man looked him over, came closer, eyed his carpetbag. "You got any Confederate money, brother?"

"No. Why?"

"Well, I wouldn't ask, but I'm collecting for General Banks. He's gonna give you good Yankee greenbacks for all the no-good Rebel money you got."

The ornery cuss looked like a preacher, with his chickens and his hatchet and his hangdog mule, and Chad began to laugh. He just bent over and howled—the best darned laugh he'd had in months. The man watched, then he snickered and shook his head: "You one smartass, ain't you?"

"How'd you ever think that up? You ain't with General Banks, let alone—"

"Ho, ho—I sure am with the general, all of them, Weitzel, Grover, Bainbridge—they's all with me one time and another. General Banks, sure nough." He sat down on the log, put his chickens across his hatchet on the ground.

"Is that so?"

"Sure as shootin'. I work for a captain in the Twelfth Connecticut. I set up his lean-to, soap his stockings for the day's march. We's traveling fast—forced march, they calls it. I forage all along the way and by the time we ready to bivouac, I'm roasting the poultry and pounding the corn and making a little hoecake in the ashes if I can. Officers don't get rations, and the captain say he'd starve without me. The soldiers don't live on hardtack neither. Lordy, they's the worst foragers on God's green earth. Why, they'd take the tit from a baby's mouth." He shook his head sorrowfully. "There ain't a man ain't plumb wore out from the marching. Back at Opelousas we got to rest, waiting for salt beef and hardtack to come, but that's the last rest we had."

"The Twelfth Connecticut—didn't they fight at Labadie-ville, help take Bayou Lafourche?"

"You bet your boots. You from down there?"

"Uh-huh."

"What you doing up here?"

"Seeing the world," he said, not owning up. "Where you marching to?"

"Alexandria, chasing Mouton. Got orders to double-quick. General Banks is riding along. At first we was so close to Mouton you could see the cotton burning. Our skirmishers was busy, too. But them Texans on horseback was always twenty miles ahead of us. Now they're all mighty far ahead. Some from the Louisiana infantry give up on their own, just straggle back and glad to see us. They say their officers done drive them with sabres to keep them going."

"Where y'all start from?"

The big man stretched and pointed. "Down yonder on Bayou Teche. We was pestering Mouton at Camp Bisland just so General Grover could get to his rear and we could bag him, but Mouton, he pulls out in the night, some damn fool sentry didn't want to wake up Weitzel to tell him, and Massa Grover, he went to the wrong place anyway!" He gave a short burst of laughter and slapped his knee. "This here war is more like a circus than anything I seen since Carnival! I got to go catch up—see that dust cloud over yonder? Sometimes it gets so thick in the marching, them white Yankee boys turn brown!"

"How far you figure you go a day?"

"We made eighteen mile yesterday, but we waits for the rations till sunrise and then we stops to fix a bridge. I hear tell it's close to twelve mile today, and it ain't but an hour past noonday. I'll lay that mule and these hens we's gon make more'n twenty. Ain't that a holler?" He scratched his chin. "Funny, when nobody's gon catch up with nobody. Captain grumble it's a damn fool march." He mounted his mule. "We lost some soldiers, they went off to sleep on a ten-minute rest and didn't hear the marching orders or maybe played possum. I seed some walking in their sleep, sure as I live and breathe, almost like it was when I was working on the levee sixteen hour straight." He turned the beast around. "Say, take a chicken. Don't look like we gon stop much till nightfall. You might as well have it. Where you say you going?"

"Vicksburg."

"Vicksburg," the man repeated. "Well now, you watch out for Reb stragglers, they's mean as cottonmouths."

"I saw campfires back toward the river."

"Guerrillas, I allow."

Chad took the chicken, offered sweet potatoes in return.

"No, brother, I got some in my knapsack. Want to come along and get some work? Good pay and no whipping."

Chad didn't say so, but he knew he wouldn't want to be the "soldier's boy" he'd heard of—polishing a soldier's boots when he ought to be a soldier himself.

"I like you," the man went on, giving the mule a kick in the side. "You sure is a good talker. Ever think of preaching?"

Chad shook his head.

Moving out, he called back, "Just out of curiosity, what you got in that there sack?"

"A gold box."

The big man howled and rode away.

Chad watched him go. The fellow would be going north, and Chad found it was true: the Mississippi was behind him, and he was going west—damn these cloudy days! He wouldn't be surprised if, when he got back to the river, he'd still be across from Port Hudson.

TWENTY-FOUR

George Hanks was the commander's first appointment . . . His tenure as Superintendent of Negro labor was marked by an emphasis on maximizing the profits of capital and a general disregard for the rights of workers.

—WILLIAM F. MESSNER, HISTORIAN, *FREEDMEN AND THE IDEOLOGY OF FREE LABOR, LOUISIANA 1862–65*, 1978

March 1863

"That army corporal was at the meeting," said Alcibiade, sitting with Hilda at Anna's table.

She took the pot of sassafras tea off the coals and poured it into tin cups, getting satisfaction from the deep color and smell. She'd helped Alcibiade write the list of workers' complaints: too many hours, not enough to eat, paltry pay, and a few reports of incidents in the fields. He and Hilda took them up to the house. Anna didn't want to go with them, and now just hearing about it, her stomach felt half sick. It seemed she answered trouble with pains and aches and throwing up lately, and when the talk got heated she had to shut her mind, look out at a tree or something, just to stay well.

Hilda was bristling. "That man Wycliffe was mad as a hornet, but he didn't let on. He say if the crop grow good, maybe there'll be more food next year, and all the time there's that winter corn, going into the crib."

"What about pay?" asked Anna, sipping the good, hot tea.

"He won't talk about it," said Alcibiade. "He rolls his eyes like this and says, 'Ain't it a pity what war can do.' "

"Then he winks at the soldier and the soldier laughs," said Hilda. "Them men is hard as nails."

Anna sighed. "I can spare an egg or two from Hanna. We have four young chickens, too. We'll have some soup when they grow a little. You'll be welcome to it."

"You're eating for two, need all you can get," said Hilda. "Besides, it wouldn't solve a thing. We got to do something."

"Why not go to the Bureau of Negro Labor?" Alcibiade poured more tea into his cup. "Or President Lincoln?"

"The Bureau's fine with me. If that don't work, we'll walk off. Up at the Effingham Lawrence farm they had a work slowdown, calling for ten dollars a month pay and no work after supper. When he wouldn't give in, the women left the fields in a body, bless their hearts. Course he put them off again, and no telling how it will come out. I think all the hands here are willing to walk off, don't you?"

"I'm willing," said Anna. "The days go slower all the time."

Hilda patted her hand. "It's too much for you, neath that sun, honey."

Sammy and Pompée came in and sat on the floor by the door. Night shadows played on their faces.

"They're coming," said Pompée. "See that moon?"

"It's too low," said Sammy. "They ain't coming."

"Sammy, you shut your mouth!" yelled Anna, glancing at Hilda whose eyebrows were almost meeting her hair. "Get in there to bed right now! Pompée,"—he had that scared-animal look and she had to soften her voice—"don't you think you better go find a place to sleep?"

"I have a place, a fort in the woods. Even when it rains, I don't get wet."

"A fort?" said Hilda. "I declare!"

"Good night, Pompée," Anna said, "go along now."

He turned and ran. Hilda burst out laughing, then she said, "Honey, you know that man ain't fit to play with Sammy. I think you ought to do something about it."

"What?" she said, glaring. "Shoot him?"

"Come on, Hilda," said Alcibiade. "Anna's all tuckered out."

When she lay down, Sammy wasn't asleep. She was dreadfully tired but maybe what she had to say couldn't wait any longer. "Sammy boy, you heard Hilda. I think she's right."

"No! Pompée's a real good man, Anna. He's just scared."

"He tells stories."

"He don't lie, Anna. He could swear they're true."

"That's even worse, Sammy."

"No it ain't. Uncle Noah says it ain't. He says people that make up things come in two kinds, bad and poorly. The ones that don't believe what they say are the bad ones. Just ask Uncle Noah." He sniffed. "May I please play with Pompée? He can help Uncle Noah, too."

"Is he a big help?"

"Not as big as I am, but he ain't as strong."

"He's crazy, Sammy."

He began to cry. "Don't you say that, Anna. Why, he's so scared of that word he might run away, and next thing you know, they'll lock him up in the crazy house, and Uncle Noah says that's the worse place! Why, folks don't understand fellas like him!"

She put her arm around him. "How come Uncle Noah knows so much?"

"We had a talk when Pompée went to pee," he said, wiping his eyes with his fists. "Long, long ago Uncle Noah came here on a big boat across the ocean—couldn't see land, only water, and they was packed in tight. Some on the boat died and some went crazy and some, like him, had to watch." He sobbed and Anna squeezed him. "Oh, honey—" she began, but he shook his head. "Pompée and me got along right off. But I—I was afraid those fellas would come and get him till I got this funny feeling, and Uncle Noah told me yes, chances are there ain't no fellas."

"What a schooling you got."

Sammy sat up then, suddenly bright. "When you gonna get the book you promised long time ago?"

The cook shook her head above the potatoes she was peeling. "Anna girl, I always did think you had the devil in you, and now I know it!"

"But Aunt Cora, my boy wants learning so bad he can taste it, and you know they don't use all them books. I just knew you'd help, you always like the little ones."

"Well." She wiped her hands on her apron and went over to knead her dough. "I'll consider. What you doing down there with a bunch of no-good field hands, anyhow?"

Anna opened her mouth, but thought better of it. She shrugged.

"And where did you get a boy that size?"

"In a convent for orphans and sick in New Orleans."

"Do tell!" Cora cocked her head. "Why, that was right nice of you, Anna girl. I declare, maybe there's a little bit of good in you after all."

Anna smiled. She used to resent Cora's ravings but now she heard the ring of affection that might have always been there. Besides, Cora was the only one she knew who could help Sammy.

"Here, take some hot biscuits for the boy and git!"

"The book?"

"I declare, girl, come back tomorrow and we'll see."

"He does need some paper and a pencil—"

Cora glared.

"A tiny stub will do just fine."

The cook held out a bulging napkin and shook her head. "Give them an inch and they take an ell," she said.

* * *

Coming from the fields, Anna stopped by Granny Martha's chair to sit at the old woman's feet, her head against the ancient bony knees, the knees of the woman who saved Chad's life. It was a good time of day, the time between the fields and home, a time to rest and not to think.

Uncle Noah patted her shoulder, and she shook herself and saw his worried face. "What is it?"

"Don't want to scare you," he said, "but I ain't seen Sammy all day long."

"No!"

"He say last night he gon help me finish that table, but I couldn't find him and Pompée nowhere."

Anna's heart began to pound. They rounded up some folks and they searched in all directions—out the lane past the big live oak and over the road to the bayou, through the fields to the cypress swamp behind the plantation, through the lush undergrowth of the pine woods that rimmed the fields and the swamp. Uncle Noah sent Anna home and she dropped again by Granny Martha's knees, trembling. She could not imagine life without Sammy. She gave a long, wracking sob and felt a hand move ever so slightly, stroking her head with long fingers. Then suddenly here he came, a whirlwind of a boy.

She spanked him and hugged him and dragged him off, stopping only to kiss Granny Martha's cool cheek.

Pompée, trailing behind, settled on the step of the shack. "We were reading in the fort," he said.

"Oh, get out!" she cried. "There's no such thing."

"Yes there is, Anna," said Sammy.

Uncle Noah nodded. "Someone built a little shack out there in the pinewoods, Anna, got a lot of vines and moss hanging on it, and that's where Pompée's been sleeping. They just call it a fort."

Noah roasted his foraged sweet potatoes in the embers of the hearth, and they sat down at the brand-new table. Anna couldn't get over how sturdy it was: she shook it and it wouldn't wobble.

Then Sammy spoke up. "The book you got us is hard," he said, "but Pompée reads better than Sister Clarice. It's got all the stories Shakespeare wrote, and I'm going to learn to read them. Pompée says the words sing. Shakespeare is a master."

"So that's who wrote the book, huh? Well, sounds like you got a good book to learn from, Sammy. Maybe you can read to all of us sometime, Pompée. Maybe we'd all like to hear the words sing."

Almost to himself Pompée said, " 'The pale-faced moon looks bloody on the earth, / And lean-looked prophets whisper fearful change.' "

Before Anna could comment on that sorrowful-sounding declaration, he got up and said he was going back to the fort.

"They won't never find you there," said Sammy, though Anna could tell Pompée was more thoughtful than scared.

He hurried off and she shook her head. "I do wonder where he came from."

Uncle Noah took a deep breath. "One day he come down the road singing like a bird. Don't know where he belong, but he never were a slave."

TWENTY-FIVE

I would liken you
To a night without stars
Were it not for your eyes.
I would liken you
To a sleep without dreams
Were it not for your songs.

—LANGSTON HUGHES

April 1863

"Oh, the moon shines tonight on pretty Red Wing, / The wind is sighing, the night bird's crying . . ."

Anna raised her head to listen to the clear, high notes. Pompée was singing, and the sullen workers weary from the fields stopped their chores a moment. There was something fine about his tenor voice, soft and melodious and apart from the usual. She smiled to herself: she was grateful for him, his craziness and all, for he was teaching Sammy his lessons. There was a grace about him that had nothing to do with his awkward movements and his silly notions. When he spoke, she imagined he'd been to school, the kind you are sent to and come from with a diploma you hang on the wall. Maybe someday when he was sensible she'd ask.

* * *

When Pompée saw that he would have to leave the academy and journey home, he wrote himself a Letter of Protection and signed the principal's name. They were considering what to do with him as they met behind the closed doors of the office (they had said his mother, that wisp of a memory, was dead) and his soft sweet love was in there with them, betraying him, exposing what she thought was him.

With the long quill pen on the massive oak desk he wrote in formal script, tucked the pass into his shirt pocket, and softly, delicately, opening the office window, beads of sweat now on his face, squeezed over the wide, white sill.

Many days and nights he traveled south, heeding the warnings of the wind, watching for signs and finding them in the ripple of streams and the birdsong, and the way that puffy cloud sped by. Sometimes there were woodsheds or roomy barns for sleep, but often he was guest of the forest creatures, who were more friendly than the people in the towns, and less perplexed.

Living off the land had left him weak when he came upon the campfires of the village. They watched him wander in, ignoring him as he warmed himself, curled up in a knot before their fires. The men with braided hair smoked their pipes and spoke together and let him be. The women offered food and he took it, eating by himself, humming as he ate. He crouched in their corners and peered at them, but when the children came he was eased, and ran with them. Sometimes in the night he awoke with the howling of a wolf, and sang.

He stayed among them, listening, learning, until the full moon told him it was time to go. As he passed the wigwam of the chief, the old man beckoned. There by the light of the fire, the chief brought out a map, trails and distances so beautiful on bark that Pompée stared in awe. But the chief was asking what direction he traveled, and his fear welled high. Though he did not speak, he pointed, pointed south, and turned away.

Now and then, when he was with Sammy, reading or writing or mending wooden things, or eating by the hearth of Anna's shack, Pompée remembered: when he visited the villages of Shawnee or Kickapoo, Osage or Choctaw on his way down south, they knew him. Oh, the one besieged, a Chitimacha woman said as he passed through the Louisiana reservation, we are glad no harm came to you along the way. He had looked beyond her, to the children.

Anna smiled, listening:

"And far beneath the southern sky her sweetheart's sleeping / While Red Wing's weeping her heart away."

TWENTY-SIX

They must not be left to choose for themselves whether they
will work or not . . . if they refuse to work they must be *made*
to work.

——*THE NEW YORK TIMES*, 1863

April–June 1863

Hilda said she looked like a sleepwalker, and offered to help
in the shack, but Anna told her to go and take a nap. Hilda
wasn't a young woman, though she pressed through the day
like one, and Anna could see the strain of the past few weeks
on her face. She commanded respect, people listened to her,
and that was a burden for her. When the letter of protest to
George Hanks at the Bureau of Negro Labor was sent to
Colonel Wycliffe to "handle," it was Hilda who threw up her
hands and shouted "Now!" That morning the field hands
walked off in a body, Corporal Allen rode from field to field,
watching. Kane cussed at them, then took a holiday.

When Anna finished the washing she wanted to sleep, so
Sammy and Pompée took their lessons outside. Uncle Noah
snoozed in his chair in the shade. The sky was deep blue and
busy, the clouds huffing and puffing, the sun beating through

a gathered dampness with new force. Except for a few men and women talking in subdued voices, all was quiet as she went to bed. How good it was to stretch out, close her eyes, let her muscles down.

She woke with shouting: "You there!"—"Hands behind your back!"—"Line up!"

Out on the path Corporal Allen and three civil police were rounding up workers at gunpoint. As far as she could tell, they weren't after special people, but anyone who took their fancy. As they marched away with their prisoners, Allen shouted, "If you aren't back to work tomorrow, we'll come and get ten more!"

She ran around back and found Sammy and Pompée crouched by the chicken coop. "Did the Rebels come?" whispered Sammy.

"No, honey, not the Rebels. Some of us got carted off to jail, but never you mind. It won't be for long."

"Uncle Noah?"

"No, not Uncle Noah."

Pompée was smiling at Sammy. "Don't worry," he said, "they won't ever get you."

Anna laughed and took Pompée's hand, pulling him up and after her.

Uncle Noah was at the table with Hilda and Alcibiade, whose faces were drawn, their eyes saying more than their mouths ever could.

Alcibiade said as Anna sat down, "How many can that new jail hold?"

"I don't know," said Hilda, "but I allow they'll find some place to put us."

Anna yawned. She didn't want to think, just sleep, but everyone was looking at her. "I think we ought to hold out," she said, "at least till I get a little rest."

The small group outside her shack laughed with the ones at the table. Hilda patted her arm. "You ain't much more than five months along, honey. Your strength will be coming back one of these days."

Each day ten more workers were taken, and after thirty were gone, Hilda and Alcibiade went up to the house. Wasn't Colonel Wycliffe worried about the cultivation of his crop, they asked, and the soldier spoke for him: Sure, the good man is worried, but they'd soon bring in people from contraband camps who were more than willing to work, and send all the hands that were making trouble to abandoned plantations to work for the government.

That was that. Hilda lowered the curtain on her face until she could shape a good smile. The freed men and women were talking in small groups, blowing off steam and cooking up schemes, knowing they'd be back in the fields in the morning. One man outside Anna's shack said they ought to storm the house, tie up all the people until they got their terms. Another said, "Hell with terms! This here land is our land!" Anna said she agreed with them both, but they wouldn't have any more chance than John Brown had. "We'd have the whole Union army chasing us," she said with a private smile.

Uncle Noah nodded. "I know the white man's ways and he ain't gon give up easy. I declare, all of them is tarred with the same stick."

The weeks came and went in a steady stream, came and went leaving nothing changed—nothing, she thought, but the life within her, its quietude when she worked beyond her strength, its insistent leaps when she lay at peace, and its growth, bounding with hope. She came from the fields dead certain: up there at the house she didn't know the half of it. But Hilda was there to soothe her. The whippings sent her scurrying to the shade at the field's rim where she sat, head between her legs, her clammy hand in Hilda's. Workers were falling with diarrhea and pneumonia, and Hilda rushed her off to shelter her from sickness. If she felt dizzy or weak, Hilda would fetch water, sitting her down between the rows of green cane. "You oughtn't take such chances," Anna said. "You got your own life to think of."

Hilda nodded, sweat gleaming on her forehead, her upper lip. "You said it. If I can't stop to help somebody, then what's my life worth, anyhow? Mercy, child, the cane will grow without me for a minute."

Her baby fluttered with a life of its own, but she was scared for her friend. Then one day her fears were realized: Kane grabbed Hilda, curled his cowhide lash around her shoulders twice while Anna pounded his back. He cussed softly and let Hilda go with that terrible half smile on her lips. Anna was a mixture of fury and relief: he didn't put his anger in the right place, didn't crack his whip on her back.

"Go on, Hilda," she said now as the sun took her strength and she sat down with a thud. "Don't you get in more trouble." But her friend fetched water and Kane glared.

Before the week was up, the police came for Hilda. Anna kicked the shins of the officer tying Hilda's hands, and they took her arms and dragged her back.

"She's a first-class worker—you'll be sorry!" she yelled as Hilda was carted off. Eyes turned to her, wide eyes full of many things, and she knew there wasn't a worker who thought that Hilda would ever return.

She left the fields then and no one chased after her. Sammy, studying at the table, looked up with a greeting, then went back to his reading. Pompée's eyes didn't meet hers—they never did—but he got up slowly and made her tea and after a while said barely above his breath, " 'Oh, liméd soul, that struggling to be free / Art more engaged!' "

She stared at him, at his slender face, his hairline high, his eyes fixed beyond her. The tea was good, but the strange words were somehow settling. "That sounds nice. I think," she said, rubbing her temples where the tightness was, "you'd be a big help if you'd talk more, a help to me, I mean."

Sammy was smiling. "He talks to me, Anna."

Pompée smiled at Sammy. " 'Give every man thy ear, but few thy voice.' "

"I think it's from *Hamlet*," said Sammy.

That was the last straw. "Put your airs on somewheres else!" she shouted. She wanted to stay mad, to keep on being peeved with the big, lanky man, but awkwardly getting up he made her laugh.

Sammy came to kiss her goodbye. "What's funny, Anna?" He began to giggle as her laughter swelled, and holding her sides, she cried, "You are, boy—get along now!"

She laughed so hard that soon she was crying and sobbing, crying for Hilda, sobbing with her loss, but it was all right: they left while she was laughing.

The workers set a distance between Anna and them. They didn't say a thing that was nasty or whisper behind her back, but the distance was there. Goddamn, she breathed, it wasn't her fault Kane left her alone and the police just held her back when they took Hilda: what did they want from her, anyhow?

She kept on getting water and sitting in the shade when she felt weak and dizzy, dreading the time she'd have to pay but feeling she had no choice. Kane's response was a repeated back-to-work yell and an occasional infuriating swat on the bottom that was more of a feel than a slap. Finally she said to a woman in her row, "I thought I might be sitting next to Hilda by now." The woman looked her sadly in the eye and said, "Don't wish nothing on yourself. There's too much suffering already."

Her own was the least of it, she thought. Sammy was happy and she was gaining weight with Uncle Noah's cooking. Pompée, sitting on the edge of her consciousness, was always there for Sammy, and sometimes flew in front of her with a helpful cup of tea or a curious string of words she'd learned to let sink in. Then there was Alcibiade, who seemed to sit on the point of a needle, waiting to leap off. "I think," he said after Hilda was taken, "this won't last long. The news seems to say the fighting's just begun around here, and who knows—we might be liberated by the Rebels!" At least he could laugh, and Anna liked to hear it.

She knew a farm or two where the workers got their pay, but she'd never leave Sweet Haven, not until Chad came, not until they were together to stay. For whatever reasons, those around her seemed just as determined to stay and see the crop harvested.

She looked at her blistered hands and feet and the calluses where soft skin used to be and wished Chad would come before she dried up like a prune. Waking in the dark with the wind and rain or the call of a nightbird, she let doubt creep in: how do I know he'll come, why did I let myself care? Sometimes she woke in the dead of night to sweet, high notes in which she could take refuge. It was a rare gift to be aroused by Pompée's singing, and drift back to sleep on his song.

Her calico dress from the convent shimmied up around her now, and Uncle Noah brought her one he found under Hilda's mat in the longhouse. She put it on and it hung around her like a tent, but the old man's satisfied face made her smile.

"Do you know about birthing, Uncle Noah?"

He shook his head. "It's a woman thing, Anna."

"But no woman here likes me, and I wouldn't want the help of any of them!"

"Well," he said, a funny expression on his face, "if I have to learn I reckon I can, so don't you worry your head."

"I don't want Sammy around," she said.

"You have a while, Anna, just don't you fret."

He was right, of course. As far as she could tell, it wouldn't be until August, at least two whole months away. The daily rumors frightened her—Colonel Wycliffe was going to make "changes" and she'd had enough of those. But if they could only make it to the baby's birth, the war would be over, of course it would, and Chad would surely be there.

TWENTY-SEVEN

And I'm gonna put white hands
And black hands and brown and yellow hands
And red clay earth hands in it
Touching everybody with kind fingers
And touching each other natural as dew
In that dawn of music . . .

—LANGSTON HUGHES

March 1863

He crossed the Red River and marked on his map his north-east course. The land was now rolling and dry and sugar plantations were replaced by cotton.

The forests will be the same, he thought, but he was wrong. In this wide woods fallen magnolias lay like slain warriors, their split and jagged branches tangled over singed grass. Leafless hickories and live oaks broken in two, great trunks and small saplings nicked and scarred—wounded trees were dying. Earth was dug into and earth was built up. A makeshift barricade of logs stood charred in a field of torn thornbushes and trampled thistles, and blackberry thickets were thin and forlorn with a sprinkle of scraps—a hat here, a canteen there, a bayonet. Fragments of cannonballs, eighteen- or even sixty-eight-pounders, that's what those daggers were, and a rifle leaned in wait against a splintered tree. The field was somber, and sundrenched. He sat down, pondering. What was it like, this battle? Had the men marched forward with grim faces and set jaws or had they run with muskets blazing, laughing and yelling like children? How had it felt when they fell back, and how had it felt on the chase? Being killed seemed too farfetched to consider, yet death had walked here: the haphazard mounds of dirt were graves. Getting up, he shook himself, and fingered the waiting rifle.

A twig cracked and he whirled around, the rifle pointing awkwardly as a field mouse scurried through the brush. He threw the firearm down and, marking the sun's position, turned east.

He found a spot shaded by beech and ash trees and cleared a space to roast his chicken. The plucked bird looked grand hanging on a makeshift spit over the fire. He placed a sweet potato in the hot ashes, then settled back and watched. His mind was at ease until he thought of Clay and Blake, the two he knew so well, or thought he did. Blake had left in haste, there was no doubt about it, and he'd finally accepted that fact and the message Blake left. He could believe they would be reunited. But Clay's loss would be permanent, their parting final, and it left a hole as big as a cannonball in his life.

The sun blazed down from the west, changing the shadows and deepening the heat, while chicken fat dripped and bursts of flame leaped to singe pinfeathers. Still the whole world smelled of disturbed, disordered earth. Birds must have scattered to distant trees, for the waning day was silent.

Sudden footfalls through the brush startled and dismayed him as a figure in grey and yellow-brown staggered toward the fire. The slight young man halted as if in drill and stared at Chad with eyes full of hunger and fury. His face was contorted with pain, but he clutched a rifle he seemed able to use. "Don't move, nigger!" he snorted. "Unless you don't value that black skin more'n I do!"

Chad sat stock-still, his hands folded before him as they'd been while he'd watched the browning hen. He said nothing.

The Rebel edged around the fire and jabbed him with his rifle butt, his eyes too bright. "What you doing, boy, sitting like a half-ass king roasting his dinner? Look-a-here at the big sweet potato you stole!" He jerked suddenly and grimaced, then carefully sat down near Chad. "Don't you once think I can't shoot you clean dead. Why, I'd as soon spatter you all over the countryside as—draw a breath!" He drew one then, and it was labored. Chad kept quiet, let him rave.

"I likes the idea of you cooking for me," he went on, smiling a pained contortion of a smile. "Never had a slave."

A rent in the soldier's pants just above the knee trickled blood.

"Where you come from, nigger?"

The Rebel sounded country-bred. Chad said, "New Orleans."

"Ah-ha, a sassy nigger from the big city! I knows the airs of cityfolk strutting around. Everything big. Big carriages, big horses, big houses. I was there myself once, so don't tell me better. Why, you goddamn slaves eat ice cream in the kitchen!"

"I ain't a slave," Chad said before he could stop himself.

"You ain't, huh?" The soldier grinned and his rotting teeth showed. "Well, maybe you wasn't but you is now. I'm gon give you good advice. You sure enough better start acting like my slave, y'hear? Now, hand me that there chicken and I'll show you how your massa eat!"

Chad loosened the hen from the spit and slid it into the Rebel's lap. The soldier yelled and threw it in the grass. "Curse you, nigger! Trying to burn me!" He groaned and put his hand on his leg, then on the rifle's trigger. "Now go pick up that bird and tear it apart—put it right down on these here leaves with the sweet potato, nice and easy, and don't you make any false move."

The Rebel gobbled the potato and the pieces of chicken and threw the bones to Chad.

* * *

He watches Clay go, smells the supper cooking in the master's kitchen, feels his stomach wrench. Hunger is with him through his chores, beneath his mat in the slavehouse corner, under the boards where it's written in his copybook, deep inside him where it has no voice.

One of the kitchen help dishes out the hominy from the great vat, passes it through the door: Git! *He waits till a servant shakes the tablecloth from the dining room, vies with the dogs for the bones that fall, sucks them dry.*

"You're gonna bleed to death," he said.

"Do tell!" The greycoat shot a glance at the rent in his trousers, edged with fresh blood. "I got it bound up."

"Let me look at it."

The Rebel raised his rifle. "You touch it and you one nigger the South is plumb done with. You ain't gon put no voodoo curse on me!"

Chad raised his eyebrows. "I have a whole sack full of them."

The soldier looked surprised. He thought a moment, then asked, "Where?"

"Over yonder, under that bush."

"Get it."

He pulled his carpetbag from the brush and held it out, then began to unbuckle it. "Want me to show you one?"

The soldier lost what little color he had. "No! You keep that thing buckled tight, y'hear?"

"If you say so."

"This here rifle say so!" Out of breath, he scooted back to lean against a tree. His body kind of fell in on itself and he seemed to be thinking of something far away, his eyes losing their glaze, his face livening. When he spoke, his tone had changed. "Do you know where we is?"

"The Mississippi's that way—to the east." He calmed down a little, himself. "Not too far."

"Shucks, I know that." The greycoat almost smiled. "I can smell water a mile off. Ma relied on my nose, said I was as good as a hound when it come to hunting. I could scare a rabbit dead, too, without firing a shot."

"How'd you do that?"

"My catcall. I'd show you, but we don't want any horny wildcats snooping around."

Chad laughed and the Rebel shot him a glance, then went on: "Last time I made that call, I had to fight off a dozen cats."

"You don't say."

The Rebel chuckled to himself. "Pa used to make a fire in front of the house and we'd sit around nights just talking, telling one story after t'other, some true, some spun. After Pa died, we didn't make any more night fires." He gave a small pitiful cry. "When I saw my first campfire after joining up, I thought of Pa. But it weren't the same. Too big, too many fellows, none of them kin. All they could talk about was home."

Chad looked at the soldier's contorted face. "You need help bad for that leg."

"I'll be just fine in a minute. I need a little rest, that's all."

"I saw a plantation a while back, maybe a half hour away. If you can make it, they'll help you."

The Rebel shook his head. "I don't want to go to no plantation house. Them people ain't no more amiable than the Yankees."

"Where do you figure on going?"

"Guess I'll just stick with you, see you behave!" He shot a glance at the carpetbag. "Maybe we ain't such enemies, you know."

"I got no fight with you."

"Hey, y'ain't, huh?" He gritted his teeth and moved his leg. "Well, long as I'm the one with the rifle, you don't. You know anything about wounds? I mean, you ever do any doctoring without that satchel?"

"Not much," said Chad, "but I reckon I could dig out a bullet if you have a good knife."

"Ain't no bullet in my leg. A ball blew up the fellow running beside me, and one of them splinters done slice me right above the knee. They say if you gets hit wait for the hospital squad, but I say get out of there fast as you can or you'll get hit again. I seen that happen to a man. So when I got hit I picked myself up and run like the devil!"

"When was that?"

The Rebel blinked. "One, two nights ago."

"You been bleeding all that time?"

"Shucks, no. I put a good tight bandage on it before I went too far. Then I went back to look for my regiment and it was clean gone."

Chad shook his head. "Have you been fighting a long time?"

"You're looking at a real veteran. I been in battles where the smoke was so thick you couldn't see more than two, three feet ahead except in a time out to bury the dead. Then maybe you talk back and forth from the trenches." He laughed. "Funny, talking to them like over the pasture fence. One of our boys yell out, 'What happen to your Captain Rhoads?' We heard that name a lot at first, you know, messengers on horses calling him, then no more. We thought the captain was shot dead, and he was. They said so."

"Nice of them to tell you."

The greycoat scowled. "You don't know nothing about it."

"I'm going to join the Union army."

The Rebel laughed. "From what I hears, those Yankees wouldn't be caught dead with you on a battlefield." He laughed again and grimaced.

"You ain't got room to talk," Chad said. "Look what you just said about the planters—no more amiable than the Yankees."

The greycoat drew in his breath slowly, as though it gave him strength. "I don't know why I'm setting here talking to you, you and your city airs. Here I am, a poor boy all my life, just join up to get fit like my mama want me to, and there you is, one of them niggers they say makes the South what it is. Well shit, maybe I don't like what it is."

Chad sighed. "Can't say as I do, either." He thought of Elmer's ailing mother, what she said about their life on the farm and how she wanted him to take the boy with him.

The soldier eyed him suspiciously. "Put the fire out. We's moving."

He obeyed, then reached for his sack and the Rebel aimed his rifle at Chad's head. "You go near that and I swear, you has drawn your last breath." He got shakily to his feet, the blood draining from his face. "Now march!"

Chad took two short steps, then swung around and knocked the rifle from the greycoat's hands. It went off and the shot went wildly through the trees. The leaves shook, hanging on, and the soldier fell to the side, cussing and moaning.

Chad put the rifle under his carpetbag then rolled up the Rebel's trouser leg. The wound's binding was soaked with blood, and the leg around it was red. "This ain't good," he said. "I'll wrap it as tight as I can, but you ain't walking any more today."

He took off his shirt, tore it into strips, and bound the wound. "That too tight?"

"No."

"You need it sewn. I could do it with a needle and thread, and maybe we could get it from the black folks on the plantation back there, and some ointment, too. But now it's getting dark and I'd lose my way."

The Rebel was up on his elbows and his face looked haggard but full of thought. "It's okay," he said, "it's okay."

"You think you'll be all right till morning?"

"I allow so, long as you don't open that there satchel."

Chad shook his head. "I won't, Reb."

"Swear?"

"Swear."

Chad built a platform of leaves and sticks for the Rebel's leg; then he lay down. It was the quick time of day just before sunset when the curtain hangs ready to fall, and he put his hands behind his head and stared up through the purple trees.

Suddenly the Rebel reached out and tapped his arm. "What am I to you?" he asked. "I mean—what—"

"You're a Butternut to me."

"A nut?"

"No, a Butternut. The color of your uniform, grey and brownish yella. Butternut."

"Oh."

The branches swayed with a soft, welcome breeze.

"When I get home," the Rebel said, his voice small, "I got big plans. The army money I have coming is going to buy us some decent land—or a boat. I'd like that, a boat you can live on and be a fisherman, too. That'll be keen. Good food. We ain't et well on the land. Ma and Pa was slaves to it, and Pa used to say when the soil was sifted through, we got the chaff." He gave that mournful cry again, high and sharp and stifled. "Ma and Sis are tough. They'll get along till I get home. I never shoulda left, but they'll get along."

Above the trees, a lone bird circled, then swooped out of sight.

"Nigger?"

"What?"

"You hungry?"

"Yeah."

"I shoulda let you eat."

"Yeah."

"I'm particular sorry."

"Forget it."

Chad was almost asleep when he heard the soldier crying. He raised up on an elbow, asked, "Does it hurt so bad?"

"No," the Rebel said, "not all the time. I guess it feels better than it has. I just—well, I live pretty far from here, up near Alexandria, pretty doggone far."

"Um-hum." He lay back down and closed his eyes.

"In the morning—will you take me home?"

Chad looked at the slim body in the pale light and thought of Mars.

"Will you, nigger?"

"Yeah."

The soldier sighed. Chad shut his eyes against the deepening purple and went to sleep.

Before sunup, when the fog lay so thick he could hardly see the soldier lying near him, Chad awoke to a chorus of wild geese overhead. Rising to check the Rebel's wound, he found a pool of blood on the mound of brush. "Oh, my—" he said. "Hey, Reb, I'm going to get help—"

When there was no answer, "Hey—" he breathed, reaching for a bony shoulder. As he stared at the soldier's face, whiter than the fog and just as still, his vision blurred. Tears rolled down his cheeks and he brushed them angrily away: "God-damn-Reb."

TWENTY-EIGHT

The dream is vague
Without a name,
Yet warm and wavering
And sharp as flame.

—LANGSTON HUGHES

June 1863

Noah sat in the back of the wagon with his legs hanging over, holding onto the old black box he had taken from Master Wycliffe's bonfire many years before. He held it tightly because of what he once kept in it, the small, smooth stone from Africa that he'd given Chad, and because it was the only thing he owned. Against his back sat Martha who, he hoped, was spared the pain of being sent to the poor farm, a place for the infirm and a prison for workers unwilling to sign contracts.

A day or two before the wagon came, the planter walked down the path, gesturing to the Union soldier at his side. "I want to get rid of the cankerworms of the estate," he said. "Y'all have places for them, I hear, and I want them out of here."

They stopped in front of Martha, her vacant stare uninterrupted by their visit. "Morning, Granny," her former master said, and then, "I declare, she has had her day, yes sir."

They looked across the path at him. "Hello, Noah."

"Morning, Colonel Wycliffe," he said, avoiding *master* though it almost slipped out. "How is you this morning?"

"I'm tolerable. What you been up to lately, Noah?"

"Been busy doing for the children."

"Ho, ho, ho!" said Wycliffe. "When'll you learn the children can do for themselves?"

Noah tried to smile. His hands were cold and damp and he rubbed them against his thighs.

"Any more?" asked the corporal, his eyes scanning the path, a pencil ready above the pad he held.

"Didn't I hear tell y'all been keeping a vagrant, Noah?"

"Vagrant, Colonel? No sir."

"You know what I mean, Noah, boy come pestering around, don't work, just eat—big load on y'all."

"Don't know nobody like that, Colonel. If he was here, he ain't here no more."

The master looked into all the shacks, all the longhouses, on his way back. "There are a few more out in the quarters along the far fields," he said. "When you going to see to this?"

"They'll be off your hands within a week, sir," Noah heard the soldier say, and when the two were gone, he looked at Martha, cold spreading throughout his body. He sat down by her, remembering how he'd always turned to her. "We's going, Martha," he said, feeling already gone.

He set to work on the rocking chair he had begun for Anna and her baby. Hurrying's no good, but he had to hurry. He had planned to build a cradle, too, but now there wasn't time.

The hardest part of going was telling Anna and Sammy. It had to be done. He couldn't let them find him gone without a word. This was one time he wished he'd had the chance to learn to write. It would be easier to say goodbye in a letter.

That night he told them. Anna up and left for a spell, and when she came back, she said she found out where the farm was and they'd be sure to come for him and Granny Martha when Chad got back. Then she sat, stiff and peaked, lost in herself. The boy said he wished Uncle Noah didn't have to go and he'd go with him if he could, but he had promised to look after Anna just as she looked after him. Noah said, yes, Sammy, that's where your duty is, she'll be needing you.

Noah himself was the one who acted the fool when the time came. Darned if it wasn't a Sunday and a whole gang congregated around to say goodbye. He and Martha got into the wagon with a few other folks and he leaned toward Anna's ear. His breath came in spurts so the words were squeezed: "You can get along, Anna, old Martha can't—" But he cried, no two ways about it. That made Sammy turn his face into Anna's skirt, and away rolled the wagon.

Poor farm, he thought, what a damn-fool name. How can we be anything but poor, all of us? There wasn't much that made sense to his mind. He'd been stealing to feed the few he dearly loved, and he wasn't ashamed or sorry for it. But here he was now, no home, no food, nothing but a small black box.

Anna rocked back and forth in the new rocking chair, and thought of how she was greeted when she went up to the house to plead for the old man. Colonel Wycliffe seemed kindly, but wouldn't budge. She told him Uncle Noah was not a burden but was part of her family. He said Noah was getting to be a burden on the plantation, even stole from the neighbors. He spoke softly and with easy patience, grating on her nerves. He was so composed that when she raised her voice in anger, he didn't even bother to repeat his refusal.

"I want you to know, Anna," he said, "that you sure enough are welcome to come back here to Miss Laurel any time you please. She misses you, keeps asking Master Kane about you, too. And child, we sure don't hold it against you that you got yourself in trouble."

She froze. So that was it! Missy Laurel was behind all that protection in the fields. She stood up, spat out "I'm not in trouble!" and stormed away.

It was funny that Laurel should think Anna's condition was

responsible for her not wanting to be a nursemaid, for in a way, it was. She'd hated the stifling job, but more than that, she wanted to be as far away from Laurel as she could when her baby was born.

Food was meager now that Uncle Noah was gone. Seldom did they see a sweet potato, and they had no cornmeal for mush or ashcakes. Still, the hens were laying eggs and she had grown less proud. If she saw a need in Sammy or Pompée or in her own engrossed body, she went to chat with Cora.

Aunt Cora had a way of saying things. With a characteristic sniff she said that Colonel Wycliffe's wine was a less-prideful year, his table held fewer dishes, and because company had dwindled with the war, the spit seldom held a hog. She was not as unaware as Anna had supposed, and though she still sniffed when she spoke of field hands, she often puckered her brow when Anna was fagged out, muttering to herself. Finally she lifted her eyes to Anna's and said, " 'Tain't right, none of it. I know what's going on." Like as not when Anna left, she'd carry away a bundle of biscuits or even, if it was safe, a small stew boiled hurriedly in her bucket. The only thing that bothered Anna was how she'd ever pay the kindness back. Cora seemed so self-sufficient. She was married to Horace, the doorman, who spent his days sweeping and napping and fussing over guests, his nights planting and tending the small plot behind their shack, and trudging the four miles to Pugh's plantation to see their daughter, taking her food and messages from Cora. Cora couldn't walk the distance. She worked too hard in the kitchen, and her legs wouldn't take her weight come nightfall. Still she seemed so relaxed, so confident, almost as though she was in control of her life. Nothing Anna could think of would add to that.

Anna used to lie with her arms flung out or up and over her head, but now as she lay on her right side, her left arm followed her body line, lay along her hip, her thigh, lay there in comfort. She liked the feel of her smooth skin over her well-shaped bone. She moved, eased her arm along, turned on her back. Instantly the baby swam to the surface, punched at the wall, rolled over and drifted away. She climbed out of bed.

It was Sunday evening, hot and close. She set out the day's second meal of hominy and molasses for Sammy and Pompée, saying, "You two eat up. I don't feel like eating." Hilda had been right about her energy: it had returned, but only for a while. Now the weight of the baby seemed to sap her strength and she was glad for a day of rest.

Sammy looked at Pompée, and Pompée said, "Sammy has a surprise in his pocket."

He brought out several handfuls of pecans and set them before her proudly. "For you and our baby, Anna."

"I declare, they do look good!" They were soft and ripe and she ate hungrily, surprised at her sudden appetite, but there was something she had to say. "You have to go too far to get these, honey. I want you close to home, y'hear?"

Sammy gave her a don't-fret smile that was soft, nothing sassy or peeved about it.

Anna fell asleep before she could eat all the nutmeats. It was black as pitch when Sammy woke her. "A bad dream?" she asked.

"No! Listen!" he whispered.

At first there was nothing, then came a rifle report and another on its heels, a string of them followed by silence.

"I'm scared," whispered Sammy.

"It's all right. Maybe someone went gator hunting down on the bayou."

"Sounds too close."

"I don't hear nothing now, honey. Go back to sleep."

Sammy turned over and soon his breathing was deep and even, coating the air like a balm. But she lay staring at the black ceiling, stretching her hearing as far as it would go. She thought she heard running, a fast horse galloping, then a shout and more footfalls. By now her senses were overtuned and deceitful, she thought, as she drifted off.

Just before dawn, Alcibiade came stealing into the shack and woke her with a whisper: "Anna, it's me. Have to talk."

They sat in the darkness on her doorstep. Alcibiade watched her closely, took her hand and said, "You already know."

"They've come back."

"Yes. The Rebels have taken Brashear City and pushed up the bayou to Thibodeaux. The Yanks have gone back to Donaldsonville, moved out with no more'n a little skirmishing. The Rebs will soon be here."

"Oh, Alcibiade!"

"The Union corporal left in the night, and so did some of the field hands."

"What do you make of it?"

"I know one thing—Grant is closing in on Vicksburg, and Banks is beating the hell out of his troops at Port Hudson, and all the rest of it is just nothing."

"Where'd you hear all that?"

"An army recruiter showed up last night. He told me."

"What did he say about New Orleans?"

"General Emory down there has the fidgets, but no one's sending him reinforcements."

"What are you going to do?"

His expression changed: it scared her. "Join the army."

She laid her hand on his arm. "If I was a man, I guess I would, too."

"Well," he said, still solemn, "then I'll leave tonight. Things change too fast to see ahead clear, but that's what I want to do."

"Don't worry about me, I'll be fine."

He looked down. "I wish I hadn't lost touch—with the old ways. Mama tried to teach me, but it's been so long. Sometimes I can hear her chants, her prayers, and I guess they're still a part of me." He smiled at her, such a sober smile. "I wish I could protect you with a prayer."

"Maybe you just have. Do you think—Sammy will be safe with me in the fields?"

"Why, sure," he said, the Alcibiade she knew returning to his face. "No one's about to hurt a nice slaveboy."

He was being funny, but she cringed. "Pompée—won't he be in trouble?"

"I judge the Rebels won't have a chance to be nosy about who's who. By the time Taylor stops his clucking about the victory, Weitzel will come down from Port Hudson and chase him off for good."

She threw a summoned smile that having reached Alcibiade left no trace behind. "It don't hurt to fancy," she said, "when you can't do nothing but."

TWENTY-NINE

But softly
As the tune comes from his throat
Trouble
Mellows to a golden note.

—LANGSTON HUGHES

Late June 1863

"I'm bound for the land of Caanan," sang Pompée, strolling up to Anna's shack, Sammy at his side. Sammy liked to sing, but when Pompée was singing, Sammy kept still. It was as though a spell were being spun, as though a curious gypsy were throwing a sheltering song around them, like a cloak.

The man and the boy came into the shack and suddenly it seemed close and cramped. She sent Sammy off to bed. Tonight her need for privacy was greater than her need for company, and she asked Pompée to go. Thunder rumbled in the distance, but she was sure he could make it to the "fort."

The soft, wet carpet took his heavy footfalls and smothered them as he went headlong through the woods. The wind blew against his face and the tall trees swayed with the coming storm. "Go along," said Anna, and he'd gone along, her words set to music in his ears. But amidst the purple-hued pines, he couldn't find the song or see her smile. Lightning whitened the gloom and he stopped a moment, waiting for the thunder. When it came, ragged and demanding, he nodded and began to run again. He was aware that something in him tried to hold him back, tugged at the edges trying to contain the fright he carried just below the surface, the fright that was pushing him, putting terror in his step. He stumbled and fell facedown, his nostrils against the undergrowth.

He cast a blow with his fist against the ground and knew his folly. Getting to his feet, he walked the rest of the distance to the fort, but the fear rose with every thunderclap, and he wondered what form they would take and how he would know them.

There was once a house where he felt safe, a wooden house with courtyard and flowers. His memory of it was a shaft of light, and with it came a soothing voice that whispered, *Sing when you are frightened, Pompée, sing!* His song played through the years like a lyre, brightening his dark corners, overlapping into joy when the fear was gone.

Now he hummed, as he was taught to hum the scales by the strange white man with the stiff white collar who stood at the head of the class, whose eyes he met and learned not to meet. He remembered the black notes that danced away the fear: not tonight, oh God, please not tonight.

The thunder was close and its message was clear: they're coming. He hid his face in his hands, his knees bent against them.

"Your son will not be schooled abroad!" came a gruff voice from the courtyard, a voice without a face.

"I am not your slave, monsieur, remember that!" said the one who'd brought sweet tunes to the nursery. "You made a contract with my son and me. If we cannot go to France, I shall engage tutors."

"No! I've found the school for him. I'll not have him educated here, my *inamorata,* my ladylove. Not that one. *He is too . . ."*

Thunder whitened out the rest, and if it weren't thunder it would be windsong or *wararons* croaking in the swamp.

. . . sometimes he hurt so much he could not think or feel except the agony and then the singing and the joy so round and full his strength swung forward like the moon pull . . .

He was black as night against the whiteness all around: it sat behind the desks, it loitered in the hall, it played in the playgrounds, kicked balls, shouted, it slept in the beds next to his, it ate at his table, it stood like a falcon at the head of his class.

It played with him sometimes, until the big eyes watching disapproved, and then it played tricks in the playground, in the snow.

When he was older and the tune was pure, the big eyes watching were his teacher's eyes: she saw his love of poetry and song, how deep he went into the books she taught, and when his eyes met hers, they walked inside each other. He told her they would come for him, but she did not believe him. This is the North, his fair teacher said, no one's going to hurt you here.

Always in his dreaming hours when he could not dream they were on his trail—hurry, hurry, Pompée with the eyes of glass, the feet of stone—and he locked his door when he had a door against them.

Now he shook and kept his head between his hands, his short breaths still. The wind howled against the wood and vine of the fort.

Deep, deep in the night when the small Pompée was drunk with sleep, the music teacher, the stern unmusical man with baton and stiff white collar came and got him from his bed in the line of beds and took him to the shed where the tools were kept, the small tools and the thin, shimmering saw, the nails, the rope, and the iron. Tied down on a slab, he saw his mind whiten out the pain. *Sing, Pompée, sing when you are frightened,* but his mind was bare, his running legs still as the white-hot branding iron closed in. At dawning he was glad it was a dream until the teacher's naked eyes met his. Was the ritual real? Where then, was the brand? The strange man hummed the scale.

He raised his head. There was a sound that was not the storm. There was thunder that was not from the sky. Pompée sat, his hands clasped over his knees.

They lay down side by side and she was soft, the white hands on the black body were her hands on his body . . . hurry, hurry, Pompée, eyes of glass, feet of stone, they're closing in . . . Who? she asked. No, no, Pompée! She ran fast on his stony heels . . . he made her taste the water ere he drank it.

My poor mad love, you need care, you need doctors and a place to be, a special place . . .

Whose need is this? he asked in silence, looking out of clear, cold eyes: not mine.

A man apart, he walked New Orleans streets and lingered on its benches, tired from months of travel, finally home. In a courtyard he tutored young, wise mulattoes and quadroons. Their polished elders pressed gold coins in his hand: he placed his coins on open palms before the church as he sped by, sensing disapproval from its spires. Rebuke was in the sway of gentle trees, censure in the chalk that squeaked white words. But he stayed and taught, he didn't run, except through sleepless hours: oh, God, please not tonight. When, with the war, his several pupils scattered to Haiti, to France, into seclusion and up North, he left New Orleans, left with just a song.

He held his knees and whispered: " 'Alack the heavy day, / That I have worn so many winters out / And know not now what name to call myself!' "

The storm calmed, but something else was taking place. The sound of fleeting feet?

He sat very still.

His sweet Sammy never scoffed the way the others did. Sammy, his student and his friend, let be his other world: *the moon's too low, we'll paint the coop, they won't come tonight.*

The footfalls through the woods increased to a crescendo and the fright took hold. It shook him, shook him like a bag of bones. *Sing, Pompée, sing when you are frightened . . .*
And he began to sing.

THIRTY

The blue bayou's
A pool of fire.
And I saw the sun go down,
Down,
Down,
Lawd, I saw the sun go down!

—LANGSTON HUGHES

Same night in June 1863

Anna rocked slowly back and forth as the rain pelted the shack. The door groaned against its frame, the single candle on her table flickered. Sammy called and she kept rocking: told him to close his eyes and go to sleep. She was tired, she said, and wanted no nonsense. Another month and a half, maybe, and she'd be finished with this breeding business, this strange and marvelous babe that took her body for its own, feeding on her. What then would she do with a baby in the fields? They called nursing field women "suckers." The word caught like spittle in her throat.

A storm was raging outside her shack tonight, and the Rebels were coming in small waves and trickles, reclaiming the land without much fuss. It was too late to plan: she would be watchful, she would wait. Alcibiade had gone, and she was sitting like a willow in the wind. It was hard for her to imagine the kind of future Chad believed in, hard to believe in anything or anyone—hard, she said as the baby kicked, to believe in you.

The storm calmed and Anna nodded in her chair, slipping in and out of sleep. Then the door flung open and Pompée stood at the threshold a flash of time before he entered, pulling the door shut behind him. "They're after me," he said, breathless.

The sight of him! His averted eyes were full of fear and he held his arm like a broken wing. Anna got to her feet, encircled his awkward frame in her arms, saying, it's all right, no one will hurt you here, thinking, oh Lord, what demons can be carried in the mind!

But abrupt sounds outside made her stiffen and Pompée staggered to the other room, where Sammy at the doorway caught his hand and brought him down on the mat, covering him with the sackcloth blanket.

The door once more flung open and a soldier in grey and yellow brown peered in, his rifle aimed.

"Oh, massa," said Anna, holding her belly, "you done scared the daylights out of this poor soul."

The soldier smiled and entered. "Who's in there?" he asked, glancing into the other room, dark but for the dim light cast on its walls from her candle.

"Just my husband and son—we is hardworking—"

"You see a tall boy come in here, got a bullet in his arm?"

"No, sure enough didn't. What he do, massa?"

"I allow the boy was running off with something—caught him in a shack back in the woods. When we got him out, he took off like a rabbit. I declare, we never know what you folks might do anymore."

Anna saw a crimson red drop on the floor and moved to stand on it . . . *red polka dots splashing . . . blood all over a white dress . . . dripping into the bayou . . .* The room whirled.

The soldier caught her arm. "Hey, don't faint, we won't hurt you."

A greycoat by the door called in, "He plumb got away if you don't have him, Lester. He in there?"

"Naw. It don't make no nevermind anyhow, one fool Nigra."

They left, and Anna leaned on the door. Pompée came then, hesitantly. He slid into a chair and placed his wounded arm on the table. She took one of the knives Noah left and put it in the embers, and then, after Sammy gave Pompée the old honing strap to bite and held his other hand, she dug out the bullet.

Lying in bed with Sammy asleep and Pompée curled in the corner by the hearth, it all came back.

Alila's warm hands soap Anna's body as they romp and splash in the bayou. It is barely light and very still. Alila's smile is bright, her full breasts bob in the waves they make, her nipples and the deep purple circle around them are swollen in the warmth of the water.

Crashing through the brush come boots, arms pull Alila, she grabs for her dress, she kicks, fights, and Anna wildly hits at the long legs on the bank as the hairy arms hurl out . . . Blood comes from her sister's mouth, her neck, splashes on the dress she holds before her naked body, and as she sinks before the boots, drips into the bayou.

The legs and boots run off . . . Alila lies crumpled, still, red spots on the white dress half-covering . . .

Anna screams.

Sammy leaped up: "What's wrong, what's wrong?"

Pompée came running.

"A dream," she said, sobbing, "a bad dream."

"Oh, Anna," cried Sammy, "do you want to stay awake so it won't come back?"

"No, honey," she said, "it won't come when I'm asleep. It won't come back."

Sammy put his arms around her and Pompée murmured, " 'All yet seems well, and if it end so meet, / The bitter past, more welcome is the sweet.' "

THIRTY-ONE

We're coming, Father Abraham, three hundred thousand more
We leave our homes and firesides with bleeding hearts and sore
Since poverty has been our crime, we bow to thy decree;
We are the poor and have no wealth to purchase liberty.

—*SONG OF THE CONSCRIPTS*, AFTER THE PASSAGE
OF THE CONSCRIPTION ACT, 1863

March—April 1863

Chad must have walked five or six hours without stopping after he left the Rebel back there, for the sun was beating down, straight and mindless and hot as flame, when he stopped to rest.

He hadn't wanted to bury the Rebel: someone, somewhere, might like to have the body to build a funeral around. But those two black vultures settling in the trees made him mad, and so he dug a hole and put the Rebel in it. He placed the rifle on the grave with the soldier's hat and the soldier's tag and said a few words under his breath in case God needed to be notified. With so many dying lately, one poor soul could sure enough go unnoticed, one poor scared soul. He took the Rebel's canteen, slung its slim cord over his shoulder and went on his way.

He was glad to find the levee once again. The sky's soft blue heightened the green of the woods and just ahead tall pecan trees cast long shadows over a bend in the river. He said aloud, *Misachibee:* Jerry was right, its sound was as beautiful as the river, the softly flowing river, whose trail would lead him to Vicksburg.

He had stopped counting time, even days, but he kept to the levee when he could. He spent a day lying in a tree while a greycoat regiment trudged beneath him. Slumping, stumbling, hardly speaking, they kept their eyes to the ground. He skirted occupied plantations, passed over the deserted, savored the burgeoning shades of green of the bottomland.

He'd climbed the tallest pecan tree near the levee when he was startled by loud voices. Below his carpetbag, which he'd wedged in a crook of the tree, a couple of bluecoats leaned on their guns. They were talking earnestly. He moved, and one of the branches cracked. Two pairs of eyes looked up as he climbed slowly down, leaving the bag in its leafy cache.

The brown-bearded soldier aimed his rifle, but the yellow-haired one put a hand on his arm. "It's only a darky," he said. "He's harmless, Amos."

"My ass," said Amos. "We don't trust them up in New York."

"Down here they say you get a good darky, he does everything but breathe for you."

"He don't die for you, Maxwell."

Maxwell laughed, but Amos was serious. He had a surly smile, unbroken as they talked back and forth, looking at Chad sideways, gesturing toward him.

Finally he said, "I'm Chad Creel."

They looked surprised.

"Why, hallo there," said Maxwell, and resting his rifle between his legs extended his hand. Chad shook it.

"You don't shake hands with a colored boy," said Amos.

"I never met one before," Maxwell said apologetically.

Amos turned to Chad with an ornery grin. "I have. Why, I guess I met a lot of them up there since they started drafting us." He fingered his rifle. "You know about the war, boy?"

Chad nodded.

"Well, we was sent down here to set you free. Ain't that something?"

Maxwell was watching Amos with a funny look on his face. "Let go of your rifle," he said. "We got no quarrel with him."

"That's right, we ain't. You belong around here, boy?"

"No."

"Oh, a fugitive, eh? Never mind, you be real good and we won't turn you in."

"Seeing as how we're in the same boat," said Maxwell with a smile that faded with the look his buddy gave him.

"Where you headed, boy?"

"Up the road a piece."

"What for?"

"Nothing special."

"Let him alone," said Maxwell. "Let's get out of here."

Amos grinned again and Chad wished he were close enough to the river to jump in and swim across. He knew he couldn't run and make any distance without getting shot, and he didn't know what he could say that would change the menacing eyes of the bearded man.

"I don't think we want to leave our new friend," Amos said, a curl on his lips, "not if we want to get where we're going."

"Oh, maybe he does know the countryside." Maxwell turned to Chad. "Can you set our course?"

"Where you headed?"

"North. I'm from Massachusetts, and Amos here's from New York."

Amos laughed hard, cradling his rifle in his arms. "That don't mean nothing to him. But he'll come in handy, just wait and see."

"Well," Chad ventured, "if you have to look out for both sides, seems you better find some new clothes."

Now Maxwell burst out laughing. "He's not so dumb! Why didn't you think of that, Amos?"

"I did. That's just the first thing. What you got in mind, boy?"

"Well," he said, feeling his way, "I hear some of the Rebels left their clothes behind when they ran off to Texas."

Now Maxwell howled, just bent over laughing. "That'd be a sight! Bet the Texans got a kick out of that!"

Amos laughed, too, but his eyes never left Chad's face. "The nigger ain't laughing."

Maxwell turned to him. "Don't you see what you said, all those naked Butternuts—" He began to laugh again and sat down weakly.

Amos swung his rifle toward Chad. "When we think something's funny, you laugh!"

"Come on, Amos, cut it out," said Maxwell, wiping his eyes. "No one laughs at his own joke."

Chad thought of Uncle Blake's warning about laughter: how it can change with the wink of an eye, and how he knew a man who laughed with strangers and found himself strung up. Still it was a fact that whites got suspicious of a sober black. He smiled. "I was just figuring where to go to get you clothes."

Amos's eyes narrowed. "Where?"

"There's a deserted plantation about two miles downriver."

"Let's go," said Maxwell.

"Wait a minute. Maybe this nigger wants to turn us in."

"You said he was a fugitive, Amos. He'd be turning himself in."

"All right, but I don't trust him. He goes first. You keep your eye on the country, and I'll keep my rifle on him."

Chad led them to the abandoned plantation, past the gin-house and the wide cotton fields, the rows grown over with weeds. They crossed adjoining cornfields and explored the grounds by the fine, white dwelling. The flower gardens made Maxwell's eyes widen and his mouth open. "Never saw anything like this," he said, "not even when we took Mama to Boston. And the smell of it!" He began to stroll through the garden, bowing before the jasmine and oleander, holding tender buds to his nose.

* * *

"Look out! Here comes Mammy!" shouted Clay as they were chased from the flower garden. Away they ran, down the lane to the banks of the bayou, where they lay in the grass, laughing. Clay's face was red and beaded with sweat and finally he calmed down enough to ask, "What'll we do now?"

But it was Maxwell asking that, and Amos, at Chad's side, nudged him with his rifle.

The front of the house faced the river. When the white columns of the portico came into view Maxwell cried, "It's like the Parthenon! Once my father took us to a museum in Boston—"

"Shut up," said Amos, as Chad hesitated before the big front door. "What you waiting for, boy?"

He'd never been in the Wycliffe mansion, except for the kitchen in the back. When the door opened with a good shove, they walked into a large entrance hall with a high ceiling, a massive chandelier and winding stairway, and it could have been the house at Sweet Haven.

They walked from room to room, downstairs and up, and while Amos pocketed small treasures, Chad paired rooms to people. A pink and white bedroom could have been Laurel's: the large mirror above the small table could have held her image as she combed her shiny hair. And there was a room that could have been Clay's.

Everywhere he looked he saw them moving about, as much at ease as when they played hide-and-seek at the bayou. At the dining table he could see their guests: *Parties make me ache inside,* she'd said. He fancied Cecily with her pouty mouth sitting in a straight-backed chair, straightening the folds of her party dress. *I ought to tell Papa to sell him,* she says, and Clay's face wrinkles and his eyes blaze. In every room he could almost hear Laurel laugh. How he'd relished that laugh! He thought he had forgotten.

He didn't think of Anna till he walked into the kitchen, and there she was, stiff-lipped and saucy, looking out the window at him, not letting on to Cora, the cook, who sat with a friend at the table. *Miss Laurel, honey, Mis-tress Laurel.* She was nothing Laurel was, everything Laurel was not, and he didn't love her then. Even now he could not tell when his love began.

Maxwell's hand on his arm brought him back to the present: Amos stuffing his sacks, Maxwell saying, "I think we've been here long enough. There's only dress-up suits upstairs."

Amos strode over, grinning. "We'll each take a pair of good trousers and a coat to wear when we get into town. But we ought to have overalls for traveling."

They found work clothes in the big tool shed and vegetables in the cellar. Chad built a small fire in the kitchen grate, drew some water from the tall cistern, and boiled carrots and onions. Maxwell put them in cream-colored earthenware bowls on the table in the center of the room, and they sat down to eat. "This kitchen is like mine at home," Maxwell said, "except it's a whole lot bigger."

Amos was silent, his face a grumble, while they ate. Chad suspected he would not be allowed to walk away from the Yankees, but he decided to try. "I'll show you how to stay on course," he said to Maxwell. "All you have to know is the North Star. Then I'll be on my way."

"Oh, no you won't," growled Amos. "You gonna stay with us like a good boy."

"Let him go, Amos."

"How you think we're going to get up North, Maxwell, walk? Do you know how far it is? Why do you think they sent us all the way down here?"

"What's that got to do with—"

Amos pushed back his chair and stood up. He grabbed Maxwell's arm and took him to the other side of the kitchen, whispering. The blond soldier kept shaking his head, and finally Amos shouted, "It's the only way!" Maxwell sighed. "Well," he said, "I suppose you're right."

Chad walked slowly to the door and started to run. "Stop!"

Amos shouted and sent a ball whining so close to his head he stopped in his tracks. "See?" Amos snarled. "We can't trust him a-tall. Gotta tie him up." He grabbed Chad's arm.

"Here?"

"Sure. It's almost dark. We'll sleep here tonight and head out at dawn."

Maxwell looked nervous again. "Out where?"

"He'll tell us where a Rebel town is, won't you, boy?"

"All the towns down here are Rebel," Chad said.

Amos hit him across the face with the back of his hand. "Don't you lie to us. We know New Orleans is Yankee territory now. You better show us to a Rebel town or you won't live to go nowhere."

They made him lie on his face on the library floor and tied his feet together and his hands behind his back. "We'll be right over here on the rug," Amos said, "so don't you try nothing. I might as well tell you I done use a club on niggers back in New York. Hey, we must have killed more'n you could stuff this house with in three, four days' time."

Maxwell was staring at him with that funny look on his face. "When was that, Amos, when they had those draft riots?"

"You betcha it was. Ain't going to fight to free the niggers, we said. I got drafted, but you bet your boots I still feel that way."

Maxwell swallowed and his Adam's apple moved in his neck. "It isn't Chad's fault you didn't have the three hundred dollars to get you out of it."

"No? He'd be the first to want my job on the dock if he came up North."

"He'll never get up there. You just said we need money for a railroad ticket or a steamboat ride to get us anywhere near home."

"That's right. And tomorrow we'll get it when we sell him, or he won't be around to see another day."

Maxwell's sorrowful glance at Chad seemed to say he might not see another one anyway. The Yankees lay down on the rug and he could hear their muted voices. Amos seemed to be relating a story to Maxwell, who grunted in reply and now and then laughed nervously. It was fruitless for him to struggle: the rope seemed to tighten when he moved his arms or legs. After a while the soldiers stopped talking and he fell asleep.

It was pitch-dark when he woke with a hand on his arm. "Shhh," said a voice beside him, and he felt the rope part beneath the blade of a knife. "Go quiet like," whispered Maxwell.

"He'll know."

"Don't matter. He won't hurt me."

A groan from the rug made Chad's hair stand on end.

"He means what he says. You better get moving. Good luck."

"Thanks, Maxwell." He glanced around for his carpetbag before he remembered: he had a fix on the tree where he left it.

The woods were wet and deep and the night air felt soft and good, like Granny Martha's shawl thrown over him.

THIRTY-TWO

There ought to be magnolias
Somewhere in this dusk.

—LANGSTON HUGHES

June–July 1863

It was his concern for Martha that made him do it. He wanted
to be where he could keep an eye on her, watch her like a
hawk, but they had her crammed in with the other women,
and here he was with the old men, some gone blind, some so
sick they couldn't help but pee on themselves. Still, many of
them dragged out to the fields and raised corn and cotton for
the U.S. army to sell.

He got wood and nails from an old torn-down shed. Then
he up and did it, went into the women's quarters and dragged
old Martha out, the women screaming and raising such a
ruckus he thought he'd sure enough get strung up. Martha
came as fast as she was able, her steps sounding like a child's
behind him as he pulled her along. Then, of course, he had
to build a shelter for the two of them, and thank God it didn't
rain for two days till he got the roof over their heads. He had
only enough wood for three sides, but he knew where he
could get an axe to chop a tree and build the other side.

Martha sat and watched him, watched his every move, and he told her exactly what he was doing, what nail went where and why, and how the two of them would be better off alone. He spoke of more than that: he wandered back to the days when she taught him the ways of plantation life and told him tales that kept his mind alive during dark summer evenings when he yearned for home. He liked her husband, Roan, and never lusted after her, though he couldn't love another woman. These things he told her as he put the shack in order and lit a fire outside to roast a fish. He heard her sigh, but by the time he got to her, she was off somewhere again.

There was disease and folks were dying, some, he knew, from broken hearts. But it seemed to him pure pleasure alongside what happened when the Rebel guerrillas staged their raids. Then every so often the whole place was a battle-field, and Noah sat and held Martha close until it died down for the last time. Sure enough the Union guard went running, but not until he took everything he could get his thieving hands on: folks' belongings, the clothes the army sent for them and their rations, too. Nothing was coming their way now, no food, no medicine. By Joseph there was nothing now. The crops were ruined by the raids and all that was left was want. It was everywhere: in the way the people moved, in their eyes, in their shoeless feet.

But there was the river, that deep, wide, laughing river, and Noah spent a lot of time fishing.

He took Martha with him. He'd seat her on a log against a tree, clasp her hands for her and look into those hollow eyes. "I know you can see what's what, Martha," he'd say, "you ain't fooling me."

One night as he held her close to help sleep come to both of them, she took his hand and guided it under her dress. He was surprised as his hand moved over her breast and down, down until it rested on a mound of hair. His breath came short. He felt heat in his neck, his lips, and he would have bent to kiss her but he was afraid. "Martha?" he whispered. "Martha?"

She brought her face close to his. "It's time," she said. Her hand went to that soft curly thing between his legs and he felt it stretch and yawn, harden as it had when he'd given it some pulls when he was young. He kissed her and her lips were soft and warm. She tugged now at her dress and he helped her, finding the nipples on her vacant breasts. He moved close to her, then atop, resting on his elbows so not to squash her. Then in his concern it went soft, but puffed up just fine when it felt her hand. It was as though they had loved all their lives, so effortless, so grand. His wayward dreams never had a notion of the height they soared together, of the sound and motion of their flight, of the summit they reached.

"Martha?"

"Yes, Noah."

It was time for sleep.

He built the plank floor higher to protect them from the rain. He said he was glad to see so much of it: soon the green pods on the trees would ripen into nuts. But it meant slow fishing and he had to wait all day, patient as the Mississippi, until the fish bit and he hauled in their meals. Other folks fished nearby, but he allowed the old river had enough black bass and catfish to go around.

Then one day Martha, sitting close behind him, toppled off the log. When he looked back to see her she was gone and he came running to find her in the grass, her arms flaying about like a colt's new legs. He helped her up, patting her all the while, and then she smiled. She looked into his eyes and that wonderful smile spread across her face, free and easy the way it could do now. "Noah," she said, "I'm going home."

"No you ain't, not yet," he said, his voice catching, "we can't just yet. But Chad's gon come and so is Anna, the gal who liked to lay against your legs. And even Blake, that whipper-snapper who left without the boy—they's all gon come for us, and soon, real soon."

"I'm going now," she said, and closed her eyes.

He began to cry. "Don't go, don't go without me, Martha. Why, I caught the biggest catfish—"

Her eyes opened and there was light in them and a flicker of a smile. "Oh, that's nice," she said, and then she went so limp he almost let her fall.

Why she had to do it he could never tell. But he supposed there was a purpose to it: she wasn't one for giddy haste. He wished she could have waited till they were settled far away and he could give her a proper funeral.

He sat beside her all evening and would have through the night, but it began to rain and he didn't want her catching cold. He took her home and kept her until he could lay her down under the cool earth in the bright sunshine.

THIRTY-THREE

Sing, O black mother!
Song is a strong thing.

—LANGSTON HUGHES

Early July 1863

She bathed in tepid water that Sammy carried in pails from
the bayou, stretching her legs in the rough-hewn tub Uncle
Noah made, feeling her muscles curl and tighten in her
calves, grabbing them tightly and kneading, working out the
cramps. Cora had given her soap and she used it sparingly,
carefully.

Aunt Cora was a friend, even to the field hands. Before she
died she worked far into each night preparing hoecakes and
mush, anything she could lay her hands on for the workers.
Anna passed out the food and a lot of Cora's pith along with
news from the Wycliffe family and its soldier friends. Peculiar,
Cora sniffed, how the family could take to both armies without blinking an eye, just so the old man could get what he
wanted.

Since the Rebels took over, no one knew when Sweet Haven
itself might become a battlefield. A while back the greycoats

marched up both sides of the bayou and stormed Donaldson-ville in a hand-to-hand fight. They lost. Many of their troops cut through the swamp to the river to pester Yankee transports, while others made camp near Labadieville. The Yanks still held Fort Butler, but the Lafourche belonged to the Rebels.

Then one night when Anna visited the kitchen, Cora smiled that broad smile and came as close to chortling as Anna ever heard her: "News from Vicksburg ain't good, they say. Port Hudson seem to stand like a rock of ages, but Vicksburg's in trouble, slow but sure, and if it fall, Port Hudson'll lay down arms real fast. Tell the peoples out there, Anna. We ain't lost yet!"

Then Cora came down with pneumonia and, lying in a room off the back stairs to the kitchen where Anna couldn't get to her, died without a passing word. It numbed Anna. She wondered why she wasn't crying and if she'd ever cry again. Hilda was in jail and Cora was dead. Uncle Noah and Granny Martha were at the poor farm. Alcibiade off to join the army and Chad somewhere getting killed. Did any of this make sense?

Sammy put his arms around her, declaring Aunt Cora would be happy in heaven. Maybe he's right, she thought, maybe this life is just a waiting room, not a path to follow where a dream comes true. But looking at Sammy, feeling the breadth of his concern, Anna had to smile.

She stretched a leg above the water in the tub and considered it: the ankle was swollen, but it looked like a leg, looked like her leg much more than the rest of her body looked like her. She went on to Sammy, telling him how it felt to be so full of child you could hardly waddle, how she knew she didn't act quite right and certainly looked like a bloated frog, how sorry she was he had to put up with it.

All of which mattered not at all to Sammy. He loved Anna as much as he'd loved his mama, and that was a lot. He'd stuck to his mama like glue, knowing in his heart she was very, very sick and he might lose her. She'd had those sad eyes, eyes that told him that bad as it was, she couldn't do anything about it. Anna was different. Her eyes looked tired, but they never quite surrendered. She could do something about everything, almost.

He was just glad she was there to yell at him and make him go to bed at night and kiss his sores, now opening on his legs without a scratch or bump. Playing or studying with Pompée, he felt his energy run out and he had to nap there in the woods. Often Pompée didn't eat. There were no more chickens—the Rebels had long since helped themselves—and the whole countryside was bare, except for the guarded gardens. A week back Pompée disappeared for two days, returning with his pockets full of sweet potatoes and an arm grazed by a ball. After the scurry of tending to him, they had a proper feast. Anna was happy that night, even sang a song while Pompée smiled his secret smile.

But now Anna was sullen, and Sammy couldn't seem to make her laugh. He wished Chad would come and set things right again. He knew she missed Cora and Uncle Noah, too, but Chad could set things right. He thought of how she'd cried when she feared he was lost: she was his mama, and it meant he had to look out for her even if she snapped. She was tough but she was tired, and didn't need more trouble.

That's why, when he seemed to be losing all his insides and couldn't make it most times to the stinking privy, he just curled up on his bed and went to sleep, hoping it would be over before she found out.

His eyes looked like burnt holes in a blanket. He was so listless she looked away when he focused on her face: she was sure he would see the fear. Others had died of the runs, just dried up and died, and there wasn't much anyone could do once the sickness got ahold of you. Sammy's parched lips and hot skin told her to keep him bathed with cool, moist cloths and pour and pour water into him fast as it ran out. Pompée, bless him, brought the water from the Wycliff's cistern, and she would give Sammy nothing else, as a fever was tearing along the bayou and some said bad water was to blame.

She sat by the mat day and night, cleaning his bottom with the precious soap, rousing him for water, trying to make him drink. He looked at her with hollow eyes, lifting a weak hand to say *enough.* Once he asked her what heaven was like, the heaven where Cora went. She told him it might be all right for Cora, but not for little boys, not enough to do, no bayou with red-bellied blacksnake skins just molted, no fort or teacher to go with it, no hammers and nails, nothing!

His breath came short and swift, his eyes rolled back and his mouth contorted, and he began to shake. "Pompée," she cried, "water in the tub!" She took the boy and placed him in cool bayou water as he stiffened out and shook. When it was over, Sammy lay deathly still. She called sharply toward the door, "Stay with him. I'm gon get help." As she left, she heard Pompée softly singing at the bedside.

There was no Cora in the mansion's kitchen—oh, if there were, Sammy would not be so sick. She ran up the back stairs through the cook's room, down the long hall to Laurel's door and rapped on it.

"Come in," said that silky voice, and Anna went in.

Laurel was seated at her desk writing. She looked up, surprised. "Why, Anna!" She leaped to her, grabbed her hands. "What's wrong?"

They took a pile of linens down the back stairway, some molasses from the kitchen and a bowl of broth, and hurried away.

Pompée took the soiled cloths to wash, and let them alone, the two women now at Sammy's bedside. After his chore, he settled on the step, humming. The white woman made him think of *her,* whose teaching was pure, whose love was not, for she whispered about his "needs" to his enemies. He shivered and hummed at the sight of the woman called Laurel, shivered and hummed and stayed only for Sammy. Oh Lord, he prayed, don't take my only friend away.

All night they mopped Sammy's brow, made him swallow weak salt-and-sugar water as Anna knew to do, and gave him a small sip of diluted broth. Still Sammy's breath came weak and shallow, and as the night wore on, the women's eyes met less and less. Finally Anna had to sleep a while, waking as the purple dawn came through the open door. Pompée dozed on the step.

Laurel was smiling. "He's sleeping like a lamb," she said, "and I declare, I think his sheets are dry!"

Anna felt his brow and it was cool, his breath was coming in steady rhythm, and his face looked settled with dreams.

Anna cried right in front of them, and Laurel fetched tea and biscuits from old Chorly in the kitchen.

"I was sorry for you when I heard about the coming event," Laurel said as they sat at the table, "but I don't think I am, anymore. You have that boy on the cot, that—event—on the way, and a fine, loving man."

Anna blinked. Laurel was gesturing toward Pompée, still out on the step. "It's more than I have," she said. "I feel so lost, as though there will never be a life for me, never a man I can love again."

"Miss Laurel—"

"Don't stop me. It's true, sure enough. I loved Chad, truly loved him—and I guess I still do. There was talk he killed Mr. Logan before he left, but it's only talk. We know he didn't. Why, Clay and I saw him when he was on his way, and of course he wasn't armed."

Anna watched Laurel's face. "Why didn't you go with him when he ran away? Why, I spect he'd go clear to San Francisco to be somewheres with you."

"I declare, I never really thought of such a thing. Papa would have a fit. You know how they all think of me—pretty and pesky, always there to entertain company with my quick opinions that make them laugh!" She sobered as though hearing what she'd said, and Anna looked at the floor.

"Why," Laurel went on, "I wouldn't just up and leave all my—responsibilities. I have more—more—" Her face was red and she rose abruptly, stood there naked, kind of, and Anna's envy drained away.

But Sammy was calling, and they laughed and ran to feed him.

Sammy wasn't drifting anymore. The haze was gone and he could see Anna and Miss Laurel busying around, looking happy. He was still unable to raise his arm to touch Anna's face, but no matter, she was there and he could go to sleep.

"How's our fine boy?" Miss Laurel asked, and he closed his eyes, pretending not to hear. She was all right for a white woman: her hands were there with Anna's when he was so sick he couldn't talk, but he was glad when she kissed his forehead and said goodbye. Now he had Anna all to himself and he had finally made her smile.

The night after Sammy began to get well, Anna's sleep was broken by Chad's voice calling *Is that you, Anna?* She sat up straight-backed and listened, but it didn't come again. Then she heard Pompée singing (he must have been having a wandering night) and supposed she'd mistaken his song for Chad's call. She longed for Chad. The echo of his voice from the top of the levee, greeting her, aroused a strong desire. Laurel, pooh! she thought, he'd never have taken her with him, never. She didn't know what got into her, asking such a question, twisting a knife into her own heart.

She closed her eyes and saw his smile, felt his touch, his kiss, and then his arms around her, his loins placed solidly against her, his hardness finding the place to plant their child. She came, lying next to Sammy with a baby in her belly.

THIRTY-FOUR

And a new day,
Yes, a new day's
Done begun!

—LANGSTON HUGHES

May 1863

He took out his pencil and pad by the light of the full moon. Nothing could be more fetching than the Mississippi shining and swaying, letting a soft wind ripple its back, rolling its hips against the shore. Up in a tree to see but not to be seen, Chad stared at the sensuous river and longed for Anna. There, just beyond the moonlight, a portion of the water seemed deep and still, hunching in a dark space, waiting for its lover; there it reached a moonlit arm to pluck a shadow from a tree and splash the bank with laughter. He watched, entranced, sensed its tenderness, understood its strength. *Sigh and ripple in my arms,* he wrote, *sway and roll with me and we are like the river, playing in its bed.*

The morning brought a transformation. The river was calm and muddy as an old sow, and Chad was fired with a different desire. He began his march at daybreak and did not slow until the early sun commanded. This was greycoat land: camps lay in the forest, evidence of bivouacks marked the fields. He kept an eye on the foliage for Rebel scouts and pickets to avoid.

After a rest he moved swiftly, sometimes on the river side of the levee, then on a road that followed its every bend. Once in a while he crossed the road and walked in sunlit fields. Now, as he tramped through tall grass and crawling vines, he stopped, hearing a rustle just ahead. There slid a snake, and another, until he saw he had disturbed a whole city of copperheads, taking their daily snooze. He sped off in one direction, they in another: neither he nor they tarried in the field.

Cotton plantations were everywhere—dull and hot and nothing but cotton as far as the eye could see. Each had a ginhouse, and rows and rows of shacks dotted the fields. Sometimes there were longhouses, slim and grey like his old home. And sometimes everything was burned to the ground—the ginhouse, the shacks, the cotton. When he saw smoke or if the fields were newly charred, he knew the Rebels were ahead, for they left a barren country when they went.

He met the first bluecoat pickets on a plank road. They said nothing as he passed by. Here and there small bands of white Yankees marched or sat outside tents and from them he learned where he was.

Not far above a muddy filled-in trench he gazed across the river at Vicksburg, high on a bluff. To its north the smoke of battle puffed and curled and seemed not to ruffle the fortress at all.

He kept going, his eyes across the river, his feet on the levee. He'd come to Young's Point, occupied by convalescent soldiers who roamed and yawned and fished. army detachments guarding the camp let him pass through. Across the water, the mouth of the Yazoo River opened into the Mississippi. It was a main supply line for General Grant's army north of the city, a soldier told him, and now Chad saw two transports flanked by gunboats ply down the mighty river and up the Yazoo, where they were swallowed by fog.

Along the shoreline where Chad stood, mules and wagons

waited for transportation across the river to the Yazoo's gaping mouth. He kept on walking. Scattered tents dotted the land, filled with weary, ailing veterans, who hardly noticed him. The road junctioned with another going inland, and he chose to stay near the river. Now he passed a small town and its wharf called Duckport Landing, where he stopped to gaze into a huge, partly filled-in trench similar to the other one he'd seen. An old black man standing nearby said it was one of General Grant's canals. "It was sposed to stretch from here to Walnut Bayou, but the river all of a sudden shifted and dropped so much they had to stop digging. A couple of barges and dredges were plumb stuck. Don't reckon they'll worry much with it now."

"I saw another one, I think," said Chad.

"Yep. The river flooded and stopped that one dead."

Why canals, he thought, what was happening here? Then he remembered: *a siege is such a quiet thing,* Uncle Blake had said, *moving like the mole until it explodes.*

After a while a densely wooded area alongside the road called him to rest. He was attentive to its quiet, trapped in the heat, waiting for a breeze to give it release. He, too, felt hogtied and heavy. He sat beneath a tree, took a gulp from his canteen, then closed his eyes. He was awakened by the shouts of a drillmaster.

He came through the woods to an open field, where a regiment of black soldiers moved in columns, following commands. Beyond them he could see a camp nestled between two levees, one at the river's edge, the other farther inland, forming a natural breastwork. Above flew the Stars and Stripes, and his heart thumped wildly as he stared.

A black sergeant strode over. "You come to join up?"

Chad nodded.

"Come with me."

Widely spaced rows of hedges stretched inland from the encampment. The one directly in front of the forward levee stood some fifteen feet high. The sergeant was staring at him, grinning. "They're Osage orange hedges, courtesy of some

Rebel planter. Nice and thick. Thorny, too. Where you from?"

"The delta."

"The delta? Gawd, how'd you get up here?"

"Walked, mostly."

"Mostly walked?"

"Since the war started I've been thinking of chopping the South in two. They say Vicksburg is the place for that."

The sergeant grinned and slapped him on the back. "Why, I'd say you come to the right place, no ifs or ands about it. If this here post was in Rebel hands, steamers would have a real hard time getting to General Grant over there."

"I'm sure glad you're recruiting."

"Sure enough are. You're just in time. Before this day's out you'll get sworn in good and proper to the Ninth Louisiana Volunteers of African Descent. How'd you take to that?"

"Real fine."

"What's your name, son?"

"Chad Creel."

"I'm Sergeant Wilkins. Welcome, Private Creel," he said, "to Milliken's Bend."

Thirty-five

Hurling against it masses of men, no matter how gallant, was
not a good answer.

—BENJAMIN QUARLES, HISTORIAN, CONCERNING THE ATTACK
ON PORT HUDSON, *THE NEGRO IN THE CIVIL WAR,* 1953

May – June 1863

Blake sat in the top of one of the splendid magnolia trees that
forested the area of Port Hudson, rising from a bluff above
the bank of the Mississippi. The town—a church, a few
houses, and several encampments of tents and shanties—was
on the far left across a rugged valley. With his field glass he
scanned the Rebel stronghold from the south: the large fort
directly ahead; a redoubt of six pieces of artillery on its right;
a company of riflemen and six field guns on the left, ready to
blast the plain before it, covering all approaches. There was
a fifteen-foot ditch full of river backwater at the foot of the
fort's parapet, and sharpshooter rifle pits and artillery circled
the top. The earthwork fell sharply into the plain, here and
there choked with felled trees, and interrupted by gullies and
ravines. He again trained the glass on the foot of the fort:
partially encircling the parapet just before the ditch was an

abatis, an area of felled trees, their branches sharpened and directed outward.

His conclusion was immediate and unshakable: General William Dwight's hasty strategy—he'd been given the command of the black regiments that morning of May 27—might seem sound on paper, but in execution, it would be a massacre. He could find no saving element, not one offsetting factor.

Blake knew the main body of infantrymen at the center and the left wing were awaiting orders, as well as regiments of the First and Third Native Guard, numbering one thousand eighty, on the extreme right. It was to be a simultaneous assault, the black soldiers the spearhead of a diversionary attack on the left side of the Rebel fort, drawing attention from the main advance. Bombardment of the fort by the Union vessels in the river would precede the onslaught.

He returned to field headquarters with his report: the terrain where Dwight would send his troops was an open ground, covered from all directions by Rebel sharpshooters and heavy artillery. In the tent, he gave his report slowly, fully, and with weight, knowing as he talked that the decision had been made and would not be altered. *My information is vital,* he began, and when he finished, they thanked him and dismissed him. The naval assault, he heard them say, is set for seven, the infantry attack for ten.

He had been reporting to generals for over a year now. He'd watched Banks put a halt to black enlistment until pressure came from Washington (some said Vice President Hannibal Hamlin had prodded Lincoln because of a troop shortage), and he'd met General Daniel Ullmann, a rather mild-mannered fellow sent by the War Department to speed up recruitment. Ullmann had wanted black officers for black men. But Banks shrank Ullmann's growing influence by at last enlisting slaves and renaming the phalanx of three brigades the Corps d'Afrique. Blake was there through all this and most of the time his advice was heeded; when it was occasionally ignored, he was not dismayed. But today he felt despair.

Outside headquarters, he saluted Colonel John A. Nelson of the Native Guard, the man who petitioned Banks a month or so ago to let his black infantry lead the assault on Port Hudson. The request was denied. It was not until a few days ago that the Native Guard regiments were ordered to proceed from Baton Rouge to Port Hudson, and they marched north full of good cheer, given their chance to fight. Anyone with a mite of blackness in him was supposed to rejoice. A slow ache settled into Blake's belly.

A hand fell on his shoulder and a familiar voice said, "Blake, is it really you?" Captain André Cailloux of Company E, First Native Guard, embraced him. "Ah, *mon ami*, what brings you here?"

"I am always the unfortunate scout."

Cailloux gave a merry laugh. "I should have remembered. You are a natural. There is no time to talk now, but tonight we shall sit by the fire. I must say your reconnaissance has put us in good stead. We're getting our chance today, and I feel a burden lifting from my shoulders. At last I am fighting the slavery of my people. Ah, one day in New Orleans we'll celebrate this day! I shall see you later, *mon cher* Blake."

Blake looked into his friend's clear, deep eyes and could not speak.

At ten the first black soldiers formed for attack in full view of the bluff, and the Rebels opened fire.

"The two Union guns were forced to withdraw right off," Blake heard someone say. "There's no cover now." He'd been sitting on a hummock of earth trying not to think. The simultaneous attack had not been carried out by General Banks: it was put off till the afternoon.

The wounded were struggling back and a soldier standing in reserve said, "The musketry and cannonading are bad, aren't they?" in a voice you'd use to comment on the weather. "Where are you from?" Blake asked.

"New Orleans." The soldier's line moved out into the rain of grape and canister, buck and ball. The deadly direct fire was instantly joined by an enfilading cross fire, and the soldiers reeled and fell back.

Blake expected an order to retreat, but General Dwight gave an aide an alarming message: "Tell Colonel Nelson that I shall consider that he has accomplished nothing unless he takes those guns."

Blake broke into a sweat. He climbed a knoll and turned his eyes toward the plain. He was not out there but he was part of it. It wasn't clear to him how the horrors of the battle were conveyed to him in sudden rushes, and how the men who stumbled in the shellfire, dying in a noisy, smoky haze, could be vivid in his eyes and ears and like hot blades in his gut. There was not a volley from the rifles or a mortar shell that didn't find its mark in Blake. A hot, stinging energy flowed through his veins and changed only in intensity as the attack wore on. The second, the third, the fourth—oh, holy God, the seventh time his brothers were sent into the open field, his blood ran so hot it burned through his skin, leaving welts.

A group of youths tried to ford the water in the ditch at the foot of the parapet and were killed by sharpshooters at close range, falling one by one. The color-bearer's head was lifted from his shoulders by a cannonball and the scuffle for the flag cost half a dozen lives.

These were noble deeds, he knew, as those who conjure war would have it, but his feeling was revulsion. Ravaged bodies lay moaning. He stared into the blue-red flame of that night's campfire and saw only blood. It was three-thirty in the morning before the general called off the attack.

"Captain Cailloux?" he asked a survivor of Company E. "Where is he?"

The soldier, his hand on a bloody ear, shook his head. "He had a shattered arm but he stayed with us, kept walking the line, saying 'Steady.' We almost reached the ditch—" He began to cry.

"Don't say. I don't have to know."

The soldier sniffed and his chin went up. "The last thing he said was 'Follow me.' "

Blake embraced the soldier, now sobbing openly, and then he turned away.

Reports of casualties among the whites poured in. One colonel who had refused an order to lead his weary men over the crest again, had sent back a challenge: "If you want them led into that slaughter pen, do it yourself."

The days that followed brought official praise for the black regiment. Blake was unmoved. As though the acrid seal of heroism was not enough, absurd tales flashed through Union camps. Whites said the blacks fought with the desperation of tigers, on crutches some, and with reckless zeal. They said the black soldiers threw away their guns, used their bayonets, then tore the Rebel's flesh with their teeth.

A private shook his head. "If there's a way to rob us of our manhood, they'll sure enough find it. Why can't they say we're men—ordinary men who didn't flinch?"

Blake shared the anger. But he was beginning to know a wider wrong, for he saw the useless loss touch all but the planners, and the stigma of flinching under fire seemed to him the planners' ploy. "It's all a game," he said, "and the players lose, white or black. Guess it's best to keep them at each other so they don't see."

The private scratched his chin.

The bluecoats lying like straw dolls in the field could not be removed: the Rebels would allow no armistice for collecting black bodies. Blake asked if he could go after the remains of André Cailloux by night and was refused: the captain was too near the parapet. Blake ground his fingernails into his hands and his thoughts flew to André's mother, André's smile.

The long siege of Port Hudson began. The Native Guard was ordered to join the black First Regiment of Louisiana Engineers that had placed poles across trenches around Rebel lines, and was now digging trenches of its own toward the Confederate breastworks. Four or five men a day were lost to sharpshooters and far more to sickness and the sun. Blake heard that General Ullmann complained that his troops were working twenty hours a day on the trenches. But Ullmann's earlier protest that his men were dying in the swamps went unheeded, so what could he expect now?

Just as the order was given for white infantrymen to stock their cartridge boxes for a night attack on June 10, Blake was sent to New Orleans. He was glad to leave: this was not the holy business he had fancied. All he saw, all he heard and witnessed, told him that those who died were sacrificed to a barbarity as remote as a general's smile.

THIRTY-SIX

I used to wonder
About here and there—
I think the distance
Is nowhere.

—LANGSTON HUGHES

June 1863

In the large, comfortable room at the St. Charles Hotel, Blake sat with General Emory, in command of New Orleans now that General Banks was absent. There were lines of apprehension around the general's mouth. "If Taylor knows how defenseless we are, God help us! Why, I've been marching my men out of the city by night and in by morning, feigning reinforcements."

An aide remarked: "Maybe Taylor is satisfied with capturing the Lafourche and parts of the Teche while our forces are busy at Port Hudson. Maybe he won't risk losing them to attack the city."

"Perhaps," said Emory. "But I've mustered in two regiments of sixty-day volunteers from the residents. I called both whites and blacks, but only the blacks responded enough to

form any regiments. They're stationed on our perimeter."
Now he looked at Blake. "I'd like you to see all the outlying
locations."

"Yes, sir."

"You know how we feel about you, Blake. If you say our
defenses are adequate, I'll be satisfied."

"Thank you, sir."

He left the hotel, passed the flanking cannons, and went
directly to the *carré de la ville.* Jasmine sweetened the air as he
stood on the narrow pavement outside the house of Madame
Cailloux. He used the brass knocker, and when the door
opened, she stood there, tall and unwavering.

She embraced him.

"It was André's wish," she said in the courtyard, in the
patterned sun and shade. "He believed in the Union army."

"Do you?"

She shook her head. "I believe in nothing."

"Yes," he said, "that is something easy to believe in."

She looked older. She said, "Have you heard about Fort
Jackson? The soldiers have staged a mutiny, killing twenty
officers and disabling three gunboats."

He stared in surprise.

"It lasted, they say, a day or two. I've no doubt it was
justified." She laughed bitterly. "Now: what did André say to
you before he went to battle?"

"He said he was at last fighting the slavery of his people."

"He was a romantic and a fool."

"Madame Cailloux," he said softly, "André didn't mean to
die."

"But there he lies." She stifled a sob. "I want you to be
more prudent."

He sipped a cup of steaming black coffee in a corner of the
café and listened to talk about Fort Jackson. A group of loud
whites were commenting on the mutiny. One man said there
was a massacre of officers at the fort. Another spoke, as had

Madame Cailloux, of disabled gunboats. The story seemed to vary with the speaker, but they agreed to a man that it was proof of what they'd always known: blacks needed to be controlled. It did not surprise him.

Thirty-Seven

Wind
In the cotton fields,
Gentle breeze:
Beware the hour
It uproots trees!

—LANGSTON HUGHES

June 1863

The stench of rotting vegetation under green slime clung to Alcibiade's nostrils as he lifted his knife to the tangled underbrush. The hatchet was less suited to clearing his way through the swamp outside Fort Jackson. He muttered under his breath a remnant of a prayer his mother had taught him, one he now suspected was her own, asking his ancestors that he be allowed to survive the day. Her words of comfort still lay in his mind: "Never despair, for they are with you in the dark."

His mother was a devout woman. She brought him up under the vodun religion, practicing its ancient rituals. But as he grew, he saw the secrecy with which they held their ceremonies and how guarded was his mother's talk of the doctrines the white man called voodoo. He asked why. Her explanation was brief: "They fear what they do not understand."

Still, her wide knowledge of roots and herbs, carried from Africa and applied to the New World, was recognized on the plantation where Alcibiade was born. She had learned early not to combine her medicines with their corresponding rites: she had the scars of that mistake like the stripes of the zebra on her back.

Long ago, as he lay deathly ill in the cabin the master had provided for his slave mistress and his son, Alcibiade heard his mother speak in her native tongue the healing chants of his fathers. Their music stayed with him like a faraway song in his ears.

He had been favored on his father's plantation, taught to read and write French and English, and how to build a sugar-house with bricks and mortar. This, his mother often said, would never happen to the bastard son of a woman of the fields, only to the son of a princess. Then she would throw back her head and laugh and he would join in, not caring why he was laughing, only that he was laughing with her. He knew she never ceased to grieve for Africa.

His head throbbed. He had to stop a moment in the steaming swamp to get his bearings. The first tree he would chop down was just ahead, but it seemed distant and shrouded. Oh, holy fathers, he whispered, if I had known what was to come, I would not have joined the army.

The black recruiter had come across Confederate lines to fill a brigade for General Banks. When a black man said the deal was fair, you didn't question. He promised the same treatment as white soldiers got, the same training and opportunity to fight. Alcibiade left with him.

He had to leave. He couldn't have stayed. With the return of the Confederates came a paralyzing fear, an uncertainty he could not abide, feelings he couldn't jest away. He had hesitated because of Anna, waiting for a man called Chad, the father of her unborn child. But when he went to tell her he was going, she tossed her head and said if she were a man she would go, too. He had never known a woman like Anna.

His limbs were hurting now, hurting and burning, yet numb. His swollen feet throbbed against his sodden shoes.

He stopped to wipe his brow and nod to the soldier nearby. "I'll take the tree ahead," he said hoarsely, "and it will fall this way."

The soldier moved aside, and at that instant Alcibiade reeled and fell. Two men came running, wading knee-deep to lift him and carry him back to the fort.

It is too much for him, he heard one of them say, *after what he's been through. It's bad enough when you're fit,* said the other, *but he hasn't had time to recover. Damn that white-assed Benedict,* the first spit out, *something's got to be done.*

Much of it was blurred in Alcibiade's memory. That ear of corn a fellow soldier gave him looked so good in its moistened husk, getting juicy and hot in the fire. But when he pulled it out Colonel Benedict knocked it from his hand, ordered him dragged to the open ground. Under the blistering sun he was staked down. "You pilfering nigger," Benedict shouted as the aides pulled off his shoes and stockings and spread his legs apart. They took off his shirt and roped his wrists, staked his arms to the dusty ground. His mind flew to fragments of the chants that counter evil as they brought molasses in a vat and commenced to smear. They smeared until his face, chest, arms, his hands and feet were thickly covered.

The ants swarmed and feasted, crawled up his trouser legs, gathered on his cheeks, his nose, walked over his eyelids. He longed to tear the hot, sweet blanket off, to free his flesh from the itching, stinging weight, to open his eyes shut against the ants. Venom and the sun made him retch. At nightfall a pitying soldier freed him to a night of frenzied dreams, but the next morning he was again staked down.

While it was going on and even when it was over he prayed he would die. One of his buddies spread a balm over his sores and as it drew out the swelling and the heat, his mind slowly calmed and cleared. He slept through a day and a night and then returned to the swamp to hew down the cypress.

Now as the muttering soldiers laid him on his cot, his flesh was a blanket of pain. He stared at their faces, unable to convey his gratitude. All night he moaned, and in the morning no officer came to rout him from his bed. When Company

B, Fourth Infantry, Corps d'Afrique, went out to the parade grounds, Alcibiade felt peaceful at last.

He thought of Lieutenant Colonel Lewis Benedict, how complaints to other officers were ignored. Regiment Commander Colonel Drew said Benedict was efficient. So the man went on punching and kicking the soldiers in his command. The private whose brasses were not shined to a glassy finish lay in the infirmary, his face a bloody mess from the blow he was dealt by the colonel's sword. The army had outlawed the whip, but that didn't stop Benedict. Not long ago a soldier was tied up by his thumbs and given a rawhiding for the less-than-perfect polish on his boots.

Now, as he rested, to his ears came the familiar shouts of the drill sergeant. But when the air was suddenly pierced by a pitiful wail, his eyes opened and his teeth clenched. Again through his head went rhythms of his lost religion, the ancient prayers against evil he thought he had forgotten.

The soldiers returned to the barracks. They swore they'd had enough: "We'll fix the white devils," they said, and explained that Harry Williams, the drummerboy, was horsewhipped by Colonel Benedict for failing to carry out an order in the yard.

"He made the young'n take off his coat," a soldier said, "and he took a driver's whip from the artillery and give him twenty lashes right in front of the whole regiment, officers and all."

"And not one white-livered sonofabitch raised his voice to stop him," growled another.

"He didn't get as much as a sharp word from the brass," still another said.

That evening Alcibiade got up on an elbow and watched the men tramp out to the parade grounds, where they commenced firing their rifles in the air over and over, creating a charivari the likes of which he knew he'd never hear again. There must have been two hundred and fifty of them, about half the regiment. They stood there together, demanded that Colonel Benedict be handed over for punishment, said they would never give up their arms. He saw a small group leave to search for Benedict and come back without him. Aflame with passion, he took his rifle and joined the crowd in the yard.

Within an hour the leaders called the demonstration to a halt and the soldiers returned to their barracks. Alcibiade felt pure delight: *Il est temps, ma mère,* he said under his breath: this is the Union army, not the plantation, and the command will listen now.

In the morning Alcibiade returned to duty. White soldiers were everywhere. The fort was crowded with them. General Banks had sent a regiment of infantry, a battery of artillery, and several gunboats to quell Fort Jackson's "mutiny."

THIRTY-EIGHT

Go out in any direction and you meet negroes . . . every one
pleading to be taught, willing to do anything for learning.
They are never out of our rooms, and their cry is for 'Books!
Books!' and 'when will school begin?' . . . Every night hymns to
God and prayers for the Government that oppressed them so
long, rise around us on every side—prayers for the white
teachers that have already come—prayers that God would send
them more.

—PRESBYTERIAN MISSIONARY IN LOUISIANA,
THE LIBERATOR, JANUARY 1864

June 1863

The letter to Chad lay on the table, unfinished. As Jerry
Labarre gained strength and his recent days of teaching
inched forward in his mind, vivid and compelling, he added
to it.

I am sick to death of teaching, he wrote, then put down his
pen. No, that was not true. He marked that out and wrote:
*I taught for a spell, and it was good fun, but not my favorite
occupation.* He left it at that. How could he tell Chad the whole
truth, that he would not teach now if he could, not because
of his inclinations: it was rather a matter of his heart. He had

never seen such sights. Packed into the camps like swarming bees, squeezed into leaky, slipshod huts, the "contrabands" faced each day with hope. Children splashed in foul-smelling swampland; mothers were ready with cleansing cloths, warning words. People were carried off in bags—the cough, they said, or the runs, or the fever with the blood-red stools—and they looked away, chins up—whoopee!—when they saw the books. Yes, books he carried brought a congregation, and his every word was greeted with a hush. The laughing children reached up to him, red puffs of gums below their flashing eyes. Haggard parents reached out to him, humming little tunes as they learned with their "chillun." Jerry was a teacher, akin to God. "Thank you, massa," and he was humbled. "One more lesson?" and he couldn't stop. He was sure if he stayed too long he'd lose his sense, for even now he wanted to wrap them all in cheesecloth to preserve them, even now he thought: if I could take them home! Where to begin and where end? He was amazed, and he could not sleep. He found it hard to eat. Their rations, he knew, were two-thirds the size of his, a ruling for the spoils of war. There must be a way, he thought, to teach them retroactively: where did the lost time go?

They sent him, heartsick, from contraband camp to army outpost, finally to the sinkhole of Camp Kenyon, downriver from New Orleans.

There the levee was used as a burial ground for soldiers who died of putrid sore throat. In these suffocating swamps where the men chopped trees and cleared the brush, he learned a lesson: blacks donned dignity with their uniforms, and pride. They reminded him of Chad.

He shared teaching chores with an officer in each regiment, but the hours for learning were short and labor in the torrid heat long. There were no black commissioned officers: any who were left from the Native Guard had been harassed out of the service, they told him. But the men here had other immediate concerns. They worried about their families in camps or on plantations, and they were seeking ways to contact them. A few were able to write letters. All were ready to learn, for most had to rely on the mercies of their officers to hear the fate of wives and children. Some ran away to find out for themselves.

But Jerry's teaching was also full of sweet memories, and these he recounted to Chad. *The few who spoke only French were delighted with me,* he wrote. *They said, "Lisez-moi cela" and piled letters and newspapers and even books on my lap. One big fellow who looked more like a pirate than a slave—he wore a black patch over one eye—spoke such impeccable French, I was self-conscious of my own. Then one day he embraced me and said, "You good fellow, no? Good-leetle-fellow!" Ah, Chad—small pleasures! These you must hoard as bees hoard nectar.*

He didn't write down the dreadful days—the days at Camp Kenyon when he'd caught a fever and lay on a damp cot in a lean-to, his head burning, his guts drying out. In his delirium, he floated down the river in a fast skiff, heading for the Gulf of Mexico and the hurricane that had taken L'Île Dernière. *Quelle heure est-il?* he kept asking, until one day he heard a private say, "It's noon." Soon he wobbled to his feet, ready to leave that place.

He went home to New Orleans, a city on the edge of fear. The siege of Port Hudson had left only a small Union force, and the streets buzzed with talk about a possible invasion. Many whites, weighted by the Union's yoke, relished the thought. Though fighting in the town would be a horror, he heard them say, they'd welcome it if it would bring a Confederate victory.

Jerry stood on the sidewalk and read the posted notice: the Union army was recruiting sixty-day volunteers for home defense, two white regiments and two black. All volunteers would receive the standard wage of thirteen dollars a month. He read the notice again, wondering how serious the Rebel threat. Chad is right, he told himself, we both know which side is against us—at least the one that can be faced on a battlefield.

But he was weak from his illness and went home to rest. At

his table he wrote letters to Paul Trevigne and André Cailloux. He told Paul he hoped they could soon meet over good wine and a hot meal at the Café du Faubourg or the Universal Republic cabaret.

Not knowing where the First Native Guard might be, he sent Cailloux's letter to his home in New Orleans. *How proud your father would be,* he wrote. *You are among the few surviving black officers.* He went on a bit, perhaps too long, then wrote that as one grows older, one is commissioned to look back. He asked André for a day after his discharge to devote to reminiscence and fresh news.

Chad's letter was the last one and the hard one to complete. He waited until he was stronger and full of resolve. *I think, Chad,* he wrote at last, *the moment calls for me not to confuse our adversaries, and fight the one I can. I think I will do what I advised you against: for what if you should come this way and find New Orleans gone? I hope you will be proud of me.*

He signed the letter, and having no address, laid it back on the table. Perhaps, later, he would add a smile—yes, perhaps a smile.

When the recruitment office opened for business that day, he enlisted in the Union army as a sixty-day volunteer to guard the fair city of New Orleans.

THIRTY-NINE

The niggers are the backbone of the rebellion. They [the Rebels] can put twice as many men in the field, for having niggers to cultivate the crops. What's the use to have men from Maine, Vermont and Massachusetts dying down here in these swamps, where you have to put stones on the coffin to sink it—you can't replace these men, but if a nigger dies, all you have to do is send out and get another one.

—P. E. HOLCOME, A NEW ENGLAND OFFICER,
U.S. ARMY, TO HIS FAMILY, 1863

June—July 1863

Blake's tour of the city's defenses began with Fort Jackson. The eyes of the men shot through or past him as he walked. He'd heard that the soldiers had welcomed the three-man commission Banks appointed to investigate the mutiny, expecting a chance to set the record straight. Colonel Benedict had been relieved of duty, but the fort was taut as a lynching rope. When he met Colonel Drew he could understand why.

Drew finished reading the commission's report, forwarded to him by Banks, and motioned Blake to a chair. "Nigger-lovers," he muttered, and then he smiled a secret smile. "Between you and me and the gatepost, I'd just as soon see the lot of them thrown back into slavery."

Blake held his tongue. It was not easy to do without biting it.

By a campfire at the northern edge of the city, Blake sat with a group of black sixty-day volunteers. Some were playing euchre. Others were deep in discussion, smoke curling from their pipes.

A lively old man named Jerry Labarre said he thought there would be a court-martial as a result of the Fort Jackson mutiny, despite the virtual pardon given by the commission's report.

"Benedict will be court-martialed?" asked a young man.

Labarre's eyes met Blake's. "No. The leaders of the protest will go on trial."

Most of the men nodded.

Labarre went on: "My newspaper friend says Banks told the War Department that Benedict's punishments were cruel and unusual and likely to bring about such results."

The young soldier frowned. "Why will he court-martial the mutineers, then?"

"It is an open question."

Blake spoke up: "The War Department could be looking to make examples of the ones who led the demonstration. And Banks would like to please them."

"Politics!" Labarre threw up his hands, and the light that danced in his eyes became a flame. "General Banks and Washington both know that built into the Corps are incompetent, self-serving officers who don't give a tinker's damn for the men in their command. Banks said as much himself."

Blake nodded.

Silence followed. The men, mostly educated *gens de couleur* and formerly well-to-do, must have known Labarre, or at least they knew his kind. They waited with Blake for him to go on, and he did: "I saw soldiers die of malaria and typhoid for no

better reason than to keep them out of the white man's hair."
He smiled. "Despite everything, we say, don't we, wait until
the black man gets his chance on the battlefield."

"Port Hudson," said Blake, softly.

"Ah, yes, of course. And over in Carolina the Massachusetts
Fifty-fourth stormed Fort Wagner. All over the country are
examples. Plain as day. I suppose the North will finally learn
the lesson."

"Or shall we?" asked Blake.

Labarre laughed and his thin frame shook. "*Touché!* Perhaps there is hope for us yet."

Later in the evening Labarre came to Blake's tent. "Were
you at Port Hudson at the time of the battle?" he asked.

"Yes."

"I thought so, from your tone of voice. I know there were
many men and this is a foolish question, but did you happen
to meet Captain André Cailloux?"

Blake felt his breath catch. "Yes, he—he was a friend of
mine."

"Was?" Labarre paled, and Blake put a hand on his arm.
"I'm sorry," he said.

"I was not in town or I would have known. Tell me, are you
from New Orleans?"

"No, I come from a plantation on the Lafourche. I met
André after I escaped."

"What did you say your name was?"

"I don't think I said. I'm Blake Durand." He extended his
hand.

"Jerry Labarre—Jerry, if you please. I have another preposterous question: do you know Chad Creel?"

"I'll be switched! He's my best friend in the world!"

"And—you are going to meet him at Sweet Haven after the
fall of Vicksburg?"

"You can lay your life on it. How do you know all this?
When did you meet Chad?"

"The bugle is playing taps and I am very, very tired, my
friend. I'll leave the telling to Chad."

Seeing in Jerry's face the fatigue he spoke of, Blake walked him back to his tent.

Blake headed northeast. General Emory wanted detailed information about troop movements deep within Confederate territory. It was a reasonable assignment, Blake thought: the border of an army is often the last to start to move. Dressed as a disabled refugee, he hitched a ride upriver to Donaldsonville, where a Union regiment was holed up in Fort Butler, leaving the Lafourche to the Rebels while the major Yankee concentration was at Port Hudson. Moving south, Blake begged from Rebel soldiers, served officers as messenger when he could. Tattered and dirty, he sat in their camps and heard their yarns, until he was certain they had no plans to invade New Orleans.

Before he caught a Union boat back, he went down the bayou to Sweet Haven. He ran much of the way, hoping to see Uncle Noah and get more word of Chad. But he saw no one he knew, and the field hands only nodded as he walked the path in the gathering night. Finally someone opened the door of a shack and looked curiously out at him.

"I'm Blake Durand," he said. "I was a field hand here."

The door opened wide and the woman beckoned him in. "I'm Anna Mead. Close the door. A new body isn't safe here."

He tried to place her face.

"You don't remember me, I know," she said. "I was Laurel's shadow, I do declare." She laughed and caught her belly with her hands.

"Oh, yes," he said, lying.

"I don't remember you, either." She smiled and looked him in the eye. "I'm Chad's woman. To be married someday."

"He's a lucky man. Where is he? Have you heard from him?"

"No, I don't know where he is. The last I knew, he was parading around in an army uniform in New Orleans. He was leaving to fight."

"How long ago was that, Anna?"

"Before he knew I was growing a baby."

"Then he doesn't know."

"That's right. But Uncle Noah, up at the poor farm at White Castle with Granny Martha, he knows, and Chad will find out when he gets here."

"He knows you're here, then. You said you saw him in New Orleans."

"No. I saw him there all right, but he don't know I'm here." She raised her head and put a hand on the back of her neck. "He'll be along. He told me you made a pact to meet here."

"Yes." He looked into her sober face and saw a question. "I'll be here," he said.

Her face crumbled and she looked like a child herself. How is it children beget children, he thought, and in such dreadful times? He took her hand.

"I hope he's not hurt somewhere," she said.

He touched her shoulder and she moved away a mite, enough for him to know she didn't want sympathy.

FORTY

I have the honor to report that, in accordance with instructions received from me, Colonel Lieb, commanding the Ninth Louisiana, African descent, made a reconnaissance in the direction of Richmond on June 6, starting from Milliken's Bend at 2 A.M. . . .

—BRIGADIER GENERAL, ELIAS S. DENNIS, COMMANDING
DISTRICT NORTHEAST LOUISIANA, YOUNG'S
POINT, LOUISIANA, JUNE 12, 1863

May–June, 1863

It was a busy day for the recruiters at Milliken's Bend, that May 22. Chad was sworn into the Ninth Louisiana Volunteers of African Descent, some men were assigned to the Eleventh, and the First Mississippi was formed. They said altogether they must have twelve hundred men, most of them raw recruits, all of them former slaves from the states of Louisiana and Mississippi.

Chad's excitement raced through him. The spirit here was so high you could fly in it.

Of all the white commissioned officers, he liked young Captain Matthew Miller of Company 1 the best. He always had a smile with his salute, and he'd stop to talk with you on the grounds. Lieutenant Colonel Cyrus Sears was kind of stiff but fair, and the commander of the Ninth, Colonel Herman Lieb, was respected. The commander of the District of Northeast Louisiana was a brigadier general by the name of Elias S. Dennis, but Chad never expected to lay eyes on him. That's the way of army brass, said Sergeant Wilkins. You know they're there only because they keep thinking up things for you to do.

The men were issued their gear during the next week, and Chad didn't care how hot it was, he liked marching in a column out on the field, showing the greenhorns how well he followed the drill sergeant. Tad Woods, a new recruit too, marveled at his skill. "Where'd you learn to do that?" he asked, squinting his eyes. "Did the massa have you shouldering arms?" He laughed heartily.

Chad was putting his rubber blanket down in the tent, for the wind was howling and the rain would soon begin. "To tell the truth, I did some fancy drilling with the Native Guard down in New Orleans. We marched to the fife and drum." Embarrassed by his boasting, he added, "We went to guard the railroad and got shot at by Yankees."

Tad nodded solemnly. "They say that can happen. You know the Illinois cavalry they talks about?"

"What about them?"

"They's camped clear out yonder. They won't have nothing to do with us."

"Ain't that too bad!"

They laughed and began to tussle the way he used to with Clay, but another soldier said to stop because the rain would get in. "It'll get in anyway," said Chad, sitting on his blanket that would be floating by morning, the way the rain was soaking the ground. Nothing, he knew, could wet his spirits down.

Tad sat beside him, squinting his eyes. "Do you think we gon march out and take a fort?"

"I don't know. Maybe."

"Where you think?" Tad was younger than Chad, not more than fourteen or fifteen, by his gangly limbs and his wide-open face.

"How about high and mighty Vicksburg?"

Tad grinned. "Yeah, see how far it falls. You know, my mama, she don't understand. She say let the Yankees do it, it their war, but Aunt Lilly know I got to go. She say, he going out there to fight for our freedom with them wonderful Yanks! Then my mama sob and hug me and what a time I has!"

"Where you from?"

"The other side of Richmond, not too far from here."

"Cotton plantation?"

Tad nodded. "I got cotton coming out my ears since I is able to walk." He squinted again, and Chad knew a question was coming. "How long you think this war gon last?"

"I don't know." The rain was gathering in little pools at their feet, the water seeming to come up from the ground as it did on the delta, and Chad sighed. "I thought the weather up here would be cool and dry."

"Who you kidding?" said Tad with a hee-haw. He sounded just like a mule. "But it ain't been so rainy that the river's real high this spring."

"No big snows up north in winter keeps the river low."

"How come?"

Chad sat there another hour talking to Tad, telling him things he didn't know, one after another. If he hadn't remembered how patient Uncle Blake had been with his own questions, he might have sent Tad packing. When lights-out came, he was ready for it, soggy bed and all. The rain had stopped, and the water had soaked into the ground so fast he could've thought he was dreaming that it ran like a river just a little while before.

On June 3, Brigadier General Henry McCulloch and his Rebel soldiers took Richmond, ten miles to the southwest, and rumors began to fly. Tad squinted all the time, a perpetual question on his lips, and Chad just listened. Some wondered if they'd go and take the town back, but others shook their heads and said the Rebel forces were many times their own. The only thing for sure was their drilling from morning to night, and their trying to learn to shoot those old rusty muskets as fast as they could.

Chad was sound asleep when Tad shook him. "Hurry, get up, we is moving," he said.

"Who says?"

"Captain Miller."

"You're dreaming," said Chad. "It's still dark."

"Git up there," yelled Sergeant Wilkins, sticking his head in the tent. "Orders from Colonel Lieb."

They formed a line on the field, had roll call, and then Colonel Lieb came before them on his horse. Riding down the line, he said the Ninth was ordered to make a reconnaissance toward Richmond. No encounter with the enemy was expected or sought, but each man must be ready for battle should the occasion arise. It was two A.M., he said, the best time for such a mission, and he urged that they march in silence. As the two hundred and eighty-five men of the Ninth pulled out, the only sound besides feet against earth was the clinking of canteens against bayonets.

They hadn't marched far when they overtook a company or two of cavalry they supposed was the Tenth Illinois that was camped a few miles out. Colonel Lieb halted his regiment while he talked with the cavalry commander, who then took his horsemen off in another direction.

"I'd just as soon they didn't tag along with us," said the soldier on Chad's left. "I hear tell they don't shoot straight."

Just as Chad saw a railroad depot's outline against the dark sky, Rebel pickets began to fire.

Instantly, Captain Miller shouted: "Halt! Dress the line! Commence firing!"

Chad aimed his rifle at the shadows ahead and fired, standing in a line of men doing the same thing. They advanced a dozen paces, stopped, and gave another volley. Chad performed mechanically, aware only of his own gun's smoke and the Rebel smoke dying down ahead as the Ninth advanced. But before they reached the depot they were ordered to turn around and march back the way they'd come.

About halfway to the Bend, the Illinois horsemen came thundering up to their rear.

"Jesus," said the soldier on Chad's left, "they're after us."

"No," said Chad, "someone's after them!"

He was right. The Ninth was ordered to dress the line across the open field, and as the cavalry disappeared into the night—never to be seen again—the approaching Rebels were sent packing by one volley of musketry. The soldiers turned again toward the river.

Back at the Bend, Tad, who had marched on Chad's right and hadn't said a word the whole time they were out there, sat clutching his musket and squinting. Chad told him not to worry, they'd done a good job or Captain Miller wouldn't have said so. Well, they'd had their first taste of battle and wasn't it like falling off a log? Chad felt too excited, too full of anticipation to sleep soundly the hour remaining before reveille.

A small reinforcement arrived that day—one hundred and sixty whites, the Twenty-third Iowa Volunteer Infantry. Now the whole camp was sure the Rebels were coming.

Sergeant Wilkins was not shy about passing along news: "Colonel Lieb just sent a messenger to General Dennis saying the enemy is advancing in strong force. Looks like we're in for it, men." He spat into the hedge.

Soon enough Lieb called out his regiment, and together with the Eleventh Louisiana, the First Mississippi, and the Twenty-third Iowa, the men were solemnly told that the enemy would soon attack. Lieb charged them with the task of holding Milliken's Bend.

The enemy hit Chad a powerful blow: the ring of it, its sinister sound played on his ears. He rolled it on his tongue, felt its drama. He had never thought of those who held him in bondage as *the enemy*, never given the Confederate army such a meaningful name. Now the stirring words fired his blood and he began to regard the waving cloth above the fort with passion. He would jealously guard his flag, fight under it, fight for it, see *the enemy*'s flag go down. He would defend at all costs this piece of ground called Milliken's Bend.

FORTY-ONE

The African regiment [was] inexperienced in the use of arms, some of them having been drilled but a few days, and the guns [were] very inferior . . .

—BRIGADIER GENERAL ELIAS S. DENNIS, COMMANDING
DISTRICT NORTHEAST LOUISIANA, JUNE 12, 1863

June 6–7 1863

Swift preparation for the impending attack by Confederate General McCulloch's Texas brigade filled the day: the men placed cotton bales on the inland levee as additional breastwork, dug rifle pits along both levees, and filled their canteens and cartridge boxes. Tad stuck close by Chad and talked nervously, his eyes wide. Chad thought of what Uncle Noah said before a giant storm that swept up out of the Gulf: "I reckon this is going to be a big one. Everyone's restless, like there's a hole in the air."

That night, under the stars, the soldiers joked about their position. "Here's this garrison backed up to the river, defended by fourteen hundred greenhorns who aim to lick the stuffing out of who-knows-how-many seasoned Rebels," said a private, chuckling. "We'll do it," said another. "I sure nough don't want to be taken prisoner, not if the stories turn out to be halfway true." At last, they said, they had their chance to fight, to show them who was boss. Then they lay down, mumbling good-nights, sighing sighs.

Tad cried out like a baby in his sleep, and Chad tossed and thought of Anna and the future beyond the coming battle. In the middle of the night he sat up and looked at the sky with its hazy moon. Even the night air was hot, hot and still, and he hurried back under his net to keep off the mosquitoes.

He wasn't sure if he had slept when the bugle blared and the sergeant hollered—Deploy! Deploy! He hustled with his buddies to the ten-foot-tall inland levee, into position on the extreme left. He climbed into his gopher hole next to Tad's.

"Withhold fire," called Captain Miller, "until they're within range." The captain moved along his line of men, patting their backs, giving them his grin.

Suddenly Chad could hear volleys, see wisps of smoke rise in the night's pale light as the Rebels advanced from hedge to hedge, coming slowly through the breaches and passways, driving the black skirmishers before them.

Finally the greycoats reached the open space and stopped about twenty-five steps from the levee. In the first mist of morning he saw them order their line, heard the shout "Charge!" and the Rebel yell went up like the howl of frantic hounds.

They rushed forward in close column. Cries of "No quarter!" rang out as the brown/grey figures moved in a cloud of dirt toward him, head-on. His heart drummed in his ears. The thought of racing out of the stampede's way flashed through his mind. Then he grasped his rifle: why weren't they firing instead of staring like a bunch of ruffed grouse?

Colonel Lieb's bell-like voice rang out—"Commence firing!"—and all along the line the officers echoed the order, Captain Miller's shout hoarse as he jumped into a shallow entrenchment and fired with the men.

The Rebels seemed to fall back, yes, some of them turned tail, but they formed their line and charged again.

Chad struggled with his gun, pounding the steel ramrod into the hot barrel, cocking and—"Gawd! It's jammed!" His fingers searched for the reason, repeating the steps like second nature, but he was shaking, lordy, how he shook. His buddies along the line were swearing at their weapons, their ramrods clanging as they pushed them frantically into the muzzles against the cartridges. As the Rebels neared and dressed their line to open fire, Chad was vaguely aware that Tad was sobbing, trying to reload his musket and sobbing until suddenly it was too late: the Rebels were upon them, the muzzles of their rifles spitting into them, their bayonets fixed. They came like a flash flood headlong over the levee, pouring into the pits, while Chad swung his rifle against the blades they pushed before them. Metal clanked, fire flashed red in the smoke of cracking rifles, as such a mess of men swept by.

A greycoat with an angry yell lurched at him with his bayonet and Chad clubbed him with his rifle butt, bludgeoned his side as if he were a swamp snake hanging from a tree. He poised his bayonet for the next one, before him in a flash, thrust the blade into his chest, and had to use his knee against the man to pull it out. Ahead came another and he saw the greycoat's face, the greycoat's pale, scared face, sweating tiny beads that glistened in the sun's rays straining through the smoke. "My God," breathed the man, "My God," his face twisting, his mouth sagged down. He was carried forward by the swift current of men, carried like a log cut loose from a flooded field, rolling, tumbling, down the frenzied river, his arms flaying about. Chad tried to shift his bayonet but the man fell into it, horror and surprise varnishing his face, blood from his belly spurting around the blade.

Blood was all around. It squirted from mouths, gushed from ears and eyes, sprayed from necks and thighs and severed legs. It splattered shirts and trousers and ran down arms and clung to blades like glue. It was everywhere he looked, even on his own hands. Especially on his hands.

His regiment fell back over running briar and tie-vines, broken limbs and tangled bodies. An arm clawed at him, a voice cried out. He tripped over a shoe filled with a severed foot, its spiked bone poking from the bloody mass.

They were down into the space between the levees where their camp had been, and distorted faces came and went: ashen faces, tired, transfixed, terrified faces, stunned. Beside him came Tad's sharp cry as he fell, fell with his assailant, each slashed in the belly, spilling down together, toward and over one another, their insides leaking out, their seams parting, landing in a dying heap, whimpering there.

"Tad!" He knelt, but with one frightful gasp, Tad stiffened, his back arched and his eyes went blank. The Rebel with him put out an arm to Chad, then sank down, quiet.

Broken bayonets lay strewn like twigs. Near Tad a Rebel soldier's brains oozed down his forehead while his chest heaved. Chad bit his tongue, was jolted by the pain: *Jesus.*

As the Ninth rallied and pushed forward, the soldier on Chad's right yelped and his face lit up amazed as his head flew off, flew like a scared catbird leaving a ruined nest. The bluecoat took a step or two, then slid to his knees.

The heat was murderous. The stench of sweat and blood clogged the air. The merciless sun made it hard to move, burnt the moisture out of Chad's limbs as hour after hour the greycoats kept coming, kept the bluecoats fighting for each inch of stinking ground. One glance above revealed a deep blue sky, white clouds tossed by a high breeze. Reeling back, he almost fell.

Just ahead, the color-bearer held the flag aloft. It kept bobbing back and about, up and around in a playful fit.

Soon the Rebels flanked the three Union regiments, and an enfilading fire rained death along the ranks between the levees. The Ninth fell back. Panting, Chad reached the top of the second levee, got down on his belly, feet toward the river, and finding a gopher hole, slid in. New waves of men came running over the inland levee, leaping over bodies, slipping on the blood and slime.

"Nasty," whispered a soldier at his ear. "Ain't it nasty."

A bullet tore between him and the man. Behind them, its

target staggered and fell forward, his arms dangling into the hole.

The soldier at Chad's side shuddered, cursed, aimed his musket and shot at the blur of smoke and men surging forward. Chad rammed a cartridge into place, fired, saw his random mark grasp his chest and fall. . . . from Chad's throat came a piercing, mournful howl.

A cannon shell burst in the greycoats' midst.

It tore apart everything in its brilliant flash, scattered splinters and chunks of flesh, blew dirt and men alike sky-high. A quick, shocked silence fell—then came the wounded's wails and the Rebels' fast retreat. The *Choctaw* had drawn up in the river behind them and sent a broadside between the levees.

Colonel Lieb appeared on his horse and waved his arm. Captain Miller shouted, "Fall in! Forward, march!" Dazed, Chad plowed into line to start the chase. He felt his heart had ceased to beat.

Behind them the gunboat *Lexington* cruised in, sending screeching grape and canister that trembled the ground while the Rebels scattered and disappeared over the inland levee.

Union soldiers at their heels went up in smoke with the flying black specks, but still Chad pushed toward them, his eyes burning, his throat and chest raw. His canteen swung and his arms hung loose: he gripped his rifle in one hand and it pointed toward the ground.

Colonel Lieb fell from his horse. The hospital squad rushed to carry him aside, and his lieutenant took up waving the men toward the Rebels and the dense and pungent smoke.

Suddenly a straggling greycoat stood in Chad's path, stood there like a fool hen, blank eyes fixed on Chad's face, musket aimed at his chest. Chad swung and knocked the Rebel's gun clear of his grasp, heard his own voice say, "You're my prisoner," and sent the soldier to the back of the line with hands up, lips moving, muttering something sing-song. Chad buckled, held his gut, as came a wistful voice from nowhere: *In the morning, nigger, will you take me home?*

* * *

Colonel Sears and Captain Miller walked among the wounded, patting their hands, whispering hoarsely to the dying, the living corpses with bodies all askew, faces blown off, legs out there in the dirt.

Then Miller came to congratulate a soldier of the Ninth Louisiana who had taken his former master prisoner. Chad heard the soldier say, "Thank you, massa, thank you kindly, sir," smiling all over his face.

The captain sat down by Chad. Chad chewed his hardtack absently, his mind jumping around without lighting anywhere for long.

"Forty-five percent of my men were killed or wounded!" the captain said. "We lost some good officers, white and black. I saw Sergeant Wilkins go down. He was a brave fellow."

Chad reached into his knapsack, feeling for his stone, and grasping it, ran his fingers along its smooth surface over and over, over and over.

Captain Miller cupped his eyes and peered out over the field, where many of the dead still lay. He sighed and took a sip from his canteen. "I am so proud of you all . . ."—his voice caught and shook—"you had only sixteen days to train . . . and glory, those terrible rifles . . ."

Chad got up and slowly walked away.

FORTY-TWO

I never felt more grieved and sick at heart, than when I saw
how my brave soldiers had been slaughtered . . . I never more
wish to hear the expression, "The niggers won't fight." . . . It
was a horrible fight, the worst I was ever in—not excepting
Shiloh . . .

—CAPTAIN MATTHEW M. MILLER, COMPANY 1, NINTH LOUISIANA
VOLUNTEERS OF AFRICAN DESCENT, MILLIKEN'S BEND

June 7, 1863

The ritual for the burying of the dead was quick. Chad stood
at attention while Tad and the rest were named heroes and
laid hurriedly into the ground before they could attract more
flies. The bugler played taps, a sound both foreign and too
late. Then the colonel, on his aide-de-camp's arm, told how
the color-bearers passed the flag to others as they fell, so it
never touched the ground. Sure enough, there it was, hardly
the worse for wear, waving palmlike in the breeze that somehow hid the blood.

Admiral Porter's flagship *Black Hawk* eased into its mooring. The shouts were shouts of a mooring ship's crew, loud,
boisterous, unmoved. Surviving soldiers walked, talked, ate,

slept. But everything had changed: the feel of the air, the smell, the color of the earth.

Most of Chad's company were dead, or waiting to be carried to the field hospital in a plantation house downriver. He walked the scarred ground where his tent had been and remembered how Tad squinted, asking questions, sitting by his side on the rubber blanket, while the rain made puddles at their feet.

If he tried, he could get away from the haunting faces, the looks of horror, even the sounds that pounded in his ears, but he could not get away from his hands.

He climbed the inland levee and down the other side where the hedges, thinned but still deep, seemed taller and more secret than ever. The Rebels must have loaded their wounded onto carts here, for wheel tracks marked the soil. Even where the earth was scorched and its foliage torn, it never seemed to hold it against you. It would still grow crops when you planted them, still spring up with new life of its own, going on doing what it was meant to do whenever you let it. Maybe it wasn't fragile like people, who died when their blood was spilled, who cried out in pain: maybe it wasn't.

You know how it is, says Elmer's ma, they hope their sons break away once they in the army, maybe have a chanct, leastways a full belly.

The times ain't favoring us, Chad, says Clay, that's all it is.

As he turned back, he thought he heard a footfall on the other side of the hedge, but looking over his shoulder, he saw nothing. It was almost time to set up camp again, erect the tents on the patient earth and make room for sleep.

Suddenly he quaked, the sound of a rifle shot met sharp pain, and he rolled over and over down the levee.

The Union soldiers on guard duty rushed forward, shooting into the hedge. He was, he remembered, looking at his hands when the bullet plowed into his hip.

* * *

He was floating far above the big live oak at the end of the path to the house. Laurel called him, and when he flew down, she jabbed him with a dagger and twisted it. He cried out.

"I got it, son," said the surgeon. "You'll be fine."

Two cavernous nostrils, a wide grin, and tired eyes were above him. His hip was stinging like blue blazes, and one of the hospital corpsmen placed a great bandage over it.

"You'll make the last ambulance going to the hospital, boy," the surgeon went on, "but I couldn't make you wait to get that ball out. It was nasty. Made a hole as big as a crater."

Chad whispered thanks, and the surgeon kept talking. "Glad I could help. So many had more than one wound, some cut up like a beefsteak, and I just sewed up the gashes best I could and let the bullets set. I'll give you another dose of opium before you go."

They had given him a dose to swallow as they ripped his trousers off. "It was the greycoat pickets, covering their retreat," they'd told him. "Our men went through the hedge after them, but they'd disappeared."

By that time he was seeing a rainbow and beginning to float up high. It didn't seem to surprise him much that it was Laurel who turned the knife.

FORTY-THREE

Life for me ain't been no crystal stair.

—LANGSTON HUGHES

June–July 1863

Sunday they brought Hilda back, let out of jail because able-bodied hands were needed in the fields. Anna hugged her so hard she huffed and puffed. "I ain't been active lately," Hilda said, "and it's took its toll."

"You ain't sick?" Anna asked.

"Just a little short of breath. Sweat out all my energy in that hole."

Anna looked her over. She'd gained weight, and her skin had an unhealthy pallor. She seemed to walk with difficulty. "Where's Alcibiade?" she wanted to know.

"He joined the army."

"I thought he would. That crazy Pompée's still around, I see." She frowned at Anna.

"He sees to Sammy while I'm in the fields. He's good, Hilda, real good."

Hilda humphed and went to lie down in the shade, said she had a headache and those pains in her legs. She knew she couldn't eat a thing tonight.

That was too bad, for Anna had chicken and dumplings from the house. She was favored since Sammy's illness but she didn't care. He was a new boy now, and she allowed the good food had healed the sores on his legs. Laurel said she'd try to get more food down to the rest of the hands, but she made such a fuss about all the reasons she might fail that Anna pursed her lips and expected nothing. It was a blessing that Laurel didn't hem and haw about food for Poor Little Thing, as she called Sammy. She said she'd tell Chorly to let Anna and Pompée have whatever was at hand to keep the family healthy, and Anna swallowed hard and took the favor, sharing whenever she could. It wasn't easy to be favored. It drew a lot of sour comments and not many friendly smiles. But Sammy and whoever was inside her were worth it.

Hilda slept through till morning under that tree, would not come inside. Anna got up three times to see it wasn't raining and how she was. The next morning Hilda said she needed exercise, had to get those sore limbs moving, that paining back oiled. She went to the fields and passed out *tôt*, as a French-speaking hand put it. They saw red spots coming on her face and arms and even more *tôt* whisked her off to a camp downstream that was set aside for smallpox victims. She and Anna didn't get to say goodbye, she was gone so fast. Anna thought it must've been a nightmare for Hilda, one of those nightmares where you're with someone and then, no warning, you're smack-dab in the middle of a whole new scene with other faces. She wondered if she'd ever find out whether Hilda lived or died, and what kind of care she'd get, what kind of care.

She'd squeezed Hilda hello: smallpox was catching, and she had to think. The more she thought about it, the more scared she was for Sammy, and she wished her baby could come and trot away from her. She took herself off to the fort in the woods, chased Pompée out, told him to bunk with Sammy until she saw how she was.

She'd never had time to sit and be Anna, and now she was almost too tired. Back in the state of Mississippi, when the army worm took the cotton and her mama had time to sit a while, she'd told Anna it was good to catch up to herself for a change. She set to thinking about her mama, whose sharp eyes had seen more than she cared to share until the night before her daughter was shipped off to the new master. Anna was sixteen. All that night her mama talked to her, told her what she had to put up with and what she'd better not, what she could escape if she knew how: feign the monthly sickness to keep her master or his sons away, cleanse herself with herbs to halt a baby if she failed. Her mama spilled over the chair in their shanty, sighed into a deep well, hard to sigh out. *Never smile or look the white man's way,* she said, *and put on a plain face when he rides by—not angry, not afraid, Anna: plain.*

Anna guessed she was pretty, and she was scared. She sat up all night, bothered by a world she didn't want to know, a world she'd witnessed at the bayou with Alila, but had shut quickly out. Her mama spoke softly of her sister, but never of her fate—*Alila could have told you*—and Anna saw the shadows in her mama's mind.

When a man love you, her mama said at last, *your smile will light his life.* There were tears toward morning and a fierce hug when they came for Anna. She'd cried all day on the straw in the wagon, all the way to the steamboat and the fog so deep she couldn't see the water.

Now Anna listened to the forest, fought bugs and watched birds, tried out her reading and felt smart, fanned herself with her tortoiseshell fan and felt grand. She didn't think about smallpox, although she marked the days with one of Sammy's pencils so she would stay no longer than she must.

Pompée brought her food. She said she felt like a spoiled white woman, but she was glad she wasn't. The white man had a hold on his spoiled women. Woman to woman, Anna felt she was freer than Laurel.

* * *

Catching time was over, but Pompée brought her breakfast anyway. "Sit while I eat it and then we'll go home," she said.

He settled against a pine, his knees up to his chin.

"Do you and Chorly get along?"

He shook his head.

She sighed. "You go get food anyhow, and that's brave. It keeps Sammy healthy—and us, too." She patted her belly and Pompée looked at it and smiled. "You know," she said, "you look nice smiling. Right manly. You ought to do it more often. Let's see you, look here."

He lowered his eyes.

"They must have been the worst in the world, whoever owned you. You can't even look a friend in the eye, except for Sammy." She chewed a biscuit with ham gravy and smiled at him. "Come on, for once look at me."

He would not, and it suddenly riled her, why, she never knew. "I thought you liked me, and you don't!" She moved to his side and cupped his chin in her hands. "Look at me, Pompée," she commanded, and he did.

His eyes flashed lights she didn't ask to see, and she dropped her hands. He began to whisper: "Doubt thou the stars are fire, / Doubt that the sun doth move, / Doubt truth to be a liar, / But never doubt I love."

She could only stare. When finally she could speak, she said, "Oh, Pompée—Pompée, that's the most beauti-ful thing I ever did hear."

A moment full of hours passed, and then she said, "You know we love you, too, Sammy and me, and so—so will Chad—"

He seemed to stiffen. His eyes got that far-off look as if he saw his demons coming, and then they went blank.

Tears filled her eyes. She took both his stiff hands and squeezed them, Lord, how she squeezed them as she rose. "What—would Sammy ever do—without you? And me, I—am—so—grateful . . ."

Pompée wasn't listening. She pulled him to his feet, that

big bag of bones gone stiff, took one of his rigid arms, and led him home.

Sammy danced around chattering and pulling at her, for a while not noticing that his friend sat motionless on the step.

They kept Pompée where they could see him, watching him, feeding him. He's been good to us, Anna said, now it's our turn. Sammy asked why he was that way, why he didn't talk or move unless they moved him, and Anna said maybe he was sick, as sick as Sammy was when he lay on the mat and couldn't eat and didn't want to smile. That satisfied the boy at first, but at the end of the week he asked Anna if Pompée would ever be right again. She said she didn't know, but surely, the way Sammy was reading to him and showing him his snakeskins and bits of string and feathers from the bayou—surely he'd get well if he could. Then she went into the bedroom and prayed. She hadn't done that when Sammy was sick, hadn't had the time. But she had to tell somebody it was all her fault and Sammy shouldn't have to suffer; she hoped God could understand that.

Sammy was the tenderest person! As Anna boiled cornmeal mush in the kettle on the hearth, he hugged Pompée and said, "It's all right. You don't have to move until you want to." She was still afraid, and she tried to prepare Sammy: what if he should stay this way?

"It don't matter anymore," snapped Sammy.

That stunned her. "What do you mean, honey?"

The boy smiled a fierce kind of smile. "No matter how he is, he's still Pompée!"

The next day Sammy went fishing with a pole Anna made. She promised to watch Pompée until he got back. Alone with the man, she lit into him something fine. It was unplanned but she guessed it had to come. She told him how selfish and cruel he was. She said it wasn't right, dying before you had to die, expecting a *whole* lot more attention than a boy ought to give, and not even taking heed of it. She raved blindly through her tears, stifling her grief. Pompée showed no sign, his face an awful blank. Finally she stepped over to hit him and kissed him instead, right on the mouth.

"Now don't go thinking nonsense, man," she said, riled as she'd ever been with him. "I love you, yes, but it's a special kind of love—one that don't fade and die when you turn your back on me!" She got on her knees in front of him, took his head in her hands. "It's what I'd feel for a brother, if I had one. But I don't, so how do I know? Oh, Gawd, Pompée, I didn't mean to hurt you!"

She stormed out of the shack and sat on the step until Sammy came home, asking, "How is he?"

"Stubborn as a mule and ready for his dinner, I allow."

Sammy didn't have to pry open that big mouth for every bite. Little by little Pompée's muscles came alive. In the next few days he began to move around, and then one day, in the midst of a big commotion—someone said Vicksburg had surrendered and the hands were clapping and singing and talking all at once—Sammy saw Pompée's face break through the cloud, and like a bell, his voice rang out.

FORTY-FOUR

Wave of sorrow,
Do not drown me now:

I see the island
Still ahead somehow.

I see the island
And its sands are fair:

Wave of sorrow,
Take me there.

—LANGSTON HUGHES

June–July 1863

Quickly feeling merry despite his pain, Chad couldn't seem to
put his hand in the right place to salute the officer saying
goodbye to him. He winked at Captain Miller and the captain
looked surprised, then burst out laughing, running a hand
through his blond hair as a stretcher-bearer said, "He's had
a dose."

He closed his eyes and slept. On the bumpy roads he woke
up groaning. Then there was nothing between him and the
wagon's canvas hood but white-hot, jagged pain.

A sprawling plantation house had been turned into a hospital, and it was a space that never seemed to fit into his world. The nurses were gentle and hurried and tired. There was just one surgeon for the whole lot, and his lantern glowed all through the stuffy nights. Every day they carried off the dead.

His hip stopped hurting after he was turned, but that was not often. A bone must've splintered, the surgeon said at last, that's why it's so long healing, but never mind, your forehead's cool and the wound looks good. After he could turn himself in bed, he tried getting to his feet. It felt strange, putting weight on that right leg of his, but he kept trying, put a little more each time, until one day he took a step. He was ready for pain but it didn't come, and he hobbled clear across the floor before one of the aides ran to help him. By golly, he said, I did it.

He took to roaming, leaning on a stick, pausing to talk to the soldiers lying on cots lined up on the floor. His own ward was large enough to be a ballroom, partitioned off with a white sheet for the colored section until it spilled over after Milliken's Bend, they said. The house was bigger than the one he'd explored with Maxwell and Amos, bigger, maybe, than Sweet Haven's mansion. And it was full of wounded men.

Down the road was another big house, taken for wounded prisoners of war. When Chad got well enough to walk outside, he wandered down there, walked past and around the house, talked to the guards, who dozed on the steps sometimes. They said there wasn't anything to guard: most of the Rebs had seen their last battle. He went inside, looked across the long rooms full of men, some sitting up, most lying on cots, just as they were up the road. The wounded looked the same down here, the nurses just as tired, and he couldn't see any more than one busy surgeon.

He walked outside again, around through the gardens, and over to the big barn. There was a sign on the door that said Quarantine, but he went on in, wondering why everything was so quiet, where the nurses were. There must have been a couple of dozen Rebels lined up on straw cots, and they were moaning like the wounded in the house. One man called for water, and Chad took him the pitcher from the stand across the floor. He was too stiff and sore to kneel: he had to plop down with his leg straight out, laughing at himself. "Here, fella," he said, "I guess you can drink from the pitcher." He put his hand under the head of the soldier.

"Chad—" came a voice, "is that you?"

God almighty.

Two soldiers over he was, his blond curly hair messed over the straw, a blanket up to his chin. Chad's heart went wild as he shimmied over. "Clay! What you doing here?"

Clay coughed and then he laughed and that brought another cough. He reached for Chad's hand. "What-do-you-know, it really is you!"

"Never thought I'd find you here, fella." He looked him over and thought how frail he looked, how spindly under the blanket.

"Took me prisoner . . . near Richmond . . . Then I got sick." He stopped talking, but he looked, frowning, at Chad's straight-out leg.

"You wouldn't believe how I got wounded, Clay. You'd laugh like the dickens." He patted a lean, pale hand. "How you feel?"

"Real bad . . . I got malaria, I think." He coughed. "You better go." His breathing was short and sounded like a cat's purr.

"You hurt anywhere?"

"Chest hurts . . . Started last night." Tears welled in his eyes. "Thirsty."

Chad gave him a few sips of water, holding up his neck, thinking how Clay's eyes used to shine with mischief.

"You still mad?"

"No, Clay." He realized he was telling the truth. The last time he'd been mad at Clay he was with Jerry Labarre, and he was at odds with himself. When he looked at the poor soul now, he could only feel a pull from the past, and a terrible hollow.

"We're blood brothers, ain't we?"

"Sure, Clay."

"We look alike, they . . . used to say."

"I heard that once or twice. It don't matter. You lie still."

"Have you heard from . . . Blake?"

Chad said, "Want some more water?"

"Have you?"

"No. Why?"

"I wish I could've . . . run and got you." He coughed into his hand. "I swear . . . there wasn't time."

"Time? The night Blake went?"

Clay nodded. "I made him go . . . gave him our pirogue . . ." He wiped sweat from his upper lip. "Laurel told on him . . . didn't mean any harm." He stopped and Chad just looked at him. It was as though what he was saying didn't matter anymore.

"Papa sold him . . . I knew it'd kill you."

Chad heard his voice like an echo: "You helped him go."

"I had to." Clay put his hand on his forehead. "For you, Chad," he whispered.

Of course Laurel didn't mean any harm. And Chad should've known what Clay was made of. He had one question: "Why didn't you tell me, after Blake went?"

"Didn't want you madder . . ." he said, moving his arms as though it helped the words come out. He sighed, and his chest growled. "Malaria's catching."

What an awful fix Clay was in now, sick as he could be. "I'll stay with you, if you want."

"They'll make you go." His voice was thinner now and Chad had to lean close to hear him. "Stay—till they come?"

"Close your eyes. I'll be right here."

Clay slept. Chad sat by him, watching his shallow breathing, remembering how he used to get out of breath running from Mammy, his laughter catching in his throat, his face beet red.

Other soldiers began to ask for water. Some raved with fever. The straw they lay on was damp and full of lice.

A nurse came in with drinking glasses and a pail of water. She had a bandanna tied over her nose and mouth, and she scolded him through it for being in the barn. Then her eyes brightened. "You're Private Creel, aren't you? The one who comes to the house from our hospital up the road? I have good news for you. You're going home! Vicksburg has surrendered, and Port Hudson, too. The whole river is in our hands now. Everyone's celebrating."

Everyone's celebrating. He looked at the shaft of sunlight coming through the barn door, thinking how bold it was.

The nurse spoke louder, as though he were deaf: "Private Creel! The South is cut in two! You're going home, I say. They expect a transport here in a week or two, and you and the others will be going down the river on it."

Chad shook his head, feeling nothing. Then he asked, "Can I take Clay?"

"Clay?"

He motioned to the cot. "He goes where I go, ma'am. Can I wrap him up good and take him home?"

"I—don't know. He's a prisoner of war."

"We all are," Chad said, "one way or another."

"Well, Private Creel, I don't know how you expect to take a Rebel with you, and a contagious one at that."

"You mean he might make Rebels out of all of us?" He was getting giddy, and he stood by Clay still asleep on the cot.

"I must ask you to leave," said the nurse.

"I can't," said Chad, and he didn't move.

The woman looked shocked. "I don't know what to say," she said, but she kept on talking. She said she couldn't imagine a slave being so faithful to his master, that it just didn't make good sense, especially if he knew enough to fight in the Union army. But she said she didn't know how they could make him go on that boat, for after all, he was honorably discharged. However, he had no right to be in the barn, absolutely none. At least, she concluded, he'd have to wear a handkerchief on his face to protect him from the fever. She dug into a large pocket and pulled one out. "To tell the truth," she said, "I could use some help in here."

The nurse made her rounds, filled the water pitchers on the stand by the door, gave a pill or two, and off she went.

Chad went back to his hospital and got his carpetbag and his blanket—no one seemed to notice—and made a place at the foot of Clay's cot.

Some of the prisoners began squawking for water. Some just wanted a body nearby, someone to talk to or yell at.

When Clay woke up, he smiled a weak smile. "I thought I dreamed you," he said.

"No, it's me. Just like old times."

"Blood brothers," Clay said. "You ain't . . . mad?"

"No, I told you. I ain't mad."

"Papa was hell-bent . . ." He took a sip of the water Chad offered. "I shoulda told you."

"Never mind. It don't matter."

He coughed hard, watching Chad with those innocent eyes so big in his face. Poor old Clay.

"I thought I could keep him . . . from it."

"Sure you did. It's okay. It all turned out just fine."

"You forgive me?"

"There's nothing to forgive."

Clay's eyes burned into his. "You were mad . . . hopping mad . . ."

"I know." He sighed. "I'm sorry, Clay. Thank you—for helping Blake."

Clay's body slackened. He eased back into his bed of straw, kind of disappeared.

The night was long and hard. Clay's fever went up and there wasn't time to do anything but wring out rags in water and put them on that hot forehead. Once he woke up, eyes bright, and told Chad to get his gold watch and chain from his knapsack. When Chad did, Clay said, "It's yours."

Clay looked so bad when Chad said no that he took it just to quiet him, put it in his pocket and Clay smiled, said something low and closed his eyes.

When Clay began to talk nonsense, Chad went to the house and got the surgeon.

"He's got pneumonia," said the surgeon, "on top of malaria, by God." He shook his head, and checked the other soldiers. After he left, two men came in with lanterns and took the one from the far end, his head covered over. On the way out they wondered aloud what field to put him in.

Clay stayed in his noisy half-sleep, only now and then opening his eyes. Whenever he saw Chad, he smiled, and once he said, "Let's go home."

Chad took him by the shoulders and gently turned him over, knowing how good it felt to be moved when you couldn't do it yourself.

Toward morning, he woke up and grabbed Chad's hand with surprising strength. Chad leaned over him. "You all right, Clay?"

"Times . . . ain't . . . right . . . that's . . . all . . ."

"I know, Clay," he said, squeezing the thin hand hard, "I sure nough know."

Clay choked a little and his hand went limp. He was staring at something so interesting he couldn't look away, just kept staring until he was no longer there.

Chad closed those empty eyes the way he'd seen it done, but he didn't put the blanket over that curly head, just around his neck, the way Clay liked it.

He took Clay's knapsack and his own carpetbag and limped to the barn door, but hearing a call, went back to give a prisoner some water.

"Thank you," said the Rebel soldier. "You're a good Nigra."

Forty-five

He lay just where he fell,
Forty consecutive days,
In sight of his own tent,
And the remnant of his regiment.

—FROM *ANDRÉ CAILLOUX*, AN ANONYMOUS POEM, 1863

July 1863

Jerry Labarre was mustered out of the U.S. army the day
André Cailloux was buried.

Around him were the furious voices of his comrades, furious, powerless, and surprised. His own voice seemed to
squeak as he was given the conditions of his discharge: "How
can it be that I served the army and am in its debt? Is that not
absurd?"

The sergeant behind the desk looked at him with distaste.
"Call it what you please. That's how it is."

"How it is," he said, "is not how it was presented."

He and his fellows had been promised the white soldier's
pay of thirteen dollars a month, but were paid seven, and
charged for their uniforms. Jerry was in debt to the army in
the amount of seven dollars after forty days of service. He was

dumbfounded, and annoyed at himself: he should not have been so gullible.

He glared at the sergeant, and softly as his rage allowed, said, "This is a crime of the first order. I shall report it, you may be sure." The sergeant, a just-doing-my-duty sort of fellow, was unimpressed, and secure in his position. Jerry stomped away.

He approached André's bier at the Church of St. Rose of Lima. Sweet blossoms surrounded the flag-draped coffin, flanked by massive candles and military guards. Father LeMaistre had performed the rites Jerry was happy to have missed. He took his place in the huge, silent crowd at the curb as the Forty-Second Massachusetts Regiment band played the funeral march and André's coffin was carried to the hearse. With military escort, the coach moved up Esplanade.

The procession was long: mounted Union officers, starched and deliberate, led columns of marching soldiers in full dress; carriages and buggies followed, full of mourners, while others trailed on foot. The onlookers stood at attention, solemn as the dirge itself, tall with pride. He braced himself and stifled a dry sob, for he felt nothing but a stinging loss.

The crowd dispersed and he stood alone. He began a slow walk down the street, then quickened his pace as he thought of Paul Trevigne. He turned the corner and saw the shop, as it was when he and Paul were young. He'd kept in touch with his friend only by letter since before the occupation, when Jerry lost his old life and slowly built a new one. But he missed Paul, and in his last letter had suggested they meet for dinner, neglecting to tell his friend that he was going to volunteer to guard New Orleans. It was just as well. He rang the small bell that lay on the counter.

Paul came from the back room, stared at him above his spectacles, spoke Jerry's name with dramatic cadence, and embraced him. "I received your letter, and answered it so long ago! Where have you been?"

Before Jerry could answer, Paul went on: *"Attendez-moi* while I tell the wife I shall not be home for supper, and we'll be off."

Jerry heard Madame Trevigne's protest from above, and would have made a polite departure, but Paul was back with palms raised in resignation: *"On ne peut plaire à tout le monde,"* he said, and found his hat.

FORTY-SIX

The victory completely paralyzed the enemy in our rear, and
enabled us to move from the La Fourche after the fall of
Vicksburg and Port Hudson without molestation.

—BRIGADIER GENERAL THOMAS GREEN, COMMANDING. REPORT
TO CONFEDERATE HEADQUARTERS, JULY 14, 1863

July—August 1863

Anna was wakened by a thudding of feet and hooves, the
rolling of wagon wheels, the moving of a presence so large she
was struck with wonder. Slowly it seemed to rumble over the
ground, spreading through the fields and the lanes until it
was right outside, surrounding the shack, tramping, rolling,
thudding. She broke into a cold sweat. She could hear a shout
here, a mumble there, until a fast horse like a whipping wind
carried a shout that brought it all to a halt, and the presence
settled in like a blight. She held her breath until she had to
breathe, and kept awake until she had to sleep, praying softly
that the door would stay shut. She ought to be used to armies
by now, she scolded, they ought not to scare her so, but she'd
never known them to come so close and in such numbers.
Pompée on the floor in the other room was all that lay between them and the swarming mass.

At dawn the bugle sounded, and Anna and Sammy were up with a start. Pompée, his eyes clear, told the boy he must stay by his side, and then Anna opened the door and looked out. Rebels were sitting everywhere, eating, cleaning rifles, building small fires. Horses were tethered to trees. Just beyond the path, big guns perched on wagons like vultures while the mules grazed. It was as though the whole world belonged to the Confederate brigade.

It was a far cry from the day when the news came that Vicksburg had surrendered on the Fourth of July, and Port Hudson on the eighth. The celebration was grand. Folks from other plantations gathered around to talk and sing, and even Horace, poor dead Cora's husband, came and played a fiddle.

Now a Rebel officer stopped by her door and peered in. "We're not here to harm y'all," he said. "Your master says y'all will help us where you can, and we could use some waterboys to fill our canteens."

Sammy looked at Anna and she nodded. After he left with Pompée, she closed the door and sat at the table, her arms wrapped around herself.

The next morning the army—including, Sammy said, three Texas cavalry regiments—made ready for attack. Yankees down from Port Hudson were marching from Donaldsonville, and the Rebels were meeting them halfway. They'd beat their britches, the cocky burghers, they'd teach them how to run, they said. They filled their cartridge boxes with ammunition and their haversacks with cartridge boxes, rolled up their blankets to sling on their backs, and away the infantry marched.

The battery rode through the formal flower garden. On the carts the brass howitzers and iron mortars made Sammy's eyes roll. Then from a distance came the roar of cannons, and smoke trailed overhead in wisps.

During the day another Rebel cavalry thundered upstream, and plantation workers coming down began to pass through

Sweet Haven. They talked about how bad the fighting was. Dead bodies were strewn across the fields clear back to the swamp, mostly Yankees, they said. The bluecoats fought from gopher holes they dug in haste and from drainage ditches in the fields. They'd tried to rally, but their flanks were pushed back, and now the Rebels were driving in their center. It was purely awful to behold, and when you saw all the Rebels won—at least three pieces of artillery, ammunition, tents, wagons, teams of horses, new Enfield rifles—it gave you an idea how big the army was that got itself licked.

Someone asked who the generals were, and the workers said Weitzel and Dwight on this side of the bayou and Grover on the other, and it was Rebel General Tom Green who walloped them. You saw Colonel Major's cavalry come through here, they said, well, he'd come from the riverbank to help Green. He'd been firing on Yankee gunboats and transports, causing quite a stir.

One man sat down on Anna's step and told about the transports full of Union troops from Port Hudson he saw arriving at Fort Butler in Donaldsonville. "They went scooting back to the fort, tails between their legs this time," he said, "but they sure ain't beat for long."

Anna walked up the path and saw Laurel with her arm around Cecily in the flower garden. They were staring at the ruins, looking shocked, not saying a word as far as she could tell, and then wiry old Mammy came out and hustled them in. "Ain't no time to cry over flowers," she hollered. "Get in here! Your mama's wrought up and your papa's having a conniption fit!" Anna remembered when, looking through Laurel's eyes, life was flowers and bows and pleasing Papa . . . and maybe seeing Chad. Thinking of that somehow riled the baby into doing cartwheels. She walked back to her shack holding up her belly.

That evening General Green's brigade came back. They laid their wounded in lines under the lean-tos they set up, and talked how fine it was they had less than two score this time.

In the night the suffering men cried out. She took pieces of the sheets Laurel left when Sammy was sick, and went to see if she could help. "Ah," they said when on her knees she mopped their faces and changed their bandages, "thank you, thank you." Mrs. Wycliffe was there. It was the first time Anna had seen the mistress work, the first time she'd seen sweat on that brow and light in those placid eyes. Of course, she'd never dared to look into Mrs. Wycliffe's eyes until they met over the body of a soldier, shot in the chest.

"He's gone, ma'am," she said.

Mrs. Wycliffe wept.

"We did all we could do."

"I know. Thank you, Anna." The slender woman got to her feet. "Miss Laurel wanted to help, but her papa wouldn't let her. I think—" She put out a hand to help Anna up. "Well, it would have been so nice if you could have stayed with her. I declare, you were such a help."

"Thank you, ma'am."

"Anna," she began, "I—I think of Chad. Do you know where he is?"

"No."

She sighed. "Where is Uncle Noah?"

"Up at White Castle."

"Oh? Oh, what a shame. What a mess we've made of everything . . . from the beginning. I'm sure Uncle Noah put a lot of blame on me. It wasn't right and I knew it, but I was young, you know. My husband just turned his back on the whole thing. Of course, that's not unusual. Most men—well, you know."

Anna was tired. She wished Mrs. Wycliffe would stop going on so, her eyes wide and mournful as she spoke: "Martha seemed to understand. She'd grown accustomed to the ways. But Noah let me know. It was the way he looked at me. Still, I was so upset I wouldn't touch the child—ever."

Anna looked at the profile that flickered on and off with the fickle lantern and thought the woman had lost her sense. "Ma'am," she said, "the soldiers are quiet now. Why don't you go and rest?"

"You must be tired, too. Forgive me. Do go along to bed now."

As Anna turned, Mrs. Wycliffe put a hand on her shoulder. "Your baby isn't fathered by—a white man—is it, Anna?"

"No."

"That's good. I'm so glad. And I do wish you—whatever it is you Nigras want."

"That's kindly of you, ma'am. Right now I can't think of anything but sleep."

They moved the wounded out in the morning, but the rest of the brigade bivouacked on the plantation, restless, wary, thankful for a respite. Some of them mumbled to themselves, others lay staring, while a few played cards or read books from their knapsacks. Most of them smiled at Sammy, and now and then he did little errands for them.

The third morning the general's aide came riding in with a message for the commanding officer. Anna heard shouted orders, and before noon, the brigade picked up its lean-tos, hitched its wagons, saddled its horses, and marched away—down the bayou. All that livelong afternoon a slow procession of regiments from up the bayou trudged by.

"They're retreating, Sammy," Anna heard Pompée say. "They're leaving, and nobody's chasing them."

Pompée was right. Workers who had scouted for the Union at one time or another scratched their heads and concluded that the Rebels were glad for a chance to get away.

A few days later the Yankees sent a contingent of men to Sweet Haven: the Union army was in control of the Lafourche District up the bayou and down.

"When's Chad coming?" asked Sammy. She wished he would be still. She had enough to think about without the daily questions: when's he coming, ain't he due, what will he look like, will he stay this time? She almost yelled at the boy, but stopped herself. After all, Sammy was just voicing what her heart kept asking.

Pompée must have seen how on edge she was, for he hastened Sammy outside: " 'Come, come away! / The sun is high and we outwear the day.' "

Well, she thought, that's Pompée.

Chad studied the many stars that gathered over the delta to welcome him home. The night was dry for August and a cool breeze kept the insects at bay, so he stopped to sit on the bank of the Lafourche. The *wararons,* as Jerry called the bullfrogs, chorused a greeting, and by the light of the moon he could see the nose of an alligator part the water like a riverboat.

He'd hitched a ride on a hay wagon from Donaldsonville, and now as he walked the last mile, he had to shoo away all the what-ifs that bit at him like a swarm of hungry gnats: what if Anna wasn't there, if Uncle Noah was dead, if Blake didn't come, if Sweet Haven was abandoned . . . there was no end to them.

He reached the lane that turned off to the mansion and saw lights through the windows. It looked as it had when he'd skirted its grounds as a small boy. But now it would be foolish to walk by there in the dark. The big live oak spread above him, tall and wide as ever, but he wasn't sure his leg would make the climb. He found a spot in the brush where he could stretch out and go to sleep.

Anna had a crazy dream: Chad and Laurel came laughing down the path, holding hands. Laurel saw Anna. She broke loose and ran to her, calling, *Anna, you were right, all I had to do was ask, and now we're going away together, far, far away.* Chad stood back smiling like a perfect fool and when she stared at him, all the tears she owned rolling down her cheeks, he kept on smiling.

FORTY-SEVEN

If there is no struggle, there is no progress. Those who profess to favor freedom and yet depreciate agitation, are men who want crops without plowing up the ground. They want rain without thunder and lightning. They want the ocean without the awful roar of its many waters . . . Power concedes nothing without a demand. It never did and it never will.

—FREDERICK DOUGLASS, IN A LETTER
TO A FELLOW ABOLITIONIST, 1849

July 1863

Jerry wondered how it would be, seeing Paul Trevigne after over two years of occasional letter-writing, their paths so divergent they'd had no occasion to cross. But the gap between them closed the moment they met: old friends, he thought, I should have known.

He suggested they go to the Gasthaus zum Rhein platz, for it offered a friendly atmosphere and Paul's favorite beer. He watched his friend's slight, straight figure as they walked: he didn't look a day older, except that his tidy mustache had turned grey and his hair had thinned. The imprint of his visor's headband still showed below his hat.

"Well," said Paul, turning to him, "how do I look?"

"Time has treated you well. Better, I think, than it's treated me."

"You look fine to me, Jerry. A little skinny, but fine." He frowned. "A little peaked, maybe."

They chose a table by the wall, and at once Paul wanted to know how things were "in the country" and what kept Jerry looking young. The waiter, bringing steins of beer, said, "Two young friends? What could be better!"

They ordered Wiener schnitzel and salad, and strudel for later, with *café noir*.

"If I have any youth left, it's because of a couple of young-sters, Chad and Anna," Jerry said. "They took me back to bygone days. Sometimes I think memories can preserve a man."

"I don't know. I've been too busy to find out, I guess. The newspaper business is hectic as ever." He shook his head. "We've printed a lot on wallpaper, you know. It's been touch and go with supplies."

"How did you like Chad?"

"Oh, he's a fine young man, but I'm afraid I wasn't able to give him much guidance. I was disappointed when he left to join the army. I had plans for him."

Jerry chuckled. "Remember when you were young?"

"My mother wanted me to be a doctor." Paul drank deeply from his stein. "But that's not the point."

The waiter brought the food and Jerry took a bite of veal, then a swallow of beer. "I did hope you'd be able to influence him, but he was bent on the army. The last I saw of him he was headed for Vicksburg to find a fighting brigade."

"Ah! I pictured him somewhere in the cypress swamps. I hoped he'd come back to me. Have you heard from him since the fall of Vicksburg?"

Jerry shook his head. "I don't think—I ever will." When Paul shot him a glance, he smiled. "It's just that we said our goodbyes."

Paul gave the waiter a nod and he brought more beer with

a flourish, smiling through his thick mustache, wiping his hands on his starched apron.

Jerry stared at the white tablecloth. "You've heard about the Rebels torturing black prisoners of war? And killing them? Is it so, Paul?"

"There's no doubt about it. Lincoln has threatened retaliation. But the prisoners taken at Vicksburg were paroled, Jerry, so lay your mind to rest." He raised his stein to his lips. "There's nothing better than German beer! It helps one face cold realities."

"So Lincoln threatened retaliation, eh? I think of Wendell Phillips, the abolitionist who often travels with Frederick Douglass, you know. I hear he said if Lincoln grew, it was because they watered him!"

"I know, Lincoln is a politician, but he's a good man, too, Jerry."

"A 'first-rate second-rate man,' according to Phillips."

"I disagree. He's honest about wanting to save the Union at all costs—slavery or no. He hates slavery but separates his personal view from his duty."

"Balderdash!" Jerry's eyes flashed. "What about his duty to see that his generals enforced the Confiscation Act—all those slaves could've been freed July of last year if he'd done his precious duty!"

"Well, he kept his word on emancipation."

Jerry sniffed. "Limited as the proclamation was."

Paul laughed and raised his stein: "May our friendship know no limits!"

"Amen!"

They ate in silence until Jerry gave a deep sigh. "I just came from the bier of André Cailloux, Paul. I'd heard he'd been killed, and thought his funeral would have been long ago. It was a shock."

"I told you in my letter he was to be brought home, and that Father LeMaistre will be denounced by the archbishop for his part in the funeral." He leaned across the table. "Tell me, who is more villainous, one oppressor or the other?"

Jerry swallowed. "It is an open question."

"But Jerry, didn't you read my letter?"

"It's probably waiting for me. I haven't been home yet."

"Where have you been? I thought your teaching was over when you wrote to me."

"It was." He smiled. "I was one of those sixty-day volunteers they recruited when they thought New Orleans was in danger."

"Uh-oh."

"Allow a friend a mistake."

"Such a big one, I don't know."

"It wasn't so bad. I met people, had a lot of campfire *esprit de corps,* and no invading army showed up."

"But did you get paid?"

"Then you know. Let them try to get that measly seven dollars!"

"I was appalled when I heard. It's strange what the Union army can get away with: it's as though it wants to alienate the black population."

"It has, believe me. They'll play hell recruiting in the future." He ate with gusto and finished his plate. "Tell me, what has been happening in my absence?"

"Everything and nothing."

Jerry settled back. "It's *good* to see you, Paul." He took a sip of his beer.

"If you would not be such a hermit, we could do this often, and then you would know everything I know, right off the wires!"

Jerry cleared his throat. "I hear the Corps d'Afrique has been acting up."

"True. They claim their rights as members of the army, and the more they're beaten, stabbed, spat and shot at, the more they assert themselves."

"Are they still trying to ride the white streetcars?"

"Ha, ha, you haven't noticed? That started back with the Native Guard, you know, and it finally made General Banks write to the president of the city railway asking why black soldiers were not allowed on all streetcars."

"So?"

"The soldiers are now allowed to ride on all the cars. But we other *gens* still must take the star cars." He chuckled. "Everything and nothing, *n'est-ce pas?*"

"How did the court-martial at Fort Jackson come out?"

Paul swallowed his last bite of veal and shook his head. "Banks suspended the death sentence of the two soldiers who led it and sent them to Fort Jefferson in Florida. I have no doubt they'll be worked to death there." He wiped his mustache. "But I must say some army officers recognize the outrage."

"And we should applaud," Jerry said flatly.

"My friend, a sense of justice is a rare thing."

"*Oui*, it is." Jerry motioned and the waiter came smiling, fresh steins of beer in hand. "Gentlemen," he said, "you have a healthy thirst."

"Did I tell you about the draft riots in northern cities?" asked Paul.

Jerry shook his head.

"The first posted list of drafted men touched off four days of bloodshed. Blacks were hunted down and killed by drunken whites armed with clubs. One Quaker home for colored orphans was set afire and evacuated out the back way just in time. Children's heads were bashed against lamp posts, people were drowned. It was hideous in New York, Detroit, and elsewhere. The law says you can buy your way out of the draft, so the rich are the favored ones, but the blacks took the brunt of it."

Jerry looked out toward the courtyard of the restaurant. "If you can't see beyond your own window, Chad says, you've lost the world."

"And as for us, old friend—even in our finest hour, we couldn't ride the streetcars."

"I suppose," said Jerry, stretching, "always a few of us will be allowed to ride."

"An illusion, Jerry: the ride."

The waiter brought the strudel and coffee, and the two men consumed it slowly and thoroughly. Then Jerry rubbed the palms of his hands together and said, "I expect Chad will prosper."

FORTY-EIGHT

Love is a wild wonder
And stars that sing,
Rocks that burst asunder
And mountains that take wing.

—LANGSTON HUGHES

August 1863

"Someone's coming, Anna, someone's coming," called Sammy, "come see!"

He went running. Anna stepped outside and stopped, her heart pounding: who was that limping down the path, holding out his arms and swinging Sammy around and around? She had to look away or run to him herself. She looked away.

"Anna," called Sammy, pulling ahead of Chad, pulling his arm, "look who's here!"

She felt light-headed but she stood her ground. Sammy sometimes teased her: frail is a woman's name, Pompée says so. And here she was, suddenly fluttery and scared. Controlling another impulse to run to them—waddle! she'd ridiculously waddle!—she stood still, focusing on Sammy's shining face.

"I didn't know you for a minute," he said, that Chad. He looked a little older (there were furrows where he smiled) and thinner, lordy, he was thin.

"There's two of us now," she said, tossing her head and blushing, wanting to touch him, wanting him to touch her.

"I see so," he said, his lips creasing at the corners as though a laugh wanted out. "Well, well."

"There's a baby in there, Chad," said Sammy, pointing. "Pretty soon I'll have a brother."

"Ain't that nice," said Chad, standing on one foot and then another.

Is that all he's going to say, she thought, but she said, "Come on in and have coffee."

"Coffee? Been a long time since I had coffee."

"I got it from Chorly up at the house—" She stopped, thinking of Laurel, remembering her bad dream. As a rule she took no stock in dreams, but this one was so real, and besides, hadn't she put a bee in Laurel's bonnet?

"Anna," he began, "it's real good—" But Pompée was coming out of the shack, softly singing, and she hurried in, cutting off Chad, that voice of his.

"Look who's here, Pompée, it's Chad!" cried Sammy.

Pompée walked right past them and down the path, the big Shakespeare book cradled in his arm.

"Don't worry," said Sammy, "he'll be back. He just don't talk much, that's all."

Chad's face seemed to fade before Sammy's eyes: he opened his mouth but didn't say a thing as he watched Pompée go. Sammy tugged at his arm: "Anna said to come get coffee, Chad, come on." Something was wrong, but Sammy couldn't tell what. No one was acting right. He felt like pushing Chad and Anna together, the way they were at Congo Square. That's how it ought to be, how he pictured it every night before he went to sleep: lots of hugs and kisses, with him right in the middle of it.

* * *

Anna knelt over the embers, warming the coffee in a pan, fuming that he'd not been surprised and happy to see her here. "Maybe you'd just as leave have coffee at the house," she snapped, instantly wishing she'd held her tongue.

"No he wouldn't," cried Sammy. "He don't want to go there!"

Now she turned on the boy: "Let Chad speak for himself, Sammy!"

Sammy looked at her with shock on his face, and Chad blinked, looking down at his hands. "If you—want, Anna—I won't stay."

"Go, then!" she commanded. "Go find your sweet little Laurel!" She stiffened, then, with pain, grabbed her belly and eased into a chair.

Chad shook his head. "I didn't come here for Laurel. I wonder why I came here at all."

"You came for us," cried Sammy, tugging wildly at his sleeve. "Remember? We gonna be a family!"

"He didn't know we were here!" Anna caught her breath and Sammy ran to her side. "Are you hurting, Anna?"

Earlier that morning, she'd had the kind of pains Chorly told her to look out for, but they were mild and stretched so far apart they'd almost slipped her mind. This one was wracking. She was sure it meant business. "I reckon, honey," she said, "it—is—time—for the baby."

Chad stared at her so blankly she might as well have spoken French, and Sammy leaped around like someone on a spring.

"Should I get a field woman?" Chad asked.

"No. I don't want a one of them." She stood up, and water ran down her legs and made a puddle on the floor.

"Oh, Anna's sick!" cried Sammy. "I better get Pompée!"

"I'll get him," said Chad, leaving fast.

"Fine father he is," she said. "Help me to bed, honey, and then go tell the cook."

Chad had to hunt for Pompée, and by the time he found

him sitting on a log reading, he had drawn such a picture he could have knocked him cold. "Anna's having her baby," he said, his voice edged like a knife. "You better go to her."

Pompée kept his eyes on his book. "I don't know how to bring a baby."

Chad was beside himself. He'd come all this way for what? "You sure enough better learn," he yelled. "If you gonna make them, you better learn how to bring them!"

Pompée closed his book and stood up. " 'Conceit in weakest bodies strongest works,' " he said, and looked Chad in the eye. "You ought to know who the baby's father is."

Chad lowered his eyes. He'd known coming down the path, seeing Anna, of course he had, but then everything went haywire. "I'm obliged," he murmured, and Pompée coughed and settled down to read.

He ran into the shack past Sammy, who was going for water, and almost bumped into a fat little woman. "Whoa, there," she cried, "what you doing here?"

He moved around her and into the other room where, by Anna's mat, sat Laurel, cross-legged, her hair all over her shoulders.

At the sight of him, she stood up. "Chad! You're back! Why, I declare, I can't believe my eyes. I was in the kitchen when Sammy came for Chorly, but no one told me you were hereabouts!" She crossed the room, her eyes brimming with tears. "Oh, look at me, I'm bawling like a baby. But it's been so long, so long!" She laid her head on his shoulder and before he could move, Anna was up on her elbows, bellowing like a buffalo: "You get out of here! Get out!"

"She's right, Chad," said Laurel, stepping back and smiling. "This is no place for a man."

"I belong here, Laurel," he said, seeing what a fix he was in. "I'm going to be a papa."

"You!" Laurel turned ashen. She backed up and stared first at Chad, then at Anna. She leaped to the mat and kneeling, slapped Anna across the face, splat. Chad grabbed her, swept her up and carried her away while she cursed and tore at him.

The cook stood openmouthed as Laurel broke loose and ran, yelling at her to follow. Chorly mumbled to herself and put a kettle on the fire.

Anna was crying softly. Chad took her in his arms, felt her lovely wiry hair, so electric, so alive, her high forehead, her sweet lips. "I love you, Knucklehead," he said. "I love you, my crazy lady, I love you."

"If it's just because of the baby—" she wailed, her hands on his back, his shoulders, feeling now his face, "if it's just because of what we done—"

"Oh, what we done!" he said, kissing her lips hard and long, moving to her nose, her cheeks, her eyes. "I knew you were here, Anna, I found out, I'm here because you are, I came for you . . ."

She arched with a contraction, grabbed his arm and squeezed it as Chorly came in and felt her belly, shooed Chad away, and told her to grunt.

Less than an hour later, as Chad and Sammy sat by the door of the shack listening to birthing sounds and great oaths from Anna, while the heat closed in with a hard ten-minute rain and Sammy squirmed and Chad sat stock-still, the baby was born.

"You be the papa of a good-looking girl," announced Chorly, wiping her hands on her apron and smiling. He smiled back. She said, "Just a minute more."

They went in together, Chad and Sammy, stood there feeling silly until Anna invited them over and they gazed in awe from either side of the mat at the pale baby in her arms.

"What's her name?" asked Sammy, and Anna said they'd see what she seemed to answer to.

"Here-After-This is who she is," said Chad, and he took the gold snuffbox from his carpetbag and set it on the bed. "It's a present from Jerry Labarre."

"Ohhh, ohh, how lovely, how fine!"

"Is that her name?" asked Sammy, frowning. "Here After?"

"I thought we'd give her a new name, a brand-new name," said Anna. "Is that all right, Sammy?"

"We wouldn't want two Annas," he said earnestly.

Chad began to laugh. "One Anna is about all you and me can handle, Sammy, that's right." He kissed her then, before that temper of hers could flare. Anna pulled his head down to her breast and giggled. "Sammy and me have two babies to look after now, don't we—Chad and Here-After-This."

The boy put his chin in his hands and smiled.

Chad and Sammy were chopping wood when Pompée tiptoed in and placed a bouquet of lilies at her feet. "How pretty they are!" she said. "You have a new student, Pompée. Come and see her."

He leaned forward and peeked, but he didn't come close, and Anna suspected he barely saw the child, for his eyes were beginning to glaze with that haunted look of his. "It-is-all-right, Pompée," she breathed, "they won't dare come today."

A faint smile crossed his face. Then he began to look at her, not into her eyes, but at her just the same, as though he was taking in the whole of her, baby and all. And she had the fleeting notion that as the time went by, Pompée would always be there, looking at her.

FORTY-NINE

O, I drug ma wings
All through the fire.
But the angels wings is white as snow,
White
    as
        snow.

—LANGSTON HUGHES

August 1863

In the knapsack were Clay's old red bandana, his daily journal, a stubby pencil or two, a good shirt and trousers, family photographs, some money, and an army hat. Chad almost left that hat behind, but then he said no, maybe they'd like to have it.

He had Clay's knapsack under his arm and wouldn't give it to anyone but Laurel. The old doorman didn't take kindly to that, but when he explained what the purpose was, Horace said "Mercy. He was just a child," and opened the door. "Miss Laurel, she be in the library. Go through the doors there, across the hall."

A long divan held her and her book. She looked protected by her fort of tall bookcases, thick rugs, and polished tables. When she saw Chad she let out a hostile cry that startled him.

"It's about Clay," he said. "I have to tell you about Clay."

Her face drained of color. She told him to sit down and he sat uneasily in a straight-backed upholstered chair. Maybe it was easier to say these preposterous things in this preposterous place than it would have been on the bank of the bayou, where everything was green and alive.

He began hesitantly, but then it came naturally, because Clay was between them.

She listened, looking pale and small, and nodded when he told her about Clay's gold watch and chain. "It was his to give," she said.

After he finished, she put her head in her hands and sobbed. "Oh, Chad," she said at last, "I'm so grateful you were there with him."

All that ever passed between them came flooding back, and he wanted to tell her what she'd meant to him, how he had counted on her.

"Clay and I—" she said, "well, we had a falling out. He stormed at me after I told Papa you could read. I hoped Papa would let you help Clay with the books but he wouldn't, wouldn't even listen. He said he was sick to death of your name, and couldn't wait to get rid of that troublemaker Blake. Clay was so upset when Blake got sold, it's a wonder he didn't hold it against me. But he didn't. I confess I was mean to him, meaner than he could be to anyone. I just couldn't see how that slave meant so much to him and said so. Blake was Chad's friend, not yours, I said, and who cares?" She glared at him. Then she bent over, almost rolled up, crying.

Suddenly she raised her head and smiled as she might have smiled at her father's guests. "I am indeed pleased and appreciative of your coming with the tidings," she said, "and I'd show you out, you know, but this has been a great shock to me. We received word that my brother was taken prisoner by the Yankees, but we did think he'd be coming home." She looked through him. "Thank you, and good day."

He would have said something, anything, but he had no words. It was as though a New Orleans street cleaner had taken a broom and swept his mind clean.

FIFTY

Gather out of star-dust
Earth-dust,
Cloud-dust,
Storm-dust,
And splinters of hail,
One handful of dream-dust
Not for sale.

—LANGSTON HUGHES

September rode in on a thunderhead, working magic with light and sound, digging ruts and building ridges with its pockets full of rain. Chad noticed that Sammy held his ears when it thundered. Pompée listened, looking wise. Anna, cradling Marra, the newly named, had the storm's excitement on her face.

She was sitting in Uncle Noah's rocker nursing the baby, and she looked so damned beautiful it was hard to bear. He knelt beside them, told her as soon as he could find a good wagon and a horse or mule they'd be on their way, and they'd stop for Uncle Noah and Granny Martha up at White Castle. It was good she'd found out where they were, he said. Then he had to kiss her and it was hard to stop.

* * *

She pushed him softly off, though her whole body said not to, and told him he'd better go foraging tomorrow: the Wycliffes had cut off the rations, and Chorly was not allowed to give handouts anymore. (She'd sneaked down some biscuits, but you could tell she was scared, and Anna told her not to take such chances.) It had been hard for the lot of them to survive under the Yankees, then the Rebels, and now the Yankees again. Today a mess of okra was the best Pompée could do. It was in the pot over there, stewing.

"I'm not hungry," he said, putting his arm under Sammy, who had leaped onto his back. "I'm going out again to look for a wagon. I'll forage on the way back."

"Can I go?" asked Sammy, and when Chad said no, Sammy's frown almost made it rain again.

She kissed Chad goodbye, the baby on her breast between them, and felt the teasing ache between her legs. They'd have to wait until she dried up, Chorly told her, but it was hard, and every time the baby nursed, she wanted to reach for him.

They were close, so close, except when she asked about the war. Then he broke away or hid behind a shrug, and even laughed about his hip that took a bullet when the battle was through. She didn't prod: it was enough that he was here and he was hers.

"I'm glad the storm is over," she said, and Chad pulled back his shoulders as if someone had yelled *Attention!* She patted his hand, ran her fingers over his wrist. "I didn't mean to make you jump."

She saw his face twist and his gaze go to his hands. It was what happened when something made him think the dark thoughts that were a part of him now. Since the day he arrived, she'd watched him wander through the new rooms of his mind, saw him leap from terrible corners to laughter when she brought him Marra. "Little To-Marra," he'd say, holding the baby tenderly, "we will clear a road where you can learn how to walk." When Anna would say she liked the way he talked, he'd smile that wonderful smile of his. But often when she seemed to look away, he would slip through those private doors and she'd see that he was staring at his hands.

Now he said, "It's time for us to get out of here."

"But Blake's not here yet. He said he'd come."

"Sometimes a man can't do what he means to, or he changes his mind."

"He wouldn't. I think you should trust him."

"Trust don't enter in. It's what a man can do, and what can happen to change the look of things." He touched her cheek. "I'll be back late."

She watched him leave, limping that limp, throwing back that smile.

Labadieville was a busy place. There was a lot of trading in the shops, a lot of traffic in the streets. Union soldiers were everywhere and shopkeepers welcomed them, glad, he supposed, that the fighting had stopped and they could open their doors. He looked around, wondering where to go to buy a horse and wagon. He would be lucky to find anything he could pay for, but he could work for it. Then he saw a covered wagon. It looked as though it could have traveled across the country in '49, when all the white man thought about was gold. A For Sale sign hung on it and he peeked in, scanning its roomy inside with its hooks holding pots and pans, baskets and sackcloth, its cookstove at the rear, and the rifle leaning against the rim of the canvas. He wondered if it was the old Conestoga wagon Blake had described, but thought not because the floor didn't curve up at the ends. Whatever kind it was and no matter how old, it would be perfect for his family's journey.

"What you doing here, boy?" came a voice behind him.

"Looking," he said, turning slowly, fixing his eyes on one of the provost marshal's men, "just looking."

"Look up your ass," yelled the officer. "Scat!"

He walked past the big wheels in back so he wouldn't pass near the glaring, gun-holding man. The covered wagon would be perfect, all right, but he couldn't imagine trying to buy it in this fool town.

He set out through the fields over the countryside. It was

kind of peaceful, out in the warm, wet wind of a late summer's evening, the rot of sodden plants and fresh-cut corn striking his nose at the same time. It was familiar ground. And here in the sudden darkness, apart from his new family, he could see himself.

He was not the same man who left the plantation to cut the South in two, wasn't the greenhorn soldier who took up arms against *the enemy* and spilled the blood of men. He wasn't sure, if Blake did come, he would know what to say. It had nothing to do with his friend, nothing to do with all the love and respect between them. It was rather the way he was now: a different man.

He slipped into the shack with his carpetbag full of vegetables, past Pompée and Sammy near the hearth, into Anna's bed. Marra, his Here-After-This, three whole days old, was sleeping soundly in the old dresser drawer Chorly brought her the day she was born. What love she had kindled! It was new to him and heavy with care. He counted his family, excluding for the time being Uncle Blake, and including the strange new one called Pompée, for whom he'd learned a warm regard. Sleep took him in then, gently.

He was moaning and tossing beside her. She tried to wake him but he held fast to his dream until he gave a frightening cry and sat bolt upright. "The blood," he whispered, and she put her arms around him, felt him shake.

She got to her knees, pulled his head to her breast, wiping the cold sweat from his brow. "I know."

"How could you know? I'm glad you never will."

"I know one thing," she said, rubbing the back of his neck where the muscles were in knots, "we're never going to put up white curtains with red polka dots in our house."

He relaxed against her. "Curtains," he said, and repeated the word. "Imagine that!"

*   *   *

Steam rose from the hot earth and gathered into a thick morning fog. Voices bounced and echoed, and sounds from the wet road seemed so close he didn't think those wagon wheels had turned into Sweet Haven's lane. Then through the mist came the thud of horses' hooves and the blur took shape: Uncle Blake drove in with a team of horses pulling a covered wagon, a mule and a goat tethered behind.

Uncle Noah leaped off the wagon. He flung his arms around Chad: "Oh, Chad boy, Martha's gone and I's so joyed to see you."

Blake's arms wrapped around them both, his voice ringing out like a chime: "This prairie schooner was up for sale and I sank my money in it . . . The rain sure rutted the road, and that goat's slow as molasses."

Everyone gathered around. Anna was laughing, climbing in and out of the wagon, holding up a pot, a ladle, while Sammy was prancing and patting the horses, and Uncle Noah was recounting his first sight of Blake at the poor farm.

He felt a smile on his face, heard his own voice say "Well, well. Ain't it grand!" as they went into the shack to drink Anna's sassafras tea. Pompée followed them and stood silently in the corner, looking at him curiously.

FIFTY-ONE

Slaves hung on determinedly to their selves, to their love of family, their wholeness.

—HOWARD ZINN, HISTORIAN, *A PEOPLE'S HISTORY OF THE UNITED STATES*, 1980

Uncle Noah sat in the rocking chair, holding Marra, saying how he'd hone the rockers smooth and make a cradle, too. Uncle Blake spread out a map to chart their course and Sammy pulled at Chad's arm, pointing to the map. Anna made ashcakes out of cornmeal from the wagon and boiled Chad's foraged greens, bright-eyed. Pompée slid down in the corner, still staring at him, while they all drank tea.

It was like a dream, and he didn't know if he was in it or just watching. Everything was all set, all laid out fine.

Blake raised his cup high: "Here's to the dream!" he said.

Chad gulped his tea, then he walked outside and stood there. The sun made archways in the mist.

"What is it?" Blake asked, coming alongside him like a tugboat in the river.

He shrugged and turned to watch someone come down the path, picking her way, holding her skirts.

"It's Mrs. Wycliffe," said Blake.

They bowed a little, the way they'd always done, and she

smiled. "I see you're back, Chad," she said, looking past him. "I've wanted to talk to you for a long time. And—you are?"

"Blake, ma'am."

"Oh, yes, Blake. We heard you scout for the Union."

"I did."

"Well, I declare, time does move on in curious ways. May I come in for awhile?"

When Mrs. Wycliffe walked through the door, Uncle Noah got up with the baby and Anna's face came to a halt. Pompée slid up the way he'd slid down and made a swift departure, Sammy right behind him.

"I'm sorry to shoo off your company. Oh, Anna, how lovely she is! Chorly told me you had a baby girl!" She sat down in the rocker. "I daresay I'm glad to see you, Noah. Where is Martha?"

"She's gone, Missy Wycliffe. I buried her up there."

"Oh, I'm so sorry. You oughtn't to have gone to that farm, but everything was so upset, I just lost track." She sighed. "Noah, of all our dear folks, you are going to like what I've come here for. It's just so long overdue." She smiled at Anna. "I have a proposal to make. Chad, I'd like you to stay with us, you and your family. I'm asking you to manage the plantation. I know you can read and figure, and what you don't know we'll get someone to teach you. It will be a hard job, but I think we owe it to you."

No one said anything. She went on: "And you, Blake, since you're back and Chad's good friend, you will help him, be his associate, so to speak. I hear you can read and write, too. And of course, Noah, you'll always have a home with us. It will be the nicest thing, just like old times, having all of you . . ."

Chad cleared his throat. "Does Miss Laurel know you're saying all this?"

"Oh, heavens no. She's stricken by Clay's death, and she isn't herself at all. I didn't dare speak to her about it. But the colonel, I declare, he agreed without much fuss. He knows he needs you at last, Chad." Her eyes were on the baby in Noah's arms. "You can start right away."

Anna's face was so closed, he thought of the days when she was Laurel's maid, standing like a ramrod under the tree. "No, ma'am," he said, "we have other plans."

Mrs. Wycliffe looked shocked. "But—oh, we didn't discuss wages. Of course there'll be good wages. Negotiated, the way you folks like it."

"Thank you, ma'am. I'm obliged. But the answer is no."

"That rickety wagon in the lane—is that part of your plan?"

"Yes, ma'am."

"Well, I can't see how you can turn this good offer down for a—such an unknown future. Think about it, Chad." She was looking at the floor. "Talk to Blake and Anna. Let me know later."

"No, ma'am. I'm letting you know now."

"If it has anything to do with Miss Laurel not knowing, don't worry your head about that, she'll approve. It's true she has bad feelings toward you lately, Lord only knows why, but—"

"Miss Laurel don't enter in."

"Then what is it?"

"We know what we want, that's all."

She stood up. "Well!" she said, looking right at him for the first time. "I declare, the colonel was right all along—half Nigra is all Nigra!"

She stalked out and up the path, and Pompée, standing with Sammy by the step, stared in, his eyes meeting Chad's with a tender look.

Anna said, "So that's what she was going on about the night I was tending the wounded. I was too tired to really listen, but I did wonder. Sounded to me like she was a little addled."

Chad's eyes turned toward Noah. "When I asked you about my papa, you said maybe Granny Martha would say sometime."

"No good would come of telling you, and no good has."

"Clay—"

"He didn't know."

"And Laurel!" cried Anna. "Why, Chad—" She saw the look on his face and stopped.

"I'll have no more talk of it," he said, and the room was suddenly full of everybody's silence but the baby's.

FIFTY-TWO

To break this shadow
Into a thousand lights of sun,
Into a thousand whirling dreams
Of sun!

—LANGSTON HUGHES

"What was it you were going to tell me, Chad?"

He and Blake sat on the step under a yellow moon so low he thought if he reached high enough, he might just pluck it from the sky. "I don't know."

"It was before the missus came this morning. I asked you what was wrong."

"Wrong?" He felt like shouting, but he kept his voice low and the word came out flat and hoarse: "Everything."

"That's a lot."

He looked Blake full in the face and couldn't hold it in: "I don't believe in anything anymore."

"What don't you believe in?"

"Anything. The dream. The enemy. War. I don't believe in war." He was trying not to breathe so fast. "I've changed a lot, but maybe—maybe you haven't, Blake. You come here all fired up, all full of make-believe freedom, and you think that's all it takes. Well, it ain't."

"I know that." Blake was very calm. "Don't you like the wagon?"

"Sure I like it. Maybe it's the one I saw in Labadieville, the one I wanted."

"I got it there." Blake smiled. "It don't matter who got it, Chad. It belongs to all of us."

He sighed, allowing that was part of it, knowing he'd wanted to be the one who got the wagon. But it was a small thing, a detail. He wasn't sure he was up to trying to explain. Maybe it didn't even matter. "It's more than that," he said.

Blake scratched his chin. "How's it been for you all this time?"

"How's it been for you?"

"Oh, tolerable. I was a scout in the army. Did a little spying, too."

Chad wanted to say something, make some comment, but he couldn't. He just stared at the moon.

"You got a fine woman since I saw you, and a baby, too."

"Yes." He turned to Blake. "I—I'm scared for them, for us all."

"That makes sense." Blake cleared his throat. "I came by a while back and met Anna. She didn't know where you might be. Where were you?"

"Depends. New Orleans, Baton Rouge, Milliken's Bend—"

"My God! Is that where you got that limp, Milliken's Bend?"

Chad nodded. "Crazy thing—" He stopped, thinking of Clay, thinking of everything.

"It was bad, wasn't it?"

"Yes."

"So was Port Hudson, unholy foul."

"But you were a scout, you said. The blood wasn't on your hands."

Blake's response was so fierce it surprised him: "Oh, yes it was! I knew what would happen if they attacked over that open plain." Beads of sweat gathered on his brow. "I didn't raise a ruckus, Chad. I didn't make them change the plan."

"You think you could? A scout, a black scout? What a dumb fool you are."

"I gave my report and then I was quiet, as always." He shuddered. Then he cleared his throat. "I could have raised a fuss."

"You wouldn't have stopped a thing, any more than I could've stopped that fool flood of men rushing on me—that sea of faces—"

Blake sighed. "I played their game, and they never saw my face." His forehead was silver-grey in the moonlight. "They praised me and threw insults at blacks. They never saw—"

Chad put his arm around Blake's shoulders. "Well, I guess we know a thing or two now, don't we?"

There was a rustle behind them and Blake turned to him and grinned. "You don't believe in anything anymore, you say? We'll see."

Anna came then, smiling.

Author's Note

I'm aware of the great responsibility associated with writing a novel based on history, and so I've tried to be accurate with historical facts, people, places, dates, setting and things. To the best of my knowledge I took liberties only twice: the Fort Jackson "mutiny" actually took place on December 9, 1863, not in June; and though *L'Union* was a black Creole newspaper of great importance and indeed printed General Butler's black recruitment notice, I've taken latitude with its timing: it was first published in French in 1862, and not in French and English until July 1863. These liberties were taken at the request of my main women and men, purely fictional, who have great powers of persuasion.

About the Author

Mildred Barger Herschler was born and grew up in Mounds-
ville, West Virginia, spent a year each in Phoenix and Denver,
began serious writing at the age of eight. After Bethany Col-
lege, West Virginia, she lived a snowy year near Buffalo, then
moved to Huntington, Long Island. There she wrote *Frederick
Douglass,* a biography for children, and was an editor in New
York City. Several of her poems were published in *the Crisis.*

She now lives in a border community in the foothills of
western North and South Carolina, where she continues to
write. *The Walk Into Morning* is her first novel.

DATE DUE	
READING THIS BOOK IS A FINE ACTIVITY...ONLY IF YOU' RE LATE !	
JUN 0 8 1993	
JUL 2 2 1993	
AUG 0 5 1993	
AUG 2 8 1993	
SEP 11 1993	
OCT 0 9 1993	
10/30/93	
OCT 2 8 1993	